H.H. Laura

Larkspur

sensate nine moon saga

Larkspur
Sensate – Book 1

by H. H. Laura

Published by RNL Associates
November 2011

This is a work of fiction. Names, characters, places, and incidents either are the product of the author's imagination or used fictitiously. Any resemblance to actual persons, living or dead, events, or locals is entirely coincidental.

Sensates.com

Larkspur
Sensate Nine Moon Saga

by H. H. Laura

2nd Edition

Published by RNL Associates
February 2013

Cover art copyright by Cora Graphics, Inc.
January 2013

ISBN No.: 978-0-9846678-3-3

License Notes

Dedication

To Mackayla and Reeselynn:
May all your dreams come true.
-GC

Preface

Larkspur began as reflections of my childhood and drew inferences from the good and bad experiences of my life. Then, as the characters became real to me, the story took on a life of its own. I was surprised when Alexandra spoke and led me in a direction completely different from originally intended.

Being a first-time author, I found it quite revealing to let the conversations just happen. As I wrote *Larkspur,* the next two books formed in my mind.

In keeping with my core beliefs, my books will always adhere to certain principles: true love is pure, it harbors no guile or pretense, and it endures an eternity. I believe in what lurks between the lines and the process of 'fade to black,' and finally, that good shall always prevail over evil. These concepts and beliefs offer the writer and reader boundless options limited only by their depth of imagination.

Teens, Christians, Iroquois, and those between the ages of first and last love, should find common ground within the adventures of the Nine Moon Saga. I loved creating my characters and hope you enjoy my Sensates.

Table of Contents

Prologue

"The real voyage of discovery consists of not in seeking new landscapes but in having new eyes."
- Marcel Proust

Living for centuries permits a sufficient amount of time to develop clarity of hindsight and an appreciation for the wrong turns in our lives. Each step we take becomes a path forward and a step nearer our end. Confidence walks alongside me even when the path is not clear.

The obstacles halting my progression are internal questions, which require an answer from my core: Are we basically good? Does love conquer all? Under what conditions could I take a human life?

Although the current path is strewn with certain adversity, I'm not worried... goodness shall prevail.
-Alexandra

Chapter One

Waynesburg, Pennsylvania – Spring 2013

The instant her toe caught Alexandra braced herself for the impact. Her body made contact but the surface gave way. A scream escaped her lips as she tumbled downward through a dark shaft. The descent ended abruptly with a belly flop into icy cold water.

Water gushed up her nose and into her mouth; she thrashed until her foot touched bottom and her head cleared the surface. Coughing and straining to expel the foul water, she gasped for air to fill her burning lungs. She drew in a normal breath, shoved the hair out of her eyes and blinked to help adjust to the subdued light.

Grimacing from the throbbing ache in her left side, she rubbed her arm, instantly jerking as pain shot through her hand. A toothpick-sized splinter stuck out of the fleshy part of her palm. Gritting her teeth, she pulled it out and squeezed the hole to make it bleed. She wiped the blood away on her shirt.

Fear mounting, she spun around and took in her surroundings. The hole in the cover where she had crashed through was the only light entering her pit. A cistern! Waist-high water, four solid walls, ten feet to the top, and no way out.

"No," she whispered, fully grasping the severity of her situation. Panic set in and her breathing quickened.

She walked around each side of the old well and rubbed her hands over the walls to feel for protrusions, anything to use as hand or toe holds. Nothing. Knowing beforehand that the idea had little chance of success, she dragged her foot across every inch of the floor searching for some type of drain plug.

Next, she stretched her arms and legs to the limits and tried to reach across the opposite walls. No way could she stretch the additional six inches to brace herself and shimmy upward.

Cupping her hands around her mouth, she yelled, "Help! Can anyone hear me?"

She listened, but even with the use of a bullhorn, she doubted anyone would hear her cries for help. Her arms dropped to her side and she whispered, "Mom, Dad, if you are watching out for me, I'm really in trouble this time. I didn't tell anyone where I was going, and no one's around for miles."

Alexandra closed her eyes and tried to block out the cold. Spasms started in her chest and escalated throughout her body. By holding her breath and hugging her arms to her chest, she was able to quell the jittering so she could once again concentrate on escape.

"Mom, I s-should've known better. I might take your 'no man's an island' reminders to the grave." She set her jaw. "Dad, if the chant from the commercial is coming from you, c-cut it out.

It's bad enough without, 'Help, I've fallen...' re-v-verberating in my head. I n-need help, n-not you t-tweaking my n-nose."

Her breathing came in pants, and her stomach seemed to jump up and down below her ribs. She looked at her watch. An hour had passed and she still hadn't figured out how to escape or even if it was possible.

The list of bad far outweighed the good, but she concentrated on the good nonetheless. It was too cold for snakes, no creepy-crawly things moved about in the pit with her, she didn't have to tread water, and she still had the majority of daylight left.

Reining in her panic and shivering with cold, she canvassed the pit and wracked her brain once more for any method of escape. She focused her eyes on the dark walls. Who would spend so much time to build such a flawless pit? There were no uneven sections or defects to mar the intricacy of the walls. Just her luck to fall into something so exquisitely built it had no ledge to grasp. Finding no route of escape, she chastised herself for the foolish venture that landed her in this mess.

She yelled for help every fifteen minutes, knowing no one would answer, and as the hours passed, she felt her body warmth dissipate. No longer able to feel the pain from her injuries, she moved about and rubbed her arms trying to stop her body from going numb. Her panic returned ten-fold when shivers escalated into non-stop uncontrollable jerks and her breath came in small gasps.

Growing more and more uncertain of her future, she knew no one would ever find her body in this blasted cistern. More likely, they would locate her Jeep and never figure out what happened to the owner high on this secluded mountain. A lump filled her throat; there would never be a sign stating, 'Here lies Alexandra Higgins, who died in a cistern'.

She cursed and berated herself for getting into such an idiotic situation and for bringing about her own death. Anger welled up inside and she slapped and kicked at the water re-soaking her face and arms, which initiated another round of core-shuddering spasms.

"N-not very smart," she stammered.

The sun's rays, almost directly overhead, filtered more light into her prison. Stunned, her eyes spied an opening she hadn't seen earlier - a perfectly shaped hole, chest high in the wall, which measured about six inches wide and four inches tall. Her heart skipped a beat as adrenalin shot through her veins. She stepped closer to examine the enigma. Precision walls with a hole, it made no sense. The mystery became an obsession.

Frantically, she grabbed a small stick floating on the water and probed the hole. It struck something and could go no further, so she wiggled and gouged hoping to dislodge the offending item, but only succeeded in moving it from side to side.

Dropping the stick, she slowly placed her fingers and then her hand into the hole. The space felt slippery and a bit slimy, but otherwise smooth and rectangular. Inching her hand further, she touched a smooth, round, *warm* object.

Alexandra yanked her hand out fast as a shiver

went down her spine. Warm? Her heart beat faster as her eyes raced over the cistern walls and came to rest again on the hole. Drawn to it by the sheer oddity of its existence, and revitalized that perhaps it might be an avenue of escape, she slid her hand back inside to further investigate. As her hand closed over what felt like a stone, it got warmer.

She jerked her hand out and rubbed her shriveled fingers.

"Whoa, no way." Her pulse increased as the obsession grew.

"Wait." Shaking her head to clear her thoughts, she tried to make sense of the situation. No, it made no sense.

Still obsessed, Alexandra grabbed the bottom of her shirt to use as a pocket. She inhaled a deep breath, and then quick as lightning, reached in, grabbed it and dropped it into her shirt. An innocent-looking brown stone rolled around and came to rest.

"A stone." Her pulse steadied.

She picked it up in her shaking hand and looked at it more closely. As it grew warmer, she felt a tingling in her palm. Her heart race quickened.

Instantly an idea flashed in her mind. She hurriedly scanned her surroundings. Remnants of wood planks floated all around her. She grabbed a long piece that looked sturdier than the others, shoved it in the hole, and wedged it tight. The plank proved solid when she hung from it, so she tried to pull herself onto it by leaning against the side of the cistern for support.

She slipped off the slimy wall, lost her footing and fell backwards into the water. Jumping up quickly, her body went into spasms. Unable to stop her teeth from chattering, she clenched her jaws tight and rubbed her arms to get the blood circulating.

Her heart pumped harder and faster as she grabbed the plank again. The brace of her foot against the wall held this time, but when she started to pull herself up, her hands slipped from the plank and under she went.

She sprung from the water, with her hair covering her face and her nose filled with the thick sludge from the bottom of the well. Coughing and gasping for breath, she spat and cleared her throat and forcefully shoved the hair out of her eyes.

"Your ass sucks canal water!" she yelled at the top of her lungs. Her hand flew to cover her mouth. She couldn't believe her dad's curse had slipped from her lips.

Gritting her teeth she hissed, "Sorry."

Once again, she leaned against the wall of her adversary and set her mind to the task. She gripped the board, and with unwavering willpower, pulled herself up to finally perch on the slippery board.

As her breath came in choppy spurts and she shook with cold, hope returned. From there she could reach the top cover of the cistern, and although she had fallen through a rotten section, some lengths of wood appeared strong enough to support her weight.

By opening and closing her fists, rubbing her hands together, and slowly blowing into her cupped hands, they began to warm. Once feeling returned, she stretched on tiptoe and secured a solid hold on the lid's cross-member. Pushing aside thoughts of plunging to the bottom, she focused solely on escape.

"Here goes." Giving a mighty spring upward from her perch, she clung to the cross-member, and with adrenalin-enhanced strength, pulled through the opening to her waist. She struggled to lean forward grateful the boards supported her weight. Fully aware the added stress could be her undoing, she kicked her legs for leverage and strained the muscles in her arms to shimmy her hips upward. After a few endless minutes of hanging precariously on the edge between failure and escape, she gave a final kick, pushed forward, and miraculously came to rest flat on what remained of the cistern top.

Quickly rolling off onto solid ground, she closed her eyes and offered up a small but heartfelt prayer, and only then let out a mighty sigh of relief.

As the sun caressed her cold, aching body and the beating of her heart returned to normal, Alexandra soaked up the gentle rays until her shivering subsided, and warmth, blessed warmth, spread throughout her limbs.

Chapter Two

Alexandra didn't consider moving from her position next to the cistern until her heart rate returned to normal. Pearly white spring beauties, the first blossoms of the season, surrounded her as she basked in the warmth of the sun.

"Teater," she said, sighing, "I have to wonder if I am meant to uncover your mystery."

A rustle of wings flapped overhead. Hurrying across the sky, she saw a pileated woodpecker, the only witness to her near-death experience.

Taking a breath, she rose to her feet and tried to regain a semblance of mental decorum. The scrapes on her arms and legs had started to ache and bleed again, but they weren't deep. A good cleaning and some antiseptic and they would heal.

She pulled her twisted shirt around and rung the water from her long hair. Glancing into the cistern, she inhaled, ready to fling an oath in its general direction, but caught herself. With one curse under her belt for the day, she reconsidered, and turned toward her Jeep, putting the ordeal behind her.

She rummaged around in the back of the Jeep and found a plastic trash bag. After spreading the plastic on the front seat to protect the fabric, she grabbed the hand support and climbed behind the wheel. The familiar surroundings soothed her wounded spirits. She leaned forward gripping the wheel and inhaled a deep breath. The key turned easily in her cold hand as the engine roared to life. Cold air blew up her legs from the heater fan, so she hurriedly reduced the flow until it warmed.

Pulling down the visor, she winced at the reflection of matted hair, smudges of grime, and cheeks that dripped mascara. Further assessment revealed ripped khakis and a shirt stained so badly it would end up discarded.

A shiver began, but before it could take hold, she rubbed her arms to generate warmth. Her eyes fell on the cell phone glaring obstinately at her from the console and her temper flared.

"Don't look at me like that." She grabbed it and inspected it for a signal. Her heart fell.

"Three bars. Great. Just what I needed, a cell phone giving me the raspberries."

Life deserved a kick in the pants, if that was even possible, but she knew her karma, life would kick her back twice as hard. Luck had never been her friend. Until today! Hah, she'd gotten out of that cistern hadn't she? Maybe her luck was turning.

She tossed the phone onto the passenger seat, vowing to take the darned thing with her if she ever went wandering again. Immediately rethinking the last action, she grudgingly picked it up and put it back in the console. The bumpy ride down the mountain would bounce it to the floor in seconds and she'd have to get on her knees to find it. It nagged her that she had to 'baby' things. If she'd had it with her, would it have survived the dunking?

Probably not. At least she fared better than a cell phone, and no one 'babied' her.

The tedious journey up the mountain felt quadrupled traveling back down. She could feel the weakness throughout her body from hours of exposure to the cold. Each bump threatened to jostle the wheel from her hands, so she tightened her grip and slowed her pace even more. The trek took a while, but by the time she reached the main road, the heater had warmed her thoroughly.

At the hotel, she chose the side entrance to keep from prying eyes. Thankfully, she made it to her room unnoticed.

The hot shower must have originated in heaven, for the bliss that grew from within elevated her spirits and warmed her bones. Pieces of algae floated down the drain as she sudsed her hair a second time. Laughing at the irony, Alexandra figured that next to being in the womb, she had never spent so much time in one day surrounded by liquid.

She left the shower reluctantly and tended her elbow and knee, blow-dried her hair and then piled it high on her head leaving wayward curls to frame her face. Once dressed in blue jeans and a lacy t-shirt, she headed to a local diner she had passed on her way into town. Her stomach growled and as she rubbed it to calm the noise, she thought of a phrase her father used to say, 'I'm so hungry I could eat the ass off a dead horse.' Shaking her head at the thought, she wondered why her father's sayings always referred to the posterior end of something or other. She smiled as his kind face entered her mind.

The popular diner brimmed mostly with gray-haired patrons, a few quiet families, and the typical diner curmudgeons at the counter. A tiny, silver-haired woman and her escort on their way out caught her attention. The woman carried herself with determination, poise, refinement, and exuded a quality of upbringing that made Alexandra smile. As she watched them making their way to the door, the tall escort spun around and caught her stare, almost belligerently. His eyes softened a bit. The corner of his mouth raised slightly, he nodded, and…

As their gazes locked, time stood still. Although she could feel her chest expand to take in breath, her body froze as her mind raced to accommodate a whirlwind of dancing emotions. Pleasant. Unfamiliar. Exciting. Depth. Vastness. Eternal.

The man's features etched in her conscious mind. She knew him, every inch of his chiseled jaw, the violet hue of his eyes, and the curve of his cheek. Knew him, but didn't. Familiar as an old shoe, but unrecognizable at the same time. A dizzying number of conflicting senses came into focus and just as quickly faded, soon replaced by another. She had never seen him before, yet a feeling of trust washed over her senses.

Fear went by the wayside. Instincts that initially wanted to run and hide held firm and met him on common ground. He was comforting. He was safe.

The clamoring of dishes broke through as she realized her surroundings. The man and woman were gone. Alexandra tried to calm the emotions escalating through her mind as her eyes darted back and forth searching for a tangible hold on reality.

What the devil just happened? The man pierced the very shell of her existence and had entered her mind. She was sure of it. Her heart began to race. As she looked around at the other diners, nothing or no one appeared out of the ordinary. This was beyond anything she'd experienced in her twenty-two years.

Old wives' tales told of harrowing experiences that turned your hair white. She fumbled in her purse for a mirror, half-expecting to see a visible change. Familiar eyes stared back, dilated in wonderment. Pinching her cheek fully zapped her back to reality.

She shook, trying to throw off the uncanny familiarization that had taken place without her permission. It didn't make sense. On one hand, she felt invaded, but on the other, the feeling had been incredible.

It wasn't his looks that caught her eye, although he certainly deserved a good ogle or two, it was the caring way he escorted the elderly woman. They both had the same engaging presence and seemed to live in a world of their own.

The bolt of magnetism that pulled her to him caught her off guard as she experienced the first stirrings of male attraction. Up to this point, Alexandra hadn't found the pressing need to delve into the male/female bonding ritual as her friends had. Over the years she had listened as other girls' thoughts of romance dominated conversations, but she could never truly contribute. Although her lack of interest in boys concerned her parents, she considered herself completely normal and even content, without having any desire for male companionship.

That part of her persona just turned a one-eighty. She had finally become a card-carrying member of the female race. That dark-haired Adonis with rippling muscles and mesmerizing eyes had caused her nerve endings to fire on all eight cylinders and flipped her mind in a completely new direction. If asked, she could describe him down to the exact curve of his jaw.

The yearning that pulled her toward the opposite sex shocked her very foundation. All the movies made sense now. Pheromones, she could sense them after all, but she still found it odd that someone fifteen feet away could cause a chemical reaction that rattled her bones.

* * * * *

Jediah ran his fingers through his thick black hair pondering his predicament; he had felt strange eyes on Nancy Jane, sensed the intrusion and locked onto her gaze without thinking.

Eyes, the color of new spring moss and golden hair glimmering like wheat in the wind - he was mesmerized. Tiny freckles dotted the bridge of her nose enhancing the softness of her ivory skin. He recognized her immediately.

Her arrival initiated a string of occurrences foretold many years ago that would culminate in

Nancy Jane's release. Stricken with remorse at the thought, Alexandra's presence signaled a turning point in all their lives, personally affecting Nancy Jane the most. He knew she would arrive this spring and had waited patiently for her as he had for many years.

She didn't know... yet.

* * * * *

Alexandra placed her order, which consisted of her usual diner fare: a bacon cheeseburger, French fries and gravy, and a black and white shake. As she gave the order, she sent a small 'thank you' to her lucky stars (if she had any left after today), that allowed her to eat her fill and not gain weight.

The waitress proved efficient, leaving little time to recap the day's adventures before her meal arrived. However, by the end of the fries, she found herself reliving the ordeal in vivid detail with a barrage of questions at the forefront of her mind.

Alexandra found it hard to believe she engineered the board in the slot, it actually held her weight, and she possessed the strength to pull herself up and out of her pit. Those types of occurrences happened to the heroine in some fictitious novel, but never in real life. Although she sat there as living proof, she questioned her ability to devise her escape.

Luck didn't seem to be a strong or exact enough word to describe the day's events. A tremor of fear passed through her as the hair on her arms stood on end. The proximity to a near-death experience

stunned her as she decided she didn't care for the
trial-by-cistern one bit.

She grabbed her purse, left money for the check
and tip on the table, and then sought the comfort of
the hotel.

On the floor of the bathroom lay the discarded
pants and shirt. Alexandra retrieved the plastic
dirty clothes bag from the closet and gathered up
the damp clothes to place in the trash. As she
picked up the pants, the stone from the cistern fell
from the pocket and onto the floor at her feet. She
had forgotten it completely and only vaguely
remembered placing it in the pants pocket.

Picking it up, she took it to the sink and washed
it off. After drying it with a towel, she placed it on
the nightstand.

She pulled her 'bear' from her overnight bag
and laughed at the ridiculous gray flannel nightshirt.
Two sizes too big and long-sleeved, it hung to her
knees and was at least eight years old. The well-
worn material had a pea-sized hole at the hip, and
on the front, the fuzzy bear wearing a plaid shirt,
had one wiggly eye missing. She'd found the eye
though, and planned to sew it back on.... well,
sometime. Pushing her head through the neck and
shoving her arms up the sleeves, she hugged herself.
Her bear symbolized home.

All snuggly, she grabbed her eReader, plopped
on the bed and downloaded a new book that
appeared in seconds. Using two of the five pillows
the hotel supplied, she propped herself up in bed
and started to read the intricate tale. The story
slowly replaced the harrowing day on the mountain

and as she read, her confidence regained its natural foothold.

Getting angry twice within the first hour with the contrived plot twists, she turned off the eReader and decided to call Cassie. No matter what stunts Alexandra pulled, she could always count on her cohort since kindergarten to lend moral support. Reaching for her phone, she pressed speed dial number one and pressed the 'speaker' button. On the second ring, a friendly warm voice said, "Hello?"

"Cassie, it's me."

"Where the heck have you been? I've been trying to catch up with you all day."

Not wanting her to worry, Alexandra stalled. "I went exploring here in Waynesburg and lost track of time. I left my phone in the Jeep."

"Waynesburg, like in Pennsylvania? Is it Teater again? I thought you were going to relax a bit before your masters."

"Teater is my way of relaxing. It's just a small trip, and I found the farm, but not the cemetery. I'm going back there tomorrow to scout around some more. Want to join me?" She hopped off the bed and routed through her overnight bag.

"Sure, I have no pressing social life anyway."

"You don't want one." Gotcha. She pulled out a box of Junior Mints and opened the end.

"Nothing here in the valley tempts me. You should talk; you live the life of a nun. At least, I had a date a few months ago."

"That was no date, Cinderella. You met your insurance agent for supper to go over the terms of your policy." She reminded her. "And isn't he married? How are his twins?" she said as she popped a delicious mint onto her tongue.

"Okay, but that's still more activity than you've seen in five years."

"I've been concentrating on finishing up my masters, remember?"

"Yeah, I know. Hey, what are you eating? You're chewing in my ear."

"I'm not chewing; I'm sucking on a Junior Mint."

"If you save me some, I'll come up first thing tomorrow?"

"Okay, but you only get half. I'm counting them out now. Let's see there's twenty-three left. I bought them so I get the odd one."

"But you already ate one."

Hmm, leave it to the moppet to keep her in line. "Then get here early. Junior Mints have a mind of their own."

"I will."

"I have a room with two queen beds, so you can bunk with me if you decide to stay the weekend."

"Sounds good. I'll go pack now so I can get an early start."

After giving Cassie the address for the GPS and wishing her a safe trip, she snuggled back in bed and returned to her book. The day's events took their toll. Not many minutes passed before the words on the eReader looked like the back of her eyelids.

Yawning, she caught the glimmer of a faint

blue light on the nightstand. Reaching over to turn the light of the clock away from her vision, she noticed it wasn't the clock at all. A bit startled, she sat up in bed - the blue mysterious light came from the stone. What in the world? She turned on all the lights and the blue color disappeared. Thinking her eyes were tired and playing tricks on her, she rubbed them, and looked at the stone again. Too tired to wonder anymore, she shut the lights off only to see the stone glowing once again.

She picked up the stone and started across the room to the desk lamp. The stone got warm and sent tingles into her fingertips and up her arm. Alexandra dropped it and rubbed her hand.

"What the heck? This is too weird." She knelt on all fours and scrutinized the stone.

It appeared to be nothing more than a river-worn rock. She hesitantly picked it up and once again, the sensation began anew. This time she held on and opened her palm to look at the stone, which now emitted a bright blue light. The tingling continued to race throughout her body like tiny electric charges searching for something. She caught her reflection in the full-length mirror. A blue aura wrapped completely around her.

"Ouch!" she yelled and dropped the stone as a searing pain burned her shoulder. Stunned a bit, she sat up cross-legged and rubbed her shoulder, then went to the bathroom and pulled down her shirt to see what hurt. A blazing red welt the size of a quarter presented itself where only freckled flesh should be.

She turned on the cold water, soaked a

washcloth, wrung it out, and then pressed the cool cloth to her shoulder. She hated pain! Any little ache seemed quadrupled in her, and this thing hurt.

After the stinging sensation started to ease, she turned, half expecting another go-round from the stone. It lay on the floor, looking quite innocent. She walked around the stone but kept her distance.

"Okay, what in Hades just happened? Stones don't glow blue or any other color and they certainly don't burn circles on you."

The stone wasn't talking.

Alexandra considered herself well grounded, yet here she stood, talking to a stone that glowed, burned circles, and refused to answer.

A thread of sensation pricked at the edges of her mind, then grew stronger. It mirrored an idea then became clear.

Tell no one.

What? Looking from side to side, she backed against the wall. Although it felt like someone whispered in her ear, she stood there alone. The day's trauma must have pushed her over the edge, yet the sensation persisted.

Tell no one.

She froze. Her eyes darted around the room. The muscles in her legs tightened as she prepared to bolt from the room.

Alexandra swallowed and licked her lips. "Who would believe me anyway?" she whispered.

Boy, the things she should have asked her parents and didn't have a chance to could fill a box car. Mental illness didn't run in her family, at least she didn't think so. The sensation that someone was with her started to ease.

"What ever this is," she said, "I want no part of it. Leave me alone."

She could feel the presence no longer. Her knees buckled and she sagged against the wall. No words came to mind to describe what just happened. Voices in her head was... unnatural, to say the least. It wasn't a threat, she realized, just a strong suggestion. The voice hadn't been menacing, it was more a sense of caution, like steering a child from fire.

Each time she thought to call Cassie and share the experience, the sensation came forth to keep the tale to herself. In an attempt to rationalize the strange events, she could find nothing to connect reality to the eerie activities that occurred today. She was glad Cassie was coming. If she was losing her mind, she wanted company.

Some time later, after two cups of chamomile tea and some deep soul-searching, she began to relax.

She struggled to read a few chapters but after an hour or so, she gave the stone one final glance, turned off the eReader, rolled over and finally fell into a tormented sleep.

Chapter Three

Alexandra awoke to the sun shining on her face from a gap in the curtains. Smiling, she stretched her arms and legs. Umm, that was the best sleep she'd had in ages. She pulled back the drapes of her hotel room window and gazed at the early morning mist nestled in the lowlands as it gave way for the dawning of a new day.

Stepping in the shower, she let the hot water run over her skin and invigorate her body. She noticed her shoulder no longer stung yet the strange red mark remained. Even though she scrubbed it viciously, it failed to wash off.

Once out of the shower she leaned closer to get a better look at the tattoo in the mirror. The pattern was deep maroon and contained four intricate arcs. The stone put the mark on her shoulder. But why, how? As she began to breathe rapidly, momentary apprehension engulfed her, replaced in a split second by a feeling of peace. The mental confusion brought pain to her temples. Emotions of a conflicting nature battled inside her psyche, but, after a moment, peace reigned.

Wrapped in a towel, Alexandra climbed onto the center of the bed. "Mom, we need to talk. I don't understand what the heck is going on." She glanced toward the stone.

"I know I talk to Cassie about everything, but

something inside insists I keep quiet about the stone and the tattoo. Last night, I heard a voice in my head telling me to 'tell no one'." She held her head in her hands.

"I sure wish you and Dad were here. I think it has something to do with Teater. Why didn't you tell me about my relatives? Why did you leave me so alone?"

As soon as she felt the ache in her chest, she caught herself and pushed the weakness away. Nothing she could do or say would change anything, and for some reason that remained unclear, the burden rested with her. She knew she would not share the strange occurrences with Cassie, and she wondered why she found peace with that decision.

Sitting in front of the mirror, she pinned her long blonde hair back on each side with combs. Moisturizer, light foundation, a tiny blush to her cheeks, a coat of mascara on her long lashes, and poof, a ready-for-the-day Alexandra smiled back at her. She was just adding a spritz of perfume, when a knock on the door reminded her to hide the Junior Mints. She made a mad dash and hid the box before opening the door to Cassie.

The two hugged and started talking at the same time.

"Hey, you smell good," said Cassie.

"Thanks. Look at you. I don't know how you can appear so bright and bubbly early in the morning."

"You know my curls have a mind of their own. Today they decided to behave instead of mimicking a wild child of nature." Cassie shook her curls for effect.

"No one could ever mistake you for a child, perhaps a Romanesque model, or brick outhouse, but never a child."

"Oh, so you have no aversion at all to the descriptor 'wild'?" Cassie asked with a twinkle.

"None, whatsoever." Alexandra winked.

Cassie looked around the room. "Hey, where're my Junior Mints?"

"You're like an elephant. You never forget anything," she said as she retrieved the mint box from under the pillow and handed them to her. Drat. Now she'd have to replenish her supply.

"Okay, spill it. Why did you decide to run away in search of Teater all of a sudden?"

Alexandra sighed. "It wasn't really all of a sudden. You were working and it's my last break from school before I graduate and have to get serious about a job somewhere. I had some time on my hands and now was as good a time as any."

Cassie plopped down in the middle of the bed, sat cross-legged, popped a mint then twisted an errant curl around her finger. "Okay, then, Teater it is. Where do we start?"

"I think we should begin with breakfast. I'm really hungry. Looks like you might be too the way you're gobbling down those mints. Probably has something to do with the air over here."

"Air? You're a bottomless pit," Cassie said. "I just popped two or three tiny mints. If I ate like you, I'd be rolling instead of walking."

"You will never roll anywhere. You have too

much self-control. The mere mention of a flabby body part causes calories to run for cover."

"I'm not that bad."

"Are too, but you do look fabulous." With Cassie's totally engaging personality, Alexandra wondered how long it would be before some dashing fellow stole her friend's heart away.

"Thanks. Where are we heading for breakfast?"

"I found a diner in town where the parking lot is always full. It's shaped like a rounded train car and reminds me of some place from the fifties. You'll love it. They even have miniature jukeboxes on each table and you can select songs for a quarter."

"Sounds perfect."

She sat next to her friend. "Before we go I need to tell you what happened to me yesterday."

"You look so serious. Are you all right?"

"Yes, but…" and within a few minutes, she had shared yesterday's experience with Cassie, without disclosing details about the stone or her new tattoo.

Once Alexandra completed her tale, she stopped to gauge her reaction.

"Good Heavens, you could have died. I didn't even know you were coming here, and from the sound of it, I'll bet no one would have found you any time soon. Why did you risk your life like that? Weren't you scared?"

Alexandra picked at her nails, unwilling to meet Cassie's eyes. "I've been almost obsessed with discovering why my great-great grandfather left his family." She raised her head to meet

Cassie's gaze. "Yes, I was scared, and don't think I wasn't seriously concerned about getting out of that darned hole. Those hours felt like days."

"You were alone and cold for all that time." Cassie spoke softly, and reached over and placed her hand on Alexandra's arm. "I can't imagine being in that situation."

"I can, now." Alexandra hugged her.

Finally, Alexandra spoke. "I don't ever plan on doing anything so stupid again. Believe me, I've learned my lesson. From now on I'll communicate, and take my cell phone."

"Good. I don't want to have to worry about you, okay?"

"No complaints from me. Thanks for coming up. After yesterday, it feels really good to have you here." She kissed Cassie's cheek. "How about heading out for breakfast? I need a good cup of tea."

"Sounds great, I didn't bother with anything but decaf before I left. It was too early."

As Alexandra grabbed her purse and phone, Cassie said, "Hey, what's this?"

Before Alexandra could stop her, Cassie picked up the stone from the floor and held it firmly in her hand.

"You're throwing rocks on the floor now?" Cassie asked.

As her heart raced, Alexandra responded calmly, "It came from the cistern. I thought I'd keep it as a reminder to always keep in touch."

Cassie placed the stone on the nightstand. "Maybe you should paint a skull and crossbones on it."

Alexandra shot her a look. "Not a bad idea," she said as they left the room.

The morning brought forth a fresh perspective and added a participant to the quest. After enjoying a hearty breakfast, they set out for the abandoned farm.

Cassie's eyes popped. "You came up this gut-wrenching road yesterday all by yourself?" she exclaimed. "You deserve a good cuffing just for driving this goat path on your own."

"It's not so bad once you get used to dodging the ruts."

"You've got some nerve calling these canyons ruts."

"Cassandra Hudson, where is your sense of adventure?"

"I dropped it off going over that last crater when only two wheels were on the ground."

"Those ones are a bit exhilarating, aren't they?" She winked.

"Keep your eyes on the road!"

"What road?"

"Exactly. Will these ruts, twists, and turns never end?" Cassie held tight to the Jeep hand supports.

"Don't complain about the ruts. If it weren't for them, I wouldn't be able to find my way through the trees and brush."

"Somehow, I get the feeling we'll come upon a gun-toting, overall-clad figure guarding a copper still with a shotgun, and we'll be at the end of his barrel."

She laughed. "The thought never entered my mind. There's no doubt it's possible."

Rounding the crest of the hill and entering the clearing, they arrived at their destination.

The breath-taking view of the town and valley below overwhelmed Alexandra. The seclusion she felt amid the rolling tops of neighboring mountains stretching for miles and miles in all directions wrapped around her and filled every pore. Gazing up at the clear blue sky, she inhaled the scent from spring blossoms. They lifted her spirits to a new high. Today might be the day she found the answer to Teater's riddle.

"What a trip!" Cassie's audible relief filled the air as she exited the Jeep. "I can't say I'm not sorry that's over. The worst part is: knowing we have to return the same way."

"Why Cassandra Hudson, have you turned into a girlie-girl on me?"

"Not so much a girlie-girl as a female thankful for making it to the top alive."

She smiled, and then sobered immediately. "Hey, we're not alone." She nodded in the direction of the crest of the hill.

Two men stood near the cistern and both turned when they heard the doors of the Jeep slam. Not willing to lose a chance for information, she headed toward them at a quick pace with Cassie trailing slightly behind.

She wanted to start out on the right foot so she waved and began. "Hi, I'm Alexandra Higgins, and this is my friend, Cassandra Hudson. Please forgive us for trespassing, but I'm looking for the old

Higgins Cemetery. Do you know where it is?"

As she drew closer, she recognized the tall dark-haired man as the one who had caught her staring at his companion and had glared back at her in the diner. She slowed her pace and fidgeted with her pack. First, she had been caught staring, and now, trespassing; she wobbled on poor footing once again.

The older, shorter, sandy-haired man spoke. "Ms. Higgins, this is not a safe place for you to go poking around. People put up *No Trespassing* signs for a reason, not just to inconvenience you. Best you and your friend get in your little red Jeep and mosey on back the way you came."

She frowned, strode toward him and stated firmly. "It's important I find the cemetery and I'll not be put off. I am a direct descendant of the Higgins family and need to learn as much as possible about my ancestor. My trail has run cold and this is the only place I can begin anew. I assure you, my intent is honest in nature. Are you the owner of this property?"

Her heart raced. The dark-haired man hadn't taken his eyes off her since their arrival, nor had he moved an inch from his original stance. Throughout her mini-tirade, she glanced back and forth between the two men, and each time she caught the dark-haired man's eye, he seemed transfixed on her.

Not typically scrutinized so deeply, the hairs on the back of her neck stood on end, and heat crept up her neck reaching the follicles of her hair.

"No, ma'am, I'm not the owner; that would

be..."

"Someone else," said the dark-haired man, cutting him off.

His voice resonated in her ears. Looking directly at him she could barely breathe. She reminded herself to take in air.

Time stopped once again. All went still. Instantly she found herself alone with him in an orb of shimmering light. Millions of flickering rays nearly blinded her until she adjusted to the brightness. Devoid of all sound, quiet mocked the unprepared girl who felt as light as air. Before fear could take root, his beautiful nature pervaded her senses creating familiarity where none should exist. She absorbed the vastness of eternity and infinite compassion he exuded. Serenity overcame every other emotion and held her suspended, completely at peace.

Consumed by his presence and experiencing emotions on an intimate level, she plunged into a new state of awareness. Her existence melded with his; they stemmed from the same life force. With neurons firing throughout her body, she sensed each microscopic cell of grass and tree surrounding them. The exchange crammed her senses to overflowing, the exhilaration grew too large for her to grasp or comprehend. She swirled amid the lights, becoming dizzy and getting lost in the endless bounty.

Mesmerizing violet eyes emerged in the foreground amid the lights and slowly tethered the floundering innocent. Focusing on the translucent color steadied the whirlwind of senses and returned

Alexandra's footing to solid ground. The compelling experience dissipated as the beginnings of a smile hinted on his lips and a wink solidified it all.

"Do you know where the family cemetery is located?" Alexandra heard Cassie ask.

No longer in the orb and standing next to Cassie, she noted everyone acted as if nothing out of the ordinary had happened. Unable to grasp the here and now, she stood, still somewhat transfixed, not wanting the effects to fade.

"Sure do, and you can call me Terry. I'm the caretaker here and I need to get to a bit of taking care of this cistern cap. Looks like it just gave in; someone could get hurt wandering around here. Didn't know you were family." He directed toward Alexandra. "I'm sorry for being so gruff. There aren't many Higginses left in these parts anymore. This here fellow," he said nodding at the dark-haired man, "is Jediah Saffle and I think he can help you two ladies in your search."

Terry walked off to get supplies from his truck.

Jediah. He had a name, but, despite his effect on her psyche, he had no right to transport her from reality to heaven-only-knows-where, no matter how pleasant the experience.

She couldn't understand the pressing need to keep her mouth shut. A knock-your-socks-off event just took place, and, although her mind performed somersaults in exhilaration of the discovery, she stood there calmly as if it were an everyday experience.

Cassie looked intently at Jediah. "Mr. Saffle,

we're sorry for the intrusion."

Still mummified, Alexandra peered at Cassie, who couldn't have possibly seen the orb. She glanced back at Jediah for acknowledgment, but he appeared as unconcerned with what just transpired as Cassie. Surveying the cistern, he just rubbed his jaw with a perplexed look on his face.

Alexandra's heartbeat hammered in her ears and pounded in her chest. It had to be sensory overload. Without a doubt, she knew that seconds ago she had occupied a mystifying sphere of light with Jediah Saffle. Odd as it seemed, she had shifted onto an extraordinary pathway, and although she had nothing to fear, the action taken without her permission grated on her very last nerve.

Sound waves interrupted her thoughts. Those sculpted lips spoke. "James Dawson, who has an office on Main Street in the center of town, can help you locate information about the Higgins family. He's an attorney whose family has been here for generations. He may be able to head you in the right direction. Now, if you two will forgive me, I need to help Terry get this old cover mended and back in place."

"Jediah, before you go, could you point us in the direction of the Higgins Family Cemetery?" Cassie inquired.

"It's on the other side of that rise to the left," he said pointing. "On the 'morning side of the hill'." He tossed the words over his shoulder, already heading toward Terry and the truck.

She felt Cassie grabbing her arm, jerking her gaze from Jediah and guiding her to the rise he had pointed out.

"What's wrong with you? Are you feeling all right? You look odd. He certainly was good looking, and I know we both live like nuns, but that's no reason to be dumbstruck."

"You, um, didn't notice anything odd?" she asked as she stumbled toward the hill.

"Well, they had a right to be a little firm with us, we are trespassing. They ended up being nice enough."

"Yeah, he was nice."

Cassie stopped and stared at her friend, "He was nice? For heaven's sake, snap out of it. Are you okay?"

"I'm sorry." Even if she could tell her what just happened, how would she put it into words? "I just never noticed someone like him before." Holy cow, why wasn't she spilling her guts? As her breath quickened, she realized she didn't know why. Just like the stone, she wanted to keep this to herself. Wanted? No needed, she clarified.

"Oh my, when you engage, you knock down all fences. So it finally happened; a male got under your skin."

Alexandra flushed, caught off guard. "So that's what all the fuss is about." Heat crept up her neck.

"I tried to tell you, but you've never been interested. Not a bad choice for your first infatuation."

"Did you see the color of his eyes?" As soon as the words left her lips, she felt her cheeks burn.

"Yeah, while you were standing there like a love-struck teen, I had the opportunity to check out every inch."

"He was comfortable in his own skin, wasn't he?"

"Whoa, now you're beginning to worry me. Cassie stood directly in front of her and snapped her fingers in front of Alexandra's face. "Are you in there?"

Somewhat irritated that Cassie forced her attention from Jediah's collision of senses, she forced herself to normalcy. "Oh my, I'm a train wreck."

Cassie held her mouth and laughed. "You're no train wreck. I've had tons of guys affect me for years in small increments. I just think all your increments hit you at once."

"Sheesh," she replied, trying to regain composure. "I was totally unprepared for that. Why now? Why him? I don't even know him. How could someone have that much impact?"

"Well, you have been saving it up for some time. And, if I were to choose someone to jolt me into reality, Mr. Saffle with his wind-tousled hair and hunky body looks like he could do the trick."

"Mmm, he did look like a bit of heaven stuffed in that t-shirt, didn't he?" Not a fan of 'pretty boys,' she immediately amended her male categories to include gorgeous and hunky and perhaps, eccentric. He exuded refinement, manners, confidence, and clearly, a presence that drew her unlike anything she had ever experienced before.

"He sure did," Cassie said while taking in her surroundings. "Wow, it's beautiful here. A mountain meadow complete with chirping birds and wildflowers."

"Don't get too caught up in it. When I did, I fell in a hole."

"Okay, Alice," Cassie said, "I'll keep an eye out for rabbit holes."

Alexandra rolled her eyes and continued around the knoll of the hill, stepping over briars and wading through knee-high grasses.

Keeping all the strange incidents from her best friend and cohort didn't make sense. She trusted Cassie above all others, so why the need to hold her tongue? Nearly bursting at the seams to share, her inner gut demanded she keep her mouth shut. Once the decision to do nothing settled in, she let her thoughts turn to more pleasant matters.

Jediah Saffle certainly sported a bag of tricks. The calming effect he maintained over her emotions irritated her. With that type of power, she should be afraid of losing control. Instead, she had readily accepted it. His essence forced her to trust him, and, as far as she was concerned, he hadn't earned that right. He would remain an unsolved mystery until she placed the orb and harrowing sensory overload in a real or imaginary realm.

Although Alexandra didn't know how she did it, she pushed all vagrant thoughts aside to delve into the search at hand.

"Hey," Cassie said, "I think that's it right over there. See the markers in the weeds?"

"Oh, I think you're right!"

She walked over to a partial clearing, which looked out over the town of Waynesburg in the distance. Although overgrown, the location caught the first morning sun and maintained a solemn air, a perfect atmosphere for a final resting place. Twenty or so markers grouped together created the family cemetery. No fence encompassed the graves, leaving them open to the entire side of the hill and the view below. The weathered stones leaned awkwardly in different directions due to erosion and covered an area about thirty feet square.

"The weeds are almost as tall as the markers." Alexandra said. "It's a good thing we got here in early spring; another three weeks and they would be hidden until fall."

"Yeah, you're right. I'll take the first row."

"Do you see any Higgins gravestones?" asked Alexandra after reading each one in the second row.

"No, all the ones I've look at so far are marked Madison."

"That's all I've seen too. Then why call it the Higgins Family Cemetery?"

"Doesn't make sense, does it?"

Twigs snapped and leaves crunched as she walked through the grass to a short marker. "Oh, here's one." Alexandra pointed to the first marker in the third row, as she stared at a small stone with the inscription, *Infant Higgins, born: November 30, 1938, died: November 30, 1938.*

She jotted down the information. "Such a shame. I don't see a marker for the parents, do you?"

"Not yet. Could they still be living?" Cassie asked offhandedly.

"They'd be close to a hundred years old, probably not. I'll add the child to my search list.

Let's check the remainder, there has to be more Higgins."

As she checked the markers, she couldn't stop her mind from wandering back to Jediah. The attraction knocked the wind from her, but instead of rendering her gasping for breath, she had experienced fulfillment to a cosmic degree. While in the orb, she had connected on a cellular level with the nature around her and with Jediah. Still feeling some of the after-effects, she felt the tingling of air from breathing all the way to her fingertips. As she touched the markers, she could almost sense the essence of the person. The stone, the tattoo, Jediah's orb, they all had to be connected.

Completing her search, she sighed, and then yelled to Cassie, "I was certain he would be here. Let's go through them one last time. Push the weeds aside and make sure we're not missing any."

"Okay. I'm glad I wore jeans. These sticker bushes are grabbing my legs. I'd hate to be all scratched up for work. I've been gearing up for wearing sandals and sun dresses."

"I'm sorry. I thought it was going to be easier than this."

Alexandra walked around the outside perimeter of the site looking at it from all angles trying to get a feel for the layout. As she stepped down a small incline, she tripped, landing full pelt on her belly and grazed her knee. Crap. Really?

"Hey! Where'd you go? You okay? I heard a thud," Cassie yelled.

"Yeah, just checking it out from ground level,"

she said as she popped her head up above the weeds. "No cistern over here."

"You're a goof, an educated one, but a goof no less." Cassie laughed.

"I'm not a goof. I'm witty." She sat back to brush off the knees of her jeans and then leaned over to see what had caused her to trip. A grave marker laying flat, situated some thirty feet from the others, loomed at her feet. The unexpected stone rested far outside the imaginary border she'd surmised. She pulled away the prickly briars and brushed the leaves and debris away.

"Cassie, I found one over here that fell over face down. Come help me, we need to roll it over."

"Coming, just give me time to plow through the weeds."

"The ground is soft," Alexandra said. "I think I can get my fingers under the edge. When I lift it, grab hold of the edge so I can get a better grip."

"Ok, got it. Let me know when you're ready to flip it."

"Ready. Lift."

"Watch your fingers!"

It landed with a soft thump. Alexandra brushed the soil away. The plain, oblong marker carried the inscription, *Theodore "Teater" Higgins 1859 – 1928.*

"I was about to give up hope."

"It's about time," Cassie said, "I was beginning to think he was a figment of your imagination."

"No," she said, pondering an earlier episode. "This one's for real."

"There's not much to go on," noted Cassie.

"Well, I know Teater was a nickname for Theodore and he died here in Waynesburg. That's more than I knew before. I'd still like to know what made my great-great grandfather leave his family and come back here. At least I can search the records by his proper name."

"One step closer," Cassie said while picking briars off her socks.

"A trip to town to see attorney Dawson is next. He might know something of Teater's history. He may even have family who remember something."

After snapping a few photos of the area, gravesite, and Teater's marker, they headed toward the Jeep.

"You were really lucky to find that gravestone. If you hadn't tripped over it, we would have missed him completely," Cassie said.

"I wonder why it was so far from the others?" Alexandra picked her way through the bushes with Cassie following close behind.

"That was odd, wasn't it?"

"Yeah, we can add that to the list of weird things that happened in Waynesburg."

Alexandra laughed at her comment. Cassie had no idea how true her statement really was.

As she rounded the hill toward the Jeep, she saw Terry working on the cistern cover and altered her path to walk nearby. When she got close, Terry's gaze met hers.

"Did you find what you were looking for?" he inquired.

"Yes, thank you," responded Alexandra. "I'm sorry we barged in on you like we did. I really didn't intend to ignore posted signs for trespassing, but I couldn't locate an owner to request access. We found the gravestone I was looking for and it's enough to fill in some gaps."

"Good. I don't have to worry that you girls will get into any more trouble running around up here, do I?"

"No, we've concluded our search," Alexandra responded.

"Have a good day."

"Thank you for your time."

He waved them off as he continued the repairs. As they turned toward the Jeep, Alexandra sensed him watching her, and when she glanced over her shoulder, he quickly looked away.

The little hairs on the back of her neck stood up, giving her a chill. She shrugged it off as getting away with trespassing and let it go at that.

"I'm not looking forward to going back down that road," Cassie said while getting into the Jeep.

"It's not so bad. Close your eyes."

"And miss seeing the end of our days?"

"Well, you can't have it both ways. Seat belt buckled?"

"As if I would forget that with those ruts looming before me; I'm buckled and ready."

The trip back down the mountain, though lengthy, proved uneventful.

Chapter Four

Alexandra walked up to the doorway of James Dawson, Attorney at Law with Cassie trailing slightly behind.

"I feel funny walking into his office with no appointment," Cassie said.

Alexandra knew her friend hated confrontation and preferred to do things by the book. "Don't worry, if it's not convenient for hm to see us, we can come back later," she said pushing open the heavy wood door with cut glass sidelights.

"Okay." Cassie sighed.

A well-dressed middle-aged woman raised her head from the computer screen, and said, "May I help you?"

Alexandra stepped closer. "Yes, I don't have an appointment, but I was hoping to speak with Mr. Dawson."

"Certainly, dear. Your name please?"

"He doesn't know me. My name is Alexandra Higgins."

"Won't you two please have a seat? I'll be right back," she said and turned to enter the inner office.

"He has a comfortable office," Cassie noted as she chose a seat in a tufted chair.

"And exquisite taste in watercolors." Alexandra said while examining them. "These paintings are all by the same artist. All have the same floral subject matter and use similar colors so they blend beautifully with the surroundings. They're absolutely stunning."

"The room makes you feel calm, doesn't it?"

Smiling, Alexandra nodded and took a seat next to Cassie.

"I hope he knows something about Teater."

"Me too, maybe then you can concentrate on something else, like, maybe Jediah."

Her face got warm. "Heck, he hardly noticed us. He was more interested in a hole in the ground than he was in me."

"Maybe your specific type of pheromone takes time to be absorbed. Besides, what counts is that you noticed him."

"Don't remind me. I must have come off like a school kid."

"Well, I have seen you handle yourself better. I thought you were kinda cute."

"Cute?" Her shoulders slumped.

"You don't let go enough. It was nice seeing you a bit off your game."

Alexandra let out a groan and hung her head. "I didn't know I had game."

The receptionist came back to the front desk. "Ms. Higgins, Mr. Dawson can see you now. Would you come this way?" She led them down the hall and into a book-filled, mahogany-trimmed office.

Stepping forward, he smiled, and extended his hand. "Hello, I'm James Dawson. I've been awaiting your arrival. Jediah said you would be dropping by."

Alexandra gave a small involuntary jerk, and then took his hand. "Good afternoon, I'm Alexandra Higgins and this is my friend, Cassandra Hudson."

"I'm pleased to meet you both. Ladies, please have a seat. I apologize for having you wait, but I needed to get some papers in order before seeing you."

"I'm sorry for the intrusion, Mr. Dawson. Mr. Saffle led me to believe you might know something about my ancestors. In particular, I've been looking for information regarding my great-great-grandfather, Teater Higgins."

Mr. Dawson beamed. "You are going to find this visit somewhat shocking and very rewarding. Jediah stated you were searching for information regarding the Higgins family. I'll need to see some identification, and, if you don't mind, your Social Security Number before we can proceed."

"Why do you need my social?"

"Before I can speak to you further, I need to verify your identification."

After handing Mr. Dawson her driver's license, and sharing her Social Security Number, he excused himself from the room.

"Holy smoke, what the heck's going on?" Cassie asked. "Why did he want your Social Security Number? That seems weird."

"I haven't a clue, but I feel I'm exactly where I'm supposed to be, if that makes any sense."

"No, it doesn't, but I'm glad I'm here. I would hate to miss this."

"Mr. Dawson seems likable," Alexandra said as

she scanned the contents of his office. "The pictures on either side of the fireplace look like original tintypes."

"Leave it to you and your 'old soul' to be drawn to the antiques in the room."

"Every time you tell me I have an 'old soul' it makes me feel like somebody's grandmother."

"I can't help it. You know I love you, but you have always acted so much older than the rest of us. Remember when you had to write 'What I Did on Summer Vacation' in front of Mrs. McDonald in third grade because she said your mother wrote your paper for you?"

Shaking her head, she grumbled. "Why do you always remind me of things I wish to forget?"

Cassie shook with laughter. "And then, when you finished, she still gave you a bad grade because she said you memorized it?"

Alexandra couldn't help but find the humor in the memory. "All right, what's your point?"

"You had an amazing vocabulary and spoke like an adult even then."

"I can't help who I am. I'm just me, and I've always liked words."

"Admit it, your soul has been around a long time and absorbed the wisdom of the ages. You are definitely an 'old soul'."

"Thanks a lot."

Just then, Mr. Dawson reappeared accompanied by a uniformed police officer.

She quickly stole a glance at Cassie, who also appeared baffled.

"Ms. Higgins," Mr. Dawson said, "this is

Officer Johnson of the Waynesburg Police Department. He is here at my request to verify your identity."

Her brow furrowed. "I don't understand."

Mr. Dawson continued. "He will need to match your fingerprints to those on your birth certificate. I know this seems a bit odd, but if you bear with me just a little while longer, I'll be able to answer all your questions."

It took all the poise she could muster not to break out in a tantrum and demand to know why this was necessary. Taking a deep breath, she quelled the inner stirrings and shot Cassie a determined look to do the same. Her instincts told her an outburst would not help. Mr. Dawson merely followed some sort of protocol, but what the devil for – she had no idea.

Alexandra swallowed hard as Officer Johnson laid his portable fingerprinting kit on the edge of Mr. Dawson's desk. He pressed Alexandra's thumb on the inking mat and then rolled it onto the card. Each finger received the same treatment, and finally, he handed her a cloth to wipe the ink from her fingers.

"Thank you, Ms. Higgins."

"You are welcome, Officer Johnson. Now, I know how a criminal feels." She shot Mr. Dawson a look to let him know she was at the end of her patience.

After nodding to Mr. Dawson, Officer Johnson retrieved his kit and departed.

"Was that really necessary?" inquired Alexandra.

"Yes, my dear. Please accept my apology for the intrusion into your privacy. I'm certain that wasn't pleasant for you. Soon, I'll be able to tell you why." His demeanor changed to one of genuine friendliness.

"Surely you can imagine my confusion," she said more softly.

"Yes, I can. While we're waiting, can you tell me what brought you to Waynesburg in search of Teater?"

A little unsure where to begin, she hesitated. "I've always been interested in my family's genealogy and have traced my family back to the seventeen hundreds with complete documentation. Teater has been my only stumbling block."

Over the next half hour, Alexandra shared the tale to a very interested lawyer.

"I performed numerous searches on the web, logged umpteen hours in genealogy sites, even scoured old family Bibles, all to no avail. Teater, the young son of the large Higgins family had grown up somewhere other than Wheeling or the nearby surrounding area.

"It appeared Teater left his home as a young lad, but returned to Wheeling several years later, married Mary Wilkinson and fathered two sons, only to leave them again before the boys were fully-grown.

"I uncovered information regarding a Higgins cemetery in Waynesburg in one of the old journals and decided to hunt for the cemetery and check local records for any reference to him. With land deeds, census records, marriage certificates, and local news stories within the reach of my fingertips, I hoped important clues to Teater's puzzle might surface.

"So, you see, uncovering his whereabouts after he left his family in Wheeling is a personal quest."

"I see," he said. His phone rang. "Excuse me, won't you?" He answered the phone, "Hello? Yes? Thank you for your time."

She exchanged a glance with Cassie and watched as he smiled, then hung up the receiver.

"Alexandra Higgins," he began, "after checking with the Department of Motor Vehicles, performing a background check on your Social Security Number, and verifying your fingerprints, it appears you are who you say you are. We can now move forward and wrap this up."

He handed her license back and she read relief in his friendly smile. "We've been waiting for some time for you to appear. Let me say, that I'm very pleased to meet you. I'm excited you showed up on my watch."

A shiver of excitement went up her spine. Even though she had no idea what was in store, his excitement was contagious.

"To make it simple," he said, "Teater left a little something for you."

She looked at Cassie, who raised her eyebrows and grinned.

"Please continue, Mr. Dawson," she said shaking her head in disbelief, her eyes wide. "This trip has already been a bit off kilter to begin with, now you tell me that Teater, who died in 1928, knew I would be coming to see you, and that he left me something?"

"He didn't know it would be you exactly, but he hoped for a descendant. You see," he said, "my family has been practicing law here for nearly three hundred years. Teater's will was handed down through generations to be read to one of his descendants, but only if the descendant came looking for him specifically. Our hands were tied, since we weren't permitted to search for you. Teater wanted someone who cared about family to be the beneficiary of his will. I'm his executor, and a packet was placed in my family's care along with the will. The packet is being retrieved at this very moment from a bank vault and will be here shortly. Do you wish Ms. Hudson here at the reading of the will?"

Mr. Dawson grinned from ear to ear as he sorted through the papers on his desk.

She grabbed Cassie's hand. "Cassie is all that I have to call family in this world. I want her to be present."

"I assumed as much, and requested two copies of the will so you both could follow along." He handed a copy to each.

He sat at his desk, opened the original will, which had yellowed slightly with age, cleared his throat, and winked. "Shall we begin?"

The first part contained the standard 'of sound mind' and stipulated the witnesses; the next executor part detailed the restrictions placed on Mr. Dawson's family regarding finding a relative. Teater had taken great pains to ensure the claimant searched for him, and him alone. Amid the legal jargon came a place where Teater had written in his own hand:

I'm certain you will have many questions regarding your fate. I do not take my responsibilities lightly and have left you a guide in safekeeping. Know that all you need is within you.
– Teater.

A soft knock broke their concentration. Mr. Dawson murmured, "Come in."

His secretary walked into the room and handed him a leather-bound packet and a single sheet of paper, and then left the room. He reviewed the document, smiled, rose from his seat and with great reverence handed the packet to Alexandra, and then returned to his desk and finished the contents of the will. After she heard her great-great-grandfather had left her his estate, Alexandra failed to acknowledge little else.

Minutes later, while she tried to grasp the gift her ancestor had bestowed, she came back to the present when Mr. Dawson cleared his throat, a bit too loudly.

"Ms. Higgins, to summarize, Teater left his land in Waynesburg, the monies from his estate, and the packet to the first descendant to come looking for him."

"Mr. Dawson, this is surreal. I can't believe this is really happening and least of all, to me."

"It's real all right; all completely legal, and witnessed by my family throughout the generations."

Alexandra signed the remainder of the forms Mr. Dawson presented, obtained her copies, and thanked him before rising to leave.

"Ms. Higgins, I'll be in touch once the monies are ready for disbursal. I'm sorry, there's no way of knowing the exact amount at this time, you caught me a little off guard. Welcome to Waynesburg as our newest citizen and landowner. Please feel free to call on me if I can be of further assistance."

As they left the office, she clung to the packet tightly as her heart raced wildly. She'd found Teater, and been delightfully surprised that he'd wanted to be found. Excitement tingled throughout her body as she warmed and felt connected to her ancestor, even though he had long since passed on. He had reached from the grave, in essence, to make her welcome in his world.

"What the heck was that?" Cassie asked. "Boy, talk about a shocker!"

Alexandra was grateful Cassie had held her exuberance until they were out of earshot. "Can you believe it? These two days have been the most peculiar ever. From near death to land ownership - who would have guessed things like this happened in real life?" Yeah, and a glowing stone that burns tattoos and a hunky guy who puts you in a ball of light; try those on for size.

"Totally amazing! What's in the packet? Aren't you going to open it?"

"Not yet. Let's have lunch first. I'm starved and I don't think I can get my mind around much more right now."

Lunch consisted of diner food, per Alexandra's suggestion, and conversation regarding the unbelievable turn of events.

"I still can't believe this day, Cassie. I couldn't have made this up in my wildest dreams."

"The hand-written part of the will was a bit odd, don't you think?"

"Yeah, it was. What do you suppose he meant by 'a guide'?" she questioned Cassie.

"I don't know, maybe a book or something. You'll probably find out when you open the packet. Man, I'm super glad you asked me to come here. Your great-great-grandfather left you his estate, and if you hadn't come to Waynesburg looking for him, you would never have known. Too weird!"

"Did you think it strange Jediah Saffle called ahead to tell Mr. Dawson we were coming?"

"No, it was a nice courteous thing to do."

"Hmm." Nice and courteous, that's what she thought too.

"You're thinking too hard again, what's up?"

"Nothing really, just going over the additional shock my psyche had today. I didn't know someone of the opposite sex could have such an impact."

"I wish I had taken a picture of you." Cassie smiled. "You. Were. Stunned. I've never seen you smitten before."

"I wasn't smitten, just pleasantly surprised."

"Call it what you will, Ms. Master's Degree, you were definitely not yourself."

"Who would you have me be, then?"

"Let's see, Cinderella or a zombie? Hard to tell which."

"You're comparing me to a cartoon or Halloween character?"

"Okay, how about Julia Roberts in *Pretty Woman?*"

"Hah, now there's a gal who got what she wanted."

"Did you?"

"Did I what?" Alexandra toyed with the jukebox on the table.

"Find what you wanted?" Cassie asked.

Before she could reply, she looked up and winced to see Jediah standing next to their booth.

"Good afternoon ladies," he said, not missing a beat. "Did you lose something?"

"Err, no, I didn't lose anything." Alexandra felt his intensity and blushed. "It was a rhetorical question, there is nothing to find." Geesh, could it get any worse? The brute mocked her.

Jediah smiled brilliantly. "Ms. Higgins, were you able to meet with James Dawson?"

The big bully enjoyed teasing her, and that fact rankled her female instincts. Recovering quickly, she said, "Yes, thank you for sending me to him. As it turns out, he did have valuable information regarding my ancestor." She searched her feminine wiles and tried to determine what to say next. It didn't help that his shirt clung to his chest, and when he shifted his weight, his muscular thigh filled every inch of his jeans. Summing up courage, the words slowly came out of her mouth. "Would you care to join us?"

"Thanks for the invitation, but I am otherwise engaged, perhaps another time?"

Crashed and burnt to a crisp. She swallowed hard, and nodded. "Certainly."

"Great." He nodded, and then headed to a booth behind Alexandra and sat down.

Cassie peeked around her and said, "He's sitting with an older woman in the corner."

"Quit staring," Alexandra scolded, yet she knew, full well, she ached for the information. Her scorched ego burnt to ashes. She'd pushed forward to invite him and had received singed feathers for the attempt. If being turned down affected her this much when she barely knew him, she couldn't imagine being rebuked if her heart was involved.

"I'm not staring, but I can see them using peripheral vision."

"Okay. Then what are they doing?" Alexandra busied herself folding her napkin in her lap.

"Just talking, they're almost finished with their meal."

"Quit looking. I feel bad that you're spying."

"Okay, you're the boss. We almost got caught talking about him anyway, you know."

"Yeah, I know. I think he guessed we were doing it anyway. He looks at me like he sees right through me."

"I noticed that."

Alexandra saw Cassie's eyes widen. "What's going on?"

"Shush, they're leaving."

As Jediah and the older woman left, they passed Cassie's and her booth. Alongside, the older woman looked directly at Alexandra and smiled. Alexandra returned the smile. Jediah nodded to them as the couple left the diner.

"I'm kinda glad that's over," she said to Cassie.

"He did take the time to speak to you earlier. That can't be a bad thing."

"He was just being nice. It didn't mean a thing."

"If you say so…"

On the way back to the hotel for the unveiling of the packet, Cassie's cell phone rang. She picked it up, and noted the caller ID.

"It's my mom, I'm putting it on speaker. You have to tell her what's going on." Cassie clicked a button, "Hello, Mom?"

"Yes, honey, it's me. I don't think it's anything too severe, but I'm having some abdominal pain that is pretty strong. I've called the ambulance and I am going to Wheeling Hospital."

"Mom, I'll start home right away and meet you at the hospital's Emergency Room. Did you call Dad yet?"

"I left a message on his cell. He must have been in a meeting. Listen honey, I have to go, the ambulance is here."

"I love you, Mom. See you soon."

"I love you too, honey. Be careful driving home."

Alexandra drove her to the hotel and Cassie retrieved her bag from the room.

"Hold on, I'm coming with you."

"Oh no you're not. You need to stay here and finish with Teater."

"Teater's been gone a long time, I think he will keep."

"Girl, you are smack dab in the middle of a mystery. You haven't opened the packet yet. You might have to be here to do something else."

"No way. Since my parents died, you and your family are all I have."

"And we'll still be there when you finish up here. It's probably nothing, so quit worrying. You know Mom would tell you the same thing. I'll call you and let you know what's going on. You're only an hour away and you can dash home if you need to."

She'd be lying to herself if she said she didn't want to stay. "Promise me you'll call as soon as you know anything, anything at all?"

"Yes, I will." Cassie rushed out the door leaving her alone.

She dropped face down on the bed. Too much was happening too fast. What kind of friend was she to let Cassie go home alone? She should have gone with her, but something stronger than the commitment to her friend held her in Waynesburg and festered in the back of her mind.

She was alone in her room with the stone, packet, and a foreign mark on her shoulder. The time had come for some serious contemplation regarding the mystery that surrounded this place and Teater.

The well-worn leather packet tied together with string sat on the coffee table, unopened, holding the unknown. She sat up, picked up the stone from the nightstand and tossed it between her two hands while she considered her next steps. Arriving at a decision, she placed the stone next to the packet and moved to the small couch. She untied the string, and set it aside. The soft leather unfolded like an envelope. Before her lay the contents: a photograph, a key, and a document.

Performing a cursory inspection, she noted that although yellowed with age, the photograph possessed amazing clarity and depicted two men standing side-by-side. The small, thick key contained a beautiful intricate pattern on the grip, crafted she supposed, by a gifted artisan. The document was wax-sealed with the same insignia she now wore on her shoulder.

Breaking the seal, she unfolded it and revealed the following:

"September 30, 1925,

If you are reading this, I am no longer accessible to you. You will need a little history in order to understand why I have left this legacy to you. Unknown to my family, I have led quite an extraordinary life. It began when I was a lad of just ten years. I was the fifth of nine children in 1869 and Ellis, the ninth child, had just been born. The Union was in shambles following the Civil War, and many farming communities were torn apart. Our family had survived well, but due to our size, we were struggling. The two oldest sons, William and John, worked the farm while our father worked in the lumber mill. I was placed with a distant cousin's family in Waynesburg, who were unable to have children and needed help on their farm. At first, I was angry to have been separated from my brothers and sisters, and I missed our home, but as time went by, I grew fonder of Ben and Ada Madison, and they of me. I made a difference in their lives, and together we worked and saved the farm. As each year went by, I saw my birth family less and less.

When I was sixteen, I met an intriguing woman who changed my life forever. She gave me a special gift I hope to share with you.

At twenty-eight I returned to Wheeling, married Mary Wilkinson, and fathered two sons, Lawrence, your great grandfather, and George. I left Wheeling when I was forty, leaving behind my sons and wife of just twelve years. I didn't desert them because I didn't love them, it was exactly the opposite. I left them because I did love them so very much. I don't expect you to understand my reasoning yet, but someday you will. Until then, don't think too harshly of me.

Alexandra, it is my wish..."

What? Alexandra? He'd written her name? Surely, he couldn't have meant her. Her heart began to race as she continued.

"for you to continue in my footsteps, if you so desire. You have already found the stone..."

The stone! This couldn't get any freakier. She threw the pages down on the table and paced the room. In 1925, Teater knew she would fall in the cistern and find the stone? She needed to calm down; a good explanation would be forthcoming. Walking to the door, she checked the lock and threw the dead bolt and security latch closed. After making a strong cup of tea, she took a healthy swig, and sat down to resume the missive.

"and no doubt have the mark on your shoulder. Your journey has begun. I couldn't let you die in that cistern just because you wanted to know about

66

me. *Although it wasn't permissible to save you, I interfered just enough to let you save yourself.*

You are part of an extraordinary phenomenon you will soon be experiencing. You can choose to embrace it or let it fade away. This gift is not handed out lightly for in the wrong host, devastation can ensue.

Not wishing to be cryptic, but wary of discovery, I leave you this final thought: the key unlocks the guide; seek Jediah.

Warm regards,

Teater Higgins, 1925."

Chapter Five

'Not wishing to be cryptic?' What an understatement! While re-reading the note from Teater, Alexandra picked up the key and fingered the design work with her thumb. 'The key unlocks the guide'.

She now had proof the stone gave her the tattoo. Teater planned it all. What had he gotten her into?

The photo, though old and yellowed, possessed startling clarity. Both men were in their thirties; Alexandra studied the first man in great detail. A Higgins, no doubt; same nose and eyes she saw every morning in the mirror; light hair, and a welcoming smile that acknowledged her as kin. Teater wanted her to know him.

The second man in the photo, "No, it can't be. He's the spitting image of Jediah." She held a photo of her great-great-grandfather standing next to Jediah's ancestor. Shaking her head, she wondered if there could possibly be any more bumps in her harrowing day.

Glancing back at the key, she picked it up and fingered it once more. If it unlocked a guide, she should keep it with her at all times. Unfastening the necklace she always wore, she threaded the end through the loop at the end of the key and refastened it about her neck.

Too many strange things happened all at once. The orb, an inheritance, and now, without time to absorb anything, she needed to find a guide. Couple all that with a psychic great-great-grandfather who knew she would come to near death in a cistern and provided her the means to escape, Alexandra found herself swirling in a vortex of too many unbelievable occurrences for one day to grasp.

She sat on the sofa and rubbed her temples. The beginnings of a migraine pounded. She couldn't even bounce theories off Cassie because an undetermined something-or-other forced her to hold her tongue.

Although elusive, Jediah could provide the answer to her questions. He understood every tiny distinction that made up her being. Hold that thought. How did she know that? Her pulse quickened as she realized she had inklings of information she never had before.

Reading and re-reading the note from Teater only unearthed new questions and she already had a boatload that festered, unanswered.

Two hours had passed since Cassie left for the hospital. She hoped nothing serious had happened. Mrs. Hudson had brought her under her wing after her parents' accident and shielded her from the press during her time of need. Nothing bad can happen to such a good woman, she had to be okay. She reached for her phone and placed a call to Cassie.

"I haven't heard from you. How's your mom?"

"She had appendicitis."

"Is she okay?"

"Yeah, they caught it before the appendix burst."

"Thank goodness," she breathed a sigh of relief.

"They rushed her into surgery. I'm waiting to hear something." Cassie took a deep breath. "She should be in recovery soon."

"I feel bad not being there. I'm going to pack up and drive down."

"Don't you dare. She's fine. Besides, there's nothing you can do here. Dad's here too. He said it was her fault for eating spicy food; like that had anything to do with it. Dads can be goofy sometimes."

"He was probably trying to ease her fears. You know how much he loves your mom. Tell her I was pulling for her, okay?"

"I will," Cassie said. "When are you coming back?"

"In a few days."

"Hey, did you open the packet?" Cassie's voice held excitement.

"Yeah, no guide. But, the mystery continues. There was an antique key, a picture, and a letter from Teater in it."

"Did the letter tell you how to find the guide?"

"Of course not. That would have been too easy."

"Oh, sorry, Allie. I'll have to hear the rest of this later, dad wants me to go to the cafeteria with him for coffee. He says they took her to recovery and the doctor says everything went fine."

"Good. I'm glad to hear that. Hug your mom for me."

"Sure will. I'll catch up with you when you get home."

Alexandra rubbed her eyes and the back of her neck trying to alleviate the stress. As the tension eased, she went back over the days' events, and smiled. Even with all the eerie things that had taken place, she felt more alive than she had since her parents' accident.

Stomach growling, Alexandra got a fast shower, applied make-up with care, donned a fresh shirt and jeans, and braved the cool evening air while heading for the diner and comfort food. The waitress recognized her and smiled when she entered, but before she arrived at the table to take her order, Jediah slid into the opposite side of the booth.

"I hope you don't mind if I join you. You did invite me earlier. Was James Dawson able to assist you regarding Teater?"

Laughter bubbled beneath the surface; Alexandra found it hard to contain the emotion. Gosh, he smelled good. And those eyes... Wait, she didn't come to town to lust after the local hunk, but the attraction was so darned strong. What drew her to him?

With a partial smile, she responded. "Why do I feel you already know the answer to your questions? Guess that's rhetorical. Yes, you may join me, and yes, Mr. Dawson was very helpful." She took a breath and met his eyes. "Are you following me?"

"No, I'm not following you, or stalking you, but I was hoping you would get hungry and come here again. The Silk City Diner seems to be the only decent place to catch a good home cooked meal in Waynesburg, in case you hadn't noticed. And like you, I migrated to the diner with the most cars parked outside. The food, although a bit rich, hasn't disappointed me yet, and their chocolate cream pie has made me an addict," he said breaking into a boyish grin.

The waitress stopped by to take their order; Alexandra added a piece of chocolate cream pie, and when she did, Jediah winked at her. Not able to resist, Alexandra smiled. "You may end up being a bad influence on me."

"I can assure you, it's not my intention," he said flashing perfect white teeth.

Before she got caught up in the hormones dancing around her she checked herself. Did fate have to make it this hard on her? Couldn't he have had greasy hair or some stubble he'd missed while shaving? Bad breath would have worked. Anything. Not this guy, perfect in every detail. Defeated, she sighed. He might be the most amazing example of alpha male on the planet, and the attraction toward him carried the force of an electromagnet, but she would not play his game. She needed answers.

"Look, can we cut to the chase? What the devil is going on here? What connection do you have with Teater, James Dawson, and me? I don't like playing games, and I find myself questioning my sanity for the first time in my life, so if you could shed some light on the mystery surrounding me now, I'd certainly be grateful."

He met her gaze straight on. "Why don't you tell me what has happened, then, perhaps, I can help you."

She fired back at him. "I'm supposed to just open myself up and tell you everything that has happened to me since I came to Waynesburg? I don't think so. Why should I trust you? Even I have heard of the Wernersville State Facility for the mentally compromised in Pennsylvania. Nobody here knows me and I could easily be committed in a flash. I think you should begin."

"Alexandra."

The sound of her name on his lips was like a caress. Time slow to a crawl; once again the sphere of shimmering light encompassed them. Her fears fell away and peace enveloped her. Alexandra looked directly into his violet eyes and found they searched hers.

What are you doing to me? She conveyed without speaking, which puzzled her.

You told me to begin. His thoughts entered her mind.

You heard me. How is this possible?

Ask what you really want to know.

Who are you?

I am known as Jediah.

What are you?

Ah, now we're getting somewhere. I'll need to show you the answer, but now is not the time. Will you trust me?

Don't ask me that while I'm here in this orb.

Fair enough.

The brilliant light diffused and she glanced around. They were back sitting in the booth. The patrons were eating, laughing and talking. No one noticed the display. She swallowed as thoughts raced through her mind. How was that even possible?

"Why did you do that?" she finally asked.

"I wanted you to know that what happened and what you felt earlier today was real; I didn't want you to question your sanity."

"You control the environment and the emotions in there. That seems like an unfair advantage."

"I can see where you might misconstrue as much, but I truly have no control over the environment or emotions; it is what it is." The edges of his mouth hinted at a smile.

Alexandra could feel him watching her; reading every nuance, every flicker of emotion passing through her mind.

"And just what is it?"

"It's one of our methods of communication or conveyance. I repeat. Do you trust me?"

Looking directly at him Alexandra answered, "Although I have no reason to trust you, my inner self has no fear or mistrust of you at all. I don't understand why I feel as I do, but I have no skepticism whatsoever where you are concerned. Not only do you mystify me, but my curiosity is greatly piqued as well."

"Good," he said, quite satisfied.

The waitress brought their meal. She ate in grudging silence but her mind battled over an overwhelming list of questions and the blasted need to hold her tongue. Never before had she experienced such bizarre circumstances.

Alexandra continued her brazen scrutiny of Jediah and allowed her eyes to burn every detail of his features deep in her memory. The silence continued until she took a bite of her pie. When the creaminess hit her palate, she closed her eyes and couldn't repress the "Mmm" that escaped her lips. Opening her eyes she caught Jediah smiling at her as his eyes twinkled.

"Every time I come here, I have to have a slice of their chocolate cream pie," he said. "I think they call it Chocolate Silk. It should be one of the Seven Wonders of the World."

Alexandra laughed at his ease of admitting his love for the pie. "You'll get no complaints from me. It's utterly delicious."

The calm Alexandra felt at his close proximity baffled her, but she instinctively knew he spoke the truth when he stated he did not control the emotions or environment in the orb. However, could he control those things and others while not in the orb? As soon as the question entered her mind, she knew the answer. She knew, without a doubt, he could control many things, shape things, and although a great benevolence exuded from him, the possibility existed of massive violence and total destruction, destruction on a scale unimaginable. He possessed great power.

The newly acquired knowledge hit home like a ton of bricks. Her breathing increased, and her gaze avoided contact with any part of him. Uncontrolled apprehension seized her by the throat, but just as quickly, it grew less and faded.

How many more times could her heart go through these opposing emotions without bursting? Irritation welled up inside as the torture of the unknown ate at her like a life-sucking disease.

She refused to allow the unpleasant emotions to take over. Calming herself, she finally raised her head and looked up at him; he radiated compassion and understanding. Her shoulders dropped as she found it impossible to display anger at such goodness.

"I know," was all he said.

Later, when he escorted her to her Jeep, a distinct question formed in her mind.

"What," Alexandra began, but the remainder of the question faded to silence as it came from her mind, once again in the orb, *are you?*

I am a Sensate and we have been around for the last two thousand years. You need to develop and tune your sensitivities, and it is best to explore your depth and limitations alone. I know you have many questions, but now is not the time to have them answered. Alexandra, the correct question should have been: 'What are we'?

'What are we?' The inference reverberated through her mind, affecting her on a mammoth scale. The orb vanished, and Alexandra found herself sitting in the front seat of her Jeep alone.

"Great. Disappearing on me when you are controlling the situation is not fair. You pump me full of wonder then pop the balloon. We need to talk about this. Get back here."

The questions Alexandra compiled earlier compared to those now formulating, created a flood of swirling, ever-changing pictures in her mind sweeping through her past and current reality base.

What had Teater set in motion back in the early nineteen hundreds? Where did devastatingly handsome Jediah fit into her uprooted world? And the biggest question of all: Why her?

Jediah gave it a name - Sensate. She was a Sensate. Her heart raced and her thoughts scattered in a multitude of directions at once. What should she do? To whom could she talk? Would she be able to call forth an orb? Did Teater pass this Sensate thing on to her, or was he just someone who they used to ensure her creation? Was Teater a Sensate, and if he wasn't, did he know of them?

Oh my, was she an alien?

Alexandra couldn't break it down into a manageable size. It proved too much, way too much, to comprehend.

Knowing it was a cop-out, she took direction from Scarlet, she would not think about it today.

She turned the key in the ignition and headed for her room at the hotel.

* * * * *

He could feel her heart and sense her heightened response to his nearness. What a challenge it would be to keep his distance while she came into being! She tempted him like no other. The impact of his first real sight of her was more than he expected. If his read of her was correct, her collision had been just as powerful as his. Luckily, he had known it was coming and was prepared. He caught her reaction on the mountain, and it was utterly delightful.

More than lovely, Alexandra Higgins leapt into his heart. Jediah smiled remembering her indignant attitude when she and her friend Cassie asked about the Higgins' Cemetery. He loved the bit of fire in her personality. And those captivating eyes; he had never seen eyes that color before. His first experience of Alexandra in real life stunned him.

He grinned from ear to ear; she thought of herself as plain and common, she didn't know she was beautiful.

Jediah's heart ached, so he closed his thoughts of her before they continued further.

* * * * *

Alexandra stayed in Waynesburg another two days researching Teater in the library and county records, all the while keeping her thoughts under close rein. Unable to locate his death certificate, which could have indicated the place and circumstances of his death, she settled for records for the land deed.

When she inquired at Attorney Dawson's office, she found James Dawson went out of town and the secretary had no information regarding the whereabouts of the handsome Jediah Saffle.

She made a fast trip up the mountain and found the cistern properly boarded over.

Disillusioned, she drove back to Wheeling.

After three days of unbelievable excitement and heart jolting events, she hit rock bottom. The leather packet and its contents offered the only proof she hadn't imagined her lost weekend.

Chapter Six

Alexandra's uneasiness regarding the return from Waynesburg rose to an apex knowing she had to face an inquiry. Every time she considered telling Cassie about the tattoo and Jediah, an invisible gag suppressed the urgency and, at the same time, alleviated the apprehension. She certainly didn't understand the mechanism, but she respected it and figured it was part of a bigger picture.

Walking around the house to the Hudson's backyard, she discovered Cassie and her mom relaxing on the deck and dreaded the half-truths that might fall from her lips.

"Mrs. Hudson, it's good to see you doing so well. Hi Cassie," Alexandra said and smiled warmly as stepped up onto the first level deck.

"Thank you, Alexandra. I'm so glad you could join us. Cassie, bring some Boston Iced Tea for us, would you please?"

"Sure Mom. Allie, I have tons of questions for you so don't start until I get back, okay?"

"Okay, Curious Cassie, I'll wait for you." She watched her friend flip-flop across the deck in short-shorts and a ragged t-shirt, and admired her shabby chic look.

Turning her attention to Mrs. Hudson. "You really do look good for someone who just got out of the hospital."

"Alexandra, you are such a dear for saying that. I thought it odd for a woman in her early fifties to have appendicitis, but I hear it's pretty common. I can't believe it happened when John was out of town, but apparently, a hot appendix waits on no man," she replied with a smile and a toss of her hand.

"Apparently not."

"It does feel good to be home."

"No doubt." Alexandra motioned to the garden, "who wouldn't prefer this view to a sterile hospital room?"

The Hudson's deck granted a respite in a city of concrete and asphalt. Lush plantings of ferns, hostas, lavender, wood poppies, Japanese holly, and roses could be accessed by meandering stepping-stones surrounded by Irish moss.

"It won't be long before everything is in full splendor again," Alexandra said while eyeing the buds on the knock out roses.

"Not long at all. I'm hoping to add some ice pansies in the fall for next spring. I seem to have an empty spot around the red stick dogwoods to the left."

"I agree they would be lovely there."

Cassie returned carrying a tray with glasses containing ice and a pitcher of tea. Tea sweetened with cranberry juice had been the girls' favorite beverage since Jr. High, when Alexandra's Mom and Dad returned from a trip and refused from then on to have sugar in their tea. Cassie poured everyone a glass.

"Umm." Alexandra drank deeply. "Great tea," she said.

Cassie nodded. "An old family recipe. Okay, girl, no more stalling, spill your guts. Tell me about the contents of the packet and what happened to Mr. Dreamy Eyes."

Mrs. Hudson leaned back in her chair, gingerly lifting her legs to the ottoman. "Yes, I mostly want to hear about Jediah. What an age-old name for a young man. Cassie told me everything that happened until she had to leave, and I read the copy of the will. But before we begin..." She looked directly at Alexandra and said, "You must promise me you will never again go gallivanting off on your own without letting us know what your plans are."

"Geesh, Mom, I already told her that." Cassie winced.

"And I promised never to be so irresponsible again." Alexandra sighed. "I thought I'd never get out of that hole. It only takes a split second for things to turn ugly."

"Okay, now that you hollered at her, Mom, do we get to hear the details about Teater and Jediah?"

Tightness formed in Alexandra's chest and then dissolved into that serene calmness she felt with Jediah. "There's not much to tell really. The packet contained a letter from Teater to whoever appeared and asked about him. It stated that he was ten when the Civil War ended. He was sent to live with the Madisons in Waynesburg because they needed help so they wouldn't lose their farm."

"What a shame and he was so young," Cassie said.

"It was common for that to happen back then, although it must have been tough." Mrs. Hudson huffed. "I wonder what Family Services would say about that now. I can't believe how much society has changed."

Alexandra nodded and continued. "He came back to Wheeling, sired my great grandfather, Lawrence, and his brother, George. After twelve years of marriage, he left his wife and sons and went back to Waynesburg. He didn't say why. He does not explain his actions, but he asked that we not judge him too harshly. I was unable to find out anything further through the county records. As a matter of fact, I didn't even find his death certificate."

"There must be more to the story. He sounds like a nice enough guy, but leaving a wife and kids alone back then makes you wonder. At least we know part of the mystery," said Cassie, shrugging her shoulders.

Alexandra scratched her head all over with both hands, and then shook all over. "Yeah, part." Some of the tension eased.

"What about the estate?" True to form, Cassie kept up with questions.

Alexandra sucked in a gulp if air, then let out a big sigh. "You know as much as I do. It's a piece of land and, I suppose, whatever money is left over after paying taxes on the land for almost 90 years. The attorney said he'd be in contact."

Mrs. Hudson had her eyes closed while listening to the conversation, and spoke without opening them. "We'll just have to wait and see."

"So, what about Jediah?" Cassie raised her eyebrows.

"Not much to tell there either." She looked at the floor. "I ran into him once at the diner, found out he liked chocolate cream pie, and then never saw him again. I don't think he lives in that area; he just visits there every now and then. He certainly was pleasing to the eye, wasn't he, Cassie?"

"A Krispy Kreme is pleasing to the eye, that guy was more than that, he was drop-dead gorgeous! I know you thought so too, because I have never seen you dumbstruck before."

Cassie stood up and paced. "You didn't speak at all, and you could barely walk. I was half expecting you to call and say that you hitched your wagon to his star." She dropped back into her chair and said, "I didn't expect you to say he liked chocolate pie and you never saw him again. Man, Allie, what a let-down."

Alexandra shrugged. "Truth is stranger than fiction." She had the mark on her shoulder to prove that one.

Mrs. Hudson leaned up and placed her hand on Alexandra's shoulder. "I'm sorry, honey. Sometimes things work out differently than we expect, but they always work out."

"Oh, it's okay. I guess I was just expecting more would come of it."

"Well, something came of it," said Mrs. Hudson. "You now have a piece of land."

"Yeah, that's true. When I went looking for Teater nothing like this ever crossed my mind. I'd still like to know what made him return to

Waynesburg. It must have been quite compelling, because he left behind two teenage boys and a wife."

"That will of Teater's certainly contained strange provisions for his estate." Mrs. Hudson narrowed her eyebrows.

"I just happened to be in the right place at the right time."

The conversation turned to topics not directly related to her recent trip. Alexandra let out a cleansing breath; she had made it through the inquisition without lying or sharing information she shouldn't.

After the initial shock of the events in Waynesburg wore off, time replaced the eeriness with a renewed sense of wonder. She had been part of something extraordinary.

Alexandra didn't forget what happened that weekend, but she did partition it off until she could get her mind around it and put it in its proper perspective. Waynesburg and one inhabitant in particular, weighed heavily on her mind, but in order to function and finish her Masters, she concentrated on making it through one day at a time. Her parents had impressed on her the importance of a good education. She would be the first female from her mother's side of the family to finish college. A freaky tattoo, hunky male, and a psychic ancestor would not interfere with this goal.

For the next three months, Jediah never left her thoughts, always present at the end of the day when she closed her eyes and again as the sun rose in the morning.

The day of graduation arrived. Although the Hudson family supported her accomplishment by attending the ceremony, the absence of her parents left her victory hollow.

After the ceremony, she accompanied them to dinner in her honor.

"What are your plans, Alexandra?" asked Mr. Hudson.

"I thought I'd take some time off before searching for a position. And to tell you the truth, I'm tired of living out of student housing and a studio apartment. I was thinking of taking the summer to buy a house and put down some roots."

"Oh," Cassie said, "I thought you had accepted the position with Mr. Steiner's group."

"I gave him a call yesterday and told him I'd changed my mind. Archeology will always be there."

"Why didn't you tell me you weren't sure?" Cassie whined. "We could have talked it over."

"I don't know, my mind has been so jumbled lately, I didn't really settle on my decision until I had the phone in my hand, and even then, I wasn't completely sure."

"Don't worry, honey." Mrs. Hudson patted her arm. "Just because you finished up one chapter in your life doesn't mean you have to jump right into another."

"She's right, Allie. You've been pushing yourself since the accident. It's time for some R&R."

"Then, what's the first order of business?" Leave it to Mr. Hudson to pin down a plan.

"I thought I'd check out the piece of land in Waynesburg. I received the deed in the mail almost as soon as I got back to school. I didn't even open the envelope."

"How we became friends is beyond me." Cassie placed her napkin on the table and shook her head, "if that had been me, I would have ripped the envelope open while jumping on the bed. So you had information all this time and left it unopened?"

Mrs. Hudson tried to hide a smile in her napkin. "You two are definitely worlds apart in personality, but two greater friends I have yet to lay eyes on."

Alexandra knew why she hadn't opened the letter. It was too much of a reminder of violet eyes. If she had focused on it's distraction and being a Sensate, whatever that turned out to be, she would have never been able to get through the last three months.

"Thank you, Mr. and Mrs. Hudson, for the great dinner and for your friendship and guidance." She rose from the table.

"Your parents would have done the same for Cassie had the situation been reversed." Mr. Hudson stood and hugged her. "Plus, you've grown on us over the years."

"John, you're awful. Can't you come right out and tell Alexandra she's like a second daughter to us?" She joined in the hug. "We're so very proud of you."

Misting over, she accepted the hugs.

"Okay, now that's settled, let's head home." Cassie said.

"Sure sounds good to me," Alexandra said.

"My Jeep's all packed. As soon as I change out of these clothes, I'm ready to go. You guys go ahead, I'll be about ten minutes behind you."

"Drive carefully, Alexandra. Take your time." Mrs. Hudson never failed to be motherly.

"I'll be careful."

Once back at the studio apartment in Wheeling, Alexandra tossed her keys on the table, changed into pajamas and dropped into bed. The weight of the world lifted from her shoulders and for one night, she pushed every thought from her mind and fell into a blissful sleep.

The following morning she woke, stretched her legs and back, and then wriggled her toes. The first day of freedom. No school. No job. No commitments. Her eyes bright with a keen sense of adventure, she hopped out of bed, ready to jump in the shower when she remembered the Jeep piled high with boxes that had to be brought into the apartment.

Toting the boxes into the small apartment put a dent in her enthusiasm, not a big one, but a dent that lasted until she stepped into the shower and washed it down the drain. With her hair wrapped in a towel, she threw on a robe, walked ten steps to fill the kettle, then turned and placed it on the stove to heat. As she waited for the water to get hot enough to steep the tea, she routed through the boxes until she uncovered one marked 'desk', and inside, located the unopened envelope from James Dawson, and ripped it open.

The formal cover letter stated any monies due would be forthcoming; it also indicated two attachments - the deed and a schematic of the plot. Her heart raced as she grasped the magnitude of her ancestor's gift. The wee plot turned out to be a little over twenty-four hundred acres. She stopped and read that again. Yes. Twenty-four *hundred* acres. The attached schematic widened her eyes considerably.

"Geesh, you gave me your whole mountain." Her eyes darted about the room as she tried to fit this new piece into Teater's puzzle. "What kind of person gives someone a mountain?" She blinked. "How the heck did you go from a loaned-out son to someone who owned a mountain in 1928?"

The teakettle whistled. Shifting into autopilot, she made tea and toast while consumed with awe. She tried to make sense of it all, but ran headfirst into a roadblock of questions. Sipping her tea, she found it more peaceful not to let her mind drift, to adhere firmly to the facts. Internally, she sensed all was as it should be.

Once she regained mental balance, she called Cassie and shared the morning's land mass discovery.

"I knew you should have opened that letter sooner. Now, that's a hunk of land. Is it the one with the cemetery and cistern?" Cassie asked.

"Yeah, the one and only. I'm going over today to check it out. I'll probably spend the night."

"Don't fall in any holes, okay?"

"If I do, I'll just sit tight until you come to the rescue."

"Deal."

Safely tethered to Cassie, she made hotel

reservations for the night in Waynesburg.

Dressed in a pale green mid-drift sweater, stone-washed blue jeans, and her favorite flats, she pulled her hair up into a high pony tail and held it with a gold clasp. Unruly wisps fell from her nape. Applying a whisper of blush and some lip-gloss, she glanced at the result, shrugged, filled a backpack and overnight bag, grabbed her keys and went out the door.

In Waynesburg, she stopped by to see Attorney Dawson. Alexandra studied the man. Attractive and impeccably dressed in a gray pinstriped suit, his manner conveyed his need to serve his clients with discerning loyalty and prudence. He was, by profession, a man others looked to in times of trouble. When he greeted Alexandra with a smile, he seemed genuinely pleased to see her again.

"I wondered how long it would be before we saw you again. It's good to have you back. What can I help you with today?" He gestured for her to have a seat.

She sat in a tufted leather chair, and clasped her hands in her lap to keep from fidgeting. "I was a little shocked the last time I was here, and didn't really get to thank you properly for your assistance in carrying out Teater's wishes. I'm amazed at your family's care, professionalism, and follow-through. What a burden to have carried throughout the years."

"You are certainly welcome, Alexandra." He waved his hand in the air. "It was no burden at all and actually our pleasure to carry Teater's wishes to fruition. I had no idea I would get to hand over the packet. Did you receive the deed of the property?"

"Yes, I did; that's why I'm here now. I wanted to take a better look at it. I didn't realize the extent of Teater's holdings until I took a closer look at the deed. I thought it was a small plot of land."

"Oh my. No. Teater was one of the largest landowners in seven counties. He sold the mineral rights on another piece of land to pay the taxes and ensure the safe guardianship of the land you now own. I'm just now putting the final touches on the financial accounts so I can transfer the monetary assets to you. It is quite sizable. It was a little shocking to finally have someone come looking for Teater; it had been so long, my family just figured no one would ever show up."

"I certainly never expected any of this either. I merely wanted to complete my genealogy research on my father's side. You can imagine my surprise as I can imagine yours.

She set her jaw and took a deep breath. "I'm thinking about building a house on the land. I lost my parents in an accident a few years back, which precludes me from wanting to settle where we lived, so I thought to reach out to Teater in his generosity and reconnect with my past, here, in Waynesburg." There, she got it out without hurting too much.

"I'm sorry to hear about your parents." His face softened. "I think it's a wonderful idea to put down roots and continue where Teater left off. The land is beautiful and untamed. I'm sure a home there will be filled with happiness for you."

"Thank you, Mr. Dawson. I'm glad you think it's a good idea. Could you recommend a builder?

I would like to start as soon as possible."

"I can recommend three who have worked for me in the past. Each one has a different architect on retainer, depending on your tastes. I'll write them down for you."

As Mr. Dawson compiled the list, Alexandra gazed over his office contents. A particular tintype on the wall caught her eye, so she walked over and inspected it more closely. Two men, unaware of the photographer, were engrossed in conversation and pointing to an old well. A striking woman had her arm linked through one of the men's arm, apparently quite taken by him. The photograph caused a stirring in Alexandra as it drew her into the scene. She could almost hear the conversation between the men, and felt the unconditional love of the woman. More than a photograph, it pinpointed that particular moment in time.

"Here you are, Alexandra." She jerked at the departure from her reverie.

Mr. Dawson continued. "This should get you going. All three are well-respected, so have no fear regarding your final selection."

Venturing back to the present, Alexandra opened her mouth to inquire about the tintype.

Don't ask, said the voice in her head. She complied.

"Thank you, again, Mr. Dawson."

"It's a pleasure, Alexandra. I'll send you the final paperwork regarding the monetary assets as soon as it's completed."

"You have been most helpful. I'm sure we'll be seeing more of each other in the future. You've been more than kind."

As she left his office, she questioned whether the 'voice' was real, or a strong suggestion she manifested herself. Oddly, her decision not to ask about the tintype or Jediah pleased her; restraint and Alexandra typically did not go hand-in-hand.

Stopping by the hotel, she changed out of her sweater and favorite jeans and into older clothes more suitable for trekking over a mountain. She grabbed her prepared backpack, which contained GPS, pad and pencil, photocopy of the plot, bright pink marking flags - courtesy of the local hardware - protein bars, bottled water, flashlight, cell phone, and bug spray. Tucked neatly in an inside pocket, safely ensconced in plastic, rested Teater's letter and the stone. If a mishap occurred today, she'd be ready.

When she turned the key in her Jeep, the roar of the engine echoed her own eagerness to get back on the wash-boarded road that led to the top of her mountain. She hit the steering wheel with both palms and yelled, "Wahoo, now this is exciting." She put the vehicle in gear, and pointed its nose toward the north end of town.

Although the underbrush had grown considerably, she spied the big white birch that marked the entrance to the road. Acquainted with each rut personally, she made it to the top in no time and parked the Jeep under a tree. She grabbed the backpack and began a huge clockwise square. No way could she explore the mountain on foot, so she contented herself with a relatively small section at the top. Teater had liked that spot and she liked it too. As she walked the acreage following her GPS, she placed flags at quarter mile intervals.

"So, Teater, we finally meet here on this mountain. Thank you for the gift. I don't understand my purpose yet, but it means a lot to have you as part of my life.

"It would have been nice to know you left me this land after Mom and Dad's accident. I felt severed from them and my home, and I just couldn't go back there to live. I wish I had known about your gift then; I might not have felt so alone. I'm glad you are here with me now.

"My Dad always told me to never judge someone unless you walked a mile in his shoes, and even then it should rarely be done. I hold nothing against you because you left your children and wife. My world is so different from what you dealt with during your lifetime. I wish I could figure out why you came back to Waynesburg, though. Did this mountain call to you as it calls to me?

"Were you a Sensate and did you pass your powers down to me? Did you have powers? Did my parents? I'll have to ask Jediah when I see him. If I see him." Alexandra placed a flag in the ground.

"This is a gorgeous mountain, Teater." Looking around, Alexandra realized she arrived at a truly beautiful spot. Shagbark Hickories formed the canopy and a multitude of shells crunched underfoot. A large tree had fallen years beforehand leaving the trunk smooth and weathered but not rotted. It landed across a game trail, which now re-routed around the tree.

She sat on the log to take in her surroundings. Wood ferns meshed to give a feathery carpet eighteen inches above ground. She could smell the decay of the leaves and the moistness of the earth, and closed her eyes and breathed slowly through her nose, in and out. Concentrating, she sensed the grubs in the ground, the new leaf unfurling in the gentle breeze, and the rapid heartbeat of many birds above. She felt the release of the tobacco from a grasshopper and the sticky trailing of numerous snails on dead leaves. Startled to full consciousness, she sensed the instant a walking stick grabbed its prey.

"Hey, what's going on?" She jumped from her seat and spun around half expecting to see a giant bug ready to eat her.

"Whoa, calm down." She put her hand to her chest and felt her heart pounding.

"That was really weird. I didn't really see the walking stick; I sensed it in its habitat, not mine." Could she find it again if she wanted to?

Sitting back down, she drew in a breath and cleared her mind, then began leafing through pages, going backwards until... "I found you." He chewed on the far side of the wild azalea to her right.

Questions burst forward. How did she know these things? No explanation, she just did. Did she find that odd? No, she accepted it as natural, like she always should have known, but somehow had on blinders.

"Golly, Teater, what have you unleashed in me?" She could no longer deny the instances of total clarity regarding her surroundings.

Could she do it again? Relaxed, she searched for the walking stick once more. Not only did she sense *him*, she knew he was sated. A tasty oak leaf from a nearby sapling had quenched his hunger. Disconnecting, she smiled to herself.

What else could she sense? Relaxed, Alexandra pushed further into the world around her. She selected a bird that landed so far away she could barely make it out. Could she fine-tune and feel it? Many ripples and waves passed and soon Alexandra heard a sweet song. It's a baby, just learning to fly, and its mother was nearby, shrieking urging it to take flight. She sensed the fledgling's fear of flight. The nervous juvenile worried with indecision and sang fearful tunes to its mother. Waiting, she felt the exuberance the moment the young bird left its perch and spread its wings in flight.

Unable to contain the emotion Alexandra sprung from the log and spun around her arms waving madly. She yelled, "I'm flying, I'm flying!"

Disconnecting, she hugged her arms to her chest. What a wonderful feeling. The internal peace that filled her was miraculous. She could still feel the tiny bird's exuberance as it tingled throughout her body. Wonder invaded her thoughts with endless possibilities of new and brighter discoveries all around her.

"Wow, Teater. I thought twenty-four hundred acres was large, but this feeling is mammoth."

With a large spring to her step, she continued her trek, and for every flag placement, she stopped and used her senses to see and smell various plants and animals and became one with her surroundings. Squirrels chattered either mating or digging up the nuts they buried last fall. Oddly, they remembered exactly where they put them.

Examining what she previously thought of as a single locust tree, she discovered its roots connected to each locust tree in that cluster, so that nearly 60 trees were, in actuality, one. A tiny sapling grew from the root of a massive tree some 150 feet tall. The connection to all was staggering.

Glancing at her watch, it had taken several hours to map out the square, but she finally arrived back at her Jeep. During her trek, she located a spring that might develop into a nice water source, several raspberry and blackberry patches, apple, pear, walnut and maple trees, a few sugar pear trees, and a single paw-paw tree. Overjoyed with the bounty of flavors on her mountain, she sat on a soft patch of grass to survey it once more.

"Mom and Dad, I hope you can hear me. I'm sitting on a piece of land Teater gave me. Do you remember anything about him, Dad? In his will, Teater left me a mountain. A whole mountain! I miss you so very much and wish you were here to guide me now. I felt you with me today as we walked over the land. I'm going to build a house on this land. I hope you approve, for I think you would have loved it here. All that I am I owe to you. Thank you for loving me. I welcome you to our mountain; yours, mine and Teater's."

Alexandra stood and brushed off the back of her pants. "Loved your mountain, didn't you,

Teater?"

Yes. She heard in her mind.

Teater? No response.

If you are not Teater, who are you?

All in good time, little one, came the response.

The conversation ended.

Chapter Seven

Two developments occurred in close
succession, the amazing touch with nature, and the
unidentified voice communicating in her head.

Bewildered didn't come close to describing
Alexandra's undertow of emotions. Her instincts
suggested the person behind the voice somehow
monitored her actions. Maybe the voice suggesting
she not ask Mr. Dawson about the tintype was the
same she heard later on the mountain.

Hungry, grimy, and a bit on the itchy side, she
threw her backpack onto the backseat of the Jeep,
got behind the wheel and took one last gaze at her
mountain. The clearing on top where the remains of
the homestead stood presented the best site for the
house. She gazed at the view overlooking the
valley, both serene and inspirational; the site
required no additional removal of trees. It would be
a house with lots of large windows to look out over
the land. Home, it already felt like home.

Her stomach growled as she turned the key in
the ignition and headed downhill for a shower and
something to quench her hunger.

She picked up a salad from a local deli and
took it to her room at the hotel. Further
examination of the day's adventures would have to
wait until after food and a quick shower to clear her
mind. She pulled the mini speaker from her bag,

connected her iPhone, selected the 'Bouncy'
playlist, hit shuffle, placed it on the vanity, and hit
play. Jason Mraz's *I'm Yours* filled the air.
Although it was hard to dance and get undressed at
the same time, she finally managed to jump on one
leg, kick off her undies, and get in the shower. The
playlist continued as she soaped her hair and
reached out of the shower to increase the volume
when Van Morrison's *Brown Eyed Girl* competed
with her own singing. Of course, she substituted
green for brown, as was her right, and towards the
middle of the song she switched it even further to
violet eyed guy. No way was he a boy.

She began with the dancing and singing continued as she
applied moisturizer and body lotion, towel-dried her
hair, then slid into an old robe that was as soft as a
rag.

Once refreshed, and wrapped in creature
comfort, she prepared herself for the assessment she
had long avoided.

Instead of pushing thoughts from her mind, as
she had done for the last three months, the time had
come to either embrace the changes in her life or
walk away completely. Though she bordered on
making no decision at all, a force compelled her to
delve into the unknown and explore her inner self
with more scrutiny than she ever had before.

She began with Teater's guide. A proper
indoctrination to her transition would have proved
beneficial; at the very least someone should have
offered her an instruction manual. Stumbling
around in the dark hoping to bump into it by blind
luck wasn't working. Her fear of doing something

that could not be undone held the reins taut.

Considering the words, "choice," and "fate" from his letter echoed and bounced right back. Did she have a choice? Could she choose her fate? Something of this magnitude required total commitment and a definite 'yes' or 'no'. Deep inside she'd already made the decision. Reconciling her subconscious with the untried exterior of her conscious mind presented the last hurdle.

When she compiled the various bits of information, she sensed she might be the glue that held Teater's puzzle together.

She wrestled with the secrecy issue knowing it could cause problems with Cassie, her family, and any other non-Sensate, which ended up being the rest of the world.

She had made her choice. Only time would tell if she possessed the inner strength, wisdom, and morals to uphold her Sensate responsibilities, whatever they might be.

Refreshed, sated, and at peace with her decision, she opened her laptop, connected to the Internet and queried the word 'sensate': 'able to perceive with the senses'; 'endowed with feeling and unstructured consciousness'.

Weren't we all sentient beings? She knew her five senses: sight, sound, taste, smell, and touch. How far did her gift reach?

Alexandra relaxed on the sofa, opened her mind, and waited for some clarity of thought to come, but instead, many voices entered her head, all of them talking at the same time. A bit startled, she jumped but continued to leave her mind open.

From the many conversations she could hear, she selected specific ones. Following the strings to each conversation, she separated them in her mind.

A mother chastised her son for taking money from her wallet and spending it; a man checked into the hotel and gave a false name; a little girl laughed while playing with her daddy.

Not only could she hear the conversations, she felt the anguish of the mother who knew her son had taken money from her before; she witnessed the tremendous shame of the boy who stole the money and although he was sorry, he thought he had no choice. Alexandra bordered on giggling when the little girl's daddy tickled her. She opened her eyes, closed her mind, and the voices went silent.

"Oh, I wasn't expecting that," she said as a creepy feeling made her nauseous. Shocked and ashamed of herself for invading the privacy of the people around her, the eavesdropping made her feel dirty. Why possess a gift with such intrusive aspects? Although she could think of applications for the greater good, maybe law enforcement, the use for evil could easily dominate. She remembered the phrase from Teater's letter: 'in the hands of the wrong host,' and understood the implication for the misuse of her abilities.

Her small experiment could have large ramifications if used inappropriately. What if she ended up being the wrong host and doomed herself and others? How was she chosen? What criteria decided? What were the consequences of failure? Who judged her if she crossed the line?

Too many questions swirled in her mind, and

for a second, she considered setting them aside to reconcile tomorrow. Pressing her lips together and unwilling to allow past weaknesses, she pushed Scarlet's philosophy aside and braved forward instead.

A second experiment formed. Could she zero in on a specific person and place? Opening her mind, she searched for the desk clerk of her hotel. She heard no words, but knew the clerk stepped away for a moment to get a cup of coffee - decaf, with cream.

Satisfied with the previous results, she wondered how far she could reach. Could she sense Cassie back in Wheeling a good fifty-six miles away? As she relaxed, her mind moved over the distance and located Cassie's mind with ease. She was dressing to go out on a date and taking particular care with her make-up. And she didn't tell me? As indignant as Alexandra felt, she found herself more ashamed and pulled away; she had no right to pry. Cassie would share when she was ready.

Unsure of how much she should push her new abilities, Alexandra forced herself to review parts of her ethics she never before considered. So far, her experiments revealed no boundaries except those of her own moral choosing. Before conducting additional experiments, she needed to determine personal boundaries. Were her boundaries innate and already part of her moral fiber? Would she know instinctively where to draw the line? Did the gift have more depth than being able to hear conversations and locate people?

Like Jediah, could she summon an orb and bring others into it? With unlimited areas to focus, she realized too much too soon could end badly and immediately reined in her thoughts. Until she processed the ramifications of her actions, there would be no more experimentation.

Reviewing the three builders' websites, one appealed to her more than the other two. Calling the number for the office, she made an appointment for the following day. Taking her laptop over to the bed, Alexandra sat cross-legged and entered two words into Google's search: house styles. Not really certain of her likes or dislikes, she didn't want to be at a disadvantage the following day. The American Craftsman style suited her best because the roof peaks and the porches felt most like home. She would build a home on her mountain.

What a grand thing to call her own, a mountain! She still couldn't believe her good fortune. Thinking back, she could almost feel the warmth from the sun on her face looking out over the city of Waynesburg from the Higgins Family Cemetery. It was such a peaceful view. She closed her eyes and could almost smell the untainted breeze. It had a hint of earth amid the floral scents of ... Whoosh!

A brilliant burst of light exploded all around and a gentle breeze blew through her hair.

"No way! What have I done?"

Alexandra now sat in the Higgins Family Cemetery on top of her mountain wearing nothing but her robe, and only mere seconds ago, she was in the hotel room. Her heart pounded in her chest and she breathed in pants, refusing to believe what just happened. She clutched her robe tightly around her chest, as she stared at the streaks of purple and pink blazing across the sky in a glorious sunset.

"This can't be real," she said as she shifted her weight and briars pricked her nether regions.

"Ouch, it's real all right." She stood and rubbed her backside, then stepped quickly as the rough underbrush jabbed the soft soles of her feet.

"Great. I have the worst luck."

Wasn't she just worried about this exact same thing: too much too fast? In her defense, she hadn't been trying to do anything.

"Yeah, tell that to the jury," she mumbled.

What if this had happened in front of people? A new set of repercussions filled her thoughts. What kind of people gave you a gift and let you get into messes without telling you how to fix things?

She cursed her ill fortune, and stomped her foot, landing on another briar.

"Geesh!" Moving carefully, she took a few steps away from the briars and onto a softer piece of grass.

She released a labored sigh from her lungs. "Okay, I got myself here; I can get myself back."

Think. Room. Bed. Laptop. Alexandra squeezed her eyes shut, but nothing happened. Relax. Concentrate. Nothing. She wanted to go back to her room! Alexandra felt her heart racing. Some kind of gift this was! It backfired - bigtime.

"Darn, darn, triple darn. Yoo-hoo, anybody there?" Crickets. She heard only crickets.

How the heck was she supposed to get back to

the hotel? Couldn't she have at least arrived fully clothed? Someone out there certainly had a sense of humor. Undies and a bathrobe comprised her immediate wardrobe. She certainly couldn't walk back to the hotel dressed like that.

Walk? It would soon be dark and with her luck, she would probably fall in one of those huge ruts and break a bone or something worse, and then there was the problem of no shoes.

What on earth brought her here? Did she really do this? When she thought of Cassie earlier, she didn't go there. What had she done differently? Adding the insult of ignorance to her injured pride of arriving poorly dressed for the adventure, she started to feel more than a little sorry for herself. She wondered if Jediah ever got stuck in a situation like this. She would bet not. How awful.

"Okay, I'm embarrassed enough. I promise to be a good little Sensate, so can you give me the guide now," she yelled to the wind. "Why would you give me these powers and just leave me? I'm in trouble down here!

"You know, I'm really trying to be a good sport about all of this. I think I've maintained a certain amount of decorum even though weird things keep happening to me, but to leave me to my own devices when I don't know what my devices are, seems a bit off kilter even to me. It's a good thing there's no one around. What if I had transplanted myself in the middle of the ocean?"

No answer.

"Is this really the way this is supposed to work?"

Still no reply.

"You're really messing with me here. I made promises to be careful and not to get into any weird situations."

Her brow furrowed and she pressed her lips together. "Double drat! Triple darn!"

After a few minutes of huffing and puffing over her plight, she realized, more calmly, the beauty of her surroundings. Attempting for a bit of composure, she plopped down carefully on a soft patch of grass, brought her knees up to her chest and wrapped her arms around her legs.

If her actions brought her here, at least she chose a nice place. The sun, almost gone now, left a sleepy look to the town below. Soon, the lights would come on in the houses, and the cars on the streets would start to thin out. Impending darkness up on the mountain might be beautiful, but now, she needed to feel more secure; it was getting decidedly colder.

A little voice inside wanted to whine, 'it's not fair'. She always tried to take life at face value, and didn't believe 'life was what you made of it', for life simply took control. It happened on its own terms, just like it happened to her parents three years ago, and like it did to her tonight.

As the night grew darker, she watched the crescent moon emerge low in the sky. It didn't give off much light, but presented a wondrous sight, nonetheless. Breathing in, she inhaled the same fresh scent she had been thinking about earlier. A hint of earth, grasses, and a mild floral scent from Trilliums, Sweet Williams, and Lady Slippers wafted by and caused a smile to form on her lips.

No, could it be that simple? Smell was a sense, Sensate. She had been imagining the exact smell, and had remembered it so vividly. Could it be possible she brought herself here through the sense of smell? Excited, she mentally canvassed the items in her hotel room, but couldn't think of anything that brought a specific smell to mind.

She bordered on discovering how the 'move' took place, and chastised herself for not practicing more. As her frustration revved up to wanting to kick herself, she cut herself some slack; she could just as easily ended up deep in the Amazon jungle.

What did she know or 'sense' intimately? Cassie? She knew her inside and out, but negated the idea due to possible discovery. No, Cassie would be a last resort.

An item she held dear, one located in her hotel might offer a solution to get out of this mess. Listing the things she brought with her, she happened on a possible solution.

She knew her Jeep inside and out; it wasn't in her room, but it was close enough. Its big round eyes and the funny silver door handles she originally thought were cup holders, became vivid. Closing her eyes, she concentrated on it to the exclusion of all else and pictured herself behind the wheel flipping down the visor, smelling its new car scent.

And just like that, amid the flourish of brilliant lights, she sat inside her sweet red Jeep in the hotel parking lot.

"It worked!" She raised her eyes skyward.

"Thank you, thank you, thank you."

Breathing a heavy sigh of relief, she grabbed her robe about her and walked in the front door of the hotel. She explained to the desk clerk how she'd forgotten her key while getting a soda, and asked for a new one.

An elated, happy Alexandra walked through the door of her room, closed it snugly behind her, leaned against the door, and grinned from ear to ear.

Well done! rang a voice in her head.

You knew? she raised her chin.

Yes, you were never really alone.

Why..., she started, but was cut off mid-sentence.

Think, Alexandra. Deep inside you know why I didn't help you.

A mental review of the day's events resulted in the answer to her question. Unique, no two alike, we experience life differently.

My senses and experiences are specific to me. I remember and associate them to things, people, and places with more depth when I feel them firsthand. Each sense applied personally is unlike any other.

Goodnight, Alexandra.

Goodnight.

She slid down the door and sat on the floor, consumed by the connections forming in her mind. The smell that brought her to her mountaintop might not bring another because we all perceived things on various levels.

During a grade school science experiment, she tasted some things, while others could not. It became crystal clear - no one could teach her about her own senses, it had to be a solitary journey.

When Jediah said she needed to develop her sensitivities and fine-tune them, he should have emphasized the fine-tuning part. From now on, she would disconnect from her deep senses in order to maintain a normal lifestyle. Her thoughts and abilities could not run rampant. Each sense technique unearthed required constant monitoring and control. The lesson learned tonight etched itself into the granite fiber of her mind.

As she stood, a bit of the uneasiness she felt on the mountain lessened and her normal level of confidence returned.

She needed to concentrate on one sense at a time. Since she associated smells with many good things and not too many bad, she would begin there.

As a safety precaution, she needed to associate a specific smell to her room.

"Why didn't I think of this earlier?" she said as she rummaged through her belongings and located the perfume she had used for years. *Emeraude* was a blend of jasmine, orange, citrus, floral, spices and sandalwood. When everyone else switched to designer fragrances, she remained true to her scent. She sniffed the stopper and placed the vial on the vanity. When it mixed with her skin, it became unique to her. The next time she ended up repositioned, she would return to her personal bottle of perfume, a much better alternative than ending up in her Jeep.

One problem partially solved, she moved to the next one on the list - the voice in her head that looked after her. It didn't poke her in the ribs, so it probably wasn't Jediah. Had this person watched her every move? Her gaze shot to the bathroom as all sorts of weird things flashed through her mind.

No, she shook her head, this thing, these senses, the connection to nature, it was so much more than a petty perversion. It was good, and pure. Knowing someone watched out for her gave her comfort and she relaxed considerably. She wasn't alone and going through this all by herself as she formerly thought. The race she belonged to contained kind and benevolent people, of this, she was certain.

Recharged from the self-discovery, she gathered her pad and pen, and jotted down a few notes for her meeting with the builder the following day. Before she climbed into bed, she rinsed her feet in the tub and brushed her teeth.

She drifted off to sleep with thoughts of sparkling violet eyes. It wasn't long before the eyes became the man as he came toward her.

* * * * *

She is progressing nicely, and has found some of the mechanisms quickly.

Yes. She's a delight to monitor and has such reprimanding conversations with herself. She's now considering the ramifications of her actions, something I didn't consider quite so rapidly, if you recall.

You got into many situations I wasn't sure we could remedy. Luckily, for you, back then, people were more superstitious, and mishaps could be chalked up to a variety of excuses. With the technology of today, you need to fear detection more. Everyone has a camera on them at all times, it would seem.

She's lucky she only came to the mountain. On my first journey, I ended up on a boat with a bunch of fishermen for two hours.

You were fortunate they were all drunk.

That cook wasn't too drunk. He continued to look for me for three weeks. You made me monitor him until he gave up on me as a figment of his imagination.

She gathers her senses well. On the mountain, she handled herself nicely. I have great faith in her, Jediah. She will become a great Sensate.

She has incredible inner strength.

You two are a fine match, Jediah. She thinks of you often.

I know; I sense her every thought. It's as if she has always been with me. At this stage of sense development I thought I was losing my mind; she's had that thought too, but she's too grounded to entertain that notion for more than an instant.

It won't be long before I introduce myself. As soon as she connects, we will be able to move forward. With her rate of adaptation, you should be together soon. Ah, she's dreaming of you.

Here's where I disconnect. Goodnight, Mom. Goodnight, Jediah.

* * * * *

Chapter Eight

Alexandra opened her eyes, then squeezed them shut again and tried to grasp the wisps of the dream that quickly faded to smoke. She had been walking hand-in-hand with Jediah and talking of everything imaginable. She lay in bed for a while not wanting to forget the elusive memory when he took her hand for the first time. Nothing thus far in her life gave her such a feeling of completeness. Her soul was at peace; it rested with Jediah.

A split second later, she threw off the covers and jumped out of bed. The dream had been so vivid she almost expected to find him lying between the sheets. Grabbing the sheet, she fanned it, just to be sure. She barely knew him. The actual words spoken to each other couldn't possibly amount to more than twenty-five. So why had she readily followed his lead in the dream?

Anger flared up inside. To think she allowed some guy access to her mind infuriated her. Why had she permitted him to be so friendly even though she knew nothing about him? She would never have consented to the assumed friendship if she had her wits about her. Not only did she have to set Sensate boundaries, she needed Jediah Saffle to keep his distance until she decided he was acceptable. He'd assumed she had no say in the matter and that he would be readily accepted, no matter the consequences. Well, that certainly would not be the case in the future. She would not be led by the nose like some milksop. Her parents had raised her to be sterner stuff than that.

In the shower, she scrubbed her head vigorously attempting to 'wash that man right outta' her hair. She succeeded only in having a finely washed head of hair.

Hurrying through her morning ritual, she made the meeting with Gregory Patrick, the owner of Gregg Construction, at the Silk City Diner with barely a minute to spare. Expecting that a great breakfast and interesting conversation to bury thoughts of Jediah and desensitize her from the dream, she straightened her shoulders and entered the diner.

She ran into Greg in the waiting area of the diner and guessed, by the steel-toed boots and jeans that he might be her builder. Alexandra crossed the distance, and caught his eye. "Mr. Patrick?" she asked.

"Ms. Higgins," he smiled and touched the brim of his ball cap. "Thank you for the opportunity. It's a pleasure to meet you."

"Thank you for meeting me on such short notice."

"I'm just finishing up a project here on the north end of town, so it's no inconvenience at all."

The hostess led them to their booth. Once seated and their order placed, he inquired, "What are you considering, exactly, Ms. Higgins?"

"Call me Alexandra, please."

"Alexandra it will be, and it's Greg, likewise."

"Thank you. I'm thinking of a self-sustaining home on top of a high hill. I found a spring that has possibilities for a water source, and I'd like to use a wind turbine for power. My thoughts for a home are in line with the Craftsman style; not too large, somewhere around five bedrooms, an office, sun room, eat-in kitchen with island, lots of windows, and a wrap-around porch connecting on one side to a composite deck out back. I want a view in all directions, and don't want any porch or deck railings to be visible from the inside blocking the view."

"That's quite a list," he said raising his eyebrows. "You must have been thinking about this for a long time."

"I guess I did rattle that off a bit quickly." Her cheeks flushed and she wrung her hands under the table. "My mom and I used to talk for hours about 'if we had the money, what house would we build', so yes, I've been thinking about my home for years."

"At least you know what you want, which is always a great step forward."

The waitress brought their meal and Greg took a sip of his coffee. "Do you have a building lot?"

"You could call it that," Alexandra said with a glint. "If you have time after breakfast, I could show it to you. Maybe then you could fully grasp what I have in mind."

"After breakfast sounds fine," Greg said digging his fork into his sunny-side up eggs and bacon, and dipping his toast in his yolk. "Since my crew is finishing up, there's not a lot for me to do right now. I'm yours, for a few hours at least."

"Wonderful." She took a bit of her pancake. "Wow, these oatmeal pancakes are really good." She wiped her mouth with her napkin. They actually made her mouth water.

"Yeah, they're my wife's favorite." He sat back in his seat and tilted his head a bit. "I've been looking at wind turbines for some time, but haven't had the opportunity to consider one as a complete system for power. If ample wind exists, it just might work. Are you suggesting no backup system at all?"

"I wanted to utilize storage batteries as backup, no electric to speak of, other than what I generate. Do you think it's possible?

"I won't know for sure until I have an expert check it out. I'll research the options and let you know."

After breakfast, Alexandra led Greg to the road up the mountain. As she put her Jeep in four-wheel drive, she checked her rear view mirror. Greg followed at a distance in his four-wheel drive truck. She continued to watch his progress as he smartly avoided the ruts behind her. Reaching the top, she slid out of her Jeep and met his eyes excitedly.

"We're going to need to cut a decent road up here first thing," he said, rubbing his jaw. "That," he said and motioned at the road, "doesn't really qualify."

"No, it doesn't," she conceded. She liked his sense of humor and smiled. "I probably should have warned you, but I much preferred to see the reaction on your face. You looked like a fellow who could handle it."

"I have two ATVs at home, and my daughter is already quite the four-wheeler."

"No wonder you took that hill so nicely."

"So, where are the boundaries?"

"Well, there aren't any to speak of; the whole mountain is at your disposal."

Greg whistled. "Now, this is going to be fun."

"I was hoping you would think so."

"I'm going to take a walk around, if you don't mind. I'd like to get to know this place a bit before I offer my recommendations. If I don't find the spring on my own, I'll give a yell and you can show it to me."

"That sounds perfect. I'm going to explore the remnants of those two buildings and the arbor, so if you can't find me, check there first."

"Good," he said as he walked in the direction of her first pink marker.

"Hey, I forgot to tell you, there's a cistern between us and the old house, be careful you don't tumble into it, okay?"

"I'll watch out for it; thanks for the warning."

Watching Greg trek over her mountain, she knew he would be her builder. She sensed he was self-assured, capable, and he would research items before committing to an answer if he didn't know it. He never met a stranger for his engaging personality met everyone as a potential friend.

Watching him walk away, she smiled at the sight. His sandy brown hair was a bit longer than average for a man in his thirties. Although his physique suggested his broad shoulders and trim waist were perfect for an Armani suit, Alexandra sensed he had never worn a suit in his life. No tie ever hung around that man's neck and never would.

She liked the extra little insight that stemmed from her new abilities and was glad she had opened her mind to him, if only for a second. Not knowing how her senses would react, she dared not leave them open for any length of time until she knew better how to manage them. It seemed she could allow things *in* without too much trouble, but that difficulties arose when she let senses *out*. She disconnected; she would not use her senses on Greg again.

Cautiously making her way toward the cistern, she located it, and sidestepped it. From a distance, the house looked to have possibilities, but on closer inspection, the assessment worsened considerably. Whitewashed at one time, it now weathered to a state of grayed neglect. Seeds that grew into saplings and over the years into full-fledged trees pressed close to the exterior walls threatening to obscure the home altogether. The house was one level with no basement. Stepping hesitantly onto the slatted porch, she worried she'd fall through. The two front windows had broken panes, and tatters of cloth remained indicating curtains once adorned the quaint home. Hanging sideways, the frame of a screen door leaned precariously on edge, still partially attached.

Moving aside the matted leaves and years of collected debris, she remembered her father's recommendation to knock loudly to scare away snakes. She pounded the daylights out of the door before kicking away the leaves, leaning her shoulder against the door, and pushing through.

The first room was as wide as the house and had a rough fireplace. She crossed the room and entered a doorway to the kitchen.

An iron cook stove drew her like a magnet to steel. She rubbed her hand across the rusty top, and although it contained pits, she might be able to restore it to serviceable condition. It had two areas for pots and a flat area on which to cook. The front had a door to load the wood. The stack, which had long since rusted away, lay amid the debris on the floor.

Toward the back of the room in the corner was a long enameled iron sink with a drain board to the left and a pump on the right side with the sink, which looked quite functional. Checking out the attached pump, she noted there was a place to pour water in to prime it, and the handle still moved freely. Looking underneath, she spied a wooden bucket, long since dried out and rotted and held together only by the rim. The iron plumbing from the sink went directly through the floor and, no doubt, ran into a splash basin and through a trough out the back. She wondered what her father, a plumber by trade, would have thought of this sink and plumbing.

Off to the side of the kitchen was a small room with a wooden bed frame. Slats and pieces of rough cloth were all that remained of the bedding. In size, it was slightly larger than a twin bed, but not the size of a full bed by today's standards. Someone lived here alone. What a distance up the mountain for one person to travel back and forth. Did Teater leave his family to spend years alone in this house?

She opened her mind to explore the house with her senses. Instantly, soul-wrenching loneliness filled her every pore. She gasped at the emptiness that gripped her from the inner reaches of her core and threatened to consume her. The emotion was too much to bear, so she hurriedly closed her mind. As she calmed, her heart ached for the person who suffered so much alone. She had experienced the feeling for just a few minutes and found it was impossible to comprehend a life lived with so much pain. Alexandra would probably never know what happened in the little house, but she sensed the owner had emotions beyond his control.

She took a deep breath and continued onward. Thick brier bushes blocked the back door, which had fallen off years earlier, so she turned and retraced her steps back to the front.

Looking up, the roof was almost gone and ready to fall in. As she walked back across the porch, the boards beneath her feet let out a crack, signaling it was time for her to leave.

She would salvage the sink and stove, and maybe some stones from the fireplace for use in her home to remind her of those who came beforehand.

The other building further off that she thought to be a shed, was the outhouse. As far as outhouses go, it used to be a nice one, a two-seater with oak toilet seats instead of round openings.

The last structure was the suspected arbor. Overgrown Heartseed vines had completely taken over the area. It took some time, but she finally pushed her way through to get to the inside and once encased in a floral cage, she imagined the arbor in its long-lost splendor. It was circular, maybe twelve feet in diameter, and still in excellent shape. Six areas, located evenly around the inside, looked like a seating area or a place for flowerpots.

She heard Greg call her name.

"I'm inside these vines. Hold on a minute 'til I figure out where I came in," she hollered back.

A few minutes later, she joined Greg looking across the mountain. "You've got a nice place up here. This will be a great setting for a home and an exciting project for my crew."

"Thanks, Greg. Did you find the spring?" She pulled a leaf from her hair.

"Yes, I think the supply is enough that you would never have to worry, even through a dry season, but, once developed, I'll still have a specialist check the gallons per minute, and have the health department approve its purity. I'm sure both reports will come back favorably. There's not much up here to contaminate anything."

"That's good to hear. I was checking out the old house, which is way beyond saving, but I would like to have the old iron cook stove restored and used somewhere in the design, and also the old sink and pump from the kitchen. The house has a fireplace with some nice stones, and I would like to use them as well."

"I know restoration people in the area for the stove and sink. I'll check out the stones from the fireplace and let you know where I think they might be useful. What about your fortress of vines over there?"

"It's quite intriguing. It was an arbor of some type and still in nice condition. I think I'll work on that space myself. Something about it makes me want to get in there immediately and start whacking vines back down to size. I think it will be beautiful."

"Maybe, in time. Right now, it just looks like a lot of work. Why don't I set up an appointment with my architect for you two to meet and get started on your plans?"

"It can't happen fast enough for me."

"Is there any reason for the rush?"

"Not really; I just finished college and want to get started with the rest of my life. I feel like I have been standing still for years, and to tell you the truth, I want to plant some nice roots."

"I'd be more than happy to oblige you."

"Greg, in all honesty, I was planning on interviewing two other builders, but after meeting you, I'll be looking no further."

"Thank you for your confidence, Alexandra. Let's get back to my office and get started on the paperwork."

"Good. This time, I'll follow you down the hill," she said.

"We'll need to decide where you want your access road. I'll get it done first thing."

"Why Mr. Patrick, I get the feeling you don't appreciate a good country lane." She winked.

"That country lane of yours does not qualify as a goat path. A goat has better sense." Again, the man had her laughing.

Getting into her Jeep, she yelled over her

shoulder, "I'll follow you to your office; lead the way."

Alexandra liked the people she met in Waynesburg so far. They seemed friendly and not too set in their ways. Maybe she could have walked barefoot through the center of town in her robe and not been considered a flake, but as of yet, she wasn't ready to test that theory.

Greg's office turned out to be quite the affair. From the front, it appeared to have three entrances, mostly because it looked like three separate building facades all connected together. The entrance labeled 'Main Office' was contemporary and business-like. The one on the right looked more like the worker's building, due to the navy blue Gregg Construction trucks parked outside. The state-of-the-art 'house' connected on the left hand side had her in a quandary.

Alexandra parked and followed Greg up the front steps to the office.

"Have a seat, Alexandra, this is Jesse, my office manager. She's the one that really runs this place. If you need anything she can help you. I'll be right back." He spoke to Jesse then went behind closed doors.

Sitting on the coffee table were books of completed projects. While she waited, she thumbed through them. Gregg Construction had built some of the most beautiful homes she had ever seen. Some she remembered from the website, but others, whom she figured from the stately manors, had apparently refused the unwanted publicity of having their private homes viewed on the web. She would do the same and keep her home to herself. If Greg was the type of contractor to consider his customer's privacy, he was perfect for her. She wanted privacy; maybe she even needed it. Without knowing what her future life held in store, it would be best to err on the side of caution, if possible.

A few minutes later, Greg reappeared and invited her into his office. "I took the liberty of calling Mathew Thomas, my architect. He'll be here in a few minutes."

"Thank you," she said taking a seat. "You are making this process very easy."

"You're welcome. I'm sure you will like Matt. He's a teddy bear of a guy, and well-gifted. Anything you can dream, he can get down in pen and ink, and I can build."

Alexandra helped herself to the chilled bottled water set out by Jessie, who a moment later brought documents to familiarize Alexandra with the Gregg Construction method of building a home. Again, Greg made it easy to put faith in him. He was up front on everything, and let her know what her responsibilities were and what to expect from him.

"If you have any questions after you review all the documents, you can reach me easily for clarification or resolution by calling the office. Jesse always knows how to reach me."

"It seems you've thought of everything."

"We try, but somehow something always slips through the cracks. If you want anything different than our standard, make sure you tell Matt to change it in the plans."

"I'm impressed by your standard build. It

should go well with the style of home I'm considering."

A light knock on the door sounded.

"Matt, you have tremendous timing. I'd like you to meet Alexandra Higgins. Alexandra, this is Mathew Thomas, architect extraordinaire."

"Wow, what a build-up," said Alexandra, smiling, taking his hand.

"I never know if it's going to be a remarkable introduction or a tongue-in-cheek one." Matt grinned, good naturedly. "I try to be ready for either."

By Greg's description of a teddy bear, Alexandra would have picked him from a line-up easily. He exuded confidence and friendliness from every pore of his being. Alexandra opened her senses just a bit to absorb a glimpse into him.

With his ready smile and eager-to-please attitude, Mathew Thomas was a man of many friends and loved ones. He was tall, about six-two, shaved his head, and had just enough extra weight to make him cuddly. She sensed family was very important to Matt and she knew he guarded his family with the ferociousness of a mother bear protecting her cubs. Such a man would be a pleasure to work with, and would certainly appreciate and respect her need for privacy.

Closing her senses, she said, "Thank you, Mr. Thomas, for taking time from your day to come here."

"No trouble at all, Ms. Higgins; and please call me Matt. Nobody calls me Mr. Thomas and I doubt I would answer to it in a room full of people."

"I'm Alexandra. It's nice to meet you. Greg certainly speaks highly of you, so I'm anxious to begin."

"We can use one of Greg's other rooms if you'd like."

"That's perfect."

"I'll catch up with you later, Greg," Matt said over his shoulder.

"Will do. I'll be in touch with you soon, Alexandra," said Greg, already reaching for the phone. "If that guy doesn't treat you right, just let me know."

"Thanks, Greg. I think we'll be just fine."

Matt and Alexandra got down to basics in no time at all. The other room he spoke of was actually located in the house to the left. On the inside, rooms exhibited many options from baseboard to hinges and fasteners. Various types of cabinets, flooring, tile, and bathroom fixtures were all available for scrutiny. Displayed throughout the three-story home were samples of any building material or feature she desired.

Within a few hours, and after ordering in lunch, Matt had gleaned enough information from Alexandra to start on the plans for her house. He used a digital recorder to be sure he wouldn't forget anything and asked permission to view the land. They agreed to meet the following day and drive up together.

Alexandra felt confident in both Matt and Greg, and after leaving Gregg Construction, she grabbed a soup and salad from the local Olive Garden. She rounded out the day by picking up a few essentials from the grocery store and returning to her room at the hotel.

What a great day! She met two very qualified men who would be instrumental in making her dream home come true and had taken the first steps to start the process.

She ate, showered, and felt the need to go to other worlds, so she got comfortable and clicked on her eReader.

* * * * *

She has it and probably doesn't know its importance.

They've always been secretive, blocking their minds to me. If they were so powerful, how did I exist alongside them all these years without their detection?

They hold to their customs; I hold to no man's oath.

* * * * *

Chapter Nine

Alexandra's meeting with Mathew Thomas wasn't until ten, so she took her time completing all the little steps a gal does to make herself feel soft and feminine all over.

Alexandra permitted herself one indulgence, socks. She had a penchant for socks with polka dots, argyle diamonds, stripes, leopard and tiger prints, shiny threads that sparkled, and even ones with lace or buttons on them. Her sock drawers were stuffed to brimming and didn't come close to closing. She scanned the small collection that traveled with her at all times. Her favorite ones were the solid neon colors: hot pink, lime green, florescent orange, turquoise, and a yellow that just might glow in the dark. She selected the turquoise neon socks that matched the shirt she'd picked out. As she pulled on the socks, she wiggled her toes and admired her small feet. Her grandma had worn a size five, and her dad always said she had her grandma's feet. At size six and a half, they suited her perfectly. It was good to be alive, and to have such a great collection of socks.

Alexandra stopped by the breakfast area of the hotel and grabbed fruit and yogurt and chased it down with some chocolate milk. Inwardly laughing to herself, her stomach might not enjoy the milk chaser, but her psyche yelled 'yippee'.

Walking to the parking lot, she climbed in the Jeep, started the engine, and waited for Matt to arrive. She reached for her iPod and selected John Denver's *Looking for Space.* Today she would 'fly like an eagle' up to her mountain.

When she spotted her architect getting out of his car, she lowered her window, and yelled, "Good morning, Matt."

He waved, crossed the parking lot, and slid into the passenger side of her Jeep.

"Morning, Alexandra."

"Do you have everything you need?"

"Yes, for now. I'll need to make some trips on my own later, but for now I'd just like to see how the sun moves across the land and which way you would like the house to face."

"Great, buckle up, and we'll be off then."

"Greg was telling me a bit about your land. He's excited to build up there and help you be self-sufficient. I know he's toyed with the thoughts of a wind turbine before but has never worked with an owner that has your vision."

"I'm glad the technology is there for us to use. I would prefer not drilling a well or routing electric up there. I actually think that in the end it might actually be more cost-effective, but I think the jury is still out on that one. The location is so far from the electric source that it would cost a fortune to run lines up there. Besides, I feel the least destruction of the natural surroundings, the better."

Getting better at navigating the ruts of the road, Alexandra glanced over at Matt who held onto the overhead handgrips, his eyes intent on their progression.

"Greg said he was going to cut a road up here." His eyes took in the incline.

"I'm thinking of using this same one, since it wouldn't require the removal of many more trees to make it wider. Once the overgrowth is cut back it should be very nice, and since it winds back and forth there are no really steep areas to be concerned about in the winter."

"I have a thought, since Greg will be digging a bit to get down to the level of the ruts and grading the road for water run-off, it might be a good time to consider whether or not to install some type of security at the entrance."

"That's a great idea, Matt. I never thought of that. Once you pull onto the road and go some distance, there would be no place to turn around to go back, so people who have made a wrong turn would have to continue to the top. I wouldn't like that type of intrusion."

"It would be a shame to destroy a nice entrance with a sign to keep away rubber-neckers, but a nice gate would stop them at the beginning. You could make it key card access or voice controlled."

"Another great idea. I knew I liked you. I'll look at some options tonight."

When they arrived at the top, she parked in the same spot underneath the tree.

Matt got out and smiled broadly. "No wonder Greg was excited to build here, it's an amazing property. Show me around and tell me what you envision."

Alexandra told Matt everything in her heart,

and included why she wanted to build on the land of her ancestor. She pointed out the cistern and told him how she had fallen in, and then helped him shove the cover aside.

"Young lady, you are lucky to be alive. That is one evil looking hole in the ground. The board's still sticking out of the wall."

"Looking down there, I can't believe I got out either. I'd have to agree, luck was on my side that day."

Matt stooped down and leaned into the cistern a bit to get a better look. "The structure seems very much intact. We may be able to make use of it in our design. The workmanship is very high quality." He stood and held his chin in his hand.

"What are you thinking?"

"Until I have a chance to investigate more, I'd rather not say, but if it works out, you'll have a nice surprise."

"I'll wait for your final thoughts, then. In the meantime, look at this arbor. Maybe 'arbor' is not the exact word for it, but it was the only description that came to mind."

She located the opening where she had entered before, and Matt followed her inside the mass of vines.

He pulled the vines aside and ran his hands over the upright column. "It looks like the same master mason built both this and the cistern. His work is impeccable."

"Ever since I stepped inside, I've had this compulsion to bring it back to its former glory."

Matt shook his head. "It's going to take a lot of

work."

"Come, let me show you the old house and the items I would like incorporated into my house design."

Inside the house, which Matt entered hesitatingly, Alexandra asked, "What do you think?"

"It's no wonder you want to use the sink and stove. They are both reminiscent of past times, redeemable, and will make great conversation pieces."

She led the way to the spring as Matt made notes.

"What's up with the pink flags?" he asked.

"I did a bit of exploring using my GPS and marked out my path as I went so I wouldn't get lost."

"After landing in a hole, it's no wonder you took precautions."

Matt offered many suggestions regarding placement, which took into consideration the way the sun moved across the sky and the elements of winter. Alexandra sensed fate certainly smiled when she placed her home in the hands of this thoughtful and caring man.

As Alexandra descended the mountain, he suggested they continue over lunch at a local eatery. She followed him to a reworked old hotel and Post Office. Originally established in 1827, it had the earmarks of Victorian style. On Matt's recommendation, they both ordered the special.

Lunch lasted two hours and they didn't stop talking the whole time. He wasn't only a delightful companion, his questions regarding her likes and dislikes, made for easy conversation. She found herself completely at ease in his capable hands. Matt sketched some aspects she wasn't familiar with so she knew precisely what he was thinking, and at the end of two hours, he pronounced he had her house pictured perfectly in his mind.

"Alexandra, I'm going back to my office and start on your plans while it's still fresh in my mind."

"Thanks for your great ideas, Matt," she said and shook his hand.

Alexandra stopped at the grocery store where she bought a local paper, and picked up a free apartment rental booklet from the rack at the entrance. She'd be spending a lot of time in Waynesburg and didn't want to live in a hotel any longer. When she was certain she had enough information, she went back to the Jeep to perform her research.

She spread the paper out on the passenger seat and looked for furnished apartments on the north side of town. There were only two units: a townhouse, and a two-bedroom apartment. The two-bedroom unit listed for two hundred a month less.

She entered both addresses in the GPS and performed a drive-by of the two offerings. The townhouse was very nice, located in a great section of town and close to grocery and department stores, but she found it a little too busy for her tastes.

The apartment's address took her to an old Edwardian nestled away from the bustle of city life on a street with the back of the house facing a hill.

The lot was spacious, with exquisite mature landscaping. She parked a little ways down from the house and dialed the number on the listing. A man answered the phone.

"Hello?"

"Hi, I'm calling about the two bedroom apartment for rent."

"For rent? Here? Oh yeah, I didn't know they'd listed it."

"Would it be possible to come and take a look at it?"

"Yeah, I'd be happy to show it to you anytime."

"I'm nearby, and could be there in a few minutes. Would that be okay?"

"Sure thing. I'll be looking for you. Bye." He hung up.

She drove back to the mansion and pulled onto the circular drive. Before she could reach the front steps, a voice stopped her.

"Are you here about the apartment?" Startled, she turned to see a man coming around the side of the house.

She stopped dead in her tracks, and her mouth fell open. "Terry?" she said.

She stared at the caretaker from the mountain. Her stomach rolled over. Wearing overalls, he carried two-inch shears, had on shoes stained green and covered with grass clippings, so why did her nerves stand on edge?

"Well if it isn't Ms. Higgins."

"You certainly do get around." She tried to settle the unnerving sensation creeping over her.

He looked about as imposing as a middle-aged country minister.

"As do you, young lady." He slipped the shears into his back pocket. "I look after a few properties here in Waynesburg, but this one is my favorite. I didn't know the owner had advertised the apartment, so I was a little surprised when you called."

"The property is astonishing, and the landscaping is unbelievable." Her eyes went from bloom to bloom, as her nerves relaxed a bit.

"Thank you. I have been acting as gardener here for about four years and consider most of these plantings to be family. Follow me, and I'll show you the apartment." He turned and walked back the way he came.

She followed around to the right side of the property. Behind the house, her eyes rested on a small bungalow, originally designed as the guesthouse. The 'apartment' was private, had rear alley access, modern kitchen, cozy interior, came equipped with flat screen TV, wireless Internet, washer and dryer. The stone washed walls, flower boxes, and understated fireplace wrapped up the package in astounding charm.

"I'll take it."

"Ms. Higgins, the owner is lucky to have you as a tenant. They don't stand on much ceremony here at Larkspur, so there is no lease to speak of. You may stay as long as you like. Rent is due on the first of the month with a month in advance. And if you have any problems, you can reach me at the number you called earlier."

"You probably haven't heard, but my ancestor bequeathed the land on the mountain to me. I've decided to build on the property and would like to stay here until the construction is complete."

"Yeah, Jediah said the land went to you. He told me I was out of the caretaker's job."

Her heart skipped a beat at the mention of his name. Although she ached for more information, she remained calm and said, "Oh, I'm sorry. I never considered you would lose the job."

"It's just as well, that place was a bit off the beaten track. It took me longer to get there and back again than to perform any upkeep."

"That road does take some getting used to," she said.

"I was surprised anyone ventured up there, especially young women."

Alexandra smiled. "I can give you a check for the first and last month's rent. How soon can I move in?"

"You may move in today, if you want to. The apartment is always ready."

She pulled out her checkbook. "How do I make out the check?"

"Make it out to Larkspur, Inc.; you can leave your monthly check in the drop box on the side of the back porch, if you'd like. It's convenient, and you save the price of a stamp."

"Terry, I can't believe my luck at finding this place. It certainly will be nice to spend time here while waiting on the house. Oh, I need to ask, would it be permissible to have overnight visitors? My friend, Cassie, might pop in during construction to visit."

"I remember your friend. There are no restrictions on visitors, but the owners value their privacy as I assume you do, so keep that in mind."

"I would be pleased to honor such a request."

Alexandra tore off the check for the amount specified, and handed it to him as he handed her the key.

"I'll be bringing my things over tomorrow. Thank you for everything."

She walked back to her Jeep, but as soon as she was out of his sight, she did a celebratory dance.

"Yes!" She couldn't believe her luck. The bungalow was perfect, even though it might have a not-so-perfect gardener. She would reserve forming an opinion until she could sort out her senses better.

Grinning like a Cheshire cat, she returned to her Jeep and headed to the diner. She had intended to inquire about Jediah, but that same eeriness she felt on the mountain held her back. Terry had done nothing, but he made her feel queasy. If she wanted more information regarding the elusive Mr. Saffle, she would just have to wait.

The bungalow was a treasure! Why no one had rented it was a mystery to her. Not wanting to jinx her luck, she quickly dismissed bad thoughts and concentrated on good instead. On the way back to the hotel, she stopped and picked up take-out from the diner and planned using the evening to pack her belongings and relax prior to moving into Larkspur.

Tomorrow was Thursday, day of move-out, and then move-in. Opening her laptop, she brought Cassie up to date in an email, and cringed a bit not knowing how she would receive the news.

Cassie and Alexandra had been friends for so long she questioned her decision to move so far away from her. The Hudsons were her surrogate family, but it was Cassie's family not hers; maybe that was the issue. How could she explain to Cassie the closeness she felt here? It had started with Teater, but was there something else? The rational part of her brain loudly claimed there wasn't, but that was a lie. Jediah. The attraction was both undeniable and irresistible. She didn't know him well enough to consider him an attachment, but she was more than willing to explore the possibility. That is, if he passed her secondary inspection.

Packing clothes turned into a mindless task. Her mind jumped from thought to thought in no order whatsoever, but always in relationship to Jediah. Where does he live? Does he have family? When will she see him again? The next time she ran into Terry she planned to have an arsenal of questions ready.

With packing complete, she showered, ate supper, and relaxed. Picking up her eReader, the evening filled with the completion of her book.

Hours later, sated by the author's mastery, she clicked off the eReader, and let thoughts of Jediah lull her to sleep.

The violet eyes did not disappoint - Alexandra doubted they ever would - and invaded her dreams like gale-force winds. The time she spent with Jediah in her dreams seemed endless; she became acutely aware of 'everlasting' as a state of being, they had always been, will be forevermore. She knew all, yet knew nothing.

Jediah and Alexandra walked through beautiful woodlands, they floated among clouds atop a mountain, then stepped off the face of a mega monolith only to fly on the winds as they changed from moist to arid as they later settled on a desert. She marveled at the flowering cactus amid an oasis, then, in the blink of an eye, they were walking on her mountain. She realized they were inside the arbor, not as it was presently, but as once was. Throughout all, Jediah was inviting, warm, and attentive. They sat under the vines and spoke countless words through endless time.

She woke the following morning sad and angry that the dream had ended. She wanted more, so much more of him. Did she have the right to feel this way? Her heart screamed out an ear-piercing 'yes', but common sense prevailed and cautioned her to go slowly. If he did not return her feelings, the result could be demoralizing. Letting her mind travel down that path could be treacherous; she hoped fate wouldn't be so unkind. Blanking out the current thought, she refused to allow negativity to rule the day.

Checking out of the hotel proved to be an exhilarating start to an earmark day. For the first time since her parents' deaths, she was setting down real roots. She had lived in an apartment in Wheeling, a dorm in college, and various hotels. Precious items saved from her parents' house were in storage, and she had refused, until now, to claim any one place as home. Teater's mystery led her here; Waynesburg would be her home.

After unloading the Jeep into the guesthouse, Alexandra grabbed a breakfast sandwich, some OJ, signed up for a post office box and turned the Jeep's nose toward Wheeling.

She had to load the boxes still packed from college, close out her utility accounts, submit a change of address form, and make her way back to Waynesburg. It was a list of busy items, but with luck, she could easily be back at Larkspur by mid-afternoon, with just enough time to grocery shop and settle in for the evening.

Alexandra plugged in her iPhone, selected her Fast Playlist, and sang all the way back to Wheeling, playing Sugarland's *Stuck Like Glue* three times in a row.

If she managed her time well she could take Cassie to lunch. Arriving at the Highlands shopping plaza, she pulled into the gas station to fill her tank. While the gas flowed, she punched the speed dial for Cassie's work.

When Alexandra heard Cassie's hello, she responded, "Hey there, little girl! Can I take you to lunch?"

"Allie, you're back in town?"

"Sure am, but only for a short time."

"After the bomb you dropped last night, you're only giving me lunch to get the scoop?"

"We can talk all you like later, but today I'm moving my belongings, which isn't much, to Waynesburg. I found a nice furnished place to live until my house is done."

"Lunch it is, then. I can't wait to see you."

"Me either."

"I'll pick you up at noon, and we'll go to the Bistro. Bye."

Everything went smoothly; she was even able to catch the apartment manager and settle with him. Since the apartment was furnished, she only had to load the unpacked boxes from college. She threw the remainder into the trash bin. The five-year-old vacuum made it into the Jeep, but she warned it that its days were numbered. As she looked over the paltry amount she called her own, she laughed at what a vagabond she had become.

Once she dropped off the apartment key, she had just enough time to get to Oglebay and pick up Cassie, who had secured a great position as Curator of the Oglebay Museum and Glass Institute. It probably hadn't hurt that Cassie's aunt had vacated the position and recommended her niece for the job. She was already waiting at the curb, and slid, smiling, into the passenger seat.

"Hey, Allie, I'm glad we could do lunch."

Alexandra leaned over to hug her. "You look great. Your eyes are sparkling."

"You're really leaving, aren't you?" She looked at the boxes in the back.

"I'm afraid so." When she looked from the boxes back to her friend, the sparkle had gone.

She put the Jeep in drive and started toward the Bistro. "It's only an hour away, and I promise to use my cell phone, so you can reach me anytime."

"It's going to be tough, but I've decided to support you any way I can. You've lost so much. I know how you feel about the money you received back then, and I probably would have felt the same, but I know your Mom and Dad would want you to use it to insure your future."

She pulled into the parking lot of the restaurant and turned off the engine. "It's dirty money. Money can't replace the years I lost with Mom and Dad. I hate it, but as much as it sickens me, I'll use it to build a house on the land Teater left me. I love that land; I love it like I loved my parents, and I think they'd love it too."

"It seems fast, but fate has smiled on you in Waynesburg."

"Don't you think it's about time?"

The sparkle was back in both their eyes. Alexandra met her friend's smile with one of her own.

The Bistro was a small restaurant that overlooked Oglebay's Bunny Hill for skiing in the winter and the Par 3 in the summer. Two brothers, both chefs, ran the restaurant, and in the multitude of times they had been there, they had never been disappointed with the food. The people of Wheeling kept that diamond to themselves.

"Okay, tell me everything." Cassie began after they sat down.

"I stopped by Mr. Dawson's office first. He gave me the name of a builder and architect; incredibly, they both turned out to be really great guys. Greg is my builder, and Matt, my architect. They are both very professional and I trust them completely."

"Wow that was lucky."

"I'm not so certain it was luck. Mr. Dawson seems to know the most competent people. I should know more in a week or so."

"I can't believe you are going to live so far away."

"It's not that far, and the drive is an easy one."

"I just thought we'd always live close, like it was before college," Cassie said.

"I know." She tried to soften the blow. "You know the old saying, 'you can never go home again'?"

"Yes. And I understand why you feel that way. I'm being selfish again."

"Cassandra Hudson, you don't have a selfish bone in your body. I didn't plan on this Waynesburg thing, it just happened, almost like it was supposed to happen. I don't know why I feel so drawn to that place, but it is the only place that feels like home. I can't explain it."

"You shouldn't have to explain yourself, even to me. I just want you to be happy, and if you're happy in Waynesburg, I'm happy too. Where will you be staying?"

"Oh, I got a great apartment. I still don't know how it happened, but I'm renting the guest cottage of a gorgeous Edwardian estate called Larkspur."

"Alexandra," said a silky voice over her shoulder, "where is this gorgeous Larkspur?"

Alexandra turned and looked into the steel blue eyes of Tom Magis. "Hi, Tom, it's been a long time," she said, keeping her voice level. Did he come from the woodwork?

"And if it isn't the ever-present Cassie Hudson," he said, too sweetly.

"Hi, Tom," replied Cassie, avoiding eye contact

by pretending to get something from her purse.

"Ever present? Yes, I see her as much as I can." Why didn't he just leave? Instead he took his time leering openly at her.

"Back to my original question, Alexandra." He leaned closer and said softly, "Am I to understand you warrant a guest cottage? Moving on up in the world, aren't you?"

As bile rose in her throat, she tried to downplay the bungalow, "It was either that or a two bedroom on a busy street. My choices were limited."

"I don't recall anything in Wheeling called Larkspur."

"No, there isn't. Did you want something in particular, Tom?" She tried for her sweetest non-committal voice, "I really hate to be rude, but I only have an hour for lunch and Cassie and I have a lot of catching up to do."

"Always the brush off with you, isn't it, Alexandra?" he sneered.

"I don't know what you mean, Tom." She avoided looking directly at him, thinking he might take the hint to leave them alone.

"I'm sure you don't," he sneered. "You never considered anyone but yourself."

Hating confrontations, she forced herself to remain calm. "That's not true. It was bad timing, Tom, nothing more."

"And what's wrong now?"

You're an irritating bore, that's what, tried to come out of her mouth. Instead, she replied, "As I said, I'm short of time."

Thankfully, the food arrived and interrupted the

conversation. Tom strode off, and left the restaurant. As soon as the waitress left, Alexandra looked directly at Cassie. "That guy still gives me the creeps."

"Wasn't he the one...?"

"Yeah. To this day, I can't understand what got into him. He never noticed me once all through high school, then right after my parents' accident, you would have thought he was my secret admirer all those years. He wouldn't take 'no' for an answer, even though I tried to explain to him that I wasn't ready for a relationship."

"I'm just glad he's gone. He gives me the willies."

"Me too." Alexandra agreed and shook. "He seems slimy. Let's get back to better things. I was telling you about Larkspur. You will have to come up for the weekend. It's beautiful. I can't believe I get to live there."

"I'd love to come, but I can't come this weekend."

Waiting for the reason why, Alexandra noticed Cassie had turned red. "What's going on? Why are you embarrassed?"

"Okay, fine." Cassie said, "I met someone."

"You did? Spill it."

Once the floodgates opened, she bubbled over. "Yes. Allie, he's so nice. His name is John Ryan and I met him a couple of weeks ago, at one of those fundraisers Oglebay holds every year. I went out to dinner with him the other night."

"Tell me everything." She saw Cassie's eyes sparkling.

"I was so nervous. When it came time to order, I told him I didn't think I could eat anything. He was so self-assured, he went ahead and ordered for himself and got me a glass of wine. As I talked to him, his manner put me at ease, and I felt like we were old friends. Then his food came, and I realized I was ravenous, but I didn't say a word. He insisted he couldn't possibly eat all the food the waitress had brought, so he asked for extra plates, and served me from his meal. He said, 'I know you're not hungry, but I can't sit here and eat in front of you. If you don't want it, just move it around on your plate.' Of course, I ate everything, and got dessert. It was the most considerate thing that has ever happened to me. I felt like someone cherished me."

"He sounds like a keeper."

"He might be. You ought to hear Mom go on about him. He treats her so nice; and Dad liked him right away."

"What does he look like?"

"He's about five ten, not nearly as tall as Jediah. He has sandy hair and soft brown eyes. He looks magnificent in a suit. He has firm hands and his muscles felt like iron when I held his arm. He's built like one of those rugby players, fit and all muscle."

"He sounds good so far. What does he do?"

"He's a Chemical Engineer and has his own engineering company in little Washington."

"Wow, he's established. How old?" she asked.

"He's thirty one. He started his business as soon as he got out of college. He said he had a business plan in mind and wanted to see if it would work. It did."

"Okay, now the big one, why isn't he already attached?"

"He said he'd been in a relationship in college, but it didn't work out. Until now, he'd put his energies into his business and only just recently felt he was ready for the next step."

Cassie had been talking a mile a minute. Alexandra could sense her emotions beneath the surface. Her friend was totally and completely immersed in John Ryan. She hoped John was as enthralled in Cassie, but looking across at her friend all gooey with infatuation, how could he not? She was happy for Cassie, but felt a pang of envy. Would she run into Jediah again?

Trying not to let her fears override Cassie's joy, she asked, "How did you two meet? Did someone introduce you?"

"No, it was one of those introduction-type games to melt the ice. Everyone put their favorite saying onto a piece of paper and signed it. The paper was placed in a jar, and everyone pulled one out. The person who pulled it out had to find the author of their note and come up with a response."

"What did you write?" Alexandra asked.

"You know, the one from *The Book of Psalms*, 'Weeping may endure for a night, but joy cometh in the morning'."

They shared those words to get through rough times in school.

"When he found me, all he said, as he looked in my eyes was, 'You speak from your heart'."

"You gave me chills." Her cohort was beaming. She looked closely at Cassie and saw she had already lost her heart to John. The knowledge warmed her from the inside.

"Allie, he's really nice. I can't believe my luck."

"When will you see him again?"

"We talk on the phone every night like teenagers. I'll see him again this weekend."

"Cassie, I'm so happy for you. I can't wait to meet him. You'll have to bring him up once I get settled."

"I will. Has anything happened with Jediah?"

"No, I haven't seen him on this trip. But, do you remember that caretaker from the mountain? The one who repaired the lid I fell through?"

"Yeah, Terry, wasn't it?" Cassie asked.

"Well, he's also the caretaker at Larkspur, the place I'm renting."

"You're kidding me," Cassie said.

"Not at all, and do you believe it, when I had the chance to ask about Jediah, I decided not to."

Cassie smiled and said, "You'll have plenty more chances now that you live up there."

"I hope so. I dream about him." She watched Cassie's reaction.

"You do? You must be thinking about him a lot."

"I thought that was why too, but these dreams are so very different from any dreams I've ever had. I remember the entire dream, vividly. When I wake up, it's like it really happened. The dreams are wonderful."

"Gosh, if you could see yourself right now. You are glowing. You have more light in your eyes than I have ever seen there before. You'd better be careful and not get hurt."

"I've been lecturing myself about that very thing, but in my heart, I know he will never hurt me. It's strange, and I can't explain it. I've never felt this way before. I don't act like this. It's not me. I'm cautious. I don't give my heart away easily. But I'm not afraid."

"Odd. Really weird. I don't want to put a damper on you, but you haven't seen him in months. Are you sure he's still around?"

Leave it to Cassie to hit the nail on the head. She wasn't ready to admit that maybe it wasn't meant to be. She sighed. "I know. I just have this strong feeling that everything will work out perfectly. The next time I run into that fellow, he's going to get the fifth degree. He's going to have to share a lot more about himself before I give an inch."

"Now, that's the Alexandra I know and love."

Lunch over, she drove Cassie back to her office and dropped her off.

"Thanks for lunch. Let me know when you bump into Jediah. I'm eager to hear about you two."

"The same goes for you. Don't keep me in the dark about John. I can't wait to meet him."

"I'll be watching for emails. Take care. I love you bunches."

"I love you too, honey. Say 'hi' to your Mom and Dad."

Before they parted, they decided Cassie could have her engineer, and Alexandra could have her house, and, maybe, Jediah.

Chapter Ten

Time ticked by quickly and soon Alexandra found herself unpacking the Jeep and depositing the boxes in the bungalow.

She glimpsed Terry during one of her many trips back and forth, but he was too far away to start a conversation. It was just as well, for unpacking in the heat of the day left her hair sticking to her face and arms glistening with sweat. She reprimanded herself for not getting groceries first, for now, she didn't present much of an appearance. A quick shower would be necessary before going to the market to stock her shelves.

* * * * *

The guesthouse is tucked away from the main house. The alley is perfect. I'm glad I hung around; I'll have to watch out for the groundskeeper.

It couldn't have worked out better. Since she's new to the area it will take time for them to notice her missing. Alexandra will be mine soon.

* * * * *

Two hours later, the groceries unpacked, Alexandra ate her first spoonful of yogurt in the air-conditioned luxury of the bungalow. Moving was the pits. Even with as little as she had, she placed moving on the top of her list of things to avoid.

She found the perfect place for her iPod and speakers on the sofa console between the kitchen and living area. With her soft mix playing, she walked around the little house, sat in all the comfy chairs, tested the bed in the master suite, and only then began the job of unpacking and clearing the boxes. After planning to lose only one day to moving, she realized at 2 AM, she hadn't made it.

With no alarm to wake her, she slept until nine the following morning. The day began with breakfast and a trip to the hardware store.

Ever since the dream with Jediah, she wanted to get back to her mountain. She was just entering the rutted road when her cell phone rang. She stopped the Jeep, and put on the emergency brake before answering.

It was Greg. "Good morning, Alexandra."

"Hello, Greg, what can I do for you?"

"As a matter of fact, I was wondering if I could do something for you."

"That would be good, too."

"I have a fella ready to excavate your access road. He wants to start tomorrow, and I wanted to make sure that would be all right with you."

"Tomorrow would be fine. How long do you think it will take until it is passable again?"

"These guys work fast, but I would still plan on at least a week or so before it is completed, and that's if the weather holds. I have to get down a course of large stone to begin the foundation for the road, then some finer stone on top."

"I see." She wanted her cake and to eat it too. Dang, she wanted on that mountain.

"Is something wrong?"

"No, I was just anxious to be on the site working on that arbor."

"You know, yesterday, when going over your driveway with the guys who will be running the machinery, we took our trucks up and mapped out a temporary entrance about a mile further down the road. We wouldn't put any gravel there, but with a four wheel drive, you could get to the top. It's a lot of weaving and some steep areas, but certainly negotiable until the main entry is usable."

"You are a wonder. Thank you so much." Now nothing stood in the way of that arbor and her.

"I didn't want to be hampered anymore than you did. I like a fast schedule. If you want to conceal it later, we could hide it with some natural plantings, but for now, we can both gain access without holding up progress."

"Perfect."

"Until tomorrow, then."

Already twenty feet or so up the road, she decided to explore the new access road tomorrow or later that day. Right now, she had a job in mind.

Arriving at the top, she drove through the briers and parked about twenty feet from the arbor. She opened the trunk, pulled out a rake, leaf rake, small hand loppers, large loppers, handsaw, and a pack of matches. The project began by clearing a large space free of debris where she could burn the brush. Needing a better feel for where to begin, she cleared a six-foot area around the arbor. Stepping back to view her progress, it was evident the job would take some time. She already had two piles in the burn area: one to burn, and one as extra so she could keep the fire small enough to manage on her own.

The project brought back memories of clearing the front yard of their farm in Wheeling. The house had been empty for some time when her father bought it. Her mother and she had worked days clearing berry bushes and trash from the front yard. The previous owners had several boys, and it appeared none of them liked to work, so they threw their trash off the front porch. They also liked to play with knives; the gashes in the kitchen's woodwork were living proof. She found it hard to believe people would actually sit around the kitchen and throw knives at the woodwork.

It was glorious spending the hours remembering the times with her parents. Days like this one brought their memories back clearer than ever. She missed them every waking moment.

Her mother and she worked so hard on that yard. They replanted it with thick grass and peonies that grew bigger every year. Alexandra was determined to bring the same lushness to her arbor.

Picturing the arbor as she remembered it from her dream, she started on one section, and then realized she needed to start burning before she got too far ahead of herself.

She piled the brush so the thin grasses acted as kindling. The fire caught nicely, and because some of the brush was green, it didn't burn too quickly. Alexandra added a little brush at a time, and soon had a nice bed of coals. It was only then she could turn her attention back to the arbor.

By trimming some large sections of the vines away, then slowly thinning vine by vine the overall appearance emerged wispy. Part of one of the uprights exposed beautiful carved stone construction, about eight inches wide at the bottom, and narrowing toward the top. There were six uprights in all and six benches. After working for four hours, one of the six sections appeared. She stood back looking at it with her hands on her hips.

"Well, Mom and Dad, you would be proud of the work we did here today. What do you think? Not bad for the first day."

The lack of facilities limited the time spent on the mountain to the capacity of her bladder. She'd learned her lesson years ago regarding peeing in the woods, and from that day on she lived in fear of poison ivy and poison oak. Three shiny leaves and hairy stems would be handled with nothing shorter than a ten-foot pole. With only a mid-morning snack consumed two hours ago, and three bottles of water now empty, it was time to head back to the bungalow. She let the fire die down to ashes, then shoved dirt on top if it. Tomorrow she would attack anew.

* * * * *

I need to act fast. Now that she's gone, I can see what is up that road and why she stayed so long. She won't have a chance.

* * * * *

Back home, after showering and checking for ticks, Alexandra made some lunch and sought the side yard and the small wrought iron table and chairs sequestered in the shade of a mammoth oak tree. It was there, as Alexandra sipped her tea and ate, that she opened her eReader and began a new book about dragons.

Her tastes in literature leaned toward fiction, whether it was historical romance, dragons, or Scottish highlanders. She loved just a taste of fanciful delight, a wee bit of mystery, with a tad of excitement mixed in, to take her mind elsewhere.

After reading for a few hours, Alexandra clicked off the eReader, gathered up her mess and went inside to begin supper. Chopping vegetables allowed her mind to wander, and once again, they wrapped around Jediah.

It wasn't the first time she had thought about him today, for it seemed he never really left her. He accompanied her when she thought about past times with her parents and when she watched the fire burn on her mountain. He was ever present and always in the front of her mind.

Consuming thoughts of a male were unexplored ground for Alexandra. It was both awkward to manage and a pleasure to experience at the same time. If not for the close monitoring of the reins of thought, she could turn into a babbling idiot at any moment. Sometimes she felt like there were two Alexandras: one who knew Jediah and his every thought, and the other, who didn't know him at all.

The entry of Jediah into her life combined with the newness of sense exploration, she wondered that she hadn't been crippled with emotion. Instead, she had decided to leave the area called home, build a house on a mountain, and hitch her wagon to a violet star. She could easily place herself in one of her fanciful novels with no three-hundred-page-end in sight.

Finishing the day by catching up on email, a nice note to Cassie, and reading a few more chapters of her book, she finally succumbed to the place of dreams.

This time she didn't recognize the place where Jediah took her. The village was very quaint. People gathered all around. Once amassed, at least two hundred or more, Jediah introduced her one-by-one to all, telling her something about each person as he went along. It was a relatively young group, with no one appearing to be over thirty-five or so. Except for one, the older woman from the diner was there too. They started toward her, and… she woke up.

Drat, wasn't that just like a dream? Just when it started getting good.

The dreams Alexandra experienced since coming to Waynesburg were always in color. She didn't remember dreaming in color before, or maybe she just hadn't noticed. Everything in her dreams carried a significance that somehow filled a void in her makeup that had gone unnoticed until now. Through dreams, Jediah helped her catch up to a standard of knowledge she would have gleaned naturally, if her joining the Sensate group had occurred through a more hands-on approach, like learning from parents.

During the dreams, she witnessed the Sensate abilities Jediah possessed. They gave her tremendous insight into the wide array of possibilities she might attempt someday. She also became aware of the Sensates' involvement behind the scenes in some worldwide scenarios.

One, in particular, caused her to awaken abruptly with her heart racing. Sensates had been involved in trying to prevent the assassination of JFK. They had learned of the plot and had attempted to intervene by seeding information to the authorities, but they had been unable to stop the President from being killed. Alexandra had, at her fingertips, the answers the Warren Commission sought since 1963. All the pieces fit together now. And she couldn't say a word...

The ramifications of this type of knowledge eked slowly into her mind as a new layer of responsibility bore down upon her innocent shoulders.

Before experiencing Jediah's dreams, which she remembered vividly upon waking, she could only remember one dream from childhood that she dreamt repeatedly. She was at the top of a hill amid a thunderstorm. Wind gusted, rain pounded down, and lightning flashed all around. The wind started spinning with her at the vortex pelting her with rain and drawing the lightning closer to her, the center. The flashes of lightning become so bright she closed her eyes. The rain and noise of the wind and thunder subsided instantly, and she opened her eyes to a beautiful clear day. The first time she'd had the dream, she'd been frightened and woke up with her skin wet from sweat.

There wasn'thing scary or alarming about Jediah's dreams. They were always wonderful and filled with awe, just like her most recent dream. The women had on beautiful gowns, and the men wore tuxedos. She didn't recall seeing what Jediah wore, only that his eyes, which were transfixed on her, spoke volumes.

Trucks blocked the entrance, so she drove past to locate the secondary entrance Greg mentioned. It was obscure, but the path worn by heavy equipment was easy to follow. Shifting into four-wheel drive, she slowly made her way up the mountain. The path took her around stumps and fallen trees and, had it not been for the path left by the heavy equipment, she would have lost her way. The foliage lessened and she found herself on top of her mountain, but from the opposite side. Trucks, bulldozers, backhoes, and bobcats littered the top of the hill, and, she noticed with pleasure, a Port-a-Potty. Life had just gotten even better.

She parked her Jeep close to the arbor and continued her cleanup. It was nice knowing others were up there with her. Today, she thought to bring her iPod and battery-powered speakers and listened to a wide selection of music while she worked, at least until one of the big earthmovers powered up. Luckily, the loud noise never lasted long, just until they headed down the hill.

Life continued like this for a week and a half, at

which time, Greg announced the road of sufficient quality to use.

Alexandra made fantastic headway on the arbor. With all the seats revealed, she enjoyed lunch there daily. She lost a few days to rain, but nothing daunted her effervescence for her mountain project.

Matt surprised her one day by driving up the mountain and presenting her with the completed plans.

"Oh, Matt, it's just like I saw in my mind, only better!"

"I spent most of my time trying to figure out how to incorporate the windmill and storage batteries without the design being over the top. I have placed the base of the windmill over the cistern." He pointed to the plans. "That way you still have the old with the new. I allowed access to the cistern, and plan to keep it open. I had it checked out thoroughly, and it is water-tight. After it's cleaned it can be used as storage for your spring water. We'll add filters and a cap to prevent contamination."

"What a wonderful idea. I wondered what you planned regarding the cistern and you just surpassed my greatest expectations."

"It's in fantastic shape and it would have been a shame not to use it."

"It's a super addition, Matt, and a wonderful conversion."

"Thanks. The windmill base houses the spring's pump, storage batteries, and the generator, thereby eliminating any extraneous noises from the house."

"I love the way the driveway comes between the windmill and the house. You have it perfectly situated so that my arbor ends up on the back side."

"After speaking with Greg, we were able to position the house so we only lose two large trees. I hope you don't mind. One is a diseased Chinese chestnut, notorious for shedding debris at least five times a year. The shell of the nut is treacherous to bare feet."

"I won't miss that one at all. I've had the pleasure of stepping on one of those shells before. The spikes burn when they pierce the skin and hurt like the dickens."

"The other is a wild cherry, which looks good on the outside, but the core of the trunk is gone leaving only an outer growth to sustain the massive branches on top. A strong wind could cause it to collapse. It's safer to remove that one even if it wasn't in line with the foundation."

"Thanks for caring so much about the trees, Matt. I agree that both can be cut." Alexandra scanned the remainder of the plans.

"Wow, the use of the items from the old house is really well thought out. I see you added a few ideas of your own. It's delightful. The house blends flawlessly with the environment and disturbs as little of the surrounding area as possible."

"Well, then. As soon as I have your approval, Greg can start on the foundation."

"You can have it now. Thank you, I couldn't be happier." Was it possible building a house could be this easy? She'd heard horror stories from her parents when they built their home. How was it possible that nothing seemed to stand in her way? She knew she shouldn't tweak fate's nose, but surely, soon the bottom would fall out from under her.

"You are welcome, Alexandra. Keep this copy of the plans to look over, and let me know if you find anything you'd like to change. Don't worry that you might be too picky. Remember, this is your house. It should suit you. I am here to assure you get exactly what you want."

"I can't believe I am so lucky to have you as the architect. I need to send James Dawson a gift for recommending you. Thanks, again, for being someone I can count on."

"Thanks for the kind words. I need to get out of here before my head swells so much I won't be able to get back in my truck. Have a great day, Alexandra."

"You've already made it one."

After he left, she was so enthralled, she continued on the arbor relentlessly. The completion took a full two weeks. She had uncovered six arc-shaped stone benches, each placed between two stone-carved uprights. All that remained was the removal of the packed leaves and debris from the floor. Carved-stone bricks of different hues, sizes and shapes, laid out in a circular, symmetrical pattern brought the whole arbor together. She got down on her hands and knees and removed the dirt from the design with a wooden scraper. An intricate vine and flower pattern matched from stone to stone. When she finished scraping the dirt, she used a broom on the floor the best she could. It was a beautiful work of art. The stone in the center reminded her of a keystone that held it all together. It was breathtaking. Who had taken the time to create such a masterpiece only to let the tangle of vines and whiles of time hide it from view? Each time she swept more debris away, the design became more prominent.

Ironically, the house and outhouse did not possess the same craftmanship as the cistern and arbor. What a mismatch they were! Alexandra wished for a crystal ball so she could look back in time to see what had happened on her mountain. Wait, she didn't need one.

She opened her mind to the arbor and was instantly struck with an overwhelming feeling of love. Eternal love. Timeless and endless. Tears came to her eyes and as emotion overcame her. It was so beautiful and wondrous. He had carved the arbor out of love. She closed her mind and wiped the tears away. She sat on the bench and rubbed her hand over the stone and the warmth of the emotion dissipated.

The workers stopped for the day about three, yet Alexandra continued because she was so close to finishing. She was tired, completely worn out, yet pushed to complete the task. The cleaning of the floor had taken longer than she expected, and when she looked up the sky was dark and gray clouds were thick and moving quickly across the sky. One heck of a storm was brewing; it was time to head home.

She had just made it to her Jeep when the

clouds opened up and huge drops hit the windshield. She counted her blessings that Greg's road was in place. The ruts would have quickly turned slippery making the road impassable. Safely back in the bungalow, she eased herself into a tub of scented water. Essence of lavender filled the bathroom and she languished in the bubbly water, knowing her vine trimming was finished for now and the arbor's full glory was within reach.

Chapter Eleven

The rainstorm continued for three days. Alexandra used the time to work on the ability to move from room to room without walking. She thought that if she started small, she would grow more confident, and maybe stop worrying about ending up inside a wall, which seemed infinitely more satisfying than in solid rock or an ocean. Were those things even possible? A shiver went through her and she decided not to pursue the answer.

When she sensed objects, she ensured they were within her field of vision, for if she miscalculated and ended up sending herself somewhere unknowingly, she could walk back to where she started. Before commencing any experiments, she made certain to be fully clothed. That was one lesson she didn't want to repeat.

She began slowly. The first time she moved from the kitchen to the living room. She wobbled a bit on the landing because she hadn't pinpointed the spot exactly. The move turned out to be hesitant.

Alexandra moved back to the kitchen with much more accuracy. Completing the move within her sight of vision, she then progressed to a move she couldn't see, like the bedroom. Wanting better accuracy for the landing point, she first walked to the bedroom, decided the best place to land, then went back to the kitchen to attempt it. Perfect the first time!

Using different senses, she went from kitchen to bedroom and back again. Each time she moved, she would get a feel for the sense, and after a while, she achieved a certain proficiency at adapting the sense to a given situation. At first, it required total concentration to get to a different room, but as she fine-tuned the internal mechanism, it became as simple as blinking an eye. Not wanting to fall into any unseen traps, she reminded herself not to be overconfident of this technique until someone in-the-know told her it was safe.

The next step, she decided, was to land seated in a chair. Going to the kitchen, she concentrated from there and performed the move. She landed standing on the cushion, lost her balance and fell to the floor.

"Well, that wasn't very graceful," she muttered.

Two more times she made the attempt and each time she arrived pretty much the same way. There had to be more to it. She tried picturing herself sitting in the chair, and although she arrived sitting, she was as rigid as stone, not relaxed as she intended. The result was an improvement, but not what she had in mind. She tweaked the process for an hour and could finally chalk it up as perfect.

She moved on to the same process, but moving to her bedroom and sitting on the bed. This went much quicker, and within ten minutes or so, she had the process locked down.

Next, she tried for more speed in performing the task. She moved from standing in the kitchen to

166

sitting in the living room, to standing in the bathroom, to sitting on the bed. Just when she considered herself pretty darned good, her stomach turned over, she felt faint, and she became so nauseous she had to quit for the day.

"Oh, let's not do that again," she reprimanded.

After successfully completing 'moving about' experiments, she added another component. She would hold various items and take them with her, a book, a chair, her toothbrush; after completing that step, she became curious about a living thing. If she held something living in her hand, could it go with her? She contemplated getting a pet.

By the third day of experimentation, she felt competent in her abilities, so she made a trip downtown and picked up a cockatiel with all the trappings. She named him Sebastian, and they became friends instantly. After working with him for a few hours, she sat him on her shoulder and moved them from the kitchen to the bedroom.

What had she been thinking? She scared the poor bird nearly out of his wits. Although he made the trip with her, he rescinded his friendship immediately, and lost three feathers and messed on her sofa, while flying about uncontrollably. Each time she approached him, he flew away, shaking.

"Oh Sebastian, I'm so sorry."

He made it perfectly clear he considered her something to avoid. It took her an hour to catch him and another to calm him down.

She held him in her hand and cooed softly to him while scratching the top of his head.

"Honey, I'm so sorry. I should have held you

in my hand and covered your eyes. I can't believe I was so thoughtless and didn't consider the shock to you. I promise never to do that to you again."

After that episode, he was leery of her for days. She hoped he would forgive her and learn to trust her again.

The next experiment did not work. Since she could go somewhere, could something come to her? Try as she might, and sensing everything she could think of, she could not bring anything to her, therefore, she felt she had uncovered a limitation. But, was it a limitation of the powers, or her knowledge to use the powers? That question would remain unanswered for the time being, as she started to grasp the pros and cons of experimentation.

On the fourth day, the sun shone once again. She waited until after lunch before going up the mountain. After the onslaught of water, she wanted to give the crew time to recuperate from any damage. As she began the trek upward, she noticed the gravel had shifted, but the road was still easily passable. The new road made the trip to the top at least five times faster, but it still took several minutes to climb.

The crew worked with precision. She stayed to the outskirts of the activity, but went to get a closer look when they moved to a different area.

Greg waved her over. "The rain set us back a little, but we're nowhere close to being behind schedule. We'll be pouring the basement walls next week."

"It sounds odd to 'pour the walls'," she said,

smiling. "The new technology to keep basements water-tight has really taken a turn for the better."

"You'll appreciate the walls more after a soaking like we got these past few days. I'm sorry, I have to get back to the crew, but are you available for an early supper, about four, at the Olive Garden?"

"Sure. It's two thirty now, I'll meet you there."

As Greg headed back to the crew, Alexandra made her way to the arbor to assess any damage.

The arbor had survived the dousing very nicely; in fact, it looked great. The leaves were glistening and the Heartseed's delicate white flowers were out in full bloom. Alexandra was pleased with the way it turned out. It would be a beautiful addition to the house and already offered a peaceful out-of-the-way spot to view the crew's progress.

Sitting on one of the benches and admiring the artistry of the arbor, an absolute sense of serenity washed over her; she smiled, completely at peace. Then, she noticed the floor. The pounding rain had washed all the dirt out of the floor's design and it looked brand new, untouched by age. If she thought it beautiful before, it was even more so now.

The upright stone pillars, washed clean, now stood out brightly and contrasted with the green leaves and vines. The design on the pillars was similar to the floor, but contained vines only.

The overhead area was now completely open, due to her ample trim work, and allowed a clear view of the sky. The rays of the sun poured through the opening onto the floor and her eyes locked on the center stone, which seemed to shine more than the rest. She got down on her knees for a closer look. There was an odd-shaped hole, off-center at the base of a leaf that she hadn't noticed before. All the stones fit together meticulously, allowing no area for weeds to grow or soil to settle between them, so the small hole, which was out of place, drew her scrutiny.

It looked like something fit into it. She rubbed her fingers across the opening, feeling the indentation. Her pulse quickened and her hand went to the necklace. She unclasped the latch and removed the small key. Nervously, she replaced the necklace, and then fingered the key before placing it into the small opening. It slid into the hole easily at first, but then she had to wiggle it around for quite a while before it finally gave way, turned, and released. Her eyes darted around to make sure she hadn't been seen. She removed the key and placed it in the pocket of her shorts. A stone leaf had risen about an inch on the edge of the circle; she tried pulling, then pushing it back down but it wouldn't move. Looking at the location of the leaf in relationship to the circle, she decided to try to spin the stone circle using the leaf as a handle. Left, right, she pushed, but it refused to budge. She pushed harder left, then right, and finally it gave way a quarter turn. The whole center stone, which was about three inches diameter, rose about two inches, almost as if it had a spring underneath pushing it upward. The sides of the round stone had two indentations opposite each other, which looked like finger holds. Gripping both sides, she pulled up. The stone came away completely, revealing a latch beneath.

With her heart beating rapidly, she became very aware of her surroundings and felt this was as far as she dared go with the crew nearby. She replaced the stone, rotated it, and felt it drop into place; she inserted the key and turned, and the leaf receded. After replacing the key on her necklace, she sat on the bench in disbelief staring at her discovery.

* * * * *

I will not allow her to have what should be mine. What does she know compared to the knowledge and power I possess? I can wait as long as it takes.

She's my exact opposite, the picture of innocence and all that is good in the world.

Over five hundred years - the Prophecy is about to come true.

* * * * *

Alexandra remained in the arbor until it was time to depart and meet Greg at the Olive Garden. The phrase, 'the key unlocks the guide,' kept repeating in her mind. She wondered how she seemed to just happen on things, but then reminded herself she had been drawn to the arbor; it gave her a sense of serenity. In hindsight, she had felt driven in her desire to make the arbor appear as it had in her dream. In the great scheme of things, she seemed fated to find the keystone, as she had aptly named it. It was also her fate to pull the latch and see what happened next.

Was she ready for the guide? That would be a great big 'yes'. She had been blundering around on her own long enough. It was time for some guided exploration of these new talents. Perhaps the latch opened a hidden safe and held the guide. What a wealth of information it must contain.

The time until dinner passed slowly. Once there, she wanted to rush through the supper with Greg and give her approval of all his suggestions without thought, just to return to the arbor sooner. Knowing she would be displeased with herself if she did the aforementioned, she pushed hard to remove thoughts of the keystone from her mind.

Greg had some great suggestions regarding the construction that would enhance the supporting structure of the windmill over the cistern.

"I'd like your approval before I speak to Matt since it would alter the design."

"I agree. It's a good suggestion. It looks like everything is coming along well."

"It is. I only have a few items to discuss with you. But first, let me tell you what a fine job you've done on that arbor of yours. I took a long look at it this morning; it's exquisite craftsmanship. I can't help wonder who built it."

"Thanks for the compliment, Greg. I have no idea who built it; the stonework is so intricate and precise. It's a puzzle."

"I'd like to know who carved those stone uprights and the tile on the floor. They are truly the work of a keen eye and hand; the work of a true artist."

"I'm glad you like it. I fell in love with it the first day I saw it."

"You did a marvelous job. I'll have to be sure to make your home comparable, though it will be hard to match that quality."

"Don't sell yourself short; there are those who consider you an artist in construction."

Greg smiled. "Thank you."

"I think a lot of love went into that arbor. Are you aware of the name of the vines?" Alexandra asked.

"No."

"They are Heartseed vines. As it grows, it first displays the leaves, then delicate white flowers. Once the flowers die off, a pod forms that looks like a tiny Chinese lantern. The pod contains brown seeds that have a cream heart on them."

"They sound quite nice. I've never heard of it before, I'll have to tell my wife about it; she loves unique native plants."

"It's not very common. My father used to love to discover things in nature. He's the one who told me about them."

"Well, you certainly did a beautiful job. It looks professionally done. They will be starting to develop the spring tomorrow. If the county inspector doesn't approve the spring, we haven't considered a contingency plan."

"We could drill for water in one of the deeper glens, or somewhere close to the base of the mountain and pump it to my holding tank. Does that sound possible?"

"Most things are possible if you don't mind the expense. Either of those options might work. Do you have a preference?"

"I'd prefer the glen instead of the base. I consider myself duly warned, but I'm counting on the spring."

"It's my preference as well," Greg said. "I brought along a small topographical map." He spread it out on the table. "Which glen would you prefer? I've highlighted four you might like."

"I remember this one when I walked around and marked out the section on the top. It was beautiful. I wouldn't want to disturb it."

"It was my least favorite for that same reason."

"What about this one?" She pointed to the map. "If I remember correctly, there weren't too many trees there. We could drill there and not disturb the lay of the land or trees."

"I can get a rig in there. You actually picked the perfect place. The line to the house would be easy from there as well."

"Thanks for your forethought. I'm blessed to have such great professionals to help build a dream."

"Building your dream is a pleasure." He rolled the map and prepared to leave.

"Thanks again, Greg. Have a nice evening."

As soon as they parted, Alexandra dashed back to her mountain and directly to the arbor. It was five thirty and plenty of light remained. As she stood near the center looking at the keystone, she felt her pulse quicken. She removed the key from her necklace and stared at it, wondering what new part of her life was about to unfold.

"I'll take that," said a deep voice.

Alexandra spun around with a gasp, and looked into deep-set obsidian eyes that were devoid of emotion. He was tall, dressed completely in black with black hair, and was exceedingly handsome.

She was afraid. Great power exuded from him. She tried to look away to search for some method of escape but the soulless depths of his eyes held her spellbound.

His scrutiny sliced through her. She sensed he was searching inside her for an answer.

Alexandra backed away. "Who are you and what are you doing here?" she said roughly.

"Someone you shouldn't mess with. Now hand over the key," he said stepping closer.

"No. It doesn't belong to you." She backed further away and wondered where she had gotten the courage to tell him 'no'. Her legs shook.

His eyes never blinked. "The key may not belong to me, but it was meant for me. You don't know what you are getting into. Give me the key and you can walk away." The devil stepped closer.

Her breathing came rapidly. "Every pore in my body screams for me to keep the key safe and away from you."

She was certain he would hurt her, if necessary. Teater left the key for her. He had gone to great lengths to safeguard it and her. It was hers and she would use it, not this soulless man before her.

"I will have that key!" he said springing toward her, quickly closing the distance between them. He grabbed for her.

"Jediah!" Alexandra screamed from the core of her senses, and moved herself to the kitchen of the bungalow.

* * * * *

Ryeth swore under his breath. He had made a massive, unrecoverable mistake of thinking she hadn't developed any powers. The minx had eluded him and he had given away the advantage of his existence. Now they would defend against him and be prepared for his intrusion.

He would not make the same mistake twice. In a flash, he was safely away from Alexandra's mountain and any Sensate activity.

* * * * *

Jediah appeared at her side. Alexandra shook from the experience, and was amazed her escape move worked.

"You yelled?" he said with the tiniest of smiles, but sobered instantly when he saw the concern on her face.

His serenity washed over her and she calmed measurably. "I was at the arbor ready to open the keystone when a man appeared and tried to take the key from me. He intended to hurt me to get it."

Jediah's face went stone cold. "What did he look like?"

"He was tall, had dark hair, and black eyes. I've never seen black eyes before. He said the key was meant for him."

Jediah looked at Alexandra in disbelief, shaking his head. "It can't be." He paced the floor. "I can't believe he's been out there all this time."

He turned back to Alexandra and placed his hand on her shoulder. "I'm sorry this happened, but I need you to know you will be perfectly safe from him from now on."

"Is he a Sensate? I didn't know he was there until he spoke to me."

"Yes, but we thought he had passed on centuries ago. You need to trust me. Please wait here. You will be perfectly safe. I'll be back soon." He vanished.

He left her there alone? She would be safe, but he left her? Her knees had just barely stopped knocking and he decided to poof into thin air. What kind of knight in shining armor was he? One strike for the amazing Jediah Saffle. Shouldn't he have wrapped his arms around her and told her everything was going to be all right?

What was she supposed to do if the man in black followed her home? Could he do that? Was she expected to move from place to place to avoid him until she threw up? A fine mess that would be.

Instead of pacing, she made a cup of tea and removed Sebastian from his cage to keep her company. If Jediah said she was safe, she was. She guessed.

It was half an hour before Jediah returned. "He's nowhere to be found. Now that we know he's here, we'll be monitoring the whole area to ensure you remain safe. Right now, it is very important for you to go back to the arbor and complete the task."

"What? Are you coming with me?" She couldn't believe what he was asking her to do.

"I'll be around," he said, winked, and then vanished.

No. This was terribly wrong. He wanted her to return to where evil lurked? She shook her head. A person would have to be crazy to go back there. What assurance did she have, other than Jediah's word, that she would be safe? This was certainly a dilemma.

As she finished her cup of tea, and returned Sebastian to his cage, she crossed her fingers and moved back to the arbor.

Again, she was amazed that her wish was seemingly her command, as she found herself at the arbor, her Jeep sitting off to the side, waiting.

She looked around, and opened her senses to see if she felt any evil. All she sensed was the tremendous love emanating from the arbor, which calmed her.

She closed her senses, stooped to the keystone and inserted the key. Looking at her hand, she discovered she had clenched the key so tightly it left an imprint in her palm. The leaf popped up, she twisted the stone in place, and it rose. Pulling it from the space, she set it aside, reached for the latch and gave it a sharp pull.

In a second or less, an orb of shimmering light, similar to the one Jediah manifested, encased her. The orb moved, but she couldn't see outside to know exactly where she was going. The orb came to rest, and vanished. She stood in a lovely room facing the older woman who had accompanied Jediah in the diner. She sat, quite regally, in an over stuffed chair, and smiled at Alexandra.

"Hello, and welcome, sweet Alexandra. I've been waiting for you. My name is Nancy Jane Saffle. I am your guide, and also Jediah's mother." Her eyes twinkled. She had just revealed pertinent information.

"I thought the guide was a book. Are you the one who watches over me?"

"Yes. Have a seat, my dear; we have some talking to do."

Alexandra took a seat in a chair that was as comfortable as the ones in the bungalow.

Nancy Jane began. "I'm sorry we didn't detect Ryeth. After nearly half a millennium, we weren't even sure he still existed. We think he has developed a masking power that prohibits us from detecting him."

"This is all a bit much. Who is he, and why did he want the key?"

"Both are very good questions. Like you, we selected him to join our group because of underlying ultra-sensing abilities. In my two hundred-fifty years, I have only known two Ultra Sensates to come into being, you, and my son, Jediah. There're only a handful in existence today. Including the now known Ryeth, there are only seven with your level of sensing ability."

"You are two hundred-fifty years old?" Alexandra asked incredulously.

"Yes, dear, but I am only half-Sensate. We age faster than full Sensates. Once you obtain your full powers, you will age very slowly. Our oldest Sensate is six hundred twenty-seven years old."

Alexandra felt her heart beat slow down. She reminded herself to breathe. "I'm a little lost for words, I had no idea."

"I'm sure you didn't, my dear."

"Why did Ryeth want the key?"

"The key transports the person directly to the guide, which is me. By handing the key to me, my powers unlock and are transferred to the holder of the key, you. We need to make sure I transfer my powers to you and not to anyone else."

"Why should it be me and not Ryeth?"

"You once questioned whether or not you were a good host, and what if the powers went to a bad host, remember?"

Alexandra nodded.

"Ryeth is our only poor host in over two thousand years. Although, he never received instruction on how to use his powers to their fullest capabilities, over the years he apparently amassed enough knowledge to now cause quite a disturbance. You were chosen to receive my powers because of your underlying abilities, and because my time is ending."

"What does your time ending have to do with your powers?"

"We have always transferred our powers for two reasons. First, to give greater powers to one we feel is deserving; and second, to ensure the longevity of our powers, we let none go to waste."

"What happens to you once you give your powers away?"

"I cease to be; I die."

Alexandra was appalled. "I can't accept your powers under those conditions."

"You must, Alexandra. You are the perfect host for them. I have waited patiently for you to arrive; I am more than ready to go. My body has not kept up with my mind and I am eager to seek peace and relief from pain. As I said before, I am only half-Sensate so the half that has aged has done so with regret."

"How did you become a half-Sensate?"

"I was born before my mother came into her powers, and only received powers from my father's side. It's not common, I guess they were just in too much of a hurry," she replied with a chuckle.

She continued. "You were born with latent abilities that are five times the normal Sensate. Adding my powers to yours will make you the most powerful Sensate to come into existence in over two thousand years."

She didn't want this. Alexandra wasn't even sure she wanted the powers she had so far. "Why does that have to be me? Can't you give your powers to Jediah?"

"It doesn't work that way. A mother can't give to her offspring twice. He received powers from me at birth. You are now the youngest Sensate, and if I give them to you before you come into your full powers, your powers will enhance even more. In our recorded history, this has never happened. There was never an opportunity like this to enhance powers greater than five times our normal. You could end up having seven to ten times our normal powers."

"That's too much. I don't know what I'm doing. I'm not the right person. I am not worthy of such a gift."

"It is for that very reason we are certain it is to be you. We've watched you grow up and become the woman you are today. You are without guile. Your heart is pure. Do you know how uncommon that is?"

Alexandra was embarrassed and flushed. They had been watching her for years. What unmentionable things had they witnessed?

"If Ryeth had the key, he could take my powers," Nancy Jane said, and then continued. "Luckily, you arrived here before he had another chance to get the key. The key has been safe all these years, protected in an unknown location, and waiting for you. Once it was in your possession, it was up for grabs. Although Sensates are typically very good people, any other Sensate could have stolen the key and claimed my powers. We were not concerned this could happen because it is just not our way to be devious or cruel. There has been no discourse within our kind until today when Ryeth made himself known. There hadn't been so much as an inkling of him for hundreds of years; as a matter of fact we assumed he had passed on centuries ago."

Nancy Jane added. "I gave my key to Teater for safekeeping many years ago. He was the one responsible for seeing you were born, and he could only ensure his line by going back to Wheeling and siring your great grandfather. Teater had the recessive Sensate gene, and I discovered it in him when he was sixteen. After him, it would be an additional two generations before your father would marry another with the recessive gene, thus creating you. We only had a twenty-five percent chance you would be Sensate; fortunately, our wish came true, and fate marked you not only as a Sensate, but also as an Ultra."

So much filled Alexandra's mind. Her parents had the recessive gene, but they hadn't been chosen. Only her.

Nancy Jane said with a smile, "I have to give Teater credit; he certainly worked hard to guarantee you would be here at this moment in time."

"It's a bit hard to believe my birth was orchestrated for so many years."

Nancy Jane gave a genteel laugh that contained musical notes. "Not orchestrated, my dear, ensured."

"Why was it necessary to ensure my arrival?"

"It was foretold our kind will face a dark future, and to maintain our longevity, a Sensate of unparalleled power would come into existence to avert the danger."

"What possible danger could our kind fear? It would seem we have many advantages."

"Yes, we do have many advantages. We can handle most of what is required to keep our secrets, but our greatest fear is discovery. If governments knew of us and used us to their advantage, we would lose that which we value most of all, our ability to work for the good of all, not just a chosen few. If discovered, we would be hunted, feared, misunderstood, eventually our kind would become exploited and used, and our offspring would be marked and crossbred for their powers. We know our place, and we vow to serve causes anonymously."

"I never once thought of the exploitation of the powers, just my own self-limiting moral code in using them. I can see how far reaching this could be."

"Of course you didn't, my dear. Your heart is pure, and your moral code is above such nastiness. There are others who would try to gain monetarily, those who seek power, and those who are innately evil."

The whole time Nancy Jane talked individual hairs on Alexandra's arms stood at attention. There wasn't an area on her body that wasn't covered in goose flesh; even the hairs on her head stood up.

"You consider Ryeth evil?"

"The knowledge passed down to us regarding him wasn't good. Although, we have no concrete evidence of his character, accosting you does not speak well in his favor, does it?"

"No, it doesn't. Do you think he will try to obtain the key again?" she asked.

Nancy Jane replied, "Without knowing his purpose for the use of the powers, I can't say, but it sounds like he felt the powers should be his, not yours. I can't guess whether he wants to help us or hurt us, for in hurting us, he would inevitably hurt himself."

"Are we the only group of Sensates in existence?"

"Yes." Nancy Jane acknowledged.

"And Ryeth has been out there all alone for hundreds of years?"

"Yes, so to speak. Where are your thoughts going, Alexandra?"

"I'm not sure; I just wondered how scared he must have been to have powers and no one to guide him on how to use them. What happened to his parents?"

"We don't know for sure," Nancy Jane said.

So lost in her thoughts of Ryeth, Alexandra missed the incomplete answer. "I have so many questions."

"I know you do, dear, but time is of the essence now. We must be sure Ryeth doesn't get the key. We will monitor you constantly, and you have only to speak Jediah's name for him to come to your side in an instant.

"I must transfer knowledge to you before I give the powers to you, for what good are powers if you don't know how to use them, and like all individuals, they are managed differently in each of us. Some of my powers may be similar to yours, others may enhance what you already have, and others will be completely new."

Alexandra was still absorbing the information given and processing the importance, when Nancy Jane stated, "Jediah, I'm tired, please come and see Alexandra home."

Jediah appeared on the left side of her chair. Alexandra stood and reached for Nancy Jane's outstretched hand. "It was most pleasurable to meet you, my dear Alexandra."

"No, Mrs. Saffle, the distinct pleasure was mine."

"Good night, Alexandra, until tomorrow, then?"

"Certainly."

Jediah led Alexandra to the front of the house and out the door. It was only then she realized she was at Larkspur and had been in the parlor of the mansion.

Chapter Twelve

"This is your mother's house?" Alexandra stepped onto the front porch of Larkspur with the same familiarity she had with Jediah in her dreams.

He smiled. "Yes, it's been in the family for years."

Unsure exactly where to begin, she led with her heart. "Jediah, I know it's what your mother wishes, but I cannot take her powers." Stopping halfway down the steps, she turned and faced him, unable to comprehend the gravity of what they asked her to do.

"It weighs heavily on me as well," he said. "But bestowing her powers on you is a gift she offers completely without regret. Among Sensates, it has always been this way. This is our method of ensuring our abilities survive. Think about it; we waited for you for three generations, knowing at some point two recessive genes would produce you. When you were born, we discovered you were an Ultra. You are our best hope for the longevity of our kind."

"I wish you wouldn't say that. You can't possibly expect me to accept all I've heard here tonight without any backpedaling." Dropping his hand, she sat on the steps and looked up at the sky. The stars seemed brighter than usual, until she blinked and noticed the moisture.

"Yes, I do."

"Well, I can't. It's wrong. These last few weeks were filled with self-discovery, pinpointing my boundaries, determining a code of ethics, and grasping wonder from everything around me. Now, I'm supposed to take that which I hold so dear, life itself, from your mother?"

"Sweet Alexandra," he said as he sat next to her and took her hands in his. "It has only been the strength of her powers that has enabled her to wait for you. Each day filled with the pain of an aging body, she's been counting the days until you release her from this world into the next."

"I understand, Jediah, but it still seems wrong."

"It would be a greater wrong to have her powers taken by Ryeth."

"Is that really possible?"

"Yes, it is. We were unprepared, and if it wasn't for your quick thinking and ability to obtain safe ground, my mother could have lost her life and had her powers transferred in mere seconds. All he needed was the key and the rest would have taken place."

"Oh! Why didn't you tell me of the danger?"

"We weren't aware there was any until it happened. As far as we were concerned, you were following the path Teater laid out for you, and when the time was right, you would have come to my mother. We never counted on Ryeth. Sensates have passed down his story from generation to generation as a reminder of what could happen if we select the wrong host. Once we learned of Ryeth's dark side, we had already shared some elements required to enhance powers, but not nearly all. We had no idea he had gained enough power to live anything but a normal life span. Although we shunned him, there was no way to take the powers he had already developed. Not all Sensates come into their powers. Many pass through their lives and have no idea of the power that lay beneath the surface. Ryeth exists as our one failure and a reminder of the consequences of poor selection."

Jediah stood and pulled her to her feet. As they walked to the bungalow, she remembered. "Oh, I have to go back to the mountain and get my Jeep."

"I brought it back for you," he said dangling the keys, then handing them to her.

"Thank you, is there no end to your kindness?"

"Not where you are concerned." He brushed the hair from her temple.

The touch sent shivers down her neck. "Would you like a cup of tea?" she said trying to remain collected.

"I would love to share a cup of tea with you," he said as his eyes burned into hers. His voice sounded like a caress; it deepened and was barely a whisper.

"Good." Her pulse quickened. This time there was no humiliation of being rejected. Maybe she could get used to this male/female thing after all.

Entering the bungalow, she caught the toe of her shoe on the threshold and tripped.

"Gotcha." He caught her elbow and steadied her.

She glared at the offending doorway then raised her eyes to meet his. "Thanks, come in, watch the doorway, it'll get you if you're not paying attention."

Amazed at her lack of aplomb, she took steps to correct the situation. "Have a seat in the kitchen, I'll be back in just a second."

She half ran down the hall to the bedroom and closed the door. Blood rushed through her veins heightening olfactory and gustatory senses. She sensed him so intently she could literally smell and taste him even in the bedroom. Calming her senses took a few minutes. Either he packed a wallop of an impact or she had very little defense against him. She reminded herself she had given him his first strike a few hours earlier for leaving her alone.

Alexandra returned to the kitchen with Sebastian. "Jediah, I would like to introduce you to my roommate, Sebastian."

Jediah moved close to Sebastian, placed his finger at the cockatiel's feet, and whistled a soft wolf whistle, then said, "Hello." He repeated his whistle and greeting. Sebastian responded by stepping onto his outstretched finger and looking at him with one eye, then the other.

"Sebastian, we are going to be great friends." Jediah smiled and scratched the bird's head then returned him to his cage in the hallway.

As Alexandra pulled her favorite teapot from the cupboard and filled the kettle to place on the stove, Jediah reached into an opposite door, brought two cups to the table, and took a seat.

"You're handy to have in the kitchen," she said.

From under long lashes he glanced up. "You

have no idea," he said with distinct implications.

Alexandra felt herself blushing to the roots of her hair, and turned away quickly to get the tea.

"Do you like sugar or cream?" She spoke into the cupboard, not ready to face him.

"I like both, but neither in my tea."

A second blush ran into the first. She had lost the ability to speak coherently and sounded like a blithering idiot.

He chuckled behind her. "Alexandra, you are certainly not a blithering idiot."

She gasped and spun to face him. "You can read my thoughts?"

"Not always, only the last ten years or so."

"Oh my!" If her heart beat any stronger, it would pop right out of her chest. She busied herself getting the napkins. How should she handle a situation like this?

He rose to his feet instantly, and stepped up behind her. His arms wrapped around her and she leaned into his embrace. The serenity he shared as a gift, eased her apprehension, and he became, once again, the companion of her dreams. He dropped a whisper of a kiss in her hair and then returned to his seat.

"Thank you," she said, turning to him. She could face him again. "I should keep you around for all such lapses of decorum."

"I have my uses."

That voice went through her like quicksilver. "Are you going to start that again?"

He quickly sat back down. "No Ma'am, just waitin' on my tea."

Alexandra poured the water over the tea, placed the pot in a cozy to steep, and set it between them on the table.

"Your mother is quite the lady."

"Thank you, I'm glad you think so."

"I noticed her first in the diner. She is striking, and has such presence. Not many people draw my eye for study."

"That's the day I knew you had arrived."

"I have a small confession, but you might have already guessed. I fell through the top of the cistern. I'm the one that made the hole in the cover."

His brows came together and he kept his gaze fixed on the table. "You could have been seriously injured or worse." He met her eyes. "I wondered why that plank was wedged in the wall. Now it makes sense."

"I thought you monitored me and listened to my thoughts?"

"Not all the time; just when I choose. Mostly, I check in with you every week or so, but more frequently since you came to Waynesburg."

"Hmm."

"Hmm, is your response?" he inquired.

"Yes, that's all you get. Do you live at Larkspur with your mother?"

"No, I'm just visiting."

"Hmm." Alexandra poured the tea, and then added, changing the subject. "Is this real?"

"Is what real?"

"This thing between us." She searched his eyes.

"It's as real as you want it to be," he said tenderly.

"You are in my dreams nightly, literally. I feel like I've known you a long time."

"You have known me longer than you think. I've been coming to you for years in your dreams. It's only since you came to Waynesburg I allowed you to remember our nightly get-togethers."

She was a bit startled to realize that didn't sound creepy to her. Instead, the knowledge seemed to answer some internal questions.

"You can do that?" she asked.

"Yes, you can too, if you choose."

"That's why I feel like I've known you forever, I really have. It'd seem I have some catching up to do."

"We have all the time in the world."

If anyone other than Jediah told her they'd tampered with her dreams, she would've been furious at the possibility of being controlled somehow. However, Jediah contained such compassion, strength of character, and depth of knowledge, she felt safe.

"Do all the places you took me really exist?"

He smiled knowingly. "Yes. You have an amazing appreciation for nature and her unparalleled beauty. Seeing things through your eyes was a wondrous gift. You really have no idea how special you truly are; do you?"

"I don't feel special." She felt the heat come to her cheeks.

"Your heart is, Alexandra."

His words went to her core. There was no

flattery in his voice, just deep respect and honor. She'd never been on the receiving end of such adoration, and didn't know how to handle it. She sipped her tea as the color faded from her face.

"This is all so very new to me," she said. "I'm glad I met your mother, or, my guide. I thought the guide would be a book."

"That's a fair assumption, but nothing regarding our group is ever put in print. It would be too dangerous. We have always been guides for each other. Since we are all different we have employed a method of 'I-can-do-this, can you?' Which normally results in a 'no-I-can't-do-it-that-way, but I-can-do-it-this-way kind of scenario."

"It sounds so simple when you put it that way," she said while laughing.

"Are you laughing at me?"

"No, at your words, they were almost 'I'll-show-you-mine-if-you-show-me-yours'." Realizing what she had said without thinking, Alexandra blushed to the soles of her feet.

"Oh my," she said and got up to walk around the kitchen, not really knowing what to do next.

"Hey, you forget I know you quite well. There's no need to be embarrassed with me. We have joked and taunted each other for years in your dreams. I know what you're thinking almost before you say it. Right now, you're worried I might find you fast or forward, when in actuality you're neither. It was an innocent comment between friends that was funny. I was thinking the same thing myself."

"You were?" She turned to face him.

"Yes. And I'll tell you a secret. I've always enjoyed watching you get befuddled. It's your most adorable trait."

"You should be ashamed of yourself," she chided.

"I'm not."

"I'm going to tell your mother on you."

"She already knows," he said.

"You're incorrigible."

"My mother's words exactly."

"Hmm," she said wistfully.

"You make a fine cup of tea, Alexandra."

She gave him a smile, and said, "Thank you. Maybe next time I'll have a goody to go along with it."

"I'll look forward to next time, then."

"I will too."

He stood to leave, and Alexandra got up to see him to the door, not ready for the separation.

"I'll connect with the others and see if there has been any news of Ryeth."

"How many others are there?"

"At last count we numbered two hundred-eighty three. Ryeth ups that total by one."

"Are you certain he can't come here?"

"In all honesty, no, his masking ability has us baffled since we have never encountered it before. We can sense powers, but not his, and that's what we usually hone in on. Until we can find another way, we will have to concentrate on your thoughts and position."

"Ouch!" She didn't want to be under a microscope.

"It won't be so bad, just keep your mind busy with something mundane. You could always sing along with your iPod. That really blocks us out!"

She laughed and immediately cringed, thinking of her latest escapade in the Jeep with her bouncy playlist. Darn!

He leaned over and whispered in her ear before going out the door, 'You and me baby, we're stuck like glue'. When he looked back over his shoulder, he was grinning like a Cheshire Cat.

She closed the door and leaned against it, completely flustered. He'd shown a whole new side of his personality this evening. The devil got enjoyment from seeing her embarrassed and uncomfortable, and created situations where he could rescue her from herself. What a great amount of time he must have spent in her dreams to learn all her nuances. She remained against the door a minute or two, relishing the feeling of complete euphoria. It was no wonder she hadn't found any male attractive before him. Subconsciously, she must have compared every other male to him, and he had it in spades above everyone else. He made her smile all over.

A knock on the door startled her. She opened the door expecting Jediah. A hand shoved her backwards and a foul-smelling cloth covered her nose and mouth. Everything went black.

Chapter Thirteen

Jediah tore through the bungalow scanning every room, but she was nowhere.

"Alexandra!" he shouted and at the same time, reached for her with his mind. For the first time in twenty-two years, he could not feel her presence. His heart nearly stopped beating.

I've lost her, he screamed to the others. *Help me locate her. Protect Nancy Jane.*

The others responded, *I can't sense her.*

What happened? I've nothing here either.

Not even a whisper of thought...

Panic gripped his chest as he clenched his jaw and his fists. His body became rigid as he mentally honed his mind for battle. Ryeth would pay the ultimate cost if any harm came to Alexandra.

Jediah, come to me, he heard from his mother.

As he orbed to Nancy Jane's side, he requested the high counsel to join him there.

His first thoughts concerned his mother's safety. Once he saw her sitting in the tufted chair unharmed, he turned to the counsel.

"What happened?" William asked, placing his hand on Jediah's arm. The oldest living Sensate possessed both keen senses and undeniable compassion.

Jediah fumbled to answer. "I left her in the bungalow, and made the decision not to invade her thoughts for just a few seconds - it was only the time it took me to walk from the bungalow back to the porch and up the steps. As I reached for the doorknob, I also reached for her mind. She wasn't there."

"Did you sense Ryeth?" James said, pacing. The leather soles of his dress shoes on the hardwood floor echoed in the otherwise silent room.

Jediah sucked in a deep breath. "No. Did any of you?"

All four shook their heads.

"What have I done?" Jediah's heart pounded in his ears. "She was my responsibility."

William's eyes narrowed. "We have to find her, son. Time is of the essence."

"Don't worry about me," Nancy Jane said. "I'm pretty well protected." She smiled as Val, who sat next to her, patted her hand.

"Okay, if you'll stay with mom until I return, I'm going to the mountain to trace her steps."

Jediah first searched the arbor and looked for any traces Ryeth might have left behind, but nothing was amiss. The keystone stood open, so he reset it by pushing it back into place. He scanned the mountaintop for any residual scents or objects, and communicated the lack of findings to the counsel.

Moving to the bungalow, everything looked like it did when he'd left, so he performed an in-depth search of the grounds.

Orbing back to Larkspur's parlor, he collapsed in a chair. "We need to call the police."

"I agree," William said, "but they'll think

you're crazy, she's been gone, what, ten minutes? The police don't have the capability to know she's really missing like we do."

Jediah flipped open his phone and dialed 9-1-1 and reported her disappearance.

"I'll go to alert the complete group," William said. "Jediah, join us at Balisier as soon as you can so we can work out our strategy." William left.

Jediah said, "James, you and I are the only ones who should be visible throughout this. I'll call if I need you."

"I understand," said Val. "The more we keep this low-profile, the better. It's a shame we even have to get the police involved, but we need to maintain normalcy."

"Does Ryeth know what a can of worms he's opened?" James said as he stopped his pacing, shoved his hands in his pants pockets. He pressed his lips into a thin line.

Jediah read the concern on James' face. "If he's as fixated on obtaining mom's powers as Alexandra seemed to think, he may not have considered the ramifications in the least."

James nodded. He and Val vanished from the room.

Within half an hour, the police arrived at Larkspur.

Two officers stepped from the squad car and met Jediah on the porch.

"Thanks for your quick response, officers."

"I'm Detective Mokros, and this here's Officer Johnson," he said while hiking up his pants and shifting his belt. Only then did he offer his hand in greeting.

"I'm Jediah Saffle." He shook their hands. "I made the call to alert you of Ms. Higgins' disappearance."

"Can you tell me what happened here? When did you last see Ms. Higgins?"

"She had just visited with my mother, and I walked her back to the bungalow. She invited me in for tea. I was there perhaps an hour or so, and then left. I realized I had forgotten to tell her something and immediately returned but she was gone. That was about forty minutes ago."

"What makes you think Ms. Higgins is missing? Maybe she just went out for a stroll."

"I feel there was foul play," Jediah said.

The detective raised his eyebrows. "Do you have any evidence of that?"

"When I got back to the bungalow, the door was ajar, her car was still parked out back and I have searched the grounds. Her purse is on the stand next to the door, which leads me to believe she is not out walking somewhere."

"How much time elapsed between when you left her and when you went back?

"At most, three minutes."

"You think something happened to her in three minutes?" the detective queried, looking at him sideways.

"I do."

Detective Mokros scratched his head, looked around and shrugged. "Okay, wait here with Officer Johnson while I speak with your mother."

After a few moments, he returned.

"Your mother confirms your story. Mr. Saffle, we can take down all the information while it's fresh in your mind, but we normally don't act on adult missing persons until twenty-four hours have passed."

"Thank you, Detective.

"Mr. Saffle, a million things could be going on here, so I wouldn't be too worried yet. Perhaps an old flame stopped by and they went for ice cream." He unfolded his notepad, sighed heavily, and then shook his head.

"Her full name?" the detective asked.

"Alexandra Jane Higgins."

"Her description, please?"

"She's twenty-two, about five foot six inches tall, long blonde hair, green eyes, slight of build and very pretty."

"And this is her permanent address?"

"Yes, but she just moved here from Wheeling, West Virginia."

"We'll do a standard check of the vicinity, contact hospitals, and begin a canvas of the people in the area. There's not much to go on. We'll be back tomorrow to begin a formal investigation, if she hasn't shown up by then. Here's my card. Call me if anything happens."

"That's the best I can hope for," Jediah said while glancing at the card. "Thank you, Detective Mokros. I'll be in touch if she surfaces."

"Goodnight, Mr. Saffle."

Jediah checked the bungalow for Alexandra's cell phone, scrolled to find Cassie's number and committed it to memory. He replaced the phone where he found it and moved to Balisier to continue his search from there.

"You have to quit blaming yourself, Jediah," Nancy Jane offered.

"I can't. It was my fault. Why didn't I stay with her? I told her she would be safe. How could I have been so certain we could protect her from Ryeth?"

"I know you are upset," Nancy Jane said. "Our whole community is."

"We can't lose her." Jediah said. "I can't lose her."

He walked back and forth, thinking. "What game is he playing? The whole charade with the authorities is laughable. He could literally have her anywhere in the world and we don't have a single clue where to begin."

Jediah rubbed his forehead to relieve the tension. "I can't believe we have become so complacent. We have rested on our laurels for centuries with a false sense of security that we could protect ourselves from any and all threats. We patiently waited for the one who would have the power to save us in the event a catastrophe occurred, and what do I do?" He held his palms outstretched. "At the first sign of danger, I leave her alone." He dropped his hands to his side.

"There was no way of knowing the extent of Ryeth's powers," responded Nancy Jane. "Try to remain calm, dear. We focus better with a clear mind."

"I know, Mom, I just can't believe she's gone. There has to be something we can do. I'm going to call her friend in Wheeling then gather the Ultras. Maybe if we work together we can come up with a plan."

Jediah dialed Cassie's number knowing the hour was late, and put the phone on speaker.

"Hello?" Cassie answered.

"Cassie, it's Jediah Saffle. I'm sorry for calling so late."

"Hello, Jediah, is something wrong?"

"Yes, I'm afraid so, and there's no easy way to say this. About an hour ago Alexandra disappeared."

"What do you mean 'disappeared'?" He heard her voice quiver.

"I had tea with her this evening. I left, forgot to tell her something, and when I returned three minutes later, she was gone."

"Jediah, this is awful! Are you sure?"

He could sense the concern in her voice. "Her car is still here, but even after a thorough search of the grounds, I've been unable to find her. I've alerted the police. They said if she didn't turn up they would start a formal investigation tomorrow."

Cassie's voice wavered. "It can't be." She sniffed. "She couldn't possibly have more tragedy in her life. It's not right," she said, sobbing.

Her emotion wrenched his heart even more. "I'm so sorry, Cassie. I wanted you to know as soon as possible." Words caught in his throat and he had to force them out. "You may hear from the police tomorrow. The investigation could cover both Pennsylvania and West Virginia since she moved here only recently. Cassie, I want you to know I'll do everything in my power to find her."

"I know you will. Let me know if anything at all happens. I'm going to call the West Virginia State Troopers right now. I know a trooper personally; maybe he can help."

"I'll be in touch."

He hung up the phone, and both he and Nancy Jane moved to Balisier.

The following morning Detective Mokros and Officer Johnson arrived back at Larkspur. Jediah and Nancy Jane spoke with them in the sitting room.

"I hope you don't mind the early visit," Detective Mokros said. "After checking into Ms. Higgins background, we think there is cause to start an investigation. How long have you known Ms. Higgins?" As he spoke, he removed a notepad from his breast pocket and pulled out a pen.

Jediah spoke first. "I met Alexandra in March. She came here looking for information about her ancestors. My family has been guardian of the Higgins estate since 1928. It was while checking over the grounds on the north side of town, we ran into Alexandra and her friend Cassandra Hudson who were looking for a specific grave marker."

"We?" inquired the detective.

"I'm sorry, the caretaker of the grounds, Terry Gooch, was with me. Terry is also the groundskeeper here at Larkspur."

"And you, Mrs. Saffle, when did you first meet Ms. Higgins?" the detective asked.

"I met Alexandra for the first time last night."

"Where does Ms. Higgins work?"

"Alexandra just finished college a few weeks ago," Jediah answered. "I don't believe she has found employment as of yet."

"I'll need the name of her parents and former address. Do you have that information?"

"Her parents were Alvas and Helen Higgins of Wheeling, West Virginia. You can get her address from her driver's license or from her friend in Wheeling, Cassandra Hudson. I believe Ms. Hudson works at Oglebay Park."

"Ms. Higgins' parents are deceased?"

"Yes, in an accident three years ago." Jediah, who had remained standing, shifted his weight.

"Do you know of anyone who would want to harm Ms. Higgins?" The detective looked back and forth between Jediah and Nancy Jane.

"No, but we haven't known her that long." Jediah said as he walked over to stand behind his mother. "Her friend Cassie would know more about her past than we do."

"When you last saw her, what was she wearing?"

"Light blue jeans, pink V-neck t-shirt with lace, white tennis shoes and pink matching socks," Jediah answered without faltering.

"That's quite detailed, Mr. Saffle." Detective Mokros cocked his brow.

"She always matched her socks to her outfit," Jediah said off-handedly.

"Do you have any idea what Ms. Higgins' daily routine was like?"

"She recently contracted Gregg Construction to build a home on the land left to her by her ancestor.

She spent most of her days overseeing the construction."

"And her nights with you?" Detective Mokros shot quickly.

Jediah held the detective's stare firmly and said, "Detective, I don't know what you're getting at precisely, but Ms. Higgins' character is above reproach. I'll not have you cast aspersions without just cause."

The detective fired back easily. "And you, Mr. Saffle, are your morals as unquestionable?"

Nancy Jane, who had remained quiet throughout the questioning, burst forth. "They most certainly are! My son is nothing, if not a perfect gentleman."

Jediah reached over and patted his mother's hand. He smiled sweetly at her defense of him. "Thanks for the vote of confidence, Mom, but I believe the detective was just doing his job."

Nancy Jane sniffed. "I'll never get used to the changing morality. Imagine questioning a person's moral fiber and honor when it was Alexandra who was taken!"

Detective Mokros continued. "Has Ms. Higgins had any visitors?"

"None that I know of," Jediah replied, "though I'm not around as much as you've implied, Detective."

The detective closed his notepad, and returned it to his breast pocket. "I think that's all for now, Mr. Saffle, Ma'am. Please keep yourselves available in case my men have any further questions."

"Certainly," Nancy Jane replied.

"May we search Ms. Higgins' apartment?" the detective asked, in closing.

"By all means," Jediah responded. "It hasn't been disturbed since her disappearance, except for when I went in to obtain Ms. Hudson's phone number from Alexandra's cell phone. I pulled the door shut and it locked, so you'll need to get a key from Mr. Gooch."

"Thank you for your assistance."

As the police headed toward the bungalow Jediah's cell phone rang. The caller ID indicated Cassie. He put the phone on speaker for his mother's benefit.

"Hi, Cassie," Jediah answered.

"Hello," she said. "John and I have just pulled into Waynesburg. I couldn't work. I needed to do something, anything to help."

"Come to Larkspur." He nodded to his mom. "The police are here right now inspecting her apartment for clues. They may have some questions for you."

Jediah gave directions to Cassie, and then went to the bungalow to tell the police that Cassie would be there soon. He found them in the process of questioning Terry.

"No, I didn't see anything out of the ordinary. Ms. Higgins would normally get in her car mid-morning and come back in the afternoon. She said she was building a house," Terry said.

"Did she have any visitors?"

"Nope, though when she rented the place she said she might have friends come from out of town and asked if she could have them stay overnight. No one came that I saw."

A grey sedan pulled into the circle drive in front of Larkspur. Cassie and John got out and walked toward Jediah. Her eyes were puffy from crying, but she maintained control until she caught Jediah's eyes. Tears flowed once more.

As John's arm went about Cassie, his hand went out to greet Jediah. He said, "I'm John Ryan. We're here to help; what can we do?"

Jediah took his hand and said, "Jediah Saffle. Thank you for coming, John, Cassie.

"Any news?" John asked.

"No, I'm sorry." He looked solemnly at Cassie. Her face reflected the pain she felt, and he could sense her inner battle to control tears.

Detective Mokros walked over to them. Jediah performed the introductions, then stepped away to speak to Officer Johnson.

"Is that Alexandra's friend Cassandra Hudson?" asked Officer Johnson, nodding toward them.

"Yes. She and her friend, John Ryan, came up to see if they could be of assistance. Did you find anything helpful?"

"Nothing yet. Would you know if Alexandra knows anyone other than you and your mother here in Waynesburg?"

"Her great-great-grandfather's estate was executed by James Dawson, the lawyer on Main Street, and she's currently building a house on the land left to her by her ancestor. Gregg Construction is the builder, and she frequents the Silk City

Diner."

"Where is her land located?"

"On the northeast of town, just off State Route 1003. There's no address yet. I could take you there, if you'd like."

"I appreciate the offer. I'll speak to Detective Mokros. I'm certain he would like to check out all the areas where she spent time."

Once Detective Mokros finished questioning Cassie, Jediah went to her side.

Cassie spoke. "Jediah, John and I'll be putting up posters here and in Wheeling. We have arranged for a post office box and a toll-free number where people can leave anonymous tips. Can you think of anything else?"

"Cassie, Alexandra is fortunate to have you as a friend. I can't think of anything more right now." He placed his arm over her shoulders, and spoke to her softly. "While you are away from Wheeling, please consider Larkspur your home. The house belongs to my mother, Nancy Jane Saffle, although she keeps to herself most of the time. I'll alert the staff and arrange for them to assist you."

"Thank you, Jediah." John said warmly.

"Is that the bungalow Alexandra rented here?" Cassie asked, motioning toward the guesthouse.

"Yes." Jediah nodded.

"And this estate belongs to your mother?"

Jediah caught the inner workings of Cassie's mind in her eyes. "Yes," he replied, "but she didn't know it belonged to my mother when she rented it."

"Hmm," Cassie murmured.

Jediah smiled inwardly at Cassie's unspoken

conclusions. It's no wonder they were best friends, their minds worked similarly. Oh, how his heart ached for Alexandra. He must find her quickly.

"Jediah," John said, "Cassie and I are heading to town to get the posters printed up and then post them. We'll stop back here later this afternoon."

"I'll be away as well, showing the officers Alexandra's land, and then coordinating some local people to help search the neighborhood. You can reach me by phone. Before you go, let me show you to the rooms you can use while you're here."

Jediah gave them to a suite on the second floor, which had two bedrooms, a full bath, a partial study, and a seating area. After he shared the pass code for entry, they separated to complete their tasks.

Hoping to fill in some of the gaps regarding Ryeth, Jediah sought William at his store. Living as long as William had, it was common to seek him out regarding any historical facts, including any Sensate activities.

"William?" Jediah began hesitatingly.

"You've a question?" he said looking up at Jediah from his desk.

"I need to know more about Ryeth." Jediah sat in the chair lacing his fingers across his knees. "Why did the Sensates shun him?"

Leaning back in his chair, William began. "For over a hundred years he was only spoken of in hushed tones. No one wanted to believe that one of our kind could commit such a heinous crime. We were a very small group at that time, mostly comprised of indigenous Americans, some

Icelanders, and a few Spaniards. No one actually witnessed the act. Therefore, I can only relate what I heard.

"He was born containing the recessive Sensate gene. His father was new to America like so many of us back then. They had a small tobacco farm and all three worked the fields. Many died of disease or starvation due to the harsh life. Farms were scattered far apart and the only time one farmer saw another was if they both happened to go to the village for supplies at the same time."

William rose, turned away from Jediah, and faced the wall of books. Before continuing, he ran his fingers along the bindings of a collection of literary classics. "We recognized the son as a Sensate and had very high hopes that he would end up being an Ultra, so we started to bring him into our fold." He walked around the desk and then leaned on it facing Jediah.

"Our initial contact was successful, and he began to develop his senses. All the Sensates knew him as the boy with black eyes, because they were so remarkable. Before we could set up a key and guide for him, the crime took place."

William's eyes dropped to the floor. "What went on in a single household back then was anyone's guess, so the where or why of it never unfolded. A fellow selling his wares by wagon happened upon Ryeth's family farm just after it happened, and reported both of his parents were dead, apparently at the hand of the son."

Jediah observed the strain on William's brow. "He said the mother laid face up in the field and the father, face down next to her. The boy knelt next to them with a knife in his hand and hadn't heard the wagon approach. When the man yelled, 'What have you done?' the boy jumped up and ran off.

"There wasn't much in the way of law back then, nor were there people to chase villains. When he finally surfaced and attempted to contact us, we shunned him." William drew in a long breath.

Jediah cocked a brow. "No one ever spoke to Ryeth again?"

"No."

"Is there anything else?" He needed to be sure he had all the facts.

"Well, I met the boy back in the beginning when we decided to contact him, and he presented himself well. I liked him. I didn't sense any ambivalence at all. I found it hard to believe he would do that to his parents."

Jediah rubbed the back of his neck and decided to hold onto the shred of hope that Ryeth might not be all bad. "He's out there now and he has Alexandra. If he has demands, why hasn't he contacted us? What do you think he's waiting for?"

"Without knowing his agenda, it is impossible to guess."

Jediah stood and placed his hand on William's shoulder. "I'll focus on what we can do instead of what we can't. Thanks, William."

Later that day, Jediah, John, and Cassie searched Alexandra's apartment for any potential clues the police might have missed. While John and Cassie searched with any kidnapper in mind, Jediah focused on what Ryeth might use to his advantage.

Eyes brimming with tears, Cassie began in the kitchen. "This was her mother's favorite tea pot. Allie kept it near at all times. I can't help but think we are invading her privacy."

John hugged her. "We are trying to help her. She would probably want you to do all you could to help her, no matter the cost to her privacy."

"I know, you're right," Cassie said. "It's just that she didn't keep many things of a personal nature with her, but the ones she did meant a lot. She's lost so much, it breaks my heart to think she has to have more tragedy in her life, just when she was beginning to live again."

Jediah overheard the exchange. A lump formed in his throat as he fingered the three pair of earrings lying in a glass tray on her dresser. Jediah knew each pair intimately. Her parents gave her the gold hoops when she graduated high school, the birthstone studs for her Sweet Sixteen, and the final pair had been passed down through the female line from her grandmother to her mother, and finally to Alexandra when she had her ears pierced at the age of twelve. They were Jediah's favorite because he had secretly watched her bravely present herself at the Ohio Valley Mall kiosk for the piercing.

Helen Higgins had been pestering her daughter for years to have her ears pierced, but Alexandra had staunchly refused saying, 'blondes don't need any more holes in their heads', which Jediah knew to be a massive cover-up due to her fear of needles. Finally, peer pressure and the female desire for jewelry won over. She wore the black onyx earrings that her mother promised would be hers, if she ever had them pierced, for two years straight to mark the passage into her teenage years.

These three pairs meant she wore her threaders, the ones he felt signified her character. She bought those for herself when she graduated college. The gold dangling curves caught the light, but were simplistic enough to be worn every day, and just enough to add a touch of elegance to jeans or a sundress.

Jediah agreed with Cassie and with John, it was a necessary invasion, but the hunt proved futile. Nothing was unearthed to aid in the search for Alexandra.

Three days passed with no news from tip lines or the police investigation. John and Cassie returned home under the assurance that Jediah would notify them immediately if there was a break in the case.

Chapter Fourteen

Two men, seated in the far corner of a local coffee shop in downtown Waynesburg, spoke in hushed voices and monitored the door for new patrons. The thinner one with his back to the wall, glanced around the room, located the waitress, and spoke in a firm voice. "Hey, Honey, how about warming my coffee?"

"I'll be with you in a moment, sir," she said over her shoulder.

Turning back to his companion, he leaned forward and continued. "As I was saying, I think we should probe further into both Saffle's background and Dawson's. The situation with the girl missing could work to our advantage. They will be more distracted and you might be able to search areas you could never get into before."

"It's worth a shot. I haven't been able to find one piece of evidence that these people are anything other than what they seem. I thought when the son visited, I'd catch them at something. I'll have to be on my guard with that one, nothing escapes him."

The waitress arrived with the fresh coffee. "You two need anything else? We have fresh peanut butter pie if you'd care for a slice."

"Thanks for the refill, but no thanks on the pie, just bring us the bill, please."

Placing the slip on the table she said, "There

you go. Have a good day."

As soon as she was out of earshot, the two resumed.

"Try getting closer to the mother, Terry. She just might let something slip."

"If she has anything to hide; she's not the type to let anything slip. Ray, the old woman is real sharp, I'll give her that much, but I'll try to work my way closer, anyway. It couldn't hurt to be hanging around the house more. You know, I heard Saffle and her talking about the girl and how she checked out the cemetery and the next thing I know, she's renting the bungalow out back. I didn't even know they wanted to rent the darned thing. Things fall into place just like a puzzle around these folks."

Ray sipped his coffee. "Maybe we'll finally get lucky and catch a break."

He sniffed. "Could be we're barking up the wrong tree."

"It isn't for us to decide," Ray said shaking his head. "We have our orders to find out what makes these people tick. They wouldn't have put you there this long if they didn't have a darned good reason."

"After four years hanging out pretending to have a green thumb I have nothing to show for my work as an agent. I'd hoped to end my career with something a bit juicier."

"You could be getting yourself all shot up in some dark alley." He sat back in his chair.

"At least I wouldn't die of boredom."

Ray cocked his head. "Who do they have on the girl's case anyway?"

Terry pushed back from the table and crossed his leg over his knee. "Mokros and that new guy, Johnson. He's a good enough kid, but a bit green behind the ears."

"He might flush something out while checking the girl's background. I'll monitor his logs and keep you updated."

Terry stood, taking one last gulp of coffee. "Shoot me an email if anything breaks. If I don't hear from you, see you same time, same place, next week."

* * * * *

As he looked at Alexandra unconscious and spread out on the cot, satisfaction seethed through his veins. The plan he'd worked on for three years loomed before him. No more would she be Alexandra. From now on, he would think of her only as 'the girl' and strip her of any feelings of self. She would be his.

Ah, she moved, she's coming to.

"GotakIn," she mumbled. "Majen, mjumnito."

He watched as the girl attempted to open her eyes, but lost the battle.

"You're speaking jibberish." He grabbed the girl by the shoulder and backhanded her with enough force to split her lip.

"Are you in there?" he said, shaking her. "Wake up."

She moaned and turned her head away from him. He grabbed her chin and forced her to face him. "You are to become my wife," he smirked.

"We will spend time together and you will learn to love me. No, to worship me." That thought made him smile.

"You have no idea what I have in store for you. Let's take the first step to ensure you stay mine."

He reached into his jacket pocket and brought out the prepared protein drink. He slapped her face to rouse her as much as possible, then grabbed a handful of her hair, pushed the bottle harshly to her mouth and striking her teeth beneath her already bleeding lip. Slowly, he forced the drink down her throat.

Reduced to acting as her keeper, he gritted through the process until the small bottle emptied. Once done, he tossed her aside like a rag doll. The act disgusted him. He hurriedly removed his hands from her, and cringed knowing he would have to feed her daily to keep her alive.

"I hope that was as unpleasant for you as it was for me, you privileged piece of flesh."

"Mose," she slurred.

"Man, you're pitiful." Her gleaming hair sparkled in the dim light, forcing a contradiction in his mind. Bile began to form in his throat. She had so much, and he so little. As his anger rose, he released part of it by slapping the girl so hard he knocked her head against the wall. The action eased his anger, but excited him too.

He watched as she folded in on herself, and shrank from the pain, slowly and uncoordinated.

"You will learn to do as I say, or else."

As he turned to leave, a glimmer caught his eye. Something around her neck caught the light.

"What do you have here?" An expensive gold chain hung around her neck, and hanging from it, a wedding ring. He ripped them from her neck and tossed them on the table. No reminders of her previous life must exist. Nothing.

"WishkIs," she whispered through blood-soaked lips.

"Quit talking. You don't make any sense anyway. You have no one. You have no parents to love you; you have no brothers or sisters; you only have me."

He reached for a bucket and threw its contents at the cowering lump.

"I waited for some time to have you exactly where you are right now. I planned, found you alone, and now I'll make you understand why you are here. We will spend hours together, you and I, and you will see that I am the answer to everything you wish for in life."

She didn't respond at all. He yelled at the girl, "Look at me when I talk to you."

When she didn't comply he punched her. She moaned and shrank away from him. It was her fault, wasn't it?

"You made me do that." He ran his hand through her sun-kissed hair. She was beautiful, he couldn't deny that. She might be stubborn, but she would come around eventually. Why did women always ask to be controlled? They were such weak things, he thought as he traced her lip with his thumb. She would live to serve only him. He clicked off the light and strode out locking the door behind him.

She muttered, "WishkIs," before passing out.

* * * * *

A beautiful woman with long black hair and dressed in beaded well-tanned hides walked from the mist and came toward Alexandra. Her enchanting smile warmed her heart. Never before had the girl sensed such compassion as she did in this simple Indian maid. Kayè (Grandmother) as she asked to be called, came to her when she slept. She told Alexandra to be wètasè (brave) and to nasana (be careful).

At first, she had trouble understanding Kayè because she used a strange language Alexandra had never heard before, but soon the story Kayè told became clear.

Long ago, our people lived in villages. We would move to another place when the elk ran too far for our arrows to chase. Always we lived near the pawcohiccora; now it is called a Shagbark Hickory Tree. The great tree called the squirrels to come near, for during the autumn moons and before the cold days, the pawcohiccora released its fruit for the Algonquin people. The mashed nut was a treat for the suckling papoose during the cold days when the hunting was scarce. It flavored our broths and filled our stomachs to keep our braves strong. The Algonquin people also used the bark of the pawcohiccora. The young maidens would collect the bark from the tree many times without hurting the tree. Only the wisest of our elders knew the secret of making the sweet syrup we used on our corn cakes for celebrations.

Always take care of the pawcohiccora, she grows old slowly as do we. She is wise and can offer herself to you in times of need. Like the great tree, I will stay with you against the gotakIn (enemy).

Each time Alexandra woke, Kayè's words echoed: *'Pama mine' o knowabmin'* (*I'll see you again after a while*).

* * * * *

Since Alexandra's disappearance, Balisier had been a bevy of activity. They had used this facility as a rendezvous for their group for many years. For their kind, Balisier meant freedom from pretenses. Only Sensates entered, so they were able to speak freely.

Nancy Jane and Jediah met in a small two bedroom flat with a cozy sitting area. "Being the last to see her, I've been questioned and re-questioned by the police," Jediah said. "The window of opportunity for her abduction was only three minutes at the most. I only closed my mind to give her some privacy of thought. When I instructed the others to begin monitoring, they discovered they couldn't sense her mind. Mom, Ryeth must have been watching from some vantage point and waited for me to leave."

"That's the most probable conclusion. Since we can't sense him he could have been hiding anywhere or using his ability and been in plain sight. We weren't expecting him and could have passed him on the street without even knowing."

"How could we let this happen? The thought of something like this never entered any of our minds. Alexandra is not only important to me, she's invaluable to the future of all Sensates. If the Prophecy comes true and we are not strong..." his voice trailed, "I don't want to think what might happen. We have been preparing and planning for this for hundreds of years and when the time arrived, we failed. I failed."

"My son, we have never been defeatists, and I'll not allow you to travel down that path one instant longer." She shook her finger at him like only a mother could do. "There is always hope. Alexandra's strong and smart."

"I can't sense her at all. I know her life force is still strong, but it is impossible to lock onto her mind."

"None of us can."

"Of all people, I should be able to; I've known her the longest. It's been nearly two weeks." He pounded his fist on the arm of the chair. "I've been to every place in her memory, and, even though I'm ashamed of myself for doing it, I even searched her friend Cassie's mind. I don't understand it, Mom. How could Ryeth be so powerful?"

"I don't know." She tilted her head. "Alexandra doesn't know how to block us from reading her thoughts, does she?"

"Yes, she does. I told her we couldn't read her thoughts when she was singing with her iPod and the mechanism is the same. But I'm sure she wouldn't block us, especially when she knows there is danger near. Besides, she would equate closing her mind to slapping our faces. She trusts us explicitly and she's aware of the implied boundaries we set for ourselves."

"I agree. This girl of yours has strong convictions and nearly unbreakable moral fiber."

Hearing his mother speak so highly of Alexandra made his heart wrench. He couldn't just sit there and do nothing. There had to be a way to discover her whereabouts. He continued his train of thought.

"I've been trying to enter her dreams every night since her disappearance, just as I have done for years. The subconscious is there, but I can't enter. There is no place to grasp a thought. There is no single thought. I know Alexandra's mind as well as I know my own, yet I can't connect to it. With all our powers, I can't believe there isn't more we can do."

Going in circles only led him back to the beginning. He'd considered the options a hundred times or more.

"We alerted the police within minutes of her disappearance," Nancy Jane said. "If they uncover anything, we'll know instantly. We've been monitoring the Hudson family's thoughts, just on the small chance we might pick up a clue."

"Mom, it's like she was swallowed up by the earth. What possible motive could Ryeth have to hold onto her? It makes no sense. He was after the key. Alexandra set the transfer in motion by using it."

"We really can't expect the police to find her;

they know nothing of our world. The possibilities that exist for Ryeth to hide her could literally take us centuries to uncover."

"We're left with trying to find out how Ryeth is able to avoid our detection and whether or not he can force the same ability on Alexandra." He stood, invigorated by his thoughts. "I'm going to call the Ultras together and figure out a way to match our abilities."

"All our previous attempts to combine powers have all failed, but we never had as much at stake before. Your powers are strong and our need is great; faced with insurmountable odds, the human race has accomplished great things. If there is a way, then I believe you will find it."

"Thanks, Mom. I'm going to speak to William first about an idea I have."

"Fine, dear. I'm going back to Larkspur. I don't like being away for too long in case the police stop by."

"Okay, I'll catch up with you later this evening." He kissed her soft cheek as she vanished.

A few moments later, Jediah was in William's establishment. He always found it a wise course of action to discuss plans with the eldest Sensate, who appeared to be in his early fifties, and who had garnered wisdom and a depth of mental acuity that would shatter known records.

"William, we need to figure out the mechanism Ryeth uses to avoid our detection. Touching minds and blocking against the touch are our most basic skills."

"I can have the Ultras canvas all Sensates to see

if everyone's mechanism is the same. We can separate any we find that are different, even if only slightly so. It may help in finding Ryeth's trigger."

"That's a good idea. Sometimes the simplest solution is in the things we take for granted. Surely one of us has the same ability as Ryeth."

"It's hard to say, Jediah. We are all so very different in our emotions and senses, although I would think the odds would be in our favor. We have lived sequestered for so long that perhaps, we haven't opened up to our full potential. It could be that even though we know many of our abilities, we have not identified them all; and as we progress, so do our powers. How long has it been since you tried to either enhance an old power or develop a new ability?"

Jediah thought for an instant. "I see what you mean, and to answer your question, it's been well over a hundred years. It seems we only recognize a new power when a Sensate is added to the group and he or she happened on it by accident."

Shocked by the thought, he realized they went about their daily lives and never pushed their limits to discover their true full potential. Ryeth could have mastered many elements they hadn't even considered.

"We could be at a distinct disadvantage," he admitted.

"I'll ask Reslyn and MacAila to assess our varying abilities. I don't even know what we are capable of anymore. Perhaps it's more than we imagine."

"That's nicely optimistic," he said, then

continued. "William, what I wish to discuss with you next is something we have guarded against forever. We need to create a secure area within Balisier to amass our findings."

William's eyes widened. "Jediah, what you suggest goes against our very core. We have always held to the principle that anything written down could be confiscated and used against us."

"I am well aware of the danger of such a tactic, but truly feel it is the only way we can amass our talents and work on various combinations."

"But Balisier is already secure." Jediah sensed the hesitancy in William. He had the same cautious thoughts himself, but their current situation warranted more action than they'd ever considered before.

"I know, but I'm thinking of the future as well." Jediah said. "There may come a time when Balisier is no longer safe. I would like to excavate a separate space with impenetrable access even to other Scnsates."

"I see, and in this stronghold you would develop our cross-referencing and the results of our studies?"

"Yes," he said, and at the same time pictured it in his mind. He shared the vision with William.

"It's certainly unheard of." William was still not sure. "Our commitment to secrecy has never come into question before. You may create dissention within the group, something we've been able to avoid for two thousand years."

Jediah said, "I'm aware of that, but we never had to worry about our future until now. With

Alexandra's disappearance, we can't count on her powers and abilities. I hadn't realized how much I depended on her contribution to our eventual conflict until now."

"Yes, the loss of her powers could be devastating."

"We also have Ryeth to consider. There's a chance he will not align with us, which means, if he's not with us he may fight against us."

Jediah waited for William to consider the options and sensed the battling emotions within his dear friend.

"Tell me what you have in mind." William had made his decision.

"There's an immediate need for a comprehensive list of our abilities. How can we possibly defend against an unknown to the best of our abilities when we don't know exactly how weak or strong we actually are?"

"What do you see as our immediate need?"

"First: Pool our best resources to be able to sense Ryeth; Second: Create a cross-reference of each Sensate's abilities and a grading of those abilities by strength; Last: Compile a list of groups to work together in the event we are compromised."

William looked at him straight on. "We have guarded our abilities for centuries by not writing them down. You are now suggesting we rescind what has worked for us for all this time. Jediah, I caution you against this move. Alienating Sensates by putting them into groups could prove fatal to our kind."

"Total exposure could be much more

devastating."

"I didn't say I disagreed. I just wanted you to be aware of the consequences that might ensue. How would you want to create this space?"

"The space would require a guardian. It would be someone who had great knowledge of our kind and whose honor was above reproach."

"Do you have someone in mind?"

"You." He hoped William would agree.

"Jediah." William sighed heavily. "It is too great a responsibility. I don't know that I want that amount of pressure on a daily basis."

"There is no one else I trust to uphold the ethics required for the position."

"And in all my six hundred-plus years, the only one I would choose would have be you."

"Thank you, my friend."

"Now that I have agreed, how do we begin?"

* * * * *

He unlocked the door and entered the cabin. When he switched on the light, he saw the girl on the floor.

"Nimè (why)?" She closed her eyes and turned her head away from the bright light.

"You're not so high-and-mighty now, are you? You need to learn how to respect your betters." He grabbed a hunk of her hair and dragged her close to the chair, scraping her legs against the rough floorboards.

As he sat on the chair, he tossed her head to the side. Man, how he hated feeding her. The process had gotten only slightly better with the reduced dosage. He didn't have to rub her neck to get her to swallow anymore, but he still had to force the drink down.

He took a deep breath, uncapped the bottle, and pulled her head up between his knees. Cupping her chin, he tilted her face upward and shoved the mouth of the bottle between her swollen lips. She instinctively recognized him as a source of food and drank greedily.

After she emptied the bottle, he pushed her away. Mindlessly, the girl grabbed his leg and searched for more food, sniveling like an animal. He kicked her, and when she came back, he kicked her again, harder, and just for the pleasure it gave him, he continued kicking her until she lay limp on the floor.

He smiled. Soon, the girl would break and do everything he asked, and more.

"Poor thing, no one is looking for you because no one cares. You are insignificant, useless, pitiful and disgusting. And, you smell to high heaven. I can't stand being in the same room with you. If you could see yourself now, you would realize life holds nothing for you. You are nothing and never will amount to anything."

She closed her eyes.

"You have no family, no home. What's the matter with you?" He nudged her with the toe of his boot. "Can't make a coherent thought?"

"Mbish (water)." The girl mumbled and rolled to her side.

"If you could only see what you have become.

You can't even take care of yourself. You have no one to love. I am the only one who will accept your worthless self as you are. You are nothing."

"WishkIs (I am starving)."

"You don't have a home, you drive an old Jeep, and you dress like a pauper. You don't appreciate things like I do."

He reached for the belt hanging by the door. As she inched toward him, he raised his arm and smiled as it fell across her back. It slashed repeatedly on her arms, legs and back.

To his delight, she crept toward him still. Each swing exhilarated his passion and he screamed, "You can't escape me. You are mine."

Making a grimace of disgust, he slashed one more time at the girl, who lay, unmoving and bleeding at his feet.

"Mjumnito (devil)," she gasped. "Sukmukwei, Yabwè (dream)."

He doused her with unclean river water from the bucket and then left.

* * * * *

Kayé had lived a long time and was now known as Sukmukwei, (Grandmother Earth). She walked toward Alexandra who laid sleeping in the meadow. She cradled her head in her lap and sang an Iroquois song of the memiki (butterfly). The beautiful lyrics and melody caressed the girl wrapping her in its protective cocoon.

The memiki endured the harsh winter safe and secure; and in the warmth of the spring sun, the cocoon opened. Stretching, the new butterfly tested the wings of the Old Ones against the soft breeze. It alighted on a wood poppy, growing stronger with each flutter. As the wings grew larger, they wrapped around each other and grew larger still. When they opened, the wings had turned into the arms of a delightful Indian maiden, whose beautiful voice floated across the meadow and into the mountains above.

Be strong, little memiki, do not let the face of your enemy keep you from the goodness of the Earth. It is the source of your strength. My child, feel the arms of Mother Earth wrap around you, she can teach you many things; all you need to do is listen. The song she sings weaves strength in your soul and lifts pain from your heart. She breathes life into all things and into you. Yabwè.

Sukmukwei stayed with Alexandra, told her many stories of the Iroquois squaws and braves, and in the end, shared her knowledge of the Earth's powers. She taught Alexandra how to use those powers to be strong and fit for battle.

* * * * *

Chapter Fifteen

Jediah persisted continually with experiments to enhance the Sensates' abilities. Canvassing the specific attributes of each Sensate became the largest single effort they had undertaken in their history. Completely opposite of any suspected alienation, the Sensates formed groups of their own volition to further their powers. Never before had so many concentrated on achieving a specific goal - to shatter Ryeth's masking ability and bring Alexandra home.

The effort produced countless enhanced senses and developed others to incredible depths. Experiencing a revival of sorts, Balisier bustled with chatter as it never had before.

"How did this happen?" William inquired, his brows furrowed.

"I'm not sure," Gabriel responded. "I don't know how it slipped through the cracks, but I never knew someone could listen in on my thoughts or that I could listen to others. Now that I know what to sense, I think someone has been picking through my thoughts."

William rubbed his chin. "The technique's so commonplace perhaps all your trainers assumed you had mastered it on your own."

"Could the group be at risk because of this?"

"Yes. Gabriel, we need to tell Jediah right

away. Ryeth could have used you to gain knowledge of our community, our strengths and weaknesses, and also entry into Balisier."

"While you work on mastering both techniques, I'll speak to Jediah. Hold on a minute…"

William located Jediah and shared the new piece of information. Instantly, he appeared at their side.

"Gabriel, I don't know how this slip happened," Jediah said, "but we might be able to turn it to our advantage."

He sensed the anguish tormenting the young Sensate and placed his hand on Gabriel's shoulder giving it a squeeze. "If it's Ryeth listening in on your thoughts, we could seed information to put Ryeth off the track."

Gabriel's eyes lit up. "Okay, I understand."

"I want you to leave your mind open as before and allow his access. You will need to block our newfound knowledge of this discovery and everything regarding our recent activities; you'll know where to stop his intrusion."

"I'm sorry this happened. Ignorance is no excuse, but I offer my sincere apologies for the oversight. I'll do my utmost to learn from this mistake."

Gabriel's commitment reinforced Jediah's pride in their small group. "Your mistake may have just turned the tables in our favor."

With new hope, Jediah turned to William. "I wonder if we've committed a fatal error in thinking Ryeth blocks intrusion as we do. Perhaps he uses a technique we have yet to discover. If that's so, we can reverse our technique. If Ryeth isn't adept in our method we might just slip into his mind when he listens in on Gabriel."

"It's an interesting thought." William rubbed his forehead, as a new sparkle appeared in his eyes. "You may be on to something."

"Gather the Ultras and alert all Sensates to ensure no one else slipped through the cracks as Gabriel did; any that are found need to be brought here for instruction. We'll work with everyone Ryeth has been using to obtain information. Explore this new possibility with Gabriel while I speak to Nancy Jane."

"Why do we need Nancy Jane?" Gabriel asked innocently.

William cast Gabriel a knowing smile and said, "Because she has the toughest blocking technique in our community. No one has ever been able to break through her shield."

Before leaving to speak to Nancy Jane, Jediah added some final instructions. "Begin by breaking down the components of our blocking technique, then work to insert the reversal connection to Ryeth."

"Will do," William replied.

Jediah found Nancy Jane relaxing in the solarium.

She recognized his excitement immediately. "What's happened, Jediah?"

"Our first break came in the form of a mistake by young Gabriel."

"What kind of mistake?" Nancy Jane asked.

"I don't know how it happened, but he never

learned to listen in on another or to block his mind. He thinks someone has been going through his memories and we think it might be Ryeth." Jediah could see the worry forming behind his mother's eyes.

"Oh, Jediah, we are most surely compromised."

He hurried to reassure her. "It may work to our advantage. The Ultras are working on a method to blast through to Ryeth when he is reading Gabriel's mind."

"That sounds like it might have possibilities. What can I do?"

What strength she had. "Block your mind from us for an hour or so and concentrate on a single item. We'll try to break through."

Her shoulders set firmly. "You can try; don't expect to succeed."

Sensates had used her for decades as a teaching tool. His only attempt to enter his mother's mind had ended with a mental slap so painful and fierce he'd never once considered making the mistake again. Strong-willed and determined, she would leave a hole in his heart impossible to fill. The thought became an ache.

"I love you, Mom." He kissed her soft wrinkled cheek.

"I love you too, my son."

* * * * *

The five Ultras sat around the room: William, the eldest Sensate, wise and able to see into the past; Jonathan, once he imprinted a mind, he could hear its thoughts from around the world; MacAila, clever and strong in all senses; Reslyn, super heightened touch abilities; and Jediah, who had unparalleled power behind all senses.

The whole community of Sensates knew of Alexandra's plight from the inception, so the Ultras arrived fully aware of the critical nature of their meeting.

Jediah said, "To begin, I would like to try something we've never been able to succeed in doing before. I want us to combine our abilities to achieve a synergistic goal. Since Ultras have enhanced abilities and strength, our group might uncover ways to combine and/or enhance a particular power. Our main goal: to break through Ryeth's masking or cloaking ability and locate Alexandra."

His heart pounded in his chest as he met each eye. "I'd like us to combine similar abilities in order to greater understand the mechanics or to develop new abilities of a related nature. Try anything remotely possible. We'll begin by separating into two groups; Reslyn and I'll form one group and the remaining three the second group. If you think anything might work to enter a mind, try it using Nancy Jane as a target. She will be concentrating on a single item for the next hour."

Jonathan shook his head. "Nancy Jane's mind is a steel trap. I've never been able to know her thoughts," he said. "She's a really good test."

"Then let's get to work."

Reslyn and Jediah moved off to one side of the room. She pushed some stray strands of blonde hair behind her ear and then flashed Jediah an encouraging smile. He sensed, behind those bright blue eyes, she knew how much he ached. Her beauty was breath taking, but there had never been any chemistry between them. Reslyn had been a Sensate almost as long as he had, and preferred to live among other Sensates, whereas Jediah enjoyed living among a full complement of personalities, not just those with highly developed senses. Staying with your own kind made it a lot easier to avoid detection, Jediah surmised, but he had lived among all types for so long he became adept at maintaining the balance required to keep his abilities secret.

"Reslyn, I have an idea I would like to test. He grabbed her hand. "Suppose you touch me, skin to skin, and concentrate on combining your abilities with mine, and we'll see if the ability becomes greater." He released her hand.

"I see what you mean. What limitation should we test?"

He could sense her eagerness to work together. "I have never been able to smell anything greater than a mile away. Why don't I try smelling the chocolate cream pie at the diner? I'll try it first, and then you grab my hand and concentrate on the same thing. Give me a few seconds to make sure I am at my strongest."

"Okay, go ahead."

Jediah used all his ability to push his sense of smell to the limit. He concentrated on the pie, could taste it on his lips, but could not get a whiff of the delectable delight. A huge black wall persisted in his mind. Then he felt Reslyn grab his hand, and at first nothing happened, then after a few seconds, he could feel a light surge in his powers. After a few more seconds, he caught his first whiff of the pie.

"It worked!" She squeezed his hand.

"Yes, it did. But how did you know?"

Laughing, she said, "Because I could smell it too."

Excitement surged through his veins. He had to know everything at once. "I can't believe this worked. We've never been able to combine powers before. What made it different this time? How did it feel to connect to me, and how did you do it?"

His exhilaration was contagious. Reslyn threw her hands about as she talked. "When I touched you I imagined a thin thread and then gave it more power. First, I could sense your violent push at a wall. Then, the wall seemed to get less dense, and soon it wasn't there at all. The pie was quite distinct once we got there. I've never been able to smell anything further than two hundred feet. Jediah, you are much more powerful than I knew," she said a bit sheepishly.

"Reslyn, the diner is at least five miles away, so your touch amplified my ability five times."

Why had it worked this time? Was it the combination alone or had he become more powerful? He needed more information. "Before we jump to any conclusions and report faulty information to the others, let's try reversing it. You try for the pie, and I'll assist you."

Jediah gave Reslyn a few seconds to concentrate, and then grabbed her hand. He found the weak thread reaching for the smell, and added his power to push it further along. It soon became a mad rush to the diner. The response was faster, even though Jediah controlled the amount of power he allotted to the experiment. He suggested they reverse the process one more time and they achieved an instantaneous response.

"Now, it's time to share our results," he said.

Walking over to the others, Jediah could sense they'd had no success. What had he and Reslyn done differently? After sharing their success and conferring with the others, he suggested Jonathan push into Nancy Jane's mind with maximum effort, then Reslyn should try to amplify as she had done with him.

"It's no use, it's just not working," said Jonathan.

"It doesn't feel the same as it did when I amplified you," Reslyn added.

"What do you mean? We're close, I can feel it."

Her brows knit in concentration. "The thread never connected. I expanded it like I did with you, but there was no connection."

Thoughts raced through his mind, when suddenly a possibility came to him. "Maybe it's a specific combination. Jonathan, let me try enhancing your ability. You start, then after a few moments, I'll try to push with you into Nancy Jane's mind."

Jediah grabbed Jonathan's hand and closed his eyes. A swirl of blackness flooded his mind. Although he focused all his energy on making the connection, he ran into the black wall. Opening his eyes, he let out a long breath. Alexandra needed him. Time was running out. He looked away, wondering what went wrong. "I don't get it."

MacAila jumped up. "Oh my! I do! Don't you see? It's the touch of Reslyn and the power of Jediah," said MacAila. "Jediah, have you ever been able to read your mother's thoughts?"

Smiling, Jediah remembered the one time he tried. Nancy Jane literally yelled in his head, 'Never do that again!' and he hadn't.

"No."

"Try now, with Reslyn's help."

He took Reslyn's hands in his. Closing his eyes, the black wall surfaced again. He forced his energy on the impenetrable wall with no success.

"That's exactly what I expected," MacAila said, still enthusiastic. "Jonathan, try again. When you push, Reslyn grab Jonathan's hand, then Jediah, you grab hers. I think Reslyn needs to be the 'touch' between Jonathan and Jediah."

His breath came more rapidly as Jediah understood MacAila's rational. Reslyn was the conduit and he was the power!

All was quiet as Jonathan began. Reslyn grabbed his hand closing her eyes to concentrate. Jediah reached over, grabbed Reslyn's hand. Closing his eyes, he concentrated as a flash of light flooded his mind. Initially nothing happened, the same black wall persisted, but then he located a familiar beam of light and focused every ounce of energy he had on it. The light grew and soon consumed the blackness. It exploded into a million little flashes of light as they blasted full force into

Nancy Jane's mind.

The connection broke immediately, for in front of them stood Nancy Jane holding an intricate statuette.

"How did you break through, Jediah?"

The words tumbled out of his mouth a million miles a minute. He'd never been more excited. "It was a combination of Jonathan, Reslyn, and me. I think I amplified Jonathan's ability by using Reslyn as a conduit of touch."

"That's it exactly," Reslyn said, "and because I functioned as the conduit I sensed everything too. It's quite a rush having Jediah's powers surge through me."

"I see," Nancy Jane said tersely. "Now don't do it again." She left as abruptly as she had arrived.

Laughter and congratulatory words filled the air. Jediah knew his mother had suffered a blow to her ego, but he knew it was for a great cause. He found it impossible to stop beaming at the others. Together they had achieved something quite miraculous. Now their group had a chance to strike back.

His heightened senses returned to normal as Alexandra's sweet face flashed in his mind. Grief tore at his heart and he sobered. "Let's not forget why we are here. We have taken the first step, now let's get back to work and accomplish our goal."

* * * * *

Bye (he comes).
He entered the cabin and slammed the door.

The girl jerked. She'd turned into a piece of trash before his eyes. Her hair had lost its luster and hung in matted tufts. He found it hard to believe that at one point in time, he'd actually thought her beautiful.

She cringed when he reached for her and dragged her to the chair. At least she could sit and not fall off the damned thing now. He never thought feeding her would be so disgusting.

"Sit up. Here, take this in your hands and drink it." He pressed the bottle containing the protein drink into her hands and helped her bring it to her bruised lips, all the while repulsed at her appearance. She drank quickly, gulping and choking as she hungered to swallow it before he took it away.

"Just look at you. You aren't good enough to step on. Nothing but a poor, worthless farmer who doesn't deserve anything. Your people never had anything, so why should you?"

He forced the bottle between her bruised lips. "Drink. Drink it all. That's it, that's much better now, isn't it?" He shoved the girl away from him and wiped the filth from his hands on his pants.

"It won't be long before you'll lay down for me." The leering look was lost on the shriveled mass.

"You're going to have to bathe first. You stink to high heaven."

He wrinkled his nose in disgust as he reminded himself of the impending reward of his plan. The end result was well worth putting himself through the revolting ritual of tending her.

Getting bucket after bucket of water, he threw it on the girl. She cowered away from the cold water and pulled herself onto the bed, where she huddled.

"There now, feel better? You'll need to smile when you see me coming so I know you want me. From now on, if you don't smile, I'll have to make you smile. Do you understand me?" He paced in front of the bed, working himself into the anger required to exact the punishment he planned for her.

"You're weak and you need me to take care of you. Your parents left you. You are alone in this world and need protection. No one wants you. Men don't find your lofty attitude and snooty nose desirable. You're lucky I even took an interest in you. Learn to treat me with respect and our visits will become much more pleasant."

Seeing the cowering figure helpless on the bed angered him. "I've told you before to look at me when I talk to you!" he yelled.

He pulled the girl's hands from her face and slapped her viciously. She recoiled from his touch. He grabbed her by the hair, turned her face toward him, and punched her hard.

"Look at me. Look in my eyes. You make me hurt you, because you don't give me the satisfaction I deserve. You are the cause of all these unpleasant acts. If you were the type of woman a man wanted, I wouldn't have to treat you this way. Open your eyes, you disgusting creature."

He tossed her back forcefully onto the bed banging her head against the wall and spat at her.

"Why do you always make me angry? When I

come into the room, you should come to me and show me how happy you are to see me. If you do that, things will go easier for you. Do as I say. If you do, your worthless life will have meaning."

He slammed the door shut and left the girl alone again, chained to the floor like an animal, lying amid the wet and filthy bedclothes, and drifting into a drug-induced sleep.

* * * * *

Sukmukwei came to Alexandra once again. *Wisnawen*, Grandmother Earth said, *eat.*

My daughter, long, long ago when I was an Indian maiden I would walk through the forest. The deer and elk would eat from my hand and birds came to sing on my shoulder. I could talk to the animals of the forest and I learned to listen to the flowers, trees, and grasses. My tribe gave me the name Sukmukwei.

My life was hard then. Many in the tribe liked that I could help them, but there were a few that didn't like me because I was different. They would throw stones and beat me. They withheld food and did not talk to me or treat me with kindness. The few turned the many against me and they drove me from my home.

Those bad times were very hard to bear, but I learned to be like the giant oak and bend, but not break. This is the lesson I wish to share with you. Do not let the few, or one, cloud your thoughts of the many. Always search for the place in your heart where truth lies. Wètasè, be brave.

The beautiful Indian maiden drifted into the mist once more.

* * * * *

Thoughts of Alexandra flooded Jediah's mind. To strengthen his resolve, he kept his mind open to all techniques and experiments explored by others. The gargantuan effort wore on him like a plague festering inside with no outlet.

The following day, research into the Sensates' abilities continued.

"It appears you have the power to strengthen or boost another's abilities," Reslyn said to Jediah, "maybe MacAila can do the same."

"Ready to repeat the experiment?" Jediah asked, "The one where we smelled the pie?"

MacAila and Reslyn nodded. He watched as they gripped hands, and the expressions passed over their faces.

"It worked," exclaimed Reslyn.

"Should we try to touch Nancy Jane?" inquired Jonathan.

"I think we have to try," MacAila said.

"Yes," Jediah said, agreeing.

Reslyn and Jonathan clasped their hands together. After a few moments, MacAila placed her hand on top of theirs. Jediah held his breath as he saw the various emotions cross their faces. Determination. Strength. Angst.

Reslyn shook her head and said, "MacAila, your power is just not as strong as Jediah's." She gave him a sideways glance. "I'd bet no one's is. If you had felt the surge when he connected to me you would understand."

"Are you that much stronger?" asked MacAila.

Jediah knew he had considerable power, but had always kept that knowledge to himself. Before he could formulate a response, Reslyn spoke.

"Jediah, you're at least five times stronger than MacAila. It's quite perceptible."

He could feel their eyes on him, and sensed their awe.

Like a hungry dog at a bone, Reslyn refused to give up the thought. "When we fail at something, we should try it again with Jediah. It could just be a lack of power to complete the ability," she said.

Embarrassed at being caught trying to hide his powers from those sharing everything to save Alexandra, he reddened.

"I'm sorry," he stated. "I'm so used to playing my cards close to my chest, I..."

"Not to worry, big guy." Reslyn winked and looked at the others. "We've known about you for decades. You're just so nice, we never teased you about it. I think I can speak for everyone here, though, - we're all glad you're in our corner."

Jediah separated himself from the others in the room so he could sit alone and 'listen in' on the experiments throughout Balisier.

As the hours passed, Jediah monitored many scenarios with multiple combinations. The one that proved to be the most fruitful, and caught his attention involved William, Reslyn and MacAila. Since William's greatest ability involved being able to see into the past, they had tried to sense

Alexandra at the time of her abduction and through William's eyes, the three saw everything Alexandra had seen and felt.

Jediah came to their side immediately. "Tell me everything."

"It's not much to go on, but we have discovered that Alexandra was knocked out with chloroform or some other anesthesia."

"Start from the beginning, I was only partially monitoring you, and don't leave out a single detail."

"We went back into Alexandra's past using MacAila for power, Reslyn as conduit, and me for sight." said William.

"We sensed it all, Jediah." Reslyn continued. "She opened the door and someone put a cloth over her mouth, then everything went black."

MacAila finished, rather regretfully. "There wasn't anything more after that."

The blood rushing through Jediah's veins quickened his breathing. "How can there be no more?" The strain showed in his voice.

MacAila touched his arm. "We're going to find her."

"I know this is tough, but you need to hold it together," Reslyn said softly.

Taking a deep breath, he pondered. "I have an idea, let's try it again, substituting me for MacAila, except, go back into my past right before the abduction. Find the point immediately before I left for the mansion, and then when I leave and she closes the door, switch to sensing Alexandra."

"What do you think the difference will be?" asked William.

"I'm hoping that because we connect initially through me that the connection itself will be stronger, and that because my powers have a greater strength, and I know Alexandra's thoughts so well, when we switch to entering her thoughts the connection will be more revealing."

"It's certainly worth a try," said William. "Is everybody ready?"

Jediah had no idea how invasive this request would be, and was aware he might be subject to a bit of embarrassment, but he was sure the process would reveal everything going through Alexandra's consciousness before the abduction.

William proved to be an excellent guide to past thoughts and activities. Jediah followed the trail through the expanse as they sifted out other tendrils of thought to center on the evening he spent with Alexandra in the bungalow. He sensed Reslyn's smile as her thoughts commingled with Alexandra's, William's and his. His heart skipped a beat as Alexandra came into view and the scene unfolded in his mind as if by magic:

Alexandra speaks: she thinks having many people watching her is going to be a necessary evil.

Jediah speaks: attempting to reassure her, but can't resist sharing one of his favorite memories of her; he has a mental picture of Alexandra singing and dancing to a song she loves while driving down the highway and conveys that to her. He watches her reaction to his words and it warms his heart.

Alexandra is laughing and knows Jediah shared her exuberance; she's a bit embarrassed again at being caught during a fanciful moment.

Jediah needles her with words from the song 'Stuck

Like Glue' and knows she is embarrassed again. It makes Jediah feel good that he knows her so well.

He smiles over his shoulder at her, thinking, I'm sorry for teasing you, but you are so darn cute when befuddled.

Alexandra closes the door and leans against it. She thinks: I've seen a whole new side of Jediah this evening. It was quite devilish the way he enjoyed seeing me embarrassed and uncomfortable. He created situations so he could rescue me from myself. He knows me so well he finds my trigger buttons with ease. What a great amount of time he has spent with me without my knowing, to learn all my nuances.

She remains at the door relishing the feeling of complete euphoria. She thinks: It's no wonder I didn't find any other males attractive. Subconsciously, I was probably comparing every male to him, and there is obviously no comparison whatsoever. He is delightful and charming and makes me smile all over.

Alexandra is startled by a knock on the door. She thinks: He has forgotten to tell me something.

She opens the door. Tom? What? His hair is disheveled, his eyes look like that of a madman. He's so angry! She is shoved backward and a cloth is placed over her nose and mouth; everything goes black.

* * * * *

Chapter Sixteen

Jediah broke away from the connection, knowing they had unearthed new information.

"William, it wasn't Ryeth!" Jediah said. "It was someone from her past named Tom, who she thought might be angry with her."

"He must have anesthetized her before she could call out for help," Reslyn said.

Jediah couldn't contain his excitement. This was their first real break. He had blamed Ryeth and concentrated all their efforts in the wrong direction! "If she was drugged initially it might be safe to assume Alexandra is still being drugged. Then why did he take her? There has been no request for ransom."

Jediah wrung his hands. "William, you need to go back further in Alexandra's past while I contact her friend, Cassie, for any references to an angry Tom."

"We'll monitor the police reports more closely," said William, "and sift back through what they have for any 'Tom'."

Jediah's mind worked quickly. He knew Cassie worked at a place called Oglebay in Wheeling. A quick search on the Internet produced a main phone number, which he dialed instantly. He asked to speak to Cassandra Hudson and the desk clerk transferred him to her office. Jediah heard her pick up.

"Oglebay Institute, Cassandra Hudson speaking. How may I help you?"

"Cassie, this is Jediah Saffle."

"Jediah, have you found her?"

"No, I'm sorry."

"I should never have let her go there by herself."

"Do you really think you could have stopped her?"

Cassie sighed. "No. Nor did I even try. Moving to Waynesburg was like a tonic to Alexandra. It's the most alive I've seen her since her parents' accident."

"Don't blame yourself, Cassie. She was living the life she wanted when this happened. The reason I called is that somebody remembered Alexandra mentioned a man named Tom, and that he might be angry with her. Was she seeing anyone?"

"No, she wasn't seeing anyone."

Jediah could sense Cassie's every emotion. "Did she have an argument with anyone named Tom?"

"No. She always found other ways to resolve issues."

"Anything at all regarding a man named Tom?" Jediah asked, grasping at straws.

"No, and unless it was while she was away at school, the only time she even exhibited a bit of displeasure was when an old school mate ran into us at a restaurant a few weeks ago. I could tell Alexandra would prefer he go away. His name was Tom, Tom Magis. He showed interest in Alexandra after her parents died. It was too soon following the accident and Alexandra told him she wasn't ready for a relationship. If I remember correctly, she said he wouldn't take 'no' for an answer, so he must have asked her out again and again."

"Not much reason for drastic action," Jediah offered. "Please share the information regarding Tom Magis with the Wheeling Police. It may be nothing, but we should check out everything. If you think of anything else, please let me know."

After sharing his email address, Jediah hung up the phone, hoping against all odds that this lead would pan out.

* * * * *

Jediah didn't expect anything would come of the dashed hopes of an old suitor, but planned to follow-up nonetheless.

"I'm going to Wheeling for the day to observe him." Jediah sighed. "If you come up with anything, I'll just be a thought away. Let's focus on both Ryeth and this elusive Tom to make certain we don't let anything slip through."

"Agreed. I'll keep in touch," Gabriel said.

Jediah acquired Magis' pertinent information, home and work addresses plus the places he frequented, from the Wheeling Police files. While physically observing Magis, he could also check up on Cassie.

He arrived in Wheeling just as Magis left his house for work and picked up the imprint of his mind. Monitoring his thoughts, he discovered they were crude regarding women, angry concerning life, and grandiose regarding himself. As Magis worked, his thoughts wandered to different lady-friends and what sexual advances he would make the next time he saw them. So vivid were the images in his mind, that Jediah had to stop monitoring until Magis' thoughts went in another direction, which didn't last long before returning to sex yet again.

Jediah noted Magis' spent little time cultivating his career and the majority of the time rehashing every detail of his most exciting sexual conquests repeatedly. To Jediah's disgust, Magis masturbated three separate times in the workplace bathroom, each time re-living the porn he'd watched the night before. It was too much for Jediah; the sexual content made monitoring Magis' thoughts exceedingly distasteful.

Taking a break from Magis, Jediah switched to Cassie. He discovered she cried a lot over her missing friend. Jediah felt her oppressive grief and the strength she mustered to keep it at bay. Neither she nor her family ever gave up hope. Jediah smiled, as he knew Alexandra would approve of Cassie's choice in men, for John Ryan showed extreme care in providing moral support.

Jediah resumed his mental observation of Magis later that evening. With a mixed drink in his hand, Magis leaned against the bar discussing the various attributes of the ladies with a companion. Dressed in khakis and a green silk shirt, Magis looked successful, available, and relaxed.

Jediah listened in on their conversation.

"Hey Alan, look at that girl at the edge of the dance floor in the blue skirt," Magis said, pointing.

"Yeah, I see her," Alan replied.

"Bet I could make her scream for mercy."

Alan shook his head. "Just once, can't you say something nice about a female?"

"I did say something nice. Look at her, she's just asking for it."

"She looks like a nice girl." Alan sighed and looked away.

"Yeah and they all turn into hellions. They're all nice and sweet smelling until they get their hooks in you and take all your money. I'll never make that mistake again. Women need to know their place," he said shifting his stance, "and that's right beneath me."

Magis finished his drink, sat the glass on the bar, and walked over to the girl.

"Hey, pretty lady, could I buy you a drink?" he said smiling.

She turned, was apparently pleased at what she saw, and returned the smile.

"I'm sorry, I'm here with someone," she replied, taking in the steel blue eyes and broad shoulders.

Jediah could sense Magis' reaction to the girl's appreciation of his attributes as he pressed his intentions further.

"If he's not with you now, he's not taking very good care of you. I'd never leave you thirsty and alone in a room full of wolves."

The girl leaned closer, obviously taken in by his attention. Jediah saw her reaction change instantly when she caught his sneer, as he looked her up and down.

She hurriedly looked away and mumbled into her drink. "Again, I'm sorry." She made a point of looking for her date.

Magis' reaction to his dismissal was quick and deadly. Leaning close to her ear he whispered, "You piece of trash, you don't know what you're missing."

He stepped back to the bar and ordered another drink.

The evening continued with numerous variations of the same theme. Jediah watched as Magis hit, struck out, and showed his true colors, which left him frustrated with the night's failed attempt to secure sexual release.

At the end of the day Jediah thanked his lucky stars that Alexandra had the foresight to never get taken-in by Magis. Jediah classified him as a bottom-feeder without honor. The one redeeming item in an otherwise dismal day was that Magis' thoughts contained no hint of Alexandra.

After a full day of searching through the minds of others, Jediah sought the solace of Larkspur. As he dropped into a tufted chair that seemed to engulf the weariness of his soul, he hung his head and let the sorrow ease from his mind.

Another week passed with no news of Alexandra. They had exhausted all leads, including the weak one, Tom Magis.

At Balisier, Jediah spoke to Gabriel regarding the information gleaned from the Wheeling Police investigation.

"Tell me everything the police know about Tom Magis, Gabriel."

"They've checked into his background. Mostly, he seems disgruntled. After high school, he flunked out of college. He hooked up with a girl from his graduating class and she helped him get back into college. They married; he graduated with a degree in electronics and landed a job locally. After three years, his wife divorced him, claiming she had no wish to carry a man with no ambition through life. According to her, rather than accept a job with better pay and benefits, he let her carry the weight of the monthly bills while he took a minimum salary job, because its one perk was free golf at the local championship course."

"Anything else?" Jediah tried not to let his disappointment show in his voice.

"Not much." Gabriel continued. "He doesn't belong to any organizations; his free time is spent golfing throughout the day and in the evenings he congregates in bars, drinking with friends."

"Thanks, Gabriel. It sounds as if the police turned up empty like I did."

"I'm sorry there's no news. You know I'd contact you the moment they found anything."

"I know. Thanks, anyway." Jediah sighed. He had taken little time to call his own since Alexandra's abduction. Concentrating his efforts on finding her had helped ease the pain in his chest. But, once alone, his thoughts went immediately to her and the ache surfaced ten-fold.

Jediah thought he might have the best long-range sensing ability of all the Sensates, for he had always been able to touch Alexandra's mind no matter where she traveled. A drugged stupor would account for not being able to touch a clear thought. He worked tirelessly with the Ultras and individually on her investigation, all the while attempting to touch her mind and though he could not touch it, he knew she was alive.

He missed his nightly visits into her dreams where they had become so close and the soft look of her green eyes when she smiled beneath her blushing cheeks. As he closed his eyes, he could picture her in his mind. He reached and stretched his abilities as far and wide as he could, only to be filled once more with emptiness and longing.

The following day, the police placed the investigation on the back burner.

* * * * *

Sukmukwei came to Alexandra dressed in a soft buckskin dress adorned with beads. Alexandra loved her time with Grandmother Earth who gave her strength and love, warming her like a blanket against the cold. Sukmukwei taught her many things and showed her how to fill the hole in her heart. Before Sukmukwei left she said:

My granddaughter, the time has come to tell you of another who needs your strength to survive.

She is alone. Find her and give her peace. I count on you to help your sister. Do not forget the strength of the great oak and the wisdom of the pawcohiccora. They will guide you.

As she faded into the mist, she heard,

GotakIn (enemy)! Anèmot (breathe). Wètasè (brave).

* * * * *

Chapter Seventeen

The man inched closer to the pale girl sitting on the floor hiding her face in a tangled mess of stringy blonde hair. "Get up and come over here."

She didn't move which made him angry. He grabbed the bucket, reached over the side of the boat and filled it with river water. Returning to the cabin, he tossed the contents on the shrunken mass and gloated when she responded by covering her eyes with her hands.

"Still alive, I see. You didn't remember to smile." He backhanded the girl with enough force to knock her backward to the floor.

She dragged herself back to the sitting position and leaned against the wall.

"I see we're making progress."

The weeks of tending her had severely hampered his preferred lifestyle. To his satisfaction, her total subservience neared completion. There would be no trace of his underhanded deeds once the drug flushed out of her system and she healed, and by that point, she would be forever under his control. He would be a hero when he found her, and in front of the entire world, she would seem madly in love with her rescuer. Satisfaction rippled through his body, knowing all he ever wanted was within reach.

As the repulsive work lessened, he felt his

long-lost bravado increase.

"Take this and drink it." He thrust the bottle at the girl and roughly shoved it to her mouth. She no longer shrank from his touch. Instead, she sheepishly came forward equally accepting good or bad from him.

Strutting back and forth, he watched as the girl drank.

He looked at the frail figure and became disgusted, "I have to tell you how to do everything. If it wasn't for my daily trips to see you, you would die; you need me. You have always needed me to take care of you. I'll show you how to behave and respect those who are better than you."

She would soon do anything to please him. His plan was working out better than he expected.

"Remember, you have no one to count on but me. What you want is not important. Since you are worthless, you need me to manage your affairs and do everything for you. It will be me, and only me, in your life."

In another few weeks, he would have all he had ever wished. He would have what he deserved. What did the girl know? She had no idea how to live and enjoy life. Satisfied he would soon achieve his goal, he continued his abuse with more fervor.

"Did you think I'd forgotten your daily reminder not to make me mad?" He sighed.

His favorite part of her indoctrination had arrived. The distinct feeling of power rose in his chest. Before he captured her, he would have never thought he'd enjoy training her as much as he had. He could stomach the feeding knowing his pleasure came later watching her suffer.

"If you would just do and act as I wish, we wouldn't have to use the belt, so you see, it's really your fault. Women serve men, it's that simple."

He licked his lips. "Your lot in life is to see to my desires and whims. But, you look like an animal, and turn my stomach. It will be some time before you gain my respect. Work hard to make me love you, and you will see things get much better."

He grabbed the belt hanging on the hook by the door. As he walked toward the girl, his eyes widened and he lifted his arm to let the first slash fall.

The girl huddled into a ball on the floor.

"You are filthy and disgusting. You don't deserve me," he yelled at the girl as he filled with even more distaste for what she had and what he did not.

A bright light burst forth and filled the room, nearly blinding Magis. He covered his eyes and squinted through his fingers to see a man dressed in black towering above him, and now stood between him and the girl.

"Who the hell are you?" Magis yelled. The man might be taller than him, but Magis was all muscle and he'd spent a lifetime dealing with bullies. Taller didn't alarm him in the least. He'd take down this stranger easily.

The man inched closer, not saying a word. Magis certainly wasn't afraid of some jerk dressed up for Halloween in a long black coat. Killing him could be a problem, though, since the last thing he needed was the police snooping around and finding the girl.

Magis threw a punch, but quicker than lightning, the man held him up against the wall with one hand around his neck, his feet barely touching the floor. Damn! Magis wanted no part of this stranger. Instinctively he knew he was seriously outmatched.

"What the hell?" Magis jumped away, his eyes looking furtively for an escape but he had nowhere to go; the stranger blocked the door. Magis backed further away.

Magis watched as the stranger's eyes fell to the emaciated girl now lying limp on the floor, and then turned to him narrowed with seething rage.

"Bloody Hell, what have you done to that girl?" the man yelled. "What kind of animal are you?"

Magis' spunk returned. Who was he to question him on his own property? "Who are you and what are you doing here? This is none of your business," yelled Magis, pumped with false bravado. "You're trespassing on private property. If you leave right now, I won't press charges."

The man didn't move. Magis tried another threat. "This is your last chance. Leave now. Leave before I…"

"Before you what?" The man cut him off and sneered. "Do you intend to beat me with a belt? Maybe you think you can chain me to the floor?" The man's black eyes burned into Magis.

"This doesn't concern you. You have no right to interfere." Magis clenched his fists and snarled like a cornered animal.

To his dismay, instead of meeting fire with fire,

the stranger relaxed his stance and said calmly, "Let me show you just how much this concerns me."

Magis winced and watched in horror as his hand holding the belt rose to shoulder height. His fingers opened and the belt fell to the floor. Fear crept into him bit by bit, as he could only watch as his body responded to commands from the black eyes.

His terror of the man increased. Magis' eyes darted around the room looking for a weapon of some sort or an avenue of escape. He could find none. Nor would it do him any good. As much as he tried to move his body, it refused to answer his commands.

"What are you doing to me?" he yelled, still attempting to move his legs.

"I'm controlling you, just like you controlled the girl. What? You don't like it?"

"Of course I don't like it," Magis spat, "I demand that you release me from this hold! Leave me and the girl alone and I'll forget this ever happened."

Magis' arm lowered, and panic gripped his chest. To his revulsion, his body walked itself to the chair and sat down. No matter what he thought or tried to accomplish, his body responded only to the stranger's commands. His face gave off heat from the internal rage he felt.

"Stop this!" Magis screamed. "Damn you to Hell, you black-eyed demon!" His body sat calmly, totally unaffected by the wrath spouting from his lips.

Blatant terror seized Magis as his struggle to

escape proved fruitless. His heart hammered in his ears as he felt the blood surging through his veins at an astounding rate. "Leave me alone! Get out of here! Stop what you're doing!"

The man spoke, "You've stolen the girl from those who love her and treated her quite badly from what I can see."

Pure hatred poured from Magis as he spat, "What's the girl to you? She's nobody. Who are you?"

"Who am I?" The man gloated. "I am the one who can stop you dead in your tracks and make sure you never harm another for the remainder of your pathetic life."

Still trying to flee, Magis looked furtively around for any avenue of escape. His eyes came to rest on his hands, lying lifeless in his lap. They were purple, mottled with yellow, and looked like those belonging to a corpse.

Dread gripped his very soul as Magis worked harder than he'd ever done in his life to break the hold the man had over him. Tension built between the body that calmly sat in the chair and the rage that intensified exponentially as he battled within to fight for his life.

"Let me go! Release me! I demand you let me go and get out of here! You have no right to keep me here!" Magis' blood pumped through his veins at a shocking rate and his face puffed up with the concentration of vile hatred.

"And you had no right to keep the girl here." The man replied.

"It's none of your damn business!" Magis

screamed. The man wasn't normal. Did the devil himself stand before him? He wasn't ready to die at twenty-three, but he knew he had crossed the line. He had to fight. He had to live.

The man spoke. "It is my business, more than you will ever know."

Magis grew closer and closer to bottomless fury and neared exploding internally from the vehemence seething through his veins. Death had never worried him, but now it had him within its grasp. His breath seethed, his heart raced, pounding uncontrollably. He felt the blood amassing in his face. The truth was plain to see; he couldn't win against such insurmountable odds. He would sacrifice his trophy.

"She means nothing to me. You can have her. She's useless anyway. Take her, do what you will. Look at her, she's repulsive!" screamed Magis. He looked around knowing his time was at an end. He expected to see the Grim Reaper at any moment when he realized the reaper stood right in front of him. Magis raised his eyes to meet the black, soulless ones that held him in his grasp.

"You did this to her." The man said, condemning him. "You don't deserve to live on this earth."

Magis' felt his life force ebb; he let loose a blood-curdling scream, and fell to the floor.

Chapter Eighteen

Jediah heard William's call from Balisier.
Come, we think we have something.

He appeared before them, sensing their anguish. "Go ahead."

"We were able to go into Gabriel's past using Reslyn's touch and my sight abilities," William said. "Each time we made an attempt to access the connection with Ryeth it failed. After repeating it time and time again, we got a slight connection just a few minutes ago to Ryeth. He was talking about a girl, and then... nothing."

Fearing the worst, he tried to reach Alexandra's mind; he could make no connection, but she was still alive. He reached for Ryeth but still couldn't connect. The only other he'd investigated was Magis. When he tried to reach him, his imprint fell vacant.

"Keep working on Ryeth, I'll be back soon."

In a second, Jediah was in Wheeling at Magis' place. His home was a trailer on the island between Ohio and West Virginia called Wheeling Island. He didn't sense anyone inside, but looked around for a body.

Finding nothing of value inside the trailer, Jediah took a chance and went out the back door. He looked around to make certain he wasn't observed and monitored the area for voices.

Behind the trailer, he spied a weathered dock and boat. The boat was ill-kept and badly in need of repair. Judging by the watermark on the side and heavy algae, it hadn't been moved for some time. Stepping onto the dock, Jediah worried he might fall through, but it was stronger than it looked. He leapt onto the boat and noticed it had a small cabin beneath deck.

Grabbing the knob, he jiggled it. Locked. He moved himself to the opposite side and was immediately assaulted with the stench of rot and mold. It took a few seconds for his eyes to adjust to the darkness, but as soon as they did, he saw Magis at his feet. He leaned down and touched Magis' neck; he was still alive. Jediah scanned the contents of the filthy cabin. A chain, attached to the floor with a clasp at one end, was big enough to fit around a large wrist or a small ankle. His eye caught a flicker of light. Squinting he leaned over to get a closer look and recognized the item wedged between the floorboards. His heart sank.

He heard voices outside. They were getting louder. Taking one last look before leaving, he moved instantly back to Balisier.

"Tom Magis has met with some trouble," he announced to the group. "He held Alexandra hostage on a boat behind his house."

"Are you sure?" William asked, deep concern showed on his face.

"Yes, I recognized one of her earrings on the floor."

"Where's Alexandra?" Reslyn asked.

"I don't know. She's not there now, but there's

evidence he held someone against their will. He may have moved her, or Ryeth could have gotten there first and taken her. Either way, she's gone," Jediah explained, crestfallen.

"Do you think Ryeth harmed Magis?" William inquired.

Jediah shook his head. "I don't know. I didn't have time to go over the scene for any length of time; just first impressions. I had to get out of there because I heard voices coming and I didn't want to be found there with Magis. The conditions under which she was held were horrible."

He rubbed his hand through his hair, and tried to gather his thoughts.

"Don't let your concern for her safety sidetrack you, Jediah. Now is the time to strike back and locate Alexandra." William's tone was firm.

Jediah recovered. "Were you able to break through to Ryeth again?"

"No, we're thinking the strength of his rage allowed us a greater advantage," Reslyn commented.

"Monitor the police department," Jediah said. "When they discover Magis we'll need to know where they go with the investigation. I'll be with Nancy Jane. I want to wheedle everything she knows and understands about blocking out of her. Let me know if you find out anything."

He turned to face the group that, along with him, had worked endlessly toward their goal. "Thanks, for all you've done. I can't tell you what it means to me."

"You would have done the same for us,"

Jonathan said, and the others nodded in agreement.

He smiled at them gratefully and then left.

Opening the door, Jediah smiled at his mother engrossed in one of the mysteries she loved so much.

She set the book down on her lap. "Jediah, is there news?"

"Yes, Mom," and he replayed the events from the Ultras' summons to current time.

"Oh, Jediah. I'm sorry you didn't find Alexandra. So now you think Ryeth took her? You think Ryeth had something to do with Tom Magis' incapacitation, don't you?"

"That's my best guess. I can't think of any other plausible scenario."

"Why would he do serious harm to Magis? All he had to do was come up behind him, take him unaware, and thump him on the head a little."

"Yes, but he was enraged; either at what he witnessed or for some other reason. Mom, I'm here because I really need you to help me. I know you don't like to let others into your mind," he could sense Nancy Jane's discomfiture, "but I need you to let down your guard, rid yourself of all your misgivings, and tell me everything you know about blocking your mind so we can reverse it to use on Ryeth. We're close to breaking through to him and I need the first attempt to work, otherwise he may hide her forever."

"I knew it was going to come to this, and have been dreading the day, but I know you would not ask me unless it was absolutely necessary. Ask what you wish, all that I know is yours."

What followed was an education of the mind reading senses so complete in the translation, the art of reading and blocking became a simplified exercise easily mastered in minutes. The extent of his mother's ability astonished him. Nancy Jane worked with her son for over an hour to ensure he understood every subtle aspect she now bestowed upon him. He became acutely aware of the many reasons why she had guarded her knowledge with such intensity.

Nancy Jane had developed her blocking technique as a guard against anyone tapping into the knowledge she held that could change the world, cause ultimate destruction, and kill. Kill on a scale unimaginable. He sat, staring at the delicate flower he'd called 'mom', and couldn't believe the power contained in that beautiful small frame.

"No wonder you pushed me away with such force the first time I attempted to enter your mind. I'm sorry, Mom, I never knew."

"Jediah, you are now keeper of that ability. It was always yours, but I chose not to share how to use it. Guard it as fiercely as I have. Know that it also transfers to the person who receives my powers."

"There would be no stopping Ryeth if he had this knowledge," Jediah said.

"I've never been as scared as I have been these last few months until Alexandra received my key from Teater, and I won't rest until these powers are contained elsewhere. I'm weary of the responsibility."

"Won't you let someone stay with you?"

"And have my remaining time spent with someone watching me all the time? Jediah, I am not without my own protection. I may appear frail and old, but I can pack a wallop if I need to," she said confidently.

"I don't doubt it a bit." He smiled. "Mom, I'm going to try and reach Alexandra again. I also want to try blasting through Ryeth's blocking mechanisms. You may have given me exactly what I need."

"Good luck. Find your Alexandra and bring her home."

The first stop Jediah made was Balisier. He gathered Gabriel, William, and Reslyn together and asked them to tell him everything they remembered about the small touch of Ryeth's mind. He needed to know how they used William's ability to go into Gabriel's mind to get the link to get into Ryeth's.

As he heard their individual experiences, he questioned them in great detail, ferreting through all the senses utilized for the experiment in depth. Once he was certain he had all he required, he thanked them.

"Do you need us to help?" Reslyn asked.

"Not yet, but I'll be back in touch soon. I'm going to try some small things on my own. I'll be trying them on the group, if you don't mind."

"Feel free to try. I'm willing," said Reslyn.

"Me too," said Gabriel and William, then Gabriel added, "I might not be such easy pickings as I used to be. I'll be using my best tricks to stop you."

"That's what I was hoping for, Gabriel.

Thanks, all."

Knowing Reslyn's touch would leave his new knowledge unguarded, he decided to conduct the experiments alone. The technique his mother shared was akin to adding an Intel processor to an abacus. With his power, he hoped to perform the ability alone.

He tried reaching out for Alexandra's mind using his full powers and the new techniques. He still could not reach her.

William became his first target; he used the method that made William unaware of the intrusion. He could read his thoughts easily. He watched William for any indication that William knew he entered his mind but could see none. He had to be sure. William wondered if Jediah would try to get into his mind, and if he got there, would he be able to see his secrets?

"William, I do not wish to know your secrets."

"Jediah, keep my thoughts to yourself!" Then realized what he said, and that Jediah had been in his mind without him knowing. His eyes grew wide. "What have you done?" William asked.

He held up his hand. "Hold on, I'll let you know later."

Jediah transferred to Reslyn and tried the same thing. She gave no indication she knew he was reading her. She repeated, 'think of chickens, think of chickens, think of chickens'. Jediah just laughed and moved to Gabriel.

Jediah could feel Gabriel's gaze centered on him, so he purposely turned away. Jediah didn't find his mind easily, he couldn't touch initially, which confused him a bit, but then he found it; Gabriel had projected a black, blank image and forced his mind to emptiness. One less skilled would think him unreadable.

"Good job, Gabriel! Thanks for the reminder of Occam's Razor. Thanks, everyone!"

"Hey, you didn't try me!" Reslyn pouted.

"I decided to leave you and your chickens alone," Jediah replied, and then was gone.

Chapter Nineteen

Ryeth stood in his bedroom looking at the girl he'd rescued from the boat. He was no caregiver; he was the manifestation of a centuries-long quest for revenge. Far from being the gallant knight of yore, he had placed himself in a position to act as one.

This certainly wasn't the outcome he had envisioned. His plan entailed finding the girl, getting the key, and acquiring the powers, nothing more. Baffled, he couldn't explain what process had taken over and changed his fate so irrevocably.

This girl could not care for herself and no malice existed in his heart to harm her further. His heart wrenched at the atrocities she had suffered. After five hundred years, Ryeth entered new territory.

She was barely conscious and reeked of the filth in which he'd found her. Her ankle festered where the chain tore into her skin. Gone were the rosy cheeks, and breath of sunshine he'd seen at the arbor. The stringy hair, cuts and bruises, and overall pallor had reduced the girl to a pitiful state. He started a warm bath and went back to her side.

Her clothes would have to go. Without thinking too much about what he intended, he retrieved a plastic bag from beneath the sink and spread it out on the floor. Qualms of uncertainty filled Ryeth; it was one thing to remove the clothes from a willing partner and another to remove them from a helpless shell of a girl.

As much as possible Ryeth averted his eyes, while removing each article of clothing and placed them on the bag to throw out later. When he removed her shirt, he cringed. The condition of her back sickened him and anger ballooned in his chest. Open cuts and welts completely covered the surface. Each time he'd moved her it must have caused unbelievable pain. He tried to touch her as little as possible.

Ryeth gently carried her to the tub and while holding her from sinking with one arm, lowered her into the water. With one hand, he lightly soaped the washcloth and gingerly patted her face and neck and then lathered the cloth and washed the grime from her legs and arms. He let her slide down as much as possible to rinse, soaked and soaped her hair and then let her head lean back into the water to rinse. It was a poor attempt at cleanliness, but the best he could do with Alexandra's dead weight.

Lifting her, he carried her back to the bed and laid her on the clean side, then went back to the dirty side and pulled the cover down and then moved her to the clean sheets beneath. He tossed the dirty cover to the floor, and covered her with the sheet. Obtaining a fresh towel, he dried her hair. As he worked the towel, ringlets of gold formed surrounding her face.

Even through the mass of bruises and welts, he could see her enchanting bone structure. Though he'd averted his eyes as much as possible completing his task, he had to admit the girl's body was a work of art. He might even be tempted to woo her, if circumstances were different. She was a child, barely full-grown. Fate had more fickle qualities than even he'd suspected. He shook his head. How the hell had this happened? It was a thought to consider another day.

Ryeth stood back to view his handiwork. Tidying up this girl consisted of the most effort he had put into anything, including locating the key, in many years, and he was shocked to see how tired he was from the exertion.

He made a call to his housekeeper. "Marion, please bring a tray containing clear broth. Leave it outside the bedroom door." Receiving her acknowledgement, he hung up the phone.

Marion had been with Ryeth for a few decades, was discreet, and never questioned his instructions. He monetarily rewarded her handsomely for her services over the years, and knew by now she was wealthy in her own right. They had become friends. She was the only real friend he allowed himself and didn't want her drawn into any mess because of him. The least she knew about the girl, the better.

Returning from the bathroom with antiseptic, bandages, and tape, he first used some of the antiseptic to clean the wound on her ankle, then added more to the wound, bandaged and taped it.

At the knock on his bedroom door, he knew the broth had arrived; after allowing time for Marion to leave, he quickly got the tray and closed the door.

He wasn't sure if it was possible to feed an unconscious or drugged person or not, but he decided to try it anyway. Propping her to a semi-sitting position, Ryeth got several teaspoonfuls into her, and after each, held her head so that she swallowed naturally. Several spoonfuls went down her neck, which he wiped away, but many more entered that weren't laced with drugs. The remainder of the broth was in a small thermos-like container, so he closed the lid to keep it warm.

He returned the girl to a reclining position, pulled up the sheets, and placed a blanket over her. He lowered the shades and positioned himself in a chair across the room to watch over her.

After a few hours, she started to stir a little, so he went to her. Somewhat familiar, he could still make no sense of the words she spoke, "azhèni" (angel), "yabwè" (dream), and concluded she still experienced the effects of drugs in her system. Her movements jerked and she seemed disoriented. Ryeth held her hand, which calmed her. He took the opportunity to feed her more soup. She finally fell into a deep slumber.

After setting the tray outside the door along with the plastic bag containing her clothes, he showered, shaved, dressed, and resumed his position across the room.

A few hours later, Ryeth heard the light knock on the door. He roused himself from his chair and stretched, knowing he had been in the same position for hours. His neck was stiff and sore. Rubbing it, he opened the door to reveal a tray and a package. He moved the tray to his writing desk and took the package to the side table. Unwrapping the package carefully to cause as little noise as possible, he found panties, bra, a pair of pajamas, and two sets of street clothes all in the girl's size. Marion had seen the soiled clothes and purchased fresh ones. She was worth every cent he paid her and more.

He lifted the cover from the tray and saw various options from a light to normal supper, complete with drinks and dessert.

Ryeth knew Alexandra could move herself to a safe place if she felt threatened, and that she would probably do so as soon as the drugs left her system and she could think clearly. Knowing his time with her was limited, he couldn't decide whether to stay, thinking she might need more care, or leave her to get home alone when she was ready. Her easy breathing told him she rested, so he opted for the latter and slipped from the room.

He found Marion in the kitchen.

"Thank you for going the extra mile once again, Marion."

"You are welcome, sir."

"If the girl wakes and is disoriented and comes to you, tell her she is safe. Her name is Alexandra. She may not remember who she is and how she got here. She might not come out of the room at all; if that is the case, leave her alone. Do not enter the room."

Marion nodded. "As you wish, sir."

"I'll return this evening. Feel free to leave at your normal time." He planned to return only after Alexandra was gone.

He went back up to his bedroom, peeked in the door to see the girl resting, and then moved to his forest.

When Ryeth needed to think he always went to the woods where he taught himself how to use his powers. He used the site often; it was acreage he had donated anonymously to the national park system many years ago. As he leaned against a tall oak tree, his eyes wandered over the lush ferns. The new bright green fronds partly curled and peeking through last year's fallen leaves came up outside the large ferns as off shoots. As he focused on a single frond, he emptied his mind to begin his contemplation.

Left to his own devices, Ryeth had manipulated and cajoled his way through five hundred years, waiting until the ideal time to serve up the revenge the Sensates deserved for turning him out without teaching him how to use his powers. Just when all was within his grasp, a century of planning had dissipated in an instant. A waif of a girl had brought him to his knees.

The whole village had said he was evil. Was it possible the Sensates had seen ahead? The episode with Magis would alter his life, he was certain. With no more guidance this time than the first, he had no idea where to go from here.

An Eastern Bluebird perched on a branch across the path and puffed his feathers to clean them. Ryeth, deep in his thoughts, failed to notice its vibrant colors. What caused him to do a complete one-eighty? He wasn't a 'save the world' type. His specific type had been determined long ago when the incident occurred that changed his life forever. Over the years, he had played the scene repeatedly, and each time he arrived at the same conclusion: there could have been no other outcome than what had transpired. That one event, over which he had no control, made him unworthy in the Sensates' eyes and they had turned him away.

Looking back, he had separated his life into steps toward a goal. Always existing on the fringes of their society, he knew when new Sensates came into the fold. Before they learned to block his intrusion into their thoughts, he gathered key information about their group.

He knew about Balisier, their stronghold, even though he could not enter. Through the tiny glimpses into their philosophy and knowledge, he maintained a covert connection to his kind and happened upon the Prophecy a few centuries ago.

The constant reminder of what he'd lost, his parents and his rightful place with Sensates, fueled the furnace of revenge. The journey to the now-sacrificed end had been a lonely one. Without revenge to ignite his path, he could see no discernable future. The quest for ultimate power now gone, he had no goal.

* * * * *

Jediah concentrated his thoughts on Gabriel. He blocked his own mind, blocked Gabriel from knowing of the intrusion, and pushed forward into Gabriel's mind. With exhaustive effort, he combed the contents until he found the area where memories resided, and then bit by bit, examined each overlapping fold until he found the past connection with Ryeth. He investigated the concepts used to access Ryeth, and stored Ryeth's imprint in his own memory, so he would no longer need to go through Gabriel. Satisfied he had the information he required, he disconnected from the young Sensate.

Jediah moved to Larkspur and located his mother.

"I'm ready to breach Ryeth's mind. Would you mind if I connected from here, and if anything goes wrong, would you step in? This ability is new to me and I'm still fumbling around, but I feel certain enough to make an attempt."

"Yes, I will monitor you." Nancy Jane replied.

"Okay, here goes."

Jediah positioned himself on the edge of an ottoman, and closed his eyes to block out distractions. The thread to Ryeth was easy to follow. He found his mind within a few seconds, blocked Ryeth from discovering him, and then tentatively pushed slowly into his mind.

Ryeth sat in the woods somewhere reminiscing about his childhood. Jediah's connection to Ryeth was so strong he became an empath to his adversary's emotions. He sensed Ryeth's great loneliness as a young lad and it pulled at his heart. He sensed when the loneliness grew into bitterness against those he felt were responsible, the Sensates.

Jediah could feel Ryeth's power; it was as great as his own. Reaching further, he felt Ryeth's bewilderment of having powers and not knowing how to use them, and his great sorrow when he inadvertently made mistakes that cost lives. Jediah wandered into Ryeth's controlled rage and confusion regarding Alexandra.

Alexandra! Jediah willed himself to remain calm. He weaved through Ryeth's thoughts until he located the thread to Alexandra. Ryeth was concerned about her well-being and very confused he had helped her.

Helped her? He chastised himself to remain calm once again. Jediah backtracked through Ryeth's memory, waded through the scenario on Magis' boat, and saw the instant he had taken Alexandra. He had the proof he needed. Ryeth had Alexandra!

* * * * *

Smiling, Grandmother walked from the mist to Alexandra. She took her hand and they sat on a fallen log in the forest.

My little flower, you have endured much these past weeks. Mother Earth kept you strong of spirit, but your body has suffered greatly.

What happened to me, Grandmother?

An enemy tried to enter your mind to control you. You were brave and strong. Now you must forget the pain and remember only your strength. Always remember the strength of Mother Earth. You can summon her strength to use as your own. In nine moons our tribe will count on you to defend us against great danger. Trust no one, my granddaughter, trust only your heart and our tribe will be safe from harm.

Kayè, what if I fail?

A dark cloud will hang over our kind. Our strength will be lost to the winds and our people

*will be no more. Do not worry, little one, all you
need is within.*

*I will do as you say. Thank you for staying
with me, Grandmother.*

I will always be with you.

Kayè stood and took Alexandra's face between
her hands. She bent low and kissed Alexandra on
the cheek and then she faded into the mist.

* * * * *

Alexandra tried to open her eyes but they were
too heavy. Her stomach hurt. She curled into a
ball, hugging her knees to her chest as lightning
bolts of pain shot through her body. Squeezing her
eyes tight against the pain, she willed herself to go
back to sleep, anything to make the hurting stop.
Her head throbbed uncontrollably as she rolled it
back and forth on the pillow. As she moved, her
skin felt too tight for her body, and as it cracked
open, she moaned. She opened her mouth to gasp
and felt her lips part and break. The metallic taste
of blood hit her tongue and caused her to gag.

Still unable to open her heavy lids, her
breathing came in rapid spurts as she tried to focus.
The aching consumed her as each second brought
sharper stabs.

Terror set in as her eyes flew open wide and
her arms and legs kicked wildly at an invisible foe.

She screamed uncontrollably and continued to
lash out at the air with her limbs until fatigue took
over and she fell back on the bed.

Something was terribly wrong.

Alexandra opened her eyes, and shuddered with excruciating pain as she pulled up to lean on her elbow, and took in her surroundings. She had no idea where she was or why she hurt so badly. The strong masculine flavor of the room left no doubt in her mind that she was in a man's bedroom.

Running her tongue over her lips, she discovered them to be crusty and her teeth disgustingly fuzzy.

"What?" The sheet had fallen. She was completely naked; she pulled the sheet up to cover herself. Alarm bells rang in her head.

Alexandra saw a stack of clothes on the table next to the bed. Although every cell in her body wanted to lie back and sleep for ten years, she forced herself to a sitting position and painstakingly slid her legs over the edge of the bed.

A wave of dizziness washed over her. She grabbed the mattress for support as she swayed and nearly fell over before the feeling passed and she became steady. Pushing the hair out of her eyes, her fingers caught in a tangled mess. The movement caused a searing jab that radiated down her back. Nothing was right here. Holding the sheet with one hand and using the other for balance, she took a deep breath against the inevitable pain and stood.

Once her knees quit wobbling, she turned around and let out a scream as she barely recognized herself in a full-length mirror hanging on the wall. Thinking the vision false, she moved her hand to her battered face; the reflection moved the same.

"No," she whispered.

Alexandra walked closer to the mirror and as she did, she lowered the sheet and gasped at her image. She had lost weight, her back, legs and arms were a mass of bruises and slash marks. With no way to stop it, her eyes filled with tears of pity for the poor creature that stared back at her.

Her stomach retched, and she stumbled, nearly falling, as she bent over and convulsed into head-splitting dry heaves. Each heave hurt more than the last until the spasms finally subsided.

Where was Cassie when she needed her? Where was Jediah? She just wanted to go home.

Home! She could go home. Holding the sheet tight, she screamed Jediah's name and flashed back to the bedroom of her lovely bungalow.

Chapter Twenty

Jediah moved to Ryeth's location, disappearing from Nancy Jane's ottoman, and emerging directly in front of Ryeth. Before Ryeth could react, Jediah shouted, "Where is she?"

"Impressive," said Ryeth who appeared unshaken. He raised his head and eyed Jediah coolly. "I was expecting you."

Jediah's lip curled in a snarl. "Just answer the question."

Ryeth pulled a wide blade of wild grass from the ground and calmly separated it into strips. "Last time I saw her, she was asleep in my bed."

Momentarily stunned, Jediah recovered quickly. "Did you hurt her?"

"I wanted to at one time," Ryeth said softly, his focus still on his grass.

"You cad," Jediah said.

Ryeth stared directly at him. "I've been told that before, and worse. So don't think you're wounding me in any way. I will tell you, though, someone did hurt her, but it wasn't me."

As his heart leapt for Alexandra, Jediah probed Ryeth's mind and sensed the truthfulness of his words.

"Why did you take her?"

"To get the key, of course." Ryeth smiled smugly.

"You could have had the key without taking her."

"I suppose so. I really don't know why I took her; I'm pondering that thought this very minute, or I was, until you rudely interrupted."

He bent low over Ryeth and pushed his shoulder roughly. "Take me to her."

Unfazed, Ryeth smiled. "No."

The riot of emotions Jediah sensed brewing in Ryeth left him bewildered as to the course of action he should take. He sensed both good and evil in Ryeth's thoughts over the last several hours. As far as Jediah could determine, Ryeth had done nothing wrong, other than remove Alexandra from the boat.

"When you took her, why didn't you press your advantage?"

"To tell you the truth, once I had the upper hand, I realized I didn't want it anymore." He looked at the sky then back at Jediah. "I'm having difficulty understanding myself as of late; welcome to my nightmare, so to speak."

Ryeth's attitude didn't make sense. He could stand there and bicker with him for decades, but paramount in his mind was getting Alexandra back where she belonged. He'd figure Ryeth out later. "Release her."

Ryeth let out a sigh. "I'm not really holding her. She'll go home when she's good and ready, I suppose. We both know she can do it."

Jediah's brows furrowed. "It would seem we're at an impasse. I'll just wait here with you. You do know that wherever you go, I go."

"Yes, I do know that. I prefer not to chase

about with you fast on my heels, but rather to sit here under this magnificent tree." He cocked his head and looked up to the branches high above.

Realizing Ryeth would not think about Alexandra and give Jediah an advantage, and knowing he could not deep-read Ryeth's thoughts without leaving himself vulnerable, he resigned himself to stick to Ryeth's side until the tables turned. As he leaned over to take a seat next to Ryeth, a familiar voice yelled, *Jediah.*

Ryeth read his relief instantly and said, "Guess she went home."

Jediah flashed instantly to her side

* * * * *

Alexandra sat barely upright on the bed wrapped in a sheet, leaning on one arm for support, a pathetic version of the girl he'd last seen. Jediah rushed to her and took her in his arms. She winced as his arms closed around her, and he immediately released her. "I'm sorry, I didn't mean to hurt you."

"It's okay," she stammered. "What's going on? I'm hungry and tired." Her labored breath made the words come out slowly as if she needed time to form each syllable with her lips.

The sight of her tore the heart from his chest. Moss green eyes were the only recognizable feature not damaged by the treatment she had received. He compelled his words to remain soothing, not indicating any alarm at her appearance.

"Let's get you settled."

"I'm naked," she said.

Jediah sensed her embarrassment, although her face didn't register much emotion at all. "What do you want me to do?"

Her hand lifted only slightly and pointed to the dresser.

He went to the dresser and opened the drawer. In it were worn sweat suits, soft to the touch from so many washes. Lifting shirt and pants, he took them to Alexandra and laid them in her lap.

"Are you able to dress yourself?" he asked.

Without looking up, she nodded.

"I'll just be in the kitchen heating some soup," he said before slipping from the room to give her some privacy.

Pushing his anger aside, he heated the soup and placed it and some crackers from the cupboard on a tray. He added a hot cup of tea and a small bowl of canned peaches.

"Alexandra, may I come in?"

"Yes."

Bringing the tray to the bedroom, Jediah sat it on the dresser and helped her sit up a bit higher so she could eat. He sat the tray on the nightstand.

"I know you are tired and weak, but try to get some food down before you rest."

She nodded.

He held the bowl close and as she reached for the spoon her hand shook so badly Jediah offered to assist, and she agreed.

As he fed her, she asked, "What happened?"

"You don't know?"

She shook her head. "I came home."

He noted the strain in her voice. "We'll talk

later. Concentrate on getting as much down as you can."

"I'm so tired…" Tears flowed down her cheeks as she burst into sobs.

Jediah cupped her hand in his and winced knowing it was probably the only part of her body he could caress without hurting her. He brushed the hair from her forehead.

Spent from her tears, Jediah gave her some sips of tea to bolster her spirits.

She seemed calmer. Half the soup was gone, a few crackers, and some peaches before he realized she had her eyes closed while eating. He set the tray aside and helped her lie down. Before he removed the tray from the room her breathing steadied. She fell asleep in an instant.

Anguish dug deep as his eyes surveyed the swollen and bruised face he adored. He knew her back, legs, and arms suffered abuse by the way she moved. Though he tried to hide his disgust for Magis from Alexandra, the heinous act ate at him like acid going through his veins.

The more he thought of her suffering, his loathing increased for the filthy scum who had harmed her. His emotions and senses rose to a fevered pitch. Before he knew what happened, his internal power had escalated to mammoth proportions. He wrestled to control the buildup and calm the rage, but it was too late. Realizing he couldn't contain it any longer, he moved to the massive waterfall beneath Balisier and unleashed a primal yell that transcended all decibels.

Outside the mountain, birds took flight, deer

scurried from their rest, and small rocks split in half. Sensates with heightened hearing sensed his pain, keyed in on the Sensate responsible, but did not intrude on his grief.

He fell to his knees gripping his head in his hands and reached for the loving heart of his mother.

Mom, she's been hurt so much. I don't know how to help her. What kind of savage would do this to such an innocent?

I saw through your eyes, Jediah. Give her time and let her rest. She'll know what she needs, and you can be there to help her. Let the others know she's safe.

* * * * *

At Balisier Jediah told the others she had returned home.

"Gabriel, have you heard any news from the Wheeling Police?"

He replied, "A neighbor heard a man scream horribly at Magis' address, and ran outside to see if he could help. When he didn't see anything, he went back inside his house, but was so affected by the chilling scream he called 911.

"The police arrived minutes later and pounded on the front and back doors of Magis' trailer, but no one answered. Because the neighbor was so insistent someone had to be hurt or dying, they knocked down the door to the trailer. He was nowhere inside.

"During the inspection of the grounds they

discovered a shabby-looking boat docked out back alongside the river. When they broke the lock on the cabin door, they found him inside, barely alive."

If the timeline proved correct, Jediah had been there mere minutes after Ryeth had taken Alexandra.

Gabriel continued. "The police are assuming foul play due to the circumstances and they are holding him under guard at the hospital."

"What happens next, Gabriel?" Jediah asked.

"After forensics finishes with the cabin and Magis is well enough for questioning, we will know more. The condition of the cabin left the police baffled. They say it looked as if someone had been held there in chains, and it wasn't Magis."

"Thanks, Gabriel. I need to call the police to let them know Alexandra has been found."

"They're going to ask how she got home," Gabriel said.

Jediah looked at the floor and sighed. "I know. We'll handle that one as it comes."

"Do you think Magis held her on that boat?"

"It seems that way, but so far, Alexandra doesn't remember anything, or if she does, she's not talking about it."

"You know, it might appear to the police that the person being held got the upper hand, and escaped."

Jediah rubbed his hand through his hair. How could he contain this mess? "I never thought of that, but I can see where they could come to that conclusion. Thanks for all the concentrated effort."

Jediah went back to the bungalow and called

the Waynesburg and Wheeling police to let them know Alexandra had returned home. He wanted to allow her time to rest, but needed to comply with the law.

A second call went out to James Dawson, who arrived at the bungalow within minutes. Jediah told James all that had transpired. After speaking with James, Jediah decided to bring Dr. Jellan to the bungalow at once. The three were in the kitchen when a knock sounded from the door. Jediah opened it to see the two familiar officers. He ushered them indoors.

"Officers, this is Ms. Higgins' physician, Dr. Valentine Jellan, and her lawyer, James Dawson."

"I'm Detective Mokros, and this is Officer Johnson. May we speak with Ms. Higgins?"

"Although I have not examined Ms. Higgins, Mr. Saffle has indicated she is in no condition to be interrogated," Dr. Jellan said. "She is bruised and was beaten quite badly and apparently malnourished."

James Dawson said, "Perhaps if you could postpone your interview until tomorrow morning, Ms. Higgins will be alert enough to receive you."

Jediah read the hesitancy in the detective's face and hurriedly added, "She's worn out and sleeping."

"Fine," Detective Mokros said, "but I insist we speak with her tomorrow and no later."

"Understood," said Dawson. "Thank you for your consideration, gentlemen."

Jediah escorted them out. Closing the door, he turned to his friends. "Thanks for helping out. So far, it hasn't been too bad, although I could tell the detective wasn't happy with the outcome."

"Tomorrow's a new day," Dr. Jellan said while departing. "I'll be back tomorrow morning to examine her and we'll go from there."

"Thanks, Val." Jediah shook his hand then turned to James.

"My services are at your disposal, Jediah," stated Dawson. "I can be here within minutes."

"I appreciate that, James. Maybe you should plan on tomorrow morning as well."

"Sure, let me know when." He took his leave.

He cleaned up the kitchen and then ordered some meals and hearty soups from various restaurants, some fresh produce and groceries, and had it all delivered to the bungalow. When the orders arrived, he ate one meal himself, then divided the rest into smaller meals for Alexandra and placed them in the refrigerator. At the same time he replaced the spoiled milk, vegetables, and fruit.

Jediah went to the cage and got Sebastian. He was quite the handsome cockatiel with all over soft gray feathers, and a blush of peach on each cheek. Over the weeks of Alexandra's absence, he and Sebastian had gotten to know each other quite well. He had even taught Sebastian to mimic a few sounds. Jediah smiled thinking how Alexandra would laugh. After he refilled his food and water, he placed Sebastian back in his cage.

As he sat back in a chair, relaxing for the first time in almost six weeks, he grabbed one of Alexandra's books and began to read. Five chapters into a book about an immortal highlander, he decided Alexandra read some interesting books. Alexandra, his Alexandra. Why had Magis hurt her? Why had he kept her in such a horrible, filthy place? Maybe he'll never know.

What would he have done to Magis if he'd found her first? Would he have killed him? Had he seen her bruised and hurt and Magis right in front of him, would he have lost control and struck out? He didn't know if Ryeth had harmed Magis or not. The possibility certainly existed.

Could Alexandra have harmed him? No, he found that hard to believe, but she had been beaten and, by the look of her, starved. Jediah had no idea what he would do under those circumstances, so how could he possibly know what another would do?

The Sensates needed to find out as much as possible about Ryeth; this time as he settled back, instead of reading a book, Jediah decided to read Ryeth, as deep and as much as he could. Besides, he had questions: Where had he been all these years? How had he gained so much power without help? Most importantly, did he physically harm Magis?

He touched on Ryeth's mind, but before entering, he stopped.

What right did he have to probe Ryeth's mind? Alexandra was home, and safe from the man who had taken her. Jediah reminded himself, 'just because you can, doesn't mean you should.' Crossing the line wasn't the true path for a Sensate.

Curiosity did not give him the right to invade Ryeth's thoughts or Alexandra's. Discovering more about Ryeth would have to be a task performed the old-fashioned way, without using his senses.

He seized Alexandra's book and began the next chapter.

* * * * *

Chapter Twenty-One

Terry walked into the coffee shop and saw his contact in the far corner. He rolled the newspaper in his hand and quickened his steps to the table. He slid into the opposite chair.

"What's up?" inquired the agent as the waitress dropped off the coffee.

Once she moved out of earshot Terry said, "Ray, we may have a break in the case; they found the girl."

Ray's eyes widened as he leaned in closer to ask, "Where was she?"

"They don't know yet; she mirac-u-lous-ly turned up back at the bungalow. Someone worked her over. She looks pretty bad. The odd thing is - no one knows how she got there."

Ray smiled and nodded his head. "You're right. This break may lead somewhere." He clapped his hand on Terry's shoulder. "I'll let the boss know you might be on to something. Get back there and keep your ears open. Find out anything you can. The least little thing might be valuable." He tossed some bills down to cover the tab as he stood.

Terry and Ray left the shop leaving two cups of steaming coffee untouched.

* * * * *

Later that evening Jediah heard Alexandra stirring. He went to the bedroom door and heard her mumbling. Only a few words were distinct: no, drink, pain, and sleep. She tossed and turned in her bed moving restlessly. He lightly placed his hand next to her cheek. Alexandra calmed and returned to peaceful sleep.

Each time he considered what she must have gone through his thoughts turned black and cold, and cried out for vengeance. His normal calm conflicted with the blackness and he found it unsettling. He had been fighting this war since Alexandra's disappearance and had falsely assumed it would dissipate when she returned; the two battling emotions were still unresolved.

In the past, Jediah exuded a calming effect on those around him. Nancy Jane described it as his most beautiful gift; he was able to give others peace. She said it came from inside him, from deep within his spirit.

Alexandra was so tender, how could anyone raise a hand against her? What had Magis hoped to gain? Shredded thoughts continued to torment him until he finally fell asleep.

* * * * *

Alexandra awoke to bright sunlight filtering through the curtains. She reached for the covers to throw them off but searing pain running like liquid fire throughout her body stopped her. Her eyes sought her surroundings. She was in the bungalow, but that thought did little to ease her mind, all she remembered was waking up and coming home. Her mind tried to reconcile the pain. It was best not to move or, at least, not to move in giant leaps.

Closing her eyes against the sting of her wounds, she forced herself to push up to a seated position with her legs dangling over the side of the bed. The exertion made her dizzy, so she waited a few moments until the sensation passed.

"Jediah, are you here?" she said loudly.

"Yes," she heard him say from the other side of the door. She smiled knowing he was near.

"I'm going to get a shower," she said.

"Will you be okay?"

She sensed the concern in his voice. "I think so. I feel a little better today, but I'm going to leave the bathroom door ajar in case I need you."

"That sounds good. Listen, I've asked our family doctor to come over this morning to have a look at you. The police came last night but we persuaded them to wait until today to talk to you, so they might come by this morning too."

"Oh, okay," Alexandra said half-heartedly. Her mind was clearer, and she felt better, but she had trouble remembering yesterday. It seemed fuzzy and just beyond the fringes of her ability to grasp.

She stood against the pain, removed her clothes and looked at her body. It was hard to believe the reflection in the mirror. She twisted around to see her back, and was shocked to see the welts and black-and-blue areas. There wasn't a place on her back that looked normal, even the backs of her arms were chewed and raw. She didn't remember being beaten, yet everything she saw proved it had happened. Her fingers touched her face. Her lips were severely cracked, and had bled at some time, and her eyes looked hollow and without feeling, with dark circles around them. Her cheeks had taken a few blows; some yellowish-red and bluish-black areas covered what used to be freckles. The person in the mirror couldn't be her. Something had happened and she wasn't even sure she wanted to know the details. If her mind had closed its eye, why shouldn't she do so as well?

Removing the bandage on her ankle, she wondered at the cause of such an injury.

"What's wrong with me? Why can't I remember? Why am I so blasted tired?"

Alexandra eased into the shower and scrubbed her body, causing all the injured nerve endings to burn fiercely from the water and soap.

She shampooed her hair three times and left the conditioner on a full three minutes, or so she thought; it was probably closer to ten, since it took her an inordinately long time to complete any one action. As she rinsed her hair she let water run over her body. Thankfully, the burning seemed to lessen.

Alexandra toweled off and when patting herself dry, noticed half an inch of hair or more on her legs. Whatever had happened spanned at least a month; she never let her legs go unshaven. The hair would have to grow longer still. No way was she going to take a razor to them until they healed. If she could live through the embarrassment, the good doctor should be able to handle it too.

Donning undies, she then reached for her toothbrush and toothpaste. She brushed her teeth, gums, and tongue, and when done and rinsed, she repeated the process once more. At the final rinse, she cupped her hands and had several gulps of cool water. A little clarity began to form, but she had trouble concentrating. Each action took tremendous effort. Combing her hair turned out to be a mammoth chore. When she held her arms above her head, it took energy she no longer possessed.

A fresh pair of sweats would be the outfit for the day. The whole morning routine took hours due to her restricted movements and the pauses to rest between each action. It was all she could do to keep alert. She tired too easily. Her ankle needed attention, but it would have to wait.

Once done, she gingerly made her way to the kitchen. Jediah, smiled. "Good morning," he said, and held the chair for her.

Unable to look him in the eye, she said, "Good morning," to the front of his shirt.

Jediah placed a beautiful plate in front of her containing baked oatmeal covered in mixed berries, one of her favorites, and a steeping cup of tea. "Thank you for staying last night," she said while looking at the food.

She could feel his eyes on her and sensed he knew her thoughts without reading her mind. The shame that radiated from her over her appearance and whatever happened to her couldn't have been more evident had she displayed it on a billboard for all to see.

Jediah reached over, tucked his finger under

her chin, and raised her eyes to meet his.

"Alexandra, no one can ever take away your tender heart or your deep capacity for love. You are still Alexandra Higgins and an incredible woman."

She smiled, and her eyes glistened with unshed tears. "Thank you, Jediah."

With an attempt at lightness, he said, "You should try the baked oatmeal; I spent all morning slaving over a hot stove to bake it for you."

"It looks perfect."

She concentrated on eating with sore lips and jaw. It did taste wonderful. Each bite brought her more into the present as she began to feel a little more like her old self.

When she was through, Jediah cleaned up the kitchen. Alexandra took her tea to the living room and nestled into one of the comfortable chairs. Before he joined her, he asked if she needed anything.

"I don't think so. Thank you for taking care of me and Sebastian."

"Alexandra, I know you are going to have to go through a lot today, but I think you should call Cassie and let her know you're okay."

"Oh, I never thought!" But before she could call Cassie, she had to know. "Jediah, how long has it been? To me it has only been the time it would take to go to sleep and wake up again, but I know it has been much longer."

"It was almost six weeks." His hand closed over hers.

Her heart beat loudly in her ears. "I was gone from here that long?" she whispered.

"Yes. We tried to find you, but there weren't any clues."

She sensed the anguish in his voice. What they must have gone through trying to find her she could only imagine. How Cassie must have worried.

Jediah handed her the phone and busied himself in the kitchen to give her some privacy. Since it hurt to use her arms and took strength to hold the phone, she put it on speaker on the arm of the chair and then pressed speed dial for Cassie.

"Hi Cassie."

She heard Cassie gasp and then break out crying. "Allie, oh, Allie, I'm so glad to hear your voice. What happened to you? Are you all right? Where are you?" Cassie sobbed in full force.

Alexandra smiled at the concern in Cassie's voice; she loved that moppet. "I'm okay. I don't remember much. I don't want you to worry; Jediah is here taking care of me. I got back to the bungalow last night, but I was too tired to even think straight."

"Do you want me to come up?"

Not wanting Cassie to see the condition she was in, she stalled. "Maybe in a few days. Right now, all I'm able to do is sleep and eat. The police are due here soon. Give me a chance to get through it myself and then feel free to come, okay?"

"Sure, but I'll want to hear everything. Are you sure you're okay? You had us scared to death."

"I'll be okay. It wasn't good, but I'll be fine."

"Oh, Allie..." Cassie's voice trailed.

Just then, there was a knock on the door. "Cassie, I have to hang up, someone's at the door."

"Call me later, okay?"

"Sure thing. I love you Cassie. Bye."

Jediah answered the door, escorted a small man into the living room, and introduced him to Alexandra.

"Alexandra, this is Dr. Valentine Jellan, the Saffle's family doctor."

Kind, soft gray eyes filled with compassion put her immediately at ease.

"Hello, I'm glad to meet you," she said.

He reached for her hand to help her rise from the chair and said, "Alexandra, let's go into your bedroom so I can have a look at you. Alright?"

She led Dr. Jellan into the bedroom and he shut the door. He helped her sit on the bed and then he sat next to her.

"You've been through quite an ordeal. I'll try to be as gentle as I can. Let's have a look at you, shall we?"

Dr. Jellan's exam was quite thorough. Alexandra told him she didn't know if she had been sexually assaulted or not. His examination proved she hadn't. She started to cry.

"Why are you crying, Alexandra?"

"I was afraid something had been taken from me that I hadn't wanted to give."

"Alexandra, you have been through a lot. Jediah says you don't remember anything. I'm going to do some blood tests, but if my guess is correct, I think you were drugged quite heavily. That's probably why you don't remember."

"Will I ever remember what happened?"

"I don't know. My guess would be no, which is

probably a good thing. This kind of trauma can leave its own scars that aren't so quick to heal; some never do."

He stood to leave. "I've applied a salve to your back, upper arms and thighs that will help with the stiffness and pain. You are dehydrated and malnourished; so drink all you can, and eat everything in sight. If you do, I won't have to give you an IV or admit you to the hospital. Your ankle is going to take a bit more time, since you have a nice infection going on there. I'll call in a prescription for an antibiotic and more salve for your back and legs."

"Thank you, Dr. Jellan."

"You're welcome, Alexandra. I'll be back in a few days to see how you're doing. Good bye."

Alexandra had been dreading the doctor's visit since Jediah'd mentioned it, but had worried needlessly. Dr. Jellan was very professional and had a great bedside manner. He'd spoken with a light accent, maybe Austrian, and had the sweetest face; his mama probably pinched those cheeks pink every morning. And wonder of wonders, she hadn't been violated! If she wasn't so sore and tired, she'd do a Mexican Hat Dance. One bridge crossed, and a million more to go. By the time she dressed and returned to the living room, Dr. Jellan had gone.

"The doctor called in some prescriptions to the pharmacy," Jediah said. "I don't want to leave you alone with the police coming, so I'm going to call a messenger to have them delivered."

"Thanks, Jediah," Alexandra said while gently sitting down. "I don't know what I would have done without you."

"Let's hope you never have to find out," he said with a wink as he picked up the phone to arrange for the prescription delivery.

Alexandra caught Jediah's subtle innuendo, and smiled at him. After he hung up, she asked, "What am I supposed to say to the police?"

"They will ask the questions. All you have to do is answer them truthfully."

"Okay, then how did I get home? How do I answer that one? And, where was I? Jediah, what am I to say?"

"I've considered that, and I've called James Dawson while the doctor examined you. He's coming right over. If he thinks you might be getting into trouble, he'll run interference so you needn't worry. I've found out over the years that things like this have a way of working out all by themselves."

"I wish I could believe that. There's no way for me to explain without sounding daft."

As if on cue, James Dawson arrived at the bungalow followed closely by the police. Jediah brought them into the living room, which Alexandra had once considered cozy, but now felt overcrowded.

"Ma'am," the older officer nodded to her then addressed the group. "I am Detective Mokros and this is Officer Johnson."

Jediah spoke, "This is Alexandra Higgins, and you remember James Dawson, her attorney. Won't you please have a seat?"

The detective stated, "You felt it necessary to

have your attorney present, Ms. Higgins?"

"No, but since I am new to this area, I know very few people. Mr. Dawson offered his assistance as a friend. He was instrumental in executing the will of my great-great-grandfather which resulted in my taking up residence in Waynesburg."

The detective began his questioning. "Ms. Higgins, what can you tell us about the night you were abducted?"

"Well, I answered the door thinking it was Jediah, since he had just left. Then everything becomes a bit fuzzy; I remember a cloth being placed over my mouth and nose, and that was it."

"Can you describe the person who abducted you?"

"No. I don't remember anything after that. Jediah's family physician thinks I might have been drugged. He took some blood for tests to be sure."

"He thinks you were drugged the whole time?"

"I believe so."

"Ms. Higgins, do you know of anyone who would want to hurt you?" The detective probed.

"No, I can't think of anyone."

"Do you have any recollections at all, maybe a smell, something you noticed that wasn't familiar, a voice, or any sounds?"

She concentrated trying to remember anything, then answered, "No, nothing at all, it's all a gaping hole in my memory."

"Ms. Higgins, how did you escape?"

Alexandra was shocked, she never thought of how she got away. "I don't know. I don't think I did."

"Then how did you get away?"

"I'm not sure." Now that was definitely a truthful answer.

"How did you get home?"

"I really can't explain..." Another truthful answer. Maybe this wouldn't go as badly as she thought it would.

"What do you mean, 'you can't explain'?

"I don't know how I got away." She shook her head. "And I don't know how I got home; I just arrived."

James broke in. "Detective Mokros, Alexandra is trying her best to remember, but it could be the effects of the drugs remaining in her system. According to her doctor the drugs could have either temporarily or permanently blocked the memories from her mind."

"I see," Detective Mokros stated rather dubiously. "Mr. Saffle, the name of your family physician, if you please."

Jediah replied, "Dr. Valentine Jellan."

"Yes, I've heard of him." Directing his gaze to Alexandra, he asked pointedly, "Ms. Higgins you would have me believe you were taken from your home for almost six weeks; you were beaten and drugged; you remember absolutely nothing of the incident; and you don't know how you got away from your abductor or how you arrived at home?"

"As impossible as it sounds, that is correct, Detective. Do you have any idea what happened to me?"

"I'm sorry, Ms. Higgins, I'm not at liberty to discuss that with you."

"You can't discuss my case with me?"

"No ma'am." Rising, he handed Alexandra his card. "Please call me if you remember anything at all."

"I will. Thank you, Detective."

Both he and Officer Johnson left.

James excused himself stating he had to get back to his office; soon after, the delivery of prescriptions arrived.

Jediah brought Alexandra a protein bar, an antibiotic, and a glass of Boston Iced Tea. She looked at him incredulously, and he said, "Cassie. She was here with her friend, John, putting up posters. I invited them to stay at Larkspur. During the time we spent trying to come up with clues, the subject of Boston Iced Tea came up. Alexandra, she never gave up hope that you would be found."

Feeling a little bit remorseful, she explained, "I brushed her off a little this morning. I'll call her back and this time I'll take the time to answer all her questions."

"Good. She's a remarkable girl and a true friend. Will you be all right here alone for a while?"

"Yes, I think so. I'm not scared to be alone, if that's what you mean."

"Good. I'll be listening in, so you won't really be alone." He leaned in to press his forehead next to hers. "It's so wonderful to have you back home."

"I'm glad to be back where I belong," she said and met his eyes, a bit choked with emotion.

"I'll check back later," he whispered as he dropped a kiss on the tip of her nose, and slipped from her view.

Alexandra felt the intake of breath fill her cells with fresh new life and as she began to heal from the inside out, she reached for the phone and hit the speed dial for her life-long friend.

* * * * *

The coffee shop was bustling with activity so the two men sequestered in the back corner went pretty much unnoticed.

Terry said, "Finally, something we can sink our teeth into. They don't know how she got home or how she escaped. It seems like she had help from someone. I don't think it was Saffle; he's mostly been hanging around the house. I rarely see him leave."

"The boss said this is exactly the stuff she was hoping for, except it doesn't sound like much to me. Anything else, Terry?"

"Since she doesn't remember anything, or so she says, we'll have to wait and see what happens next. Saffle has been sticking pretty close to the girl; that Dr. Jellan, who examined her, and Dawson, were both there to make sure she wasn't interrogated by the police the instant she returned home."

"They do stick together, don't they?" Ray said.

Terry asked, "Do you think the doctor is involved?"

"It's hard to say. We shouldn't discount anyone we see them with a lot."

"We'll add the doctor to our surveillance list."

"Meeting once a week is not often enough; let's step it up to Monday, Wednesday, and Friday from now on. Keep me in the loop via email if you find out anything."

"Will do."

* * * * *

Chapter Twenty-Two

The call to Cassie took over an hour.

"Hold on a second, Allie."

Cassie stepped to the door of her office and closed it pointedly. "I'm sorry, Allie, I closed the door; I didn't want to be disturbed. Okay, tell me everything, I'm ready." Cassie said.

"I don't know a whole lot. Whoever took me kept me drugged, which might be a blessing in disguise."

"You don't remember anything at all?"

"Not a thing."

"Are you okay?"

"I will be, in time. There's a good chance I was used as a punching bag."

"Oh Allie, how awful, I need to come and see you."

"Cassie, it's bad enough Jediah and the police have to see me this way, maybe you could give me a little time. Besides, I don't want you to see me and get overly worried, since the doctor said I would heal."

"It's that bad?"

"I can't find a freckle."

"I'm so sorry that happened to you. I'm not going to tell Mom, she'd never let me out of the house again."

"Agreed."

"Were you, ah, assaulted any other way?"

"No. I was worried about that too, especially since I didn't remember anything. The doctor said I was fine in that department."

"Well, that's something in your favor. Tell me about your injuries. Where are they located?"

"It's mostly my back and the back of my legs and arms. My face is only bruised, and nothing is broken or damaged so severely that it won't heal completely."

"Allie, I'm so happy to have you back, but so sad for your injuries. I really don't know how to feel. I was so worried that I'd lost you for good."

Alexandra could tell her friend was crying and had been for some time. "I'll be okay in time. I'm not worried and you shouldn't be either." And in the same breath she continued. "You should see the way Jediah takes care of me. He's so tender and thoughtful."

"Hmm, that can't be all bad."

Once she was satisfied her friend was stable and happily back at the bungalow, Cassie relaxed her interrogation.

"Guess what?" Alexandra asked. "He made me baked oatmeal, all by himself, compete with assorted berries. There's a chance I've come from Hell and gone straight to Heaven."

"It seems you're suffering a great deal at his hands."

"Agony, I'm in agony." Both girls began laughing.

"Ok, girlie, I'll give you some time before I come to see for myself that you are okay."

"Deal."

"Before we hang up, I have just one other thing bothering me," Cassie stated. "Are you afraid that whoever did this to you might still be out there?"

Alexandra gasped. "I never once thought about that. I just assumed it was all over. I'll ask Jediah what he thinks when he returns."

"He left you there alone?"

She sensed the concern in Cassie's voice and hurried to ease it. "I think he wanted to give me some privacy to talk to you. I have no doubt he is hovering nearby. He told me you and John hung posters all over Wheeling and Waynesburg. Thank you."

"Allie, everyone did all they could, but nothing worked. We couldn't find you and there were no clues. I was so scared. The police couldn't understand why there was no request for ransom once they checked into your finances. I know they set up phone taps in Waynesburg, but no calls came in."

"It doesn't make much sense, does it?"

"No, the police were throwing a wide net, though, and exhausting every avenue."

"I appreciate everything you did to find me."

"It comes under the label of 'friend'."

"I'm sorry, but I'm getting tired again. I'm going to stretch out here on the couch and close my eyes for a while. Next time we talk, I want to hear all about John, okay?"

"Sure thing, rest well, Allie, and call me if you need anything."

"I will. Bye."

Alexandra hung up the phone, grabbed the throw from the back of the couch, and was asleep within a few minutes; she smiled in her sleep as she saw Jediah coming toward her.

* * * * *

When Ryeth returned home, there was no evidence Alexandra had been there. Marion cleaned the bedroom and bathroom leaving no trace of his recent guest. What had he expected? That's what he paid her to do, to keep things the way he liked them and to be circumspect.

Ryeth smiled, glad he had been able to help Alexandra even if just a little. She was a tender and beautiful girl.

Magis got what he deserved, although the complete extermination of that snake might have been better for all concerned. He had never knowingly harmed anyone before and the thought soured his stomach.

Ryeth concluded he hadn't acted overly impulsive. When he saw into Magis' mind, it contained loathing for Alexandra and for women in general. He had planned to drug her, force her to submit to his wishes and marry him. Magis wanted to own Alexandra, body and soul. He had been taunting her, and brainwashing her into believing he was her best and only choice because no one else wanted her, and mercilessly beating her, expecting the intended outcome of her complete subservience. Moreover, his reason for his despicable actions had been money. Magis wanted all of it.

Ryeth found it ironic that Magis wanted something Alexandra hated having, the money paid to her by the mining company as compensation for the death of her parents.

Ryeth remembered when he learned of Alexandra's past. During the time he watched her work on the arbor, her thoughts often slipped into memories of her parents. Each time she thought about them, she remembered their deaths as well.

Alvas and Helen Higgins met while working at Bloch Bros. Tobacco Company in South Wheeling. Throughout the tri-state area a legacy of "*Chew Mail Pouch Tobacco*" painted barns dotted the countryside. Al Higgins, a plumber recently hired from his stint in the Navy and Helen Gellner, who worked as a tobacco sorter, entered into dating somewhat cautiously on Helen's part.

The first day Helen saw Al, even though she was engaged to Matt Kuchinka, she pulled her friend, Lillian Oberg, aside and told her she planned to marry Al Higgins, and she did.

Alexandra knew her parents loved each other deeply. She was the only proof of their existence, and she considered herself fortunate to be within their circle of love.

She finished high school early and was in her second year at Bryn Mawr when the bottom fell out of her life. Passing through the campus cafeteria, she witnessed a CNN report of a massive sinkhole that completely swallowed a home in Wheeling. As she stared at the screen, Alexandra recognized the large oak with the swing, and what remained of the garage, still standing next to a gaping hole that appeared to have no bottom. The earth had devoured her parents in the lower level of their home.

A whirlwind of news reporters, insurance investigators, police statements, funeral, well-wishers, more reporters, and lawyers followed the accident. Not remembered by local inhabitants, many years previous, the coal company undercut an area covering thousands of acres now depicted as unstable due to the eventual formation of sinkholes. The area contained the plot of land where Alexandra's parents built their home.

The Department of Highways closed the stretch of Interstate 470 from St. Clairsville to Wheeling for over a year to make repairs. The processes used to repair the damage became a 'best practice' for the undercutting of mines, and was now used all across the United States. The sinkhole topic headed local newscasts for six months.

When the dust finally cleared, the coal company's multi-million dollar settlement, deemed the largest in history, went to the survivor of #1 Dutch Lane, Alexandra Higgins.

Ryeth admired Alexandra's courage and her attitude regarding the Department of Mines compensation. It was because of this admiration that he acted quickly and without much thought to the consequences when he threatened Magis and brought him to his knees. He held Magis instantly in contempt for his acts upon Alexandra and assumed the role of judge and juror.

Ryeth had used his senses to move to the cabin, and rescue Alexandra. It wouldn't be long before they found Alexandra's DNA at the crime scene and connected her to Magis.

He would have to wait for the police to put together what happened and hoped he hadn't compromised her in any way. Ryeth could have walked away from the whole mess if he didn't think suspicion might fall on Alexandra. He would not let her suffer for his actions and decided to continue monitoring the Sensates and police for information.

* * * * *

Alexandra awoke knowing Jediah would arrive soon. She made her way to the bathroom and she was just getting back to the kitchen, when a light knock sounded on the door. She opened the door and an overpowering sense of fear and recollection struck her.

It was Jediah, but it wasn't. It was someone she knew.

Jediah saw the look of anxiety on Alexandra's face. "What's wrong, Alexandra?"

"Jediah! I remember. I saw who it was before he put the cloth over my face. It was Tom Magis, a classmate from high school. It just came back to me when I opened the door. That night, I opened the door thinking it was you, just like I did right now; but instead of you, it was Tom."

"Is that all you remember?" Jediah asked.

"Yes, it was just a flash. I should call Detective Mokros and tell him."

"Yes, you should. Do you have any idea why Tom did it?"

"I haven't the faintest idea," Alexandra responded, shaking her head, perplexed.

"Here's the detective's card. While you call, I'll get lunch ready. You need to eat."

She looked around. "Where are you getting all this food?"

"I stocked the kitchen yesterday while you slept."

"You are incredible. Lunch sounds perfect."

Alexandra placed the call. The detective wasn't in, nor was Officer Johnson, so she left a message for either to return her call.

She joined Jediah in the kitchen and sat at the table watching him while he served her. She found it pleasant to see how his strong shoulders and big hands could be so gentle with soft wheat buns. The thought made her smile and then she cringed as the pain shot through her cheek.

"One tuna on wheat ala Jediah for the most wonderful woman I know, and a full glass of iced tea," he said, then leaned over and kissed her softly on the cheek.

"Jediah, I want to thank you for the beautiful dream this morning and for being so good to me."

"Ah ha, so you caught me slipping into your dreams."

"Yes. It was nice to spend time with you."

"I've missed you too."

She bit into the sandwich. The bun was soft and chewy and the flavor made her mouth water. "Mmm. Good sandwich. Are you trying to win my heart with food?"

"Could I?"

Laughing, she said, "Right now, yes! I feel like a bottomless pit."

"I'll have to take you to the diner for a bacon cheeseburger, French fries and gravy, and a black and white shake."

"And a slice of pie?" she asked.

"Pie too? You ARE hungry."

"This sandwich is doing the trick. But that bacon cheeseburger will be in the back of my mind, waiting for you to take me there."

"As soon as you're fit we'll go. It's a promise."

Growing a bit thoughtful, Alexandra fingered her sandwich. "Jediah, I don't understand why Tom hurt me."

"What's your history with him?"

"We went to high school together. I was the typical nerd and he was a big-man-on-campus. We didn't hang in the same circles. He asked me out a few times when I was in college, right after my parents had their accident and I had taken a leave from school, and I declined each time. I was an emotional wreck and really had nothing to offer anyone looking for a relationship. I told Tom so, but he kept on trying. I went back to school, and the next time I saw him it was three years later. It was the day I packed up and moved here. Cassie and I were having lunch and we ran into him. He did act a little weird, maybe a little condescending."

"It sounds like you handled the situation without being cruel; you were firm."

"That's why I can't make much sense of it. Why would he beat me?"

"Anyone who would do what he did to you has

underlying problems. Those problems more than likely had nothing at all to do with you."

"He must have followed me here the day I moved to Waynesburg and watched me since then," Alexandra said.

"Maybe the detective will be able to share more. It could be they know more than they are telling us."

"I hope so; I would like to know why Tom would do such a thing. I barely knew him. When I spoke to Cassie earlier, she thought I should be concerned that the person who did this was still out there evading the police. I hadn't given it a thought because I was so tired and just glad to be home."

"The police had your file on the back burner because there were no recent leads, but with your return, I'm certain they are actively working the case again."

"Then there was a good chance I might never have been found?"

"The investigation wasn't going well. Even with the strong imprint I have of your mind, I was unable to connect to you for the first time in over ten years."

"What changed then? How did the tables turn?"

"Originally we thought Ryeth had you, so as the police investigated via their pathway, we considered an option they knew nothing about and centered our attention on Ryeth. We had no way to locate him or access his mind due to some blocking mechanism we couldn't penetrate. Our usual methods had no effect; it was then we decided to see if there was a way to combine or enhance our abilities to achieve a common goal.

"The Sensates were zeroing in on you through techniques we had just developed and were becoming adept at using. Our group of Ultras discovered someone by the name of Tom had taken you. I spoke to Cassie and found out you had a dubious conversation with Tom Magis the day you moved here. Trying to follow up on any lead, Cassie shared the conversation with the Wheeling police."

Jediah continued. "Some of our effort focused on identifying the Tom you saw the night you were abducted, not knowing it was the same Tom. I centered my attention on breaking through to Ryeth's mind without him knowing I was there. The group working on 'Tom' obtained his information at the same time I locked down the process to penetrate Ryeth's mind."

He took her hand in his. "As soon as we knew Magis was the culprit, I went to Wheeling and dropped into Tom's residence. He wasn't there so I searched his home and found nothing. I walked outside to search the remainder of his property and found a boat tied to a dock out back. I saw nothing there at first, but when I moved to the inside of the cabin, I found Tom on the floor. I thought he was dead."

"Oh, Jediah, how horrible!"

"I checked for a pulse and he was still alive. What was horrible was what he did to you and the condition of the cabin." He watched her reaction closely. "It had a bed, a table and two chairs, and a chain attached to the floorboards, indicating someone had been chained and held there. I heard someone coming, so I instantly moved back to Waynesburg."

"Are you telling me you think I was chained there for all that time?"

"I think so."

"But why would he do that to me? What would he hope to gain? How did I get away?"

He pulled her into his arms. After she calmed he continued. "There's more; are you ready to hear it?"

"Yes. Tell me everything."

"My assumption was that while the police and the Sensates were both looking for you, Ryeth was looking too. I'm sure he tapped into the same police files we did, and he ran across Magis' information."

He looked deeply into her eyes. "Ryeth found you first. He had been also monitoring a young male Sensate who hadn't learned to block his thoughts. Ryeth heard the name Tom Magis and acted on that information before we did. I assumed Ryeth took you from Magis' boat and hurt Magis in the process."

Alexandra found it hard to contain her emotions. She couldn't believe her ears.

Jediah cleared his throat and continued the tale. "As soon as I got back to Waynesburg and was certain I could stop Ryeth from knowing I monitored him for information regarding you, I entered his mind, and listened for any indication that he had you or knew of your whereabouts.

When his thoughts mentioned you, I moved to his position instantly. "I asked him where you were. He told me the last time he saw you, you were asleep in his bed."

Alexandra was shocked at the implication of Ryeth's words. "Jediah! I didn't know I was there. I just woke up there."

"I know, Alexandra."

"I was naked between the sheets."

"Naked? That's too much information," Jediah stated with one raised eyebrow.

"Jediah! You are making it sound so bad. I did what I could, and then got out of there. I would never..."

He watched her bluster and sputter, then broke out smiling. Alexandra looked up at him and caught his smile. "You are the devil, letting me go on like that. I forget that you know me as well as I know myself. You, better than anyone, know what I am capable of, and what I would never morally do."

He smiled at her again, and when he lowered his eyes just for a second, she hit him square in the head with a pillow.

"Did you know I was going to do that?" she asked laughing.

He leaned over and kissed her smack dab on the mouth. "Did you know I was going to do that?" He replied. It wasn't a long kiss, but one firmly planted.

"No, but you should do it again."

"Ah, once again, we see eye to eye."

As Jediah leaned toward Alexandra, she was

sorry her hair wasn't perfect, that her face was such a mess, and that her lips were still a bit sore. She wanted this moment to be perfect.

Jediah pulled away, looked her in the eyes and said, "We need to try that once more. One of us wasn't fully engaged."

This time, when he took her gently in his arms and as their lips touched, he opened his mind to her and let her sense what he was feeling. When she realized he was holding nothing back, she placed her heart in his hands and let him share her emotions as well. The elation that overcame her senses was the stuff of dreams.

She knew the regret she felt over her current physical appearance had no place usurping the memory of their first kiss. As she drew away and nestled against his chest, she said, "Thank you for reminding me what's really important."

"No problem, whatsoever," he said while brushing her hair from her temple.

Resting comfortably against Jediah was a balm to her injured body and soul. Each breath in and out seemed to nurture her bruised spirit. After a while she asked, "There's more, isn't there?"

"Yes."

"Please finish."

"Let's see, you were in Ryeth's bedroom."

"You can hurry through that part," Alexandra said. Jediah chuckled.

"Ryeth wouldn't tell me where you were, and I was unwilling to let him get away from me, so we were at an impasse. I took the opportunity to gather as much information as I could. I asked him if he hurt you. He said he hadn't but someone else had. He also said that he and I both knew you had the ability to go home whenever you wished.

"It was then I heard you call for me and I knew you were home."

"Jediah, why didn't you tell me this earlier?"

"Val, I mean, Dr. Jellan, said until he knew which drugs you were given, we should let your memory come back on its own. Once you identified Magis as your abductor, I could share what I knew with you, but if I mentioned him, the drug might predispose you to think it was Magis when it could have been someone else."

"Both Ryeth and Tom wanted me. Ryeth for the key," she said while absentmindedly reaching for her necklace, "and Tom..., oh Jediah! I don't have my necklace. I don't have the key! Is Nancy Jane safe? She trusted me and I have let her down. I must tell her right away!"

"No need to worry, Alexandra," he said while reaching in his pocket to produce the key, "you left it, as you should have, in the keystone. I retrieved it for you. Mom was never in any danger."

He placed the key in Alexandra's hand. Her eyes brimmed with tears.

"What now, Alexandra, what brings tears to your eyes?"

"My mother's engagement ring was on that necklace too. It was a tangible keepsake I kept close to remind me of my parents love."

"I'm sorry."

"In the great scheme of things, weighing my life against a token from my parents, I'm sure my parents would want me to choose my life. I shouldn't be too greedy. I do have a handsome fellow sitting next to me that I know my parents would have adored."

"Oh, you think I'm handsome?"

"Well, in a rough, exaggerated sense of the word, I suppose I do. I was just trying to be kind."

"Is that so?"

"Yes, as a matter of fact, when thoughts of you pop into my mind, I get a used fly swatter, you know, the kind with bug guts on it, and swat the thoughts away."

"You equate me to an insect?"

"Most certainly!"

"Alexandra," he said with that one eyebrow raised again.

"Yes, Jediah?" she replied softly.

"I'm thinking you must be feeling a bit better today."

"Hmm... Imagine that."

Chapter Twenty-Three

About two o'clock Alexandra's cell phone rang. Detective Mokros stated they would be dropping by in a few minutes. When they arrived, Officer Johnson spoke first.

"Ms. Higgins, do you have further information to share with us?"

"Yes. I was answering the door this morning expecting Mr. Saffle. It was just like the night I was taken. As I answered the door, I had a flash of memory. Instead of being Jediah that night, it was Tom Magis. I know Tom from high school back in Wheeling. As soon as I saw him, he shoved me backwards and placed a cloth over my mouth and nose. After that everything went black."

"So, now you are telling us you remember the person who abducted you and it was Tom Magis from Wheeling?"

"Yes. I called as soon as I remembered."

"Do you remember anything else?"

"No. I'm sorry if you were expecting more."

"Why would Mr. Magis want to abduct you?" the detective asked.

"I've thought about that quite a bit, and I truly have no idea. As I told Mr. Saffle, we barely knew each other. When we were in high school, we hung around in different circles. I wasn't even aware he knew I existed until three years ago."

"What happened then?"

"He suddenly appeared and wanted to go out with me. It was during a time in my life when I was going through some personal problems and I declined."

"That was it?"

"Well, he didn't bow out gracefully, he kept asking and asking. I gave him my reasons for not wanting to get involved, but that didn't deter him one bit. I finally went back to college at Bryn Mawr and the distance seemed to have cooled his heels. I didn't hear from him again."

"If you don't mind my asking, what type of personal problems were you going through at the time?" asked Officer Johnson.

"I don't mind you asking. It never leaves my mind anyway." Alexandra took in a deep breath, expelled the air, and began, "I was at college when the accident that killed my parents happened. A huge sinkhole swallowed our house. My parents were crushed and died instantly."

Officer Johnson nodded. "I remember that story from the newspapers. The whole section of road from Wheeling to St. Clairsville, Ohio was closed for quite a while. It turned out the coal company had undercut further than anyone suspected, and sinkholes littered the whole area. I'm sorry for your loss, Ms. Higgins."

"Thank you, Officer Johnson."

"Ms. Higgins," asked Detective Mokros, "didn't you receive a multi-million dollar settlement from the coal company?"

She lowered her eyes. "Yes, I did."

The detective continued, watching Alexandra closely. "Tom Magis was found under dubious circumstances yesterday."

"He was?" Alexandra said. "I just saw him the other day."

"You did?" the Detective queried, now very intent.

"No, I misspoke, I'm sorry. I still can't believe almost six weeks has passed. I'm sorry, Detective, it was when I went back to Wheeling to pack my apartment and move here that I saw Tom. My friend Cassie Hudson and I were having lunch and he came to our table to say hello. I still have trouble with the fact he was the one who abducted me."

"That is exactly what Ms. Hudson stated last evening."

"You talked to Cassie? I'm sorry, Detective, I'm having a hard time following you."

"Ms. Hudson mentioned to us a few days ago that Tom Magis seemed perturbed about something when he came to your table. We were checking into his background and getting ready to speak to him, when we received a call from his neighbor who reported hearing a horrifying scream. The neighbor thought someone had died. We found him unconscious in his boat docked behind his residence."

The police officers' attention now centered on Alexandra, who looked from one officer to the other. "I'm sorry if you are waiting for a response from me because I don't seem to have one," Alexandra stated. "I'm still trying to process the information. I just figured out Tom was responsible for my abduction and now you tell me you found him unconscious?"

"That's right, Ms. Higgins," Detective Mokros stated. "Do you know what happened to him?"

"No. I don't even know what happened to me."

"Then," he said reaching into his pocket, "do you know anything about these items?"

Detective Mokros held her necklace, earrings and her mother's ring in his hand.

Unable to control the flood of emotion, tears began to flow. She gasped, "My mother's ring. I thought it was lost forever."

"I can't return these items to you now; they're considered evidence in your case, but they will be returned as soon as possible. We found them in the cabin of Tom Magis' boat. We believe Magis held you captive there."

Shaking her head, she responded, "I just don't remember."

"There is evidence someone was held there against their will. We expect to find your DNA as proof it was you. There are a few items we can't explain: How you got away from him; how you got home; and how Mr. Magis ended up knocked out. It's a long way from Wheeling to Waynesburg, and we think you would have needed assistance. Who helped you escape?"

Alexandra did not respond.

"Ms. Higgins, we will find out what happened, one way or another." He handed her some paperwork and stated as he rose to leave, "You'll need to complete this paperwork. One is your official statement, the other, in case you need to file a complaint."

"Thank you."

As Jediah and she watched them leave, Alexandra was aware of the edge on which she perched. Knowing the answers to questions derived from Jediah's tale, and answering those same questions as if she had no knowledge of them proved to be a dance she had no wish to continue.

"Jediah, I wish you hadn't told me about Ryeth and what happened to me."

"Alexandra, I couldn't lie to you."

"Well, I feel like I'm lying to the police."

"I think I can ease your anguish a little. What if I were to tell you the Waynesburg Police have known everything the Sensates knew from the beginning?"

"What do you mean, 'everything'?"

"We have a Sensate on the police force who has been involved in all Sensate activities regarding your disappearance. It's our way of nondisclosure and keeping within the boundaries of the law. If this Sensate deems our activities morally wrong or criminally unjust, we answer for our involvement. Without divulging our existence, we ensure our 'white lies' harm no one."

The tension in her neck started to ease. "I'm glad you told me. It's a thin line we walk, isn't it?"

"Yes. Even after all my years experience, I still catch myself easing into areas where I should not go. We can accomplish far more than the average person can, therefore, our boundaries need to be clearly marked. We demand high moral fiber and expect it of each Sensate. I found myself pushed to the limit during your absence and almost crossed a line without thinking."

"But you seem to have such control," she said.

"Not where you are concerned," he replied as he slid his arm around her.

A silvery orb encased them and she felt it gliding soft as a whisper.

I have a surprise for you, Alexandra.

You are a surprise to me.

Look!

The front of the orb cleared, and she could see outside. They were on her mountain. Greg's crew was finishing up for the day. If she needed proof that time had gone by, then this was it. The footprint was clearly visible with foundation walls up, framing had begun, and construction materials piled high. The base of the wind turbine was taking shape and she saw the pump and tank for the water system, evidence that the spring had passed all tests. Completion was within reach.

She noted the arbor. The trimmed areas had filled in nicely with new leaves. It looked like it had in her dreams.

Jediah, thank you for bringing me to my mountain, this place is home to me.

A few more months should see you living here. Greg pushed up his timetable and has two complete crews working.

The orb window closed and, for a few seconds, she knew they were moving again. Jediah put his arm around Alexandra. When the window opened, she didn't recognize where they were.

A small window dimly lit the room. The wet, moldy odor reminded her of a swamp with rotting vegetation.

Where are we?

Look closer.

Alexandra saw the table, chairs, and bed; then her eyes went wide as she saw the chain bolted to the floorboards.

Oh, was I here?

Yes. Do you remember it?

No, not at all, and I'm glad I don't. This is worse than a bad dream. Get me out of here.

The window closed and a few seconds later, they were back in the bungalow.

"Jediah, I can't imagine why he did that to me."

"Officer Johnson thinks it might have had something to do with your money."

"Oh. I put that money out of my mind for so long I sometimes forget it's there. Jediah, I know I'm changing the subject somewhat, but after searching for me and the key with such a vengeance, why did Ryeth let me go?"

"Remember earlier when I told you that where you are concerned I seem to have trouble maintaining my moral boundaries?"

"Yes."

"I was wondering the same thing, and wanted to know if we had anything to fear from Ryeth; I caught myself wanting, no, almost entering his mind to get the answers. It was within our boundaries to search his mind to find you, but I consider it crossing the line to invade his thoughts after you were safe. It was also easy to see he meant you no harm once he found you."

"Perhaps he has given up his need for revenge."

"Maybe, for now."

"He did frighten me when he tried to take the key. I'd like to know more about him. Do you know anything?"

"He was thinking about his past right before he touched on you. He thought about the incident that caused the Sensates to shun him. Keep in mind, this was back in the fifteen hundreds, and times were quite a bit different than they are now."

"So he was ostracized from the group?"

"Yes. He was just beginning to receive instructions on what he was and how to use his powers, so he really had no idea what was going to happen to him. When he was seventeen, the town's people attempted to burn him at the stake for being a warlock, but he escaped because he accidentally moved to another place. Although he didn't understand what took him from one place to another, the action saved his life. After that episode, he sought the solace of the woods choosing to live away from others. It was during this time he developed his powers. He must have achieved the higher degree of Ultra to have lived this long; we know he is very powerful."

"What a terrible childhood!"

Jediah brought her a snack of cheese, crackers, grapes, and strawberries, accompanied by a tall glass of tea. After eating, Jediah encouraged her to rest, and while she dozed, he sought William.

* * * * *

Jediah found William at Balisier amid younger Sensates deeply engrossed in the fine art of looking back into past memories. There were only a handful of Sensates who possessed this ability and none came close to William's strength. William gave them an exercise to practice among themselves then excused himself to speak with Jediah.

"How is Alexandra?" the elder inquired.

"She's doing much better. She's asking questions about Ryeth."

"That's to be expected, Jediah. I'm sure she is wrestling with mixed emotions regarding him; I know I am."

"I wonder at his agenda. Where do we stand as a group in our treatment of him? I don't know whether to be grateful or to assume he has ulterior motives."

William said, "I guess we will wait and see. In the meantime, we need to concentrate our efforts into strengthening the core abilities as you suggested. What a difference I see in our people! They are energized. I was so wrong in thinking they might not like being singled out into groups. The process has truly invigorated everyone to reach their full potential."

"Who has been acting as scribe for our knowledge center?"

"I selected David Stillion."

"He's a fine choice, William. David has the skills to compile and organize abilities with distinct keywords for comprehensive searches."

"I've asked him to also write a program to mix

and match abilities that might achieve a common goal."

"After the team completes the fake façade of our secure area I'll complete the interior."

"The excavation is nearly complete," William said. "The entry you came up with should detract our people from questioning the stone removal. I doubt anyone will suspect our little hideaway."

"Good. Keep me posted."

Jediah checked on Alexandra and noted she was still asleep, so he took the opportunity to drive into town and pick up two antipasto salads and some spumoni ice cream from Pizza Villa. Half an hour later, he arrived just as his sleeping beauty arose.

"Feel better?" he asked with a glorious smile.

"Yes, I don't think I've slept this much in years."

"You need your rest. Your delightful little body took some nasty blows."

"I have a delightful little body? Have you been spying on me?"

"No more than usual," Jediah eluded.

Blushing, Alexandra didn't reply.

"You're no fun," he said.

"Am too, you don't spy on me really, do you?"

"If you ever finished your knowledge sessions with my mother you would know the answer to that question without even asking."

"Hah, I didn't think so. You just like to tease me to see me blush."

"I think red is my favorite color on you."

"One of these days you will get your

comeuppance, and I hope to be the one giving it to you, or at the very least, see that you get it."

"Mighty feisty words, especially aimed at the one carrying supper."

"You have food?"

And there the battle of words ended.

Chapter Twenty-Four

The following day Dr. Jellan stopped by to see how Alexandra progressed. Checking the marks on her back, arms, and legs, he pronounced her healing quite nicely, and reported that there was only a very slight chance of scarring in those areas. The majority of her bruises were starting to turn yellow at the edges, which he stated was a good sign of healing. He indicated that the area around her ankle would most likely be the last to heal due to the infection. He encouraged her to keep up with the antibiotics and salve.

"Ms. Higgins...," he said.

"Please call me Alexandra."

"Thank you, I shall. Now, Alexandra, I want to talk to you a little bit about what happened to you. I have the results of your blood work back from the laboratory."

He donned a very sober look. "First of all, I think we were very lucky you weren't under his machinations much longer. He had been spiking your food and water with a drug called Kandasil."

"I've never heard of it," she said.

"It's not common, as a matter of fact, if I hadn't specifically requested a panel for dissociative drugs, we probably never would have found it. The drug is made by crushing the dried flowers of the Tamarack Larch, which is a rare tree found here in

Pennsylvania. Used as a powder, it can be mixed with water or sprinkled on food, and has no noticeable taste."

"What did the drug do to me?"

"It can induce a death-like state of sleep, visual distortions, confusion, slurred speech, feelings of paralysis, loss of memory, and delirium."

"That's probably why I don't remember."

"I'm sure that's the case."

"Does this mean I'll never remember, or can those memories come back later?"

"I would assume you will never remember; that could be a godsend. Now, there's one other use for this drug, it would have rendered you highly susceptible to suggestions."

"Why would he want to do that?"

"To get you to do something you would not ordinarily do, and to outsiders it would look like you were a willing participant. It is my opinion that he was working with different dosages, and once he found one that allowed you to function normally, yet would maintain his hold over you, he would have achieved his goal."

"How atrocious, what a twisted mind."

"Long-term use of this drug can cause Dissociative Identity Disorder, or Schizophrenia, and death. His far reaching goal may not have been to kill you but to make you incapacitated by mental defect, then all that you possess, and you, would be his."

"Will I suffer any of these conditions in the future?"

"I don't believe so. I'm not seeing any

indications presently, and it would appear it is flushing out of your system nicely. Since I found only small amounts in the drug panel we won't even need to do any follow-up labs."

"Thank you for taking the time to explain this in detail."

"I've submitted a formal report to Detective Mokros to include in your file."

"Dr. Jellan, while under the influence of this drug, could I have overpowered my abductor and harmed him?"

"Highly unlikely, in that state of mind he would have convinced you that you deserved the beatings; you may have even asked him to beat you. And, if he was working on coercion like I suspect, you would have actually liked him and no doubt even protected him."

"This is all so sick and ugly. Now that the pieces are fitting together, I think I can put this monstrous puzzle behind me."

"Do you have any further questions for me?"

"I don't think so. Thank you for dropping by; it was so nice of you to make the house call."

"It wasn't a problem at all. I had a few minutes between patients and was certain you would want to hear the results of the labs. Have a wonderful day, Alexandra." And with that said, he vanished into thin air!

She gasped, and then broke out laughing. Dr. Jellan was a Sensate!

What a delightful group of people she met since she came to Waynesburg. Back in Wheeling, she had few people she would call acquaintances, but the people of Waynesburg were beginning to feel like friends. Her parents would have loved Waynesburg and her mountain.

She went to the bathroom and looked in the mirror, a face not ready for public stared back at her. Well, although she didn't present well, she felt better, and wanted to get into something. Maybe it was time to get back on track with Nancy Jane.

She read *Eragon* the remainder of the morning, called Cassie, had lunch, then took a walk the few steps to Larkspur and knocked on the door. She heard a familiar voice in her mind.

Come in Alexandra. I've been expecting you. Use your senses to locate me.

Can you hear me?

Certainly, child.

Entering the mansion, Alexandra took a few moments to notice the beautiful woodwork in the foyer. It had the deep luster of years of polishing and smelled of linseed oil. The sheers under the draperies had threads so fine the slightest breeze started a rippling movement that appeared as soft as the flutter of butterfly wings. The tiles on the floor where she stood were ivory with a pale design of reddish-brown inset in the center. As she scrutinized the design, it dawned on her that it was a larger version of the one on her shoulder.

As she continued her way to the parlor, she spied photographs all along the mantle of a huge fireplace.

They are all relatives, Alexandra. I value family and friends above all else.

Although she wanted to explore every picture

in detail, she maintained her path to the parlor and finally to Nancy Jane.

"Alexandra, you look a bit the worse for wear, but you are still a very pleasing sight to these tired old eyes. Come here and let me take a good look at you." She held out both hands to her.

Taking Nancy Jane's hands in hers, she knelt before the stylish elder woman who possessed so much grace. Raising her eyes to those that held the wisdom of the ages, she replied, "Mrs. Saffle, it's good to be back."

"Ah, that Magis was a vicious man. One as tender as you should never have been subjected to his cruelties. Did he hurt your spirit as he hurt your body?"

"I don't believe so. Dr. Jellan said it was good I had no memories of the events, and I'm inclined to believe him. I don't wish to be a receptacle for memories of that sort."

"Good girl." She patted her hands. "It's time we begin."

She took a seat in a comfy chair across from Nancy Jane.

What followed was a partial history of Sensates.

"The first Sensate to develop her senses was an indigenous American from the Iroquois tribe named Onatah, which means 'Daughter of the Earth'. From an early age, Onatah had a connection to the world around her that was decidedly different from the other children of the tribe. The medicine man, Otetiani, 'He is Prepared', saw the usefulness in having her by his side which made his medicine

stronger.

Onatah enjoyed a childhood of wonder. Birds flew to her shoulders and sang, deer ate from her hand, and small animals came to her feet. It was said she could talk to the Earth. All the Iroquois people held her in high regard. When it was time for her to take a mate, she chose a strong brave, Kangee, 'Raven'. As time went on Onatah shared more of her abilities with her husband, but as he learned the extent of Onatah's strange powers, he became frightened. Kangee could not stand the blow to his pride. He spread evil stories about Onatah, playing on the superstitious nature of those in his tribe.

Before long, they drove Onatah from the village. She took refuge in the caves, and when she delivered the baby she was carrying, a mark appeared on Onatah's shoulder. Many moons later, the same mark appeared on the child she named Genotah, Raven of the Earth. Onatah and Genotah spent hours each day practicing the use of their gifts, until one day, Onatah discovered she could move from one place to another. She discussed this strange event with Genotah, and before long, Genotah could move through the air as easily as Onatah.

They realized the need to keep their gifts secret if they wanted the protection of the tribe, so they made a pact never to share their abilities with another. They eventually moved to a distant Iroquois camp and both found husbands. After many years, and many babies, they appeared as young as when they had entered the camp, yet their husbands grew old. The women made themselves appear older using soot to create wrinkles and dye to grey their hair. Before the tribe discovered their ruse, they left camp and joined another, leaving the children and husbands behind. Onatah and Genotah lived thusly for many, many generations.

The seeds of the Sensates' recessive genes had been planted in many camps throughout the area we now call New England, and as far north as Iceland.

Many decades later, disguised as older women, they reentered tribes they had lived in before and sought others like themselves. Onatah and Genotah were very careful to select only those who had good hearts and who wished no evil to join them. Each swore an oath to protect the group from discovery. This Sensate core grew and eventually settled in what is now Waynesburg."

"Our current Sensate group is spread out from Iceland to Alaska, but can be convened in a split second if need be."

"What an extraordinary beginning of our people," Alexandra said. "Although I don't believe I can include this in my genealogy research."

"I would think not," Nancy Jane replied with a wink.

"I only gave you the condensed version. Once you meet our group you should seek our storyteller, Hazel, for the complete version. Hazel is a gifted Sensate who commits our history to memory. If she tells you a story, you can rest assured she's told it verbatim. Our history is well-guarded; there's no telling what the outside world would do with the knowledge if we were ever discovered."

"But I can also see the good we could do," Alexandra said.

"As do we all. And that's what makes you special. You will be torn, as I have been, all your life between the two worlds that must exist to protect our kind. If you didn't have the turmoil between the two, you wouldn't be the person meant for this gift. Your path ahead is not an easy one, but one that you are worthy to travel. Never forget that. And now, let us explore your sense of sight."

Nancy Jane talked non-stop for over four hours during which time she encouraged Alexandra to try some of the abilities as she instructed her how to use the mechanism. After she practiced and achieved the ability, Nancy Jane gave her enhancements to the ability that made it a split second task instead of one that took much thought and preparation.

She learned to think of all the senses as multi-dimensional, and not to picture them as flat lines. Sight could be seeing an item literally, or to viewing into the past or present. Sight could be a visual perception or the complete range of a mental vision. It could be the tiniest atom or the rays of the sun. Alexandra learned to use the internal mechanism that controlled her sight in small increments or to use it over a grand scheme.

The lesson that stuck in her mind the most was using the orb to see. She merely had to close her eyes, picture the orb in her mind, and open a window to view whatever she liked.

When she arrived in the bungalow after the lessons that day, she experimented a bit on her own.

She hadn't asked if it was permissible, and perhaps she should have, but the ache to see her parents won out.

She sat quietly in a comfy chair in the living room, and closed her eyes. The gazebo in Wheeling Park came into view, and in a few seconds, her parents and she arrived for a picnic lunch. They were all so happy. Her mother had packed chipped ham sandwiches from Islay's and chocolate milk. They would sit in the wooden gazebo, watch a train go by as they ate their sandwiches and then pack up and go back home. She supposed those days were some of the happiest they'd spent together. Her dad looked so relaxed, and her mom actually sparkled. Her parents held hands as they walked back to the car.

As she let the orb window fade, she felt the ache in her heart grow as tears filled her eyes. The pain of loss was as great as it had been the day they died. She couldn't control the sobbing. It hurt too much. Although she had partially healed from the loss, the window had opened a new wound.

An hour later, she was able to look back on the episode with new respect. Not all Sensate powers should be used discriminately. Some things were best left alone. She laughed out loud when another of her dad's sayings hit home, 'there's no sense in looking up a dead horse's ass'. How right he was.

Her lessons with sight continued for almost two weeks and at the end of that time, she was strong mentally and physically. When she looked in the mirror, she saw her old physical self healing nicely, but knew she possessed much greater inner strength.

Alexandra spent most evenings with Jediah. On one of those evenings, she asked him, "What do you do when you are not here?"

"Oh, you mean, what do I do for a living?"

"Yes."

"Now, or before?"

"Oh, I never thought of that. How about both?"

"Okay, let's see. I was born in 1781 so when I was ten..."

"Jediah, stop." Her eyes widened.

"Why stop?" he said with just the hint of a smile.

"1781?"

"Yes?"

She performed a fast calculation. "You are two hundred-thirty years old?"

"I am."

"Okay, wait just a minute here." She thought a second and then said, "We have a lot more to discuss here than your past jobs."

He smiled at her awe. "What would you like to know?"

"Let's just start with the normal questions a female asks a male when they are dating."

"Are we dating?" he inquired, raising that one wicked eyebrow.

She flamed red from her toes to the roots of her hair. "Are you married?" she forced from clenched lips.

"No."

"Have you ever been married?"

"You are asking this of a virile man in his prime who has lived on this earth for two hundred-thirty years?"

"Answer the question, Buck-o."

"No," he said.

"No, you're not going to answer the question, or no, you haven't been married?"

"Which would you prefer it to be?"

"Don't you dare answer my question with a question."

"Alexandra," he said in a soothing burr, "might ye be a bit Irish?"

"Oh, you! Can't you just answer the question?"

"Shouldn't it be enough to know I'm not married at this moment?"

"At this moment, like yesterday's moment you were? No, it isn't." Oh, he could really raise her hackles!

"Well, then, what's it to be, a different question, or am I to go mute." He leaned back into the cushions.

"Do you have any children?"

"Now you are questioning my honor and morals?"

"Are you refusing to answer that one too?"

"Och, now lassie, if you don't settle a bit you are going to turn your lovely blond hair red."

How did he do it? His Scottish burr was perfect, right down to the soft T's and rolling R's. He was both irritating and delightful, she had to admit. "You're not one bit cute."

"I am too, my mother told me so," Jediah said with such a pathetic pout, Alexandra burst out laughing.

"Ah, now that's the smile I love to see," he

said.

"You do know that I'll have the answers to my questions one day, don't you?"

"I do, just not today." He smiled brilliantly.

"Then tell me about the jobs." She resigned herself to the information he was willing to give.

"Okay, let's see, when I was ten, I helped my father distill our corn into whiskey. We were so far over the mountains that containers of whiskey were easier to transport than the corn. I cut tobacco for a few years, worked on a riverboat hauling goods up and down the Ohio, worked on a fishing boat, farmed some cotton and tobacco, dug coal in the West Virginia hills, set typeface for a newspaper, and ran wire for the telegraph company. I rode the Pony Express route for two years, worked on the railroad laying track, built bridges, designed buildings, worked in a pretzel factory, and trained horses. Now, I own a small engineering company that pretty much runs itself."

"You lost me at Pony Express rider. For some reason I can't get that image out of my mind," she said. What a life he had lived.

"It was a great job if you didn't mind smelling like a horse twenty-four hours a day. Eau de Horse Sweat and being fast in the saddle were not real good come-ons for the ladies," he said with a grin.

Laughing, Alexandra commented, "No, I don't suppose they were." She sobered. "What happened to your father?"

"I was twelve, we had a lot of rain that year and the mosquitoes went rampant. There was an outbreak of Yellow Fever in 1793, Dad didn't survive."

"I'm sorry. It must have been hard for you and Nancy Jane after that."

"Everyone worked from morning to night. I was no exception, I worked our farm and the neighbor's farm; we were just trying to survive. Mom and Dad were both Sensates, so our lives were better than most. Because of their abilities, over the seventeen years they were together, they were able to save $500, which was a fortune back then. The government started a land grant in 1792, which allowed people to purchase land for twenty cents an acre. We used the money to buy 2,500 acres here in Waynesburg. Of course, it wasn't nearly as populated back then as it is now."

"Then Larkspur was part of that land package?"

"Yes, it was. We've been here quite a while, though every fifty years or so, we relocate to a different place, and then in another fifty years, move back again. We try to stay out of the limelight and the newspapers."

"Oh no, guess I messed that up."

"Correction, Magis messed it up," he said.

"Agreed."

A thought began to form in her mind. "Jediah, if you are two hundred-thirty, the picture I received in Teater's packet must be a picture of Teater and you. Am I right? Did you know Teater personally?"

"Yes." She sensed, more than saw, his lips tightening.

"What? Yes? You knew Teater and you didn't tell me?" Her excitement escalated and her anger riled.

"Guilty as charged."

"Why didn't you tell me?" She couldn't believe he withheld that information from her all that time.

"I guess I always felt the timing was wrong."

She stood and paced in front of him. "Is the timing wrong now?"

"It could be better." He admitted.

"Oh, you're doing it to me. You are answering my questions like I answered Detective Mokros when he asked me how I escaped and how I got home. You're answering my questions without any real commitment."

"That's a very good assessment."

Oh, how irritating! "Why are you doing it to me?" she asked, now perturbed.

"Partly out of habit, but mostly because I've not been given the permission to speak about some aspects of him."

"You need permission to talk about my ancestor with me?" That question sounded idiotic. What type of oath could bind someone from beyond the grave?

"Yes and no. I can talk about him, but some questions I can't answer."

"Who placed this restriction on you?" she asked.

"He did."

She thought for a second. "Oh, then he can never remove it. Okay, I'll just ask away. How did he die?"

"I can't answer that."

"Why did he leave Wheeling, his wife and two sons?"

"Because he was a Sensate and he had a major role to play in our future. He spent his lifetime fulfilling a vision to ensure the safety of all Sensates."

"What was that vision?"

"You." He looked directly in her eyes.

How could one word land so heavily on her? "He spent his lifetime ensuring I would be here at this place and time?" Disbelief shrouded her.

"Yes."

So the puzzle did weave all around her. "Who were the parents of 'Infant Higgins' buried in the cemetery?" she asked pointedly.

"I can't answer that."

"I'm having trouble grasping this. Were you and Teater close?"

"Yes, very, like brothers."

She could see the pain beginning to surface in his eyes. "Jediah," she said, a bit exasperated, "I don't wish to cause you pain, but I have so many questions. This is so hard…"

"It's a little tough on me too. I'm trying to figure out if Teater knew how much pressure he was putting on me by making his requests."

"I don't want you to compromise on your oath, but I've been wondering about him for several years and finally have before me someone who knew him personally. It seems a bit like 'here's a candy bar, don't eat it' kind of thing."

"You are almost as cute when you are bewildered as you are when you're befuddled."

"Thanks, I think." She decided not to put too much pressure on their friendship. "We're not through with this conversation yet. I need to think about this."

"I understand," he said. "Now, I have a question for you."

"Go ahead."

"Would you like to go out on a date to the Silk City Diner and have a Bacon Cheeseburger, French fries and gravy, and a black and white shake?"

Her mouth watered. She'd wanted those French fries for days. "I thought you'd never ask. But don't think this gets you off the hook regarding Teater. I'll have my answers one way or another."

"I don't doubt you one bit."

* * * * *

Two agents sat on a bench in Waynesburg Park next to the university. "Ray, is this getting weird or what?" Terry asked.

Ray responded, "Yeah. It's just what the boss has been looking for. Magis found just minutes after the scream and the cabin door locked from the inside. Who locked it and how did they get out?"

"The neighbor saw nothing and nobody; I believe he's telling the truth," said Terry."

"So do I." Ray agreed. "The second big question is: How did the girl get from Wheeling back to Waynesburg? She said 'she just arrived'. Judging from the lab report she was probably still under the influence of the drugs, so, either someone helped her, or she was transported by divine intervention."

"So how did she escape that sadist and how did she get home if no one else was around?"

"Only one answer; she must have had help. It had to be another from their group." Ray decided.

"I vote for Saffle," Terry said. He's way too calm for my tastes."

"Yeah, he gets my vote too."

The two agents rose and walked off in different directions.

* * * * *

Chapter Twenty-Five

The water from the pulsating shower nozzle beat down like mini-massage fingers. Tension had set up camp on the top of Alexandra's head, a direct result of the constant worry of making a 'sense' mistake. With her eyes closed, she refused to move from the hot water's pounding until the muscles eased.

Can you hear me? The voice was faint.

Really? In the shower? She turned off the water and grabbed a towel.

Can you hear me? Barely a whisper. Alexandra sensed fear. A cold chill ran through her.

Yes. Yes, I can hear you. She wrapped herself in the towel, stepped out of the shower and waited for a response. None came. *I can hear you. Hello?*

No... The voice faded and was gone. Alexandra reached out extending as much as she could but could not reconnect.

Something was terribly wrong. Someone needed help. She tried reaching out, but received no response. She phoned Jediah as soon as she dressed.

"Did you hear the call that asked 'can you hear me'?" she inquired.

"No, I heard no such call," he said.

She rubbed her wet hair with a towel, then said,

"I know I heard it. I was in the shower. The voice was faint, but it was still there."

"What exactly did it say?" he asked.

"Just 'can you hear me' and 'no'."

"Let me ask the others." He was quiet for a few minutes, then said, "No one heard anything."

"Could it be someone playing a trick on me?" she asked.

"We don't do those type of things, normally. Do you think it could've been Ryeth?"

"I never thought of him. I don't think so. It was almost a whisper, and whoever it was, I sensed their fear. I can't imagine Ryeth showing fear."

"I'll have the others keep an ear out."

"Okay, I guess that's the best I can do. Say, since I have you on the line, what do you think about inviting Cassie and John up for the weekend? I'd love to see her and meet John."

"Sounds like a great idea, as long as you're up for it."

"I think I'm ready. The areas outside my clothing have healed so I don't look too bad," she said.

"I agree, and everywhere else?"

"Still black and blue a little, but nothing hurts anymore."

"Okay. Give them the call."

As her spirits lifted, she ended one call and began another.

It had been almost six weeks since her return to the bungalow and although she and Cassie spoke regularly it couldn't compare to the elation that filled her when she was with Cassie.

They arrived late Friday evening.. Cassie bolted from the car leaving John several paces behind, and flew into the arms of her best friend.

"Alexandra, you look wonderful."

"And you look fulfilled."

"Does it show?" Cassie asked.

"Oh my," she whispered, "you're in love with him!"

"Shh, here he comes." Cassie grabbed John by the arm and said, "Alexandra, this is John Ryan; John, my best friend, Alexandra."

"I'm so very pleased to meet you, John. Cassie has told me all about you, but surely there's something she's left out that you'll be able to share over the weekend."

"I'm afraid she's been as thorough telling me everything about you. I'll have to admit, it sure is good to have you back where you belong."

"Thank you, John. Welcome, both of you, to Larkspur. Bring your things and I'll show you two where to hang your hats."

"Allie, this place is beautiful, like it was snatched from another time. I half expect fine ladies with parasols to be walking amid this garden. When John and I were here during your abduction, I didn't notice how lovely it truly was. Mom and Dad won't believe it."

John added, "The architecture is remarkable. The bungalow is a perfect companion to the main house."

Just then, Alexandra spotted Jediah heading straight for them. Since Cassie and John where already inside the bungalow, Jediah slipped his arm around Alexandra and kissed her soundly. "You are sparkling like a Christmas tree ornament. It's wonderful to see you so happy."

"The most important people in the world are here with me right now. I can tell Cassie just adores John. I am so very happy for them."

Alexandra helped Cassie take their things to the extra bedroom while Jediah sat with John in the living room. When Alexandra introduced Cassie to Sebastian, it was love at first sight. The little male bird was totally fascinated with the dark-haired bobbin.

In no time at all Sebastian was showing his true colors. He was king of the room and he knew it. He would let out a wolf whistle, then say 'hello,' then switch to 'I love you', and add another wolf whistle. Cassie and John were amused, but Alexandra was looking questioningly at Jediah, who shrugged his shoulders like a kid with his hand caught in a cookie jar. Pretty soon Sebastian tired of his tricks, so Jediah took him back to his cage.

Jediah returned with a glass of wine for each, then grabbed the prepared tray of various cheeses, grapes, crackers, and apple slices.

The two couples told stories and reminisced until midnight. They agreed on breakfast at the diner at eight the next morning followed by a tour of her mountain.

After Jediah bid them goodnight Cassie got John situated in the guest bedroom. Cassie shared her bed, which gave the two who had been inseparable from kindergarten the chance they needed to talk about their male companions until nearly 4 AM.

A particularly tender topic came up about 3 AM when Cassie inquired about Jediah's past.

"He's so gorgeous, how did he escape the marriage noose?"

She shook her head. "I don't know that he has."

"What do you mean?" Cassie asked seemingly alarmed.

"I asked him if he was married before and he won't answer me. I asked him if he has children and he wouldn't answer that question either."

"That's odd. Why would he keep that information from you?"

"I don't know if he's seriously hiding something or intentionally trying to provoke me. He can be a little devilish at times."

"Well, he doesn't act like he has anything to hide. He seems like a well-balanced, honest-to-goodness knight on a white horse to me."

Dreamy eyed, Alexandra replied, "Yes, he seems like that to me too. And Cassie, John is so wonderful. I couldn't have picked a better man for you if I had been doing the selecting myself. He's devoted to you."

Cassie rolled on her back and stared at the ceiling. "I couldn't be any happier. He was so supportive when you went missing. I was a basket case and he was the friend I'd lost. I hope Jediah is the same for you."

"I know we'll be together for a long time, I feel it inside, and it's solid and strong. I think he feels the same way, but after the incident with Tom, he sometimes handles me with kid gloves."

"I can tell he's totally smitten with you," Cassie said. "When you're not looking, his eyes are constantly on you. I get the feeling he's memorizing every detail of your face, the way you move, and the way you speak."

"We're lucky to have such remarkable men in our lives. Let's turn in or we'll have ugly marks around our eyes tomorrow. Night, Cassie."

"Night, Allie, sweet dreams."

She thought, 'you have no idea.'

Getting the most sleep in the bungalow, John was the first to awaken, so he made coffee and quickly showered. When they emerged for the day, the girls found him outside sitting under the oak tree with Jediah talking away like old friends.

Jediah ushered all into a shiny black Hummer; they entered the diner a few minutes later.

The Super-Starter Breakfast Special with pancakes, sausage, eggs, hash browns, toast, and coffee claimed John and Jediah. The girls opted for fresh fruit and western omelets with toast and tea. All were sated when they started up the road toward her mountain.

"Wow, the road is so much nicer, said Cassie. John, when we came up here the first time, I don't know how we made it without breaking an axle."

"It's beautiful, Alexandra," John said thoughtfully, "I can see why you love it so."

"I was caught in this mountain's web of allure the very first time I came here," she confessed.

"I thought you were caught in a cistern," quipped Jediah.

"Stinker, you know what I mean," she said

pointedly at Jediah, blushing.

Jediah turned to Cassie. "You need to speak to your friend. She's forever labeling me, and I find this last one, 'stinker', totally misrepresents me."

Cassie grinned. "Jediah, somehow I think you two have met your match. You seem more than capable of fending for yourself."

"Ouch!" exclaimed Jediah, feigning injury. "The women are sticking together. John, can I count on you for support?"

"No way, Jediah, it's every man for himself, and I have no wish to rock the boat I'm in. It seems your lady fair has some underlying bone to pick with you. You will have to fish or cut bait, the choice is up to you."

They continued with good-natured banter until the jubilant foursome reached the top in high spirits.

"Smell that air? I should bottle it and sell it in New York City," Alexandra said.

"It is really fresh up here," John noted, "like the faint smell of a florist's shop."

Cassie looked wide-eyed at John. "That's exactly it."

"What? You're amazed at my keen nose?" He asked Cassie.

Cassie leaned into him. "Yes, that and the rest of you too." They held hands and walked toward the construction.

John continued, "Alexandra, you've got a lot going on all at the same time up here. Your builder must manage his subcontractors well."

Jediah fielded John's statement. "Gregg Construction has a great reputation in these parts for quality work and speedy timelines. I know Greg personally and he is a master at scheduling. I've never met anyone better."

"The site is so neat. You can view any operation and see what comes next. It's going to be a beautiful home, Alexandra," John concluded.

Jediah and Alexandra walked hand-in-hand reviewing Greg's progress while John and Cassie explored on their own.

"I really don't know very much about you. What were you like as a little boy?" Alexandra asked.

"Precocious, I suppose," he replied. "Working the farm there wasn't much time to get into trouble and with both parents being Sensates, I got caught every time I stepped over the line."

"That paints a cute picture. No little boy tricks at all, huh?"

"They knew before I even began, and usually asked, 'are you certain you wish to go down that path?' Talk about being under scrutiny. They gave new meaning to 'having eyes in the back of your head.' I thought all parents were like mine and I could never understand why other kids got away with all their minor infractions where I could never achieve even one. I figured either I was born completely without brains, or my parents were very different from other parents."

"How old were you when you found out the latter?"

"Sixteen. I was so relieved to find out I wasn't dumber than a bread box."

"You poor thing!" She laughed.

Jediah stopped and pulled her close. "I love your mountain. You've chosen the site for the house well. It will be beautiful up here."

"Thanks. What a generous gift from Teater. I still can't believe it's real. Do you have any suggestions?"

"Only one, I suggest you develop a secondary access. While Greg is here, ask him to cut one through the woods for you. Disguise both ends, the one from the top and the access from the bottom. The middle section can be finished as you wish, even paved. A home should be safe and always have an escape route."

"That's a good idea. I would never have thought of it. I could have been trapped up here."

"You could always escape danger by moving to a secure area using your senses, but if you needed to escape and guard against detection, a secondary access is the only way to go."

"I'll mention it to Greg on Monday," she said.

They reached the arbor and sat beneath the scented overhanging vines. Soon, John and Cassie joined them.

"Magnificent, Alexandra!" stated John.

"I can hardly believe it's the same place," Cassie said. "You did a fantastic job on this arbor. It was just a jumble of vines. It's a real treasure, with such a glorious breeze."

"I'm hoping the breeze will be enough to run the generator and have some left over for storage."

"Maybe you should take some wind measurements before you completely negate bringing power up here," John said.

"The turbine I selected will gather power as low as three to five miles per hour wind velocity; the average for this area is fifteen to eighteen. Perhaps I should have researched the storage criteria better."

"Not to worry, green-eyed girl." Jediah said. "Everything was measured and checked and rechecked by Greg before he began installation. He determined you would have enough to run one and a half times your normal usage for this house."

"Sounds like your battery system will work out fine," said Cassie.

"Hmm, we'll see," she said glancing at Jediah. John and Cassie turned to look at him too.

Unable to contain the pride he felt in Alexandra, Jediah jumped up from his seat, picked her up, slung her giggling body over his shoulder, and ran with her to the Hummer.

"Jediah," Alexandra yelled, laughing uncontrollably and bouncing upside-down. "Put me down!"

He slid her easily to the ground, then pinned her against the Hummer. "Yes, ma'am." He lowered his lips to hers. This was no chaste kiss like the one they had shared before, but a kiss that promised more to come, one that marked her as his; a kiss that left her breathless and weak-kneed. Her head swirled with wonderful thoughts as emotions ran rampant throughout her body. Alexandra's arms went up around Jediah's shoulders and her hands ran through his hair, down his neck, and came to rest on his arms.

When he pulled away, her lips were swollen

and red with passion, so he brushed tiny kisses over her cheeks until her breathing returned to normal. She felt like every cell in her body ignited. Although completely sated from the kiss, she found herself clinging to an invisible edge wanting more.

"All better now?" Jediah whispered, with just a hint of satisfaction in his voice, and a bit more of something she couldn't put her finger on. Whatever it was, it irked her to no end. 'All better now?' What was that supposed to mean? She wasn't sick. The hair bristled on the back of her neck.

"You think that should make things all better?" she said. She felt her chest rising and falling as she tried to maintain composure.

"You require more?" Jediah said with a grin.

Why did he look so satisfied with himself? "More? I'll say not!" she answered. She could feel anger rising but didn't understand why.

"I'm confused, didn't you enjoy the kiss?" he asked, she could see the beginnings of a smile.

What was going on here? In his arms, she was totally aware of his affection. But with his words, it felt like she was undergoing some kind of experiment where he already knew the outcome. He had taken her to the edge, and then tweaked her nose! What kind of man does that? She wanted to take him by the ear and shake him. He was acting like a boy in school teasing the girl in front of him by pulling her pigtails when the teacher wasn't looking.

Then it hit her. That was it exactly! She had asked him what he was like as a little boy, and, not only had he told her, he had given her an actual glimpse of the piece of personality that developed back then. What an extraordinary man!

She looked into his violet eyes mesmerized by the depth of affection she saw. He had been waiting for her to make the connection, and knew she had.

"Jediah Saffle." Alexandra reprimanded. "Precocious? The devil has hold of your soul. Does your mother know this?"

"I believe she does," he said with a wink. He hugged her close.

As Cassie and John arrived at the Hummer, Cassie asked, "What's next?"

The foursome took in a local winery, which turned out to be Cassie and Alexandra's first indoctrination into actual wine tasting. They purchased two bottles to enjoy later, and then enjoyed a local go-kart track where the males proved much more adventurous than the females. John and Jediah took three more turns at the track while the girls cheered them on.

Jediah constantly amazed her. He was a perfect companion, host, tour guide and, she was certain, mate.

Chapter Twenty-Six

Anonymity had been Ryeth's way of life. He knew this last incident had cost him greatly. Jediah could locate him, which meant there was a mechanism he hadn't blocked, and Alexandra could find his home.

Marion would be hard to replace. Changing locations, although messy and cumbersome, was part of an extended life span and a requirement for remaining off the radar. Jediah had located him and he had no warning of his arrival. This piqued his interest.

Ryeth had underestimated their powers, and had foolishly thought himself beyond their detection.

Until he could establish how Jediah had located him, and then guard against him, he would have to keep his distance, literally. Were their powers stronger than his? Did they have powers he did not possess?

The young Sensate he had used in order to gain information could have opened his mind purposefully to gain advantage. More research was required before he could assure security of his mind.

* * * * *

Alexandra began her week by checking on her mountain. Greg had only a few minor questions. She broached the subject of the secondary access.

"I agree with Jediah. By not planning ahead, you could become trapped by a washout of the road or a fallen tree; heck, any number of incidents could cause you to wish you had another access. What if something happened to your main access and emergency vehicles needed to get up here?"

"Oh, you just brought to mind another disadvantage I hadn't counted on. I'll need a pond large enough to supply firefighters with enough water to douse a substantial fire. We'll add water lilies, cattails and a fountain in the middle to keep it aerated."

Greg nodded. "Agreed. Access to ample water for a fire will drop your house insurance. Let's bring Matt in the loop to ensure we balance the overall look."

Satisfied the work was progressing beautifully, she planned to spend the week with Nancy Jane.

Hearing was the next sense to develop under Nancy Jane's tutelage. It encased the ability to hear another's thoughts, nature's musings, inflections of speech, and to combine this sense with sight.

The mechanisms were slightly different, but similar, and like sight, subtle nuances made the difference in perceptions and ability.

Eager to test some theories, one evening she went to her mountain and sat in the arbor. She opened her hearing to allow in the sounds of the earth. First, she heard the noise of animals jutting across the upper surface, and then, a bit lower the squeezing noise of water pressed from the soil and running off. Next, she heard roots of trees stretching out reaching further and further. The grating of stone on stone as boulders shifted and cracked was louder than she expected. She reached lower and heard the hissing of air, and water flowing. The water became louder and echoed until she thought her ears might rupture. She broke the connection and smiled.

Lastly, she turned her hearing inward to hear the sounds of her body. She began with her heart and concentrated on the lub-dub beat. Listening more closely, she could hear the blood swooshing through the arteries, then the lesser swoosh of the veins, and then the tiny rush through the capillaries.

Blocking the swoosh, she listened to the air flow through her lungs. What a racket that was!

She turned her hearing to her stomach and had to laugh. How embarrassing it would be to put that noise on a loud speaker. With so much noise going on she wondered how she'd ever been able to sleep. More thoughtfully, she wondered if this type of deep-listening could be beneficial to a doctor. She would have to ask Dr. Jellan.

The week went by quickly, and as the time passed, the bond between student and teacher became stronger. Nancy Jane would often rebuke Alexandra through mind contact. She would feel Nancy Jane's approval or discord when she erred performing a task. Her teaching techniques were a lesson themselves in how a slight push could render a form of manipulation, which used under the wrong circumstances could motivate another's actions. Again, the boundaries of the gift fell into question.

"Alexandra, you are flying through the lessons."

"I feel I have a lot of catching-up to do."

"My dear, you are already more advanced than the majority of Sensates. Your natural talent and intuition serve you well. If you but work at stretching your senses further you will soon surpass what I can teach."

"But we have only covered one of the five senses so far and have just started on the second."

"The mechanism used to trigger our senses is the same for all five. The mechanism is the true part of our ability."

Over the next few weeks, Alexandra worked daily with Nancy Jane developing her touch, sound, and taste senses. Nancy Jane was a tough taskmaster, but she proved to be an apt pupil, and before long, it was quite apparent the student had usurped the teacher in both depth of perception and sensory abilities. Without explaining a technique, when asked to perform a task, Alexandra searched her individual bag of tricks and produced a response that always completed the task. Moreover, she typically exceeded the task's requirements by adding touch of her pure spirit.

With each passing week, Alexandra could see Nancy Jane grow wearier.

"Mrs. Saffle, are you feeling all right? She asked.

"Yes, dear, thank you for asking. It is the natural order of things, nothing more. I'll see you again tomorrow."

That evening she discussed her concerns with Jediah. "I'm worried about your mother."

"I know." Before he could hide his feelings, Alexandra sensed great despair.

"I shouldn't spend so much time with her."

"My mother relishes the time she spends with you. Do not deprive her of this last pleasure in getting to know you; besides, the transfer of her knowledge is very sacred to all of us. This process is both an honor to bestow and to receive."

Feeling the subject too close to his heart, she changed to another topic that had been festering in her mind. "I want to know more about Ryeth."

"So do the rest of us."

"I need to classify him as friend or foe."

"For now, you might have to settle with a third classification, undetermined. I don't think even Ryeth knows his path forward."

Thoughtfully, she replied, "You're probably right. His actions border both sides. It can't be easy for him to have an internal conflict and not be able to share it with someone. I can't imagine what my life would have been like without Cassie, and now, without you."

Jediah turned to his pensive companion. "Part of being a Sensate is learning to balance and decide which life to choose. I'm not talking about the one you've already discovered, which requires good morals and high ethics, but the actual life you live between Sensates and non-Sensates."

"What do you mean?"

He shoved his hands in his trouser pockets.

"Some of our kind feels safer living their whole lives among only Sensates. They're worried they don't have the fortitude to live with their gifts on a daily basis among others. They don't want the responsibility of a potential slip-up on their conscience, so they live together in a protected community."

"You mean they severed ties with their non-Sensate families and friends?"

"Severed is too strong a word. It's more like they 'live away' from them. They see these people whenever they wish, but not so much they have to worry about discovery."

"I understand." Alexandra didn't like the direction this conversation was headed.

"Are you sure?" he asked. "It also means living a longer lifespan than your friends and family. Are you ready to watch Cassie and her family grow old and die, while you still look thirty?"

The anguish Jediah painted for her hit full force. No, she wasn't ready. She didn't think anyone could be ready for that. How could she be so callous?

"Oh, I'm sorry. You must be tormented greatly regarding your mother."

Jediah looked caring soft green eyes. "Only you would think of another's pain before your own."

"You're suffering now. My time will come, and when it does, I'll lean on you."

He smiled and continued. "The other group of Sensates chooses to live among both worlds. This is what I chose. I'm aware the danger my actions may present and have learned, or conditioned, myself to always be circumspect. You'll need to make a decision which life is best for you."

"I want both worlds, Jediah," Alexandra replied confidently. "The pain of loss may cripple me when the time comes, but I choose not to let one world slip from my grasp while living in the other. We still get only one life to live, and although ours may last several lifetimes, I don't want to miss anything on any go-round."

"That's my girl. I wouldn't have expected any less."

After Jediah left for the evening, thoughts of Ryeth filled her mind. He was an enigma she wanted answered. What was Ryeth's part in releasing her from her ordeal? How could a man transition from the demon who accosted her in the arbor to the rescuer who removed her from prison and tended her needs? Did he harm Tom Magis? Was he capable of killing? Why had he stopped trying to get the key he wanted so desperately?

These questions worried a hole in the pocket of her memory, and although she knew she shouldn't, early one morning, she moved herself back to the bedroom where she had awakened from the drugged sleep.

Once in Ryeth's bedroom, she was surprised to see the room freshly painted with no furniture remaining. Personal items were gone from the drawers in the bathroom; all was sterile and like new. She quickly walked through the whole house and found no trace left behind by the occupant.

Ryeth was gone.

"You could have hung around a little while. I have a lot of questions." Her voice sounded hollow, echoing off the empty walls. Since she could learn nothing more, she returned to the bungalow.

Deep in thought of Ryeth and slicing strawberries, Alexandra was startled when a knock sounded on the door. She dried her hands and opened the door to Detective Mokros and Officer Johnson.

"Ms. Higgins, we'd like to talk to you, if possible," said Detective Mokros.

"Certainly, won't you have a seat in the living room? Would either of you care for something to drink?"

"No, thank you," replied Officer Johnson for both.

Alexandra took a seat on the couch. "What can I do for you?"

"You seem fully recovered. Are you?" inquired the detective.

"My injuries have healed, and since I don't remember what happened, though horrific, I haven't had reason to suffer any mental anguish. All in all, I'd say I was pretty lucky, and recovered from my nightmare."

"We are just tying up a few loose ends, so please bear with me if I ask you some questions I asked you earlier."

"I understand."

"You still have no recollection of the details of the weeks you were abducted?"

"None whatsoever."

"You don't know how you got away?"

"No, I don't."

"And you don't know how you got home?"

"I wanted to be home, and I was there."

"Did you hurt Tom Magis?"

"I have no recollection of being with Tom, so I also don't know the answer to that question."

"The physician that attended him stated he had some sort of trauma before passing out. His eyes contained busted blood vessels that indicated his blood pressure had exceeded normal parameters for an extended period. If he hadn't screamed when he passed out, we wouldn't have found him until much later."

Alexandra lowered her eyes, and then met the detective's. "After learning of my abuse at his hands, it's difficult to muster any form of compassion, yet I can honestly say that I don't believe it is within me to harm anyone."

"Ms. Higgins," Officer Johnson said, "we found your DNA all over the cabin of the boat, so we're certain he held you there as hostage. When we spoke to some of his drinking buddies, we found Magis had mentioned he was coming into some money soon. We believe he meant to control you with drugs and take over your assets."

"It was the money? That's probably why he noticed me in the first place. It was only after the settlement that he became interested in me."

Officer Johnson continued his explanation. "When his wife divorced him, he began to fall apart. We think he meant to gain back what he thought was his proper place in society with your money. He would once again be a big man on campus. We figured he peaked in high school and wanted to recoup his lost glory."

"It's such a shame," Alexandra said thoughtfully.

"We hoped you would remember something; it is quite a distance between Wheeling and Waynesburg, but we could find no trail of your trip back here."

"I wish I could be of assistance, but as Dr. Jellan said, it's probably a godsend I don't remember anything." She sighed.

"The day of your abduction, Magis was caught speeding between Waynesburg and Wheeling on I-70," the officer said. "The trooper let him go with a warning. We believe you were in the car at that time because we found hairs matching your DNA in the trunk."

"You mean I passed right through your fingers and you didn't know it?"

"I'm sorry, we had no way of knowing you were there."

Officer Johnson reached into his jacket pocket, pulled out an envelope, and handed it to Alexandra.

She flipped open the flap and poured the contents into her hand. Her mother's ring lay in her palm.

Eyes brimming with unshed tears, she said, "Thank you for returning this to me, Officer Johnson. This one item means more to me than you can imagine."

"You're welcome. We're turning over the case to the DA's office with unanswered questions.

Magis was charged with abduction, several counts of battery, negligence, and a whole list of charges associated with crossing state lines. He's being held without bond, so you needn't fear he's on the loose. I'm sure you will be called to testify. That's about all. Thank you, Ms. Higgins. It's good to see you brimming with health. We can see ourselves out."

Detective Mokros nodded to her and they were gone.

She released a heavy sigh and fingered her mother's ring.

"Oh Mom, I wish you and Daddy were here." She would have to purchase a new necklace so she could keep the memento close to her heart. She kissed the ring and placed it on her dresser.

That evening, after a great supper at Emily's Pub, Alexandra told Jediah about her day.

"Detective Mokros and Officer Johnson stopped by today to tie up loose ends. They said they were closing the case with unanswered questions. I guess that happens all the time," Alexandra said pensively.

"Probably more than we know."

"They returned Mom's ring to me."

"Good. I'm glad it's back where it belongs."

She knew this next sentence would challenge his composure, so she watched him intently as she spoke.

"And, I popped into Ryeth's bedroom this morning." Now, that got his attention.

"You what?" he asked with a knowing smile forming on his lips.

"He wasn't there, and, as a matter of fact, it looked like he moved out."

Jediah broke out laughing and shook his head. "You could have popped in on almost anything! You didn't go to his front porch; you went to his bedroom."

"I only had knowledge of that room." Maybe she should have given it more thought...

Jediah scratched his head. "And what if he had been there, entertaining a lady-friend or walking around his bedroom au natural?"

"I suppose I would have had something to compare you to in the future," she said with a wink.

"You've been thinking of such things?"

Alexandra paled considerably, and then she felt her whole body blush. "Leave it to you to turn the conversation to your favor."

"How can it be my favor if you wanted to see someone else in the buff?"

"I didn't want to see him naked. Why are we even having this conversation? My point was that he's moved from his previous address, and if we needed to keep tabs on him, we've lost that ability."

"And now you can't find him?"

"Yes, oh, no. I don't need to find him." She was bouncing from one thought to another. "I just wanted to know his rationale for not pressing his advantage when he had one."

"Let me see, if you were in the jungle and a huge lion was about to tear you to shreds, and then it reconsidered and walked away, you would chase after it to find out why it changed its mind?"

She dropped her shoulders. "When you make

that type of comparison, of course not; Ryeth is a domesticated beast, not a wild one."

"But a beast nonetheless." Jediah pulled her into his arms.

"We don't know that," she said snuggling into his chest and peering into the eyes she loved so much.

"When the time comes, we'll find out, I'm sure. And notice the operative word in that sentence was 'we'. Please don't try to find Ryeth again without me."

The opportunity presented itself for her to gain a little of her own. "Oh, I see. You wanted to see him naked?"

"Certainly, a man needs to know his competition."

He was way too smooth and fast. She would have to hone her feminine skills. "Jediah," she said sweetly, "there is no competition." She raised her gaze to meet his and fluttered her eyelashes.

He laughed. The brute actually laughed at her.

"That's just not you. Feminine wiles don't work with your honesty. They will never go hand-in-hand."

"I can have feminine wiles if I work at it." She pouted.

"Nope. Never gonna happen." He shook his head. "You don't need them."

She retracted her bristles. "That's good to know."

His lips brushed against hers as she lowered her lashes and entered into the kiss. She felt his emotions touch her senses and she knew when he opened his mind to allow her access. She slowly entered Jediah's mind, then wandered through his cells to reach his core, his heart. A kiss that might have lasted a minute transformed into a clock without hands to mark the passage of time. His thoughts contained a vast realm of emotions and as he brought forth each one for her to examine, it searched for her yin to his yang.

Uncertainty came forward from Jediah. She sensed his questions: *Are you ready for a relationship? Will you accept me unconditionally? Can you open your heart?*

A wave of her uncertainty rushed to answer: *This is new. I need time to explore, but I want to explore with you.*

Her heart opened to Jediah, and a vast array of emotions came forth, one by one. As one half met the other with anticipation, it entwined and explored the intricacies of the unfamiliar half. Alexandra discovered Jediah as he discovered her.

The joining of the two haves combined in blissful rapture, enriching each by adding dimension and depth to each already powerful emotion. The timeless meshing of every sense to become complete continued through all senses until only one emotion remained; love.

Love, for these two individuals with ultra-developed senses, would consume endless volumes of countless descriptions, all under the one heading, and still not capture the true essence of the word.

Alexandra had loved before. She loved her parents with every cell of her being, but this love was different; it consumed her and left no room for doubt. Jediah offered this love to her. She met that love questioningly; unsure of its existence, wary of the pain of losing such a love, and needing to know it was honest and straightforward.

Jediah's love burst through and shattered her reservations, encompassing her with complete fulfillment; casting uncertainty to the wind, allowing that the loss of such a love was inconsequential compared to the emptiness of never knowing it, and replaced her reservations with faith.

He removed his lips from hers and placed tiny kisses on each closed eyelid as he whispered, "I love you, Alexandra. I've loved you forever."

As those words entered her mind, she knew what she had known innately. She was meant for him. The depth of his love had centuries to mature and reach the vastness it now encased. This was no small utterance from Jediah; it bespoke of his reason for biding time prior to her existence. She experienced loneliness after her parents' demise for the past three years, but she couldn't fathom his yearning for the other part of himself for over two hundred years.

She pulled away from him to look into his iridescent violet eyes. "I love you too. I think I have always loved you. You don't need to answer if you were married before or if you have any children."

"Really?" he said, breaking into a smile as that darned cute eyebrow rose.

"While I know you were no monk, I know you love only me. Besides, no monk could kiss like that."

"It was such a long wait. I don't think I can wait much longer," he said while reaching into his pants pocket.

He slid off the couch and landed on one knee, presenting her with a soft pink velvet box. Opening it for her to see, Alexandra viewed a large exquisite pink diamond with smaller chocolate diamonds surrounding it, set in a rose gold band.

As he watched her reaction, he said, "Please say you will marry me."

"Yes, Jediah," she said while smiling and taking his handsome face in her hands, "if only to put us both out of our misery."

He removed the ring from the box and placed it on her finger.

"It's beautiful, Jediah, I've never seen anything like it."

"I'm glad you approve of it and me."

"Was there ever really a question that I wouldn't?" she asked.

"Fate is a fickle woman and sometimes plays the part of jester. I have never been one to question fate, or to trust it without exception. Where you were concerned, I walked on egg shells until you said 'yes'."

"Then, yes, a thousand times yes! I have never known anyone with such a welcoming heart. I am happy to share our lives, and indebted to you for waiting on me."

She placed her arms about his neck and hugged him close. She sensed the expanding heart in his chest, and knew instinctively, it would hold hers.

"Can we go tell Mom? She's waited a long

time to see her son married."

She beamed. "Oh, yes, let's tell her."

Jediah stood and took her hands in his and pulled her up into his arms.

"You know," she said softly. "Right here is where I like to be."

"If that is the case, I'll have to make sure you are here quite often." He kissed the tip of her nose.

"Let's go see Nancy."

Jediah showed the courtesy of entering in the foyer, then said loudly, "Mom, where are you?"

"I'm in the library."

Jediah escorted Alexandra to the library, and said, "Mom, I'd like to introduce my intended to you."

Nancy Jane's face lit up like a candle in the night. She literally glowed. "Alexandra, I couldn't be happier. I was not sure I would get to see the two of you together. It does these old bones good to know my son has won the heart of such a lovely and talented young lady."

"Thank you, Mrs. Saffle," she said.

"Have you two set a date?"

Both Jediah and Alexandra looked at each other then laughed.

"No," they both said in unison.

Jediah then stated, "The sooner the better, as far as I'm concerned."

"Been waiting long?" Alexandra queried a bit enthusiastic herself.

"I guess we are rushing you a bit," Jediah apologized.

"How about Saturday?" asked Nancy Jane.

"Saturday, that's only four days away!" she exclaimed with disbelief.

"That seems like ample time to get things together, don't you think, Jediah?" questioned Nancy Jane with assured calm.

"Easy as picking an apple off a tree," Jediah quipped.

Alexandra looked from mother to son and back again, knowing she'd been expertly led to the foregone conclusion that Saturday would be perfect.

Giving in to the majority, she chimed, "Saturday it is!"

What followed was a hubbub of quick decisions, made easy by the knowledge of the two Saffles, regarding Alexandra's choices for flowers, food, guests, and time. All concerned knew they would find no better venue than Larkspur's south lawn. White canopies placed over tables for the food, with chairs covered in white. Alexandra's color would be violet, and Jediah's pale green, the combination of the bride's and groom's eyes.

All that remained was to call Cassie and request she take a few days off to help Alexandra find a gown.

As the soon-to-be-bride and groom prepared to leave, Nancy Jane said, "I think it's about time you started calling me Nancy Jane, don't you think Alexandra?"

As she hugged the stately woman, she said in her ear, "I'd be much more comfortable with 'Mom', if you don't mind."

Nancy hugged her tighter. "I'd be honored," she replied with tears in her eyes. She then shooshed the couple-to-be on their way.

Back in the bungalow, Alexandra looked at her soon-to-be husband. "You planned that, didn't you?"

"I hoped, sweet Alexandra, I merely hoped."

She kissed him slowly and then said, "I've got to call Cassie."

"I'm out of here, then. I don't think the pending conversation should be heard by the groom. Besides, I have some favors to call in. I'll see you in the morning for breakfast?"

"Breakfast is perfect."

"Goodnight, pleasant dreams," and he kissed her once again just enough to make her toes curl.

"Night." And he was gone as promised.

"Whew," she said, "that man certainly does leave an impression!"

Alexandra got a large glass of tea, settled into a comfortable chair, and pressed the speed dial for Cassie.

Chapter Twenty-Seven

The response to Alexandra's news sent a shockwave through the Hudson household. Cassie took off the remainder of the week and joined Alexandra immediately in Waynesburg, while her parents and John planned to arrive Thursday evening for the rehearsal dinner.

Cassie bubbled over. "Who would've thought you would be getting married this soon?"

"Does it seem too fast to you?" she asked.

"If it were anyone else I would say 'yes,' but it seems like you have been waiting for him all your life. I can't imagine you with anyone but Jediah."

At an exclusive shop in Pittsburgh Alexandra tried on wedding gowns. The fourth gown was a designer gown that fit like a glove.

"Allie, you're beautiful."

"I think this is the one. I don't like the little rhinestones at the hip, but otherwise, it's…" as she caught her reflection in the mirror, tears fell down her cheeks.

Cassie went to Alexandra and hugged her.

"I seem to be happy and sad at the same time," she confessed.

"You parents would have wanted to be here, Allie."

"I miss them so much," she said.

"I know, honey. What do you think she would

have said to you right now?"

"She would have told me to always follow my heart."

Cassie smiled. "Then you are definitely on the right track."

"Okay." She wiped the tears away. "This is the dress. Let's see if they have anything for you."

Cassie helped her out of the dress and she spoke to the sales clerk regarding the removal of the appliqué.

As the happy cohorts searched for a maid of honor dress, Cassie speculated. "You know people lie when they say you can cut the dresses off and wear them again. I don't know of anyone who ever did that."

"Me neither," she said. "Just make sure the dress is something you really like, in violet or lavender."

They found a pale violet gown for Cassie in the same shop, which hugged her figure and complemented her skin tone beautifully. It would require hemming, but the shop assured them it could be completed and delivered the following day with the wedding gown.

The hardest item to shop for was the bride's gift to her husband. Alexandra noted the constraints on time and decided to stop by Attorney Dawson's office on the way back to the bungalow. Luckily, he was there and greeted both of them with a genuine smile.

"Alexandra, you look completely recovered. We were so very happy to hear you got home. I heard of your impending nuptials, and would like to offer my very best wishes to you and Jediah."

"Thank you very much, Mr. Dawson. I see news travels quickly here in Waynesburg."

"Only in some circles. What can I help you with today?"

"Mr. Dawson, I'm afraid I require your expertise one more time. I need to commission a piece in gold for Jediah and need it done quickly."

"Oh, I see. There's a goldsmith in town that would be able to help you, I believe. He has helped me out a time or two when I have forgotten my wife's birthday, and he does exquisite work. I'll give you his address, and while you are on the way, I'll give him a call to let him know to expect you."

Dawson reached in his desk and brought out a worn business card. He copied the address and handed it to Alexandra.

"Thank you once again, Mr. Dawson. I hope to not be so bothersome in the future."

"Not at all, and, by the way, I have something for you," and handed her a bankbook. "I took the liberty of transferring all of Teater's financial holdings to you and opened an account in your name at the local bank. You'll need to stop by at your convenience and fill out the signature card."

"Again, Mr. Dawson, I find myself in your debt. Thank you. We will be seeing you at the wedding, won't we?"

"Yes, my whole family will be there."

"Wonderful. See you soon."

Alexandra and Cassie got into the car and set the GPS to the goldsmith's address. She took a few seconds to peer into the bankbook Mr. Dawson had handed her.

"Oh, Cassie, look at this!" she exclaimed. "This can't be right."

Cassie's eyes flew open wide. "Holy smokes! I'd have to count the commas first. I haven't any idea how much money that is."

"Me neither!" she said, breathing fast. "I don't know how to manage this. I need to ask Jediah what to do. I'm sure he knows a lot more about this sort of thing than I ever will."

"Aren't you excited?" Cassie asked.

"Shocked is more the word. I thought it might be a couple of thousand. I'm scared of this much money. I never did anything with any of my money until I got Teater's land. This is too much responsibility."

"Put the book in your purse for now, and don't talk to anyone about it until you speak to Jediah."

"That sounds good, out of sight, out of mind. Let's get over to that goldsmith's place before I have a heart attack."

The shop was small and unassuming, and located on the end of a strip mall called "The Crossings." A tall gentleman in his early fifties greeted them from behind the back counter. "I'll be with you in a minute."

On closer inspection, the shop contained one-of-a-kind pieces with unparalleled quality, which drew both Cassie and Alexandra into a state of awe. She found it hard to look from one piece to another since each item possessed such intricate detail. This was the work of a world-renowned artisan, not an unknown goldsmith from Waynesburg,

Pennsylvania.

Preparing to state just that fact to Cassie, Alexandra was interrupted mid-thought by a kindly voice. "I'm William Snyder, owner of this shop. May I help you?"

"You have truly exquisite items. I'm sorry, I am so taken aback. Please forgive me. James Dawson suggested I see you about a piece I would like to commission for my, ah, fiancée."

"Yes, James gave me a call. I was expecting you. What did you have in mind?"

"We don't have much time, so feel free to be perfectly frank with me regarding completion of the piece."

"How much time are we speaking of?" he inquired.

"This Saturday."

"I see, and the type of item?" he asked.

Alexandra reached in her purse and pulled out a piece of paper; she opened it and said, "A signet ring with this symbol."

Cassie said, "How intricate, did you get that from a book?"

"Not exactly."

"Very interesting." Mr. Snyder exclaimed.

"I would like it in rose gold, with the insignia having a deeper hue, perhaps crimson?"

"That's possible," he said. "By mixing various metals with gold, the hues change. But layering the crimson gold on top of the rose gold could be a challenge. If you could stop by tomorrow, I might have some colors ready for you to select, and perhaps, if all goes well, you might see a mock-up of the finished product. What about size?"

"Would it be all right if I get back to you on the size?"

"Sure, but I'll need it tomorrow in order to complete it on time."

After a quick security deposit to Mr. Snyder to get started, the bouncy Bride and Maid of Honor phoned Jediah to meet them at Olive Garden for supper.

They sat for only a few minutes when Jediah appeared.

"You got here quick, Jediah," Cassie noted. "Your office must be close by."

"It is," said Jediah. "Would you like to see it?"

At that question, he had Alexandra's full attention. She had never thought to ask about his office, somehow thinking it was 'out there' on some virtual-reality plane. Ashamed of herself, she looked at Jediah. She could see his mind working and laughing at her at the same time.

He had always seemed so much bigger than life to her, and the thought of his sitting dutifully behind a desk somewhere refused to form a cohesive image in her mind. In fact, she wasn't even sure where he went when he wasn't with her, and she couldn't guess, with any certainty, where he even slept.

How could she have been so nonchalant about these important items? Thinking back, she still knew very little about the man she was to marry. How could she know him on an intimate level of emotions, yet know nothing about him physically? Where did he keep his clothes? What was his address? Where did he park the Hummer?

What a full-blown ninny she was! How could she have gotten in so deep with so little information? It had never occurred to her to ask these questions. She was entering into one of the most important decisions of her life, totally blind.

As she caught Jediah's eye, he winked, as if to say, 'you never asked, so I didn't volunteer.'

"Sure, I'd like to see your office," Cassie responded.

"We'll go after supper, then," he said.

With their plans formulated, the ordering of supper commenced.

"How did you two do today?"

Cassie jumped in with excitement for the upcoming wedding, "Alexandra got her gown. It's quite beautiful. It only has to have a small alteration. It will be delivered tomorrow."

"And did you find something to wear as Maid of Honor."

"Yes, I only had one constraint to meet for my selection," Cassie shared, "and that was it had to be the color of your eyes." She rolled her eyes in mock agitation at the suggestion.

Alexandra blushed at the intimacy Cassie shared. Jediah picked up on the emotion instantly, and hurriedly changed the subject. "Then everything is progressing nicely. I picked out my tux today, and almost got the light blue one with shiny lapels and matching blue pants with the black stripe down the side, shiny vest with the ruffled shirt..."

At the horror displayed on both girls' faces, he could not continue.

"You wouldn't," gasped Cassie.

"What?" He asked, innocently.

Alexandra took in a huge breath of air, and when she let it out, she said, "Don't fall for that. He's messing with your mind and I almost let him mess with mine."

Cassie scrutinized Jediah's face. If it hadn't been for the barely imperceptible glint in his eyes, she would've never caught the deception.

"Jediah, you almost gave me a heart attack!"

"Sorry, Cassie, I couldn't pass that one up. You were an easy target."

"Now that I've been forewarned, I'll be forearmed. You won't catch me a second time."

"Sure about that?" he said with that one eyebrow raised.

"Oh, no, Cassie, I recognize that look from him, you have just issued a challenge I feel you'll lose for years to come," Alexandra warned her friend.

"Think so?" said Cassie.

"Most assuredly," replied Alexandra.

"Great, I'm doomed, and you've lassoed the perpetrator of my doom. Things are not lookin' good for this kid," Cassie said with chagrin.

"Shape up there kiddo, it won't be so bad. I promise to be exceedingly gentle, and not pick on you in front of more than ten people at a time," Jediah stated quite gracefully.

"Man, am I glad you guys live an hour away, Cassie said.

"These days," Jediah said, "an hour is just a blink away, so don't get too comfortable."

Alexandra could feel his intentional gaze on her, and met his eyes with a shame-on-you hint to them.

Instantly, she found herself in the shimmering orb with Jediah, he closed the distance between them and kissed her waiting lips. She heard, *I love everything about you.*

They were back sitting with Cassie.

I couldn't help myself, echoed in her mind.

With her toes still curled, she replied, *anytime.*

Good as his word, after supper they all piled into Jediah's Hummer and went to his office, which, to Alexandra's surprise, was just across the street from James Dawson's office.

The office was tastefully decorated with watercolor pictures adorning the walls. The color pallet had softer shades of blues with earth tones blended in that created a warmer atmosphere than a typical office.

"Everyone's gone home for the day," Jediah explained, "though normally anywhere from twelve to sixteen engineers would be in residence." The office was deceptively larger than it appeared from the outside due to the depth of the building.

"Here we have reception, several offices, our conference room, and break room with kitchenette." He pointed to each as they strolled through. "Our bathroom facility is equipped with a shower and changing area because my staff likes to keep in shape and many jog during their lunch break or before they start work. Finally stopping in front of a beautiful cut glass door, he stated, "My office."

Jediah's personal office was neat as a pin. The

top of his desk contained only a nameplate.

"It doesn't appear you do much work here," noted Cassie.

Jediah strode over to his desk, pushed a button, and the shiny black glass top rose to become a large touch screen, which beveled upright at another touch. They walked around to the other side so the screen was visible, and saw the mechanics for telecommunications world-wide and a map of the locations of his additional offices easily at his fingertips.

"I work sometimes," Jediah said nonchalantly.

"I put my foot in it again, didn't I?" Cassie noted.

"I get that a lot, so don't worry. My desk does look fairly clean to onlookers."

"He's quite the techie, isn't he, Allie?"

"You have no idea what this man is capable of," she stated truthfully.

"Your office is pretty impressive," Cassie said.

"Thanks, I love technology and can't imagine where it will take us in the next hundred years."

Cassie reflected. "Wouldn't it be grand to be here and see it then? This room would be something our kids would look at and laugh."

Jediah nodded. "It would be great to see."

Alexandra just watched as the scene played out before her very eyes. If no sickness or accident claimed her, she would be here to see the changes a hundred years brought, and two hundred... The thought was a lot to comprehend, yet before her stood the man she was to marry, who had already seen two hundred and thirty of those years pass. It was sad to think that Cassie, her parents, and John would not be there with her and Jediah.

What made things in life so unfair, that she alone should be given a gift and not others? It was too much to consider, so she forced her attention back to Cassie and Jediah, who showed Cassie how the telecommunication system worked.

"Isn't this absolutely incredible?" asked Cassie.

"Since meeting Jediah, a whole new world has come into focus." Alexandra looked lovingly at her mate.

"Okay, okay, enough of the dreamy-eyed mushy stuff, especially when John isn't here."

"He's coming up Thursday, right?" asked Jediah.

"Yes, and it isn't soon enough." Cassie pouted.

Jediah closed his desk and once again, it looked like he sat there and accomplished nothing. This time, on the walk back through, the girls noticed each office had a similar, but smaller rendition of Jediah's desk.

Jediah followed the girls back to the bungalow, and the three sat around the kitchen table chatting and making wedding favors for the guests.

Cassie stood and said, "I'm going to the bedroom and call John. I think you two can get along without me."

"We can, but it won't be nearly as much fun," said Jediah with a wink.

"I don't know how you did it, Allie, but you hooked yourself a keeper. Night all."

Jediah suggested they move to the couch. Alexandra grabbed the chips and dip and joined him.

"What's wrong with me that I hadn't asked about your work?" Alexandra asked.

"You did inquire several times, I just steered you in the opposite direction each time you asked."

"Why would you do such a thing? I felt positively goofy for not knowing anything about your office. I had to pretend to have been there before."

"You did a marvelous job."

"You haven't answered the question."

"The office here in Waynesburg is relatively new."

"How new is 'relatively'?" she asked.

"About a month."

"A month? You work fast. I'm not sure I'm ready for the answer, but where was your office before that?"

"Would you like to see?" he asked.

"Yes."

"Hold on tight, then, you are about to have your socks knocked off."

The shimmering orb appeared, surrounding them.

Will I be able to make an orb and travel like this?

You can probably do it now, but without the proper instruction, you could end up in it for a long time and not know how to get out. All in good time. You are already exceeding everyone's wildest dreams.

Everyone's?

Even mine.

Chapter Twenty-Eight

As he kissed her lips, the orb vanished. Alexandra opened her eyes to... well, she didn't know what.

"Welcome to Balisier," he said.

It was massive, perhaps the size of four football fields. The sides were dark and had texture. As high up as she could see, there didn't appear to be a top. There were no stars or moon, and although she sensed she was beneath the ground, the ceiling exhibited no visible means of support. The buildings were constructed from solid stone, probably hand cut from the interior, each stained a different hue from the same pallet, sand, taupe, ivory, brown, and embellished with burnished red-brown accents.

There were no streets in this small village; instead, it had wide walkways carved with the same beautiful vine and floral pattern as the floor of her arbor. A bluish glow from lanterns hanging from intricately wrought iron poles lined the walkways and rendered a dream-like appearance to the village. She could see small grocery stores, clothing shops, specialty shops, and a central park with trees and flowers. Apartments were located above many of the shops with eye-catching flower boxes just brimming with blooms. Everywhere she looked the scenery was unbelievable. The village bespoke harmony and kinship.

"It's beautiful. I feel like I'm in a dream."

As they walked down the path toward Jediah's office, and she continued to look in awe at the sheer wonder of the place, Jediah shared its history.

"Over the years our engineers used the latest engineering techniques to secure this habitat. Balisier was constructed from mostly limestone, but some places have marble streaks. The buildings are all limestone, the same stone used in the Pyramids in Egypt. We were fortunate to find this solid mountain in Pennsylvania, and have concentrated efforts over the past centuries to create the space you see.

"The lights are on a timer and simulate day or nighttime just as it is outside. A giant waterfall located in a chasm far below generates more than enough hydroelectric power to supply our village. We have engineered just the right amount of ultraviolet rays to allow for sufficient plant growth and no vitamin deficiencies so you can actually get a suntan. We produce our own breathable air which is electronically controlled and filtered for molds and noxious gases."

"It's amazing," she muttered.

They entered a stately building three stories high and took an elevator to the top floor. The doors opened to a fashionable office similar in design to the one Jediah had shown her earlier.

"Due to our need for seclusion," Jediah continued, "we have no external door, so if you haven't mastered the ability to move from place to place, you would not be able to enter. One of our veteran Sensates must bring a new Sensate to Balisier before they can gain entrance.

"We have additional protection for our group. Before we bring a newbie inside, we alert all who are currently here. At that point, they can choose to not be seen."

"What do you mean?" she asked.

"Like this." Jediah vanished from her view, yet she could hear him.

"Come back here!" she said.

Jediah appeared.

"We can become invisible? This is not something I wanted to know."

"In a manner of speaking, yes, but it's not like you think. Because we have a strong sight sense and know what generates this sense, we have learned how to control it. We typically concentrate on expanding our vision, but what if we concentrated on lessening it? It's the same technique, only utilized in the opposite direction. Once you can do this in your mind, you can do it in other's minds, and limit their view of you. In other words, you don't permit them to see you. The stronger the Sensate, the more people you can will to not see you. Most Sensates can only remove their presence from one or maybe two people at a time."

"I can't believe this. Think of the repercussions of this in the wrong hands."

"Try it on me." Jediah suggested. "See if you can block me from seeing you."

In a flash, she was gone from his eyes. Jediah laughed as he felt her arms encircle his waist, yet he didn't see her.

"Mom said you absorbed like a sponge, but man, are you fast!"

Alexandra removed the block and leaned into his chest.

"Jediah, the temptation of using that block could turn someone completely evil. It's so much responsibility. We already have a grave obligation to keep the knowledge of Sensates from the general public and to maintain a high moral code. This last bit of knowledge would seem to be the straw breaking the camel's back. The discretion required for concealment is mind-boggling."

"Remember that many have our trait, but few are of high enough moral fiber to be taken into our fold."

"That restriction is a good one." She said. "Why wouldn't the Sensates want me to see them?" asked Alexandra.

"Self-preservation. If you are not seen, your identity is safe from those who would harm us if they knew. Some Sensates may hide from you for twenty or thirty years before letting you know they are Sensates. Others are tickled to show themselves to a newbie."

"Like Dr. Jellan?" asked Alexandra.

Jediah laughed out loud, "Yes, like Val. What did he do?"

"After he examined me for the last time, he chuckled, and then vanished right before my eyes."

"Val liked you from the beginning, and trusted you immediately. He's certainly one in a million."

"I liked him too. What a kind spirit he is."

"I couldn't have described him better," Jediah said.

"Are people hiding from me now?"

"Yes, it is not yet time for your formal introduction into the group. We will come back for that later, and then if they choose, they will reveal themselves to you. As a member of the high counsel, I see all Sensates, and we are the ones responsible for inviting new Sensates into Balisier."

"How long have the Sensates been here?"

"Well, to continue with my soliloquy, we, the Sensates, have congregated and lived here in Balisier for a millennium. I have been their leader for the last 72 years. It is mostly an honorary title, but I oversee the plant operations for the continuity of our environment.

"We only need outside stores and offices if we plan to live on the outside for an extended period. The offices you visited this evening in Waynesburg are for the benefit of non-Sensates. As you can see, we take great pains to assure our acceptance as normal.

"Alexandra." He turned her to face him. "You didn't press the issue of where I worked, so I thought I might make it without the subterfuge. I wasn't quite sure I would need an office until I got to know Cassie better. Once I did, I was convinced she would ask quite innocently, and she did."

"That's Cassie, all right." She smiled and kissed his cheek. "This place is beyond belief. Where exactly are we?"

"Here's the big jolt," he said with complete candor. "We are inside your mountain."

Before she could respond, they were safely back in the orb.

I swear you use this orb to your advantage.

A guy has to use everything at his disposal with a gal like you.

'A gal like me'?

One who will shortly learn all there is to know, and who will not be as impressed by my tricks as she used to be.

I'll never know all there is to know about you. And Jediah, I'll always be impressed by you.

Good answer.

The orb vanished and once again, they were sitting next to each other on the sofa.

She whispered, "We were inside my mountain? There's a whole village down there. I can't even think of it as mine anymore."

"It is yours. Hook, line and sinker. It was no small act of consideration that entrusted it to you. The high counsel takes great pains to assure the deed transfers into the right hands. Teater was instrumental in the chain of events required for you to be the current owner."

"I have come a long way from the day I dropped into the cistern, but I still can't imagine the inner workings of a community that spans so many centuries and generations. Oftentimes, I have to stop myself from thinking about it because it literally boggles my mind."

Jediah attempted to calm her fear. "I grew up knowing my place in the plan. You are playing a quick game of 'catch-up'. All by itself, becoming a full Sensate is overwhelming. Couple that with your sidestep into the Hell Magis created for you, and I'd have to say, in retrospect, you are handling things remarkably well. It proves our faith in you as an Ultra was well-founded."

"There's more, isn't there? It sounds like you are planning to place a huge load on my shoulders."

"Alexandra," he said whispering into her hair. "You are fated for an amazing future."

"Don't tell me anymore. I'm willing to help in any way possible, but you must promise to always be by my side."

"I'll always be with you," he whispered, then nuzzled her neck.

Unable to stop the load of questions forming in her mind, she plowed right in with the first of many. "If there are no doors to Balisier how did the first Sensate get inside?"

"It's a great story and requires a small glass of wine for the telling. Would you care to join me?"

"I'd love some. Why don't we try that new bottle of Chardonnay?"

Walking into the kitchen, he found it in the counter wine rack. "Got it."

He began the tale as he got the glasses, poured the wine, and joined Alexandra on the sofa.

"One of our earliest Sensates was a young Iroquois named Papina, whose name meant 'vine growing around an oak tree.' One day Papina was walking through the forest gathering herbs and flowers when she heard the call of the red bird with the black mask. She strained her ears to hear the bird and followed its song just so she could see its beautiful feathers. As she listened, the sound got louder and louder, and it wasn't just the bird's song that got louder, the wind and the leaves got louder too. She could hear the other females in her tribe talking even though she was very far from them. A loud rushing noise filled her ears blocked out all other sounds with its pounding force. She couldn't stop the noise and soon she fell into a swoon and passed out.

"A few moments later she awoke and all was normal once again. She listened for the loud rushing noise and could hear it faintly in the distance. She followed the sound for a great time until she came to the base of a large mountain. She could go no further, for the sound came from within the mountain. She concentrated on the noise trying to figure out what it was, and in doing so, the sound grew louder once again. Her desire to find the source was so great she found herself moving through the air and into the mountain, encased in a ball of light. A faint green glow lit the inside of the mountain chasm and once her eyes adjusted to the darkness, she witnessed the source of the pounding roar.

"The vision was one of wonderment for Papina, for she had never seen anything so beautiful and powerful in nature before. She stood staring for a long while at the waterfall, then grew anxious to be back in her forest with the call of the red bird echoing in her ears. Papina's desire formed the shimmering orb and she traveled back through the mountain to the base on the outside.

"She did not tell anyone about her strange trip inside the mountain until many years later when a beautiful Iroquois named Onatah came to visit her village. Onatah walked one day with Papina in the forest and began to tell Papina many stories of special Iroquois who could do many things that others could not. Onatah told Papina they were both special. It was then that Papina told Onatah of the waterfall inside the mountain and at the urging of Onatah, Papina took her there using the round ball of light. Over time the space inside the mountain became a place the special Iroquois gathered when they needed to be alone."

Alexandra smiled at Jediah and said, "And Balisier was born. The vine pattern on the village pathways and the floor of my arbor are a tribute to her, aren't they?"

"Yes, my intuitive Iroquois descendant."

Alexandra gazed up into the timeless eyes of the man she loved. She knew that even though she was teased in fifth grade, called Higgy Piggy in high school, ostracized as a nerd, lost her parents, and was drugged and beaten, the powers-that-be had granted her a favor. For all her adversity, she was given a tremendous reward, and he sat next to her on the sofa.

"What are you thinking, sweet Alexandra?"

"You mean you aren't eavesdropping?" she asked.

"No, and I won't be doing it in the future."

"Why not?"

"It is not a normal practice among Sensates to delve into each other's minds, as a matter of fact it's considered rude and improper."

"That never stopped you before, why the touch

of conscience now?"

"Leave it to you to cut right to the heart of the matter," he said.

"And the answer is?"

"We had to put you on the fast track."

"What do you mean, fast track and we?"

"'We', are Mom, the High Council, and me. The fast track is because of Mom."

Panic gripped Alexandra in an instant. She jumped up from the sofa and went into the kitchen. "No, I can't hear this. Never mind. Forget I asked."

"We can't forget, Alexandra. Mom has one last lesson for you. She's hung on long enough, and is in considerable pain. She requests release."

Alexandra broke down, crying. "But why does it have to be me?"

"It's better by someone who loves you than by someone who doesn't care. It's her last wish and it can't be put off much longer."

"Jediah, I can't." She crushed herself to his chest, sobbing.

He wrapped his arms around her as she cried. After a while, she felt his serenity surround her to ease the anguish.

Later, snuggling on the couch next to Jediah, she remembered her visit to James Dawson's office.

"Oh, I have something to show you."
Alexandra got her purse and brought it back to the couch. She reached in and pulled out the bankbook James Dawson had given her earlier and handed it to him.

"What's this?" he asked.

"Teater's monetary means passed on to me.

Mr. Dawson gave it to me earlier today. Look inside."

As Jediah looked at the book, her eyes watched his reaction.

"That's quite a bit of pocket change," Jediah noted.

"I've never really had money before; I never did anything with the money I got from the insurance company but let it sit somewhere until I started building the house. I don't know what to do with this much money."

He closed the book and handed it back to her. "I had no idea Teater amassed such a fortune. Knowing Teater, he would want you to be prepared financially to handle any unforeseen consequences regarding the mountain. This kind of money requires its own manager. You don't want it sitting around when it could be doing some good. I've never discussed my financial situation with you, Alexandra. It's sufficient to say mine is similar as are most of the Sensates. It's another area where Sensates excel due to their longer life spans. Because we wish to stay under the radar, we spread our considerable holdings over many ventures. I've just the person to help you. It's the same person who manages my accounts."

"Doesn't anything ever shock you? When I looked at that many commas I had to remind myself to breathe."

"You forget, I've been around the block a few times."

She scrutinized him. "You are looking a bit tired. Should I get you a wheel chair?"

"I'm not that old."

Mimicking Jediah, Alexandra raised one eyebrow and said, "Says who? You could be arrested for kissing someone as young as me."

"I wondered when this was going to come up."

"You thought I would just let you continue on your merry way without me commenting on your age? Are you even still virile?"

"Virile?" Jediah stood up, puffed out his chest and sucked in his non-paunchy stomach. "You want to know if I'm virile?"

He pulled Alexandra from the couch and into his arms as she squealed in delight. Then, picking her up and kissing her, he proceeded to carry her gruffly down the hallway to her bedroom.

"What's going on out there?" said Cassie sticking her head out into the hallway. "Put her down this minute. There will be no hanky-panky going on here tonight!"

"Blast it!" said Jediah, dropping Alexandra to her feet, "I forgot about the chaperon."

"Why Jediah, aren't you going to prove your virility to me?" asked Alexandra innocently. "You're going to let some wee tart keep you from your task?"

Feigning impatience Jediah said with a frown, "Girl, you tempt the hounds of Hell with ice water, the weary with a day of rest, and the soul with peace. Kiss me, woman, and be quick about it. I've a thirst for you that will not wait much longer!"

He grabbed Alexandra, who was laughing at his phony tirade, kissed her soundly in front of Cassie, and then strode out slamming the door, leaving both girls in cheerful laughter.

"Um, mm, sure do love that man," said Alexandra to Cassie.

"It's a good thing; you're going to marry him in three days!"

"Three days! Oh, Cassie, how I wish Mom and Dad were here. I'd love for them to have met Jediah. Three days, that's only seventy-two hours. I'll be a married woman!"

"Have you two even talked about a Honeymoon?"

"No."

"Where are you going to live once you are married?" Cassie asked.

"Don't know. Don't care."

"Yep, you are stricken. Cupid hit you squarely between the eyes."

"Wow, and he's all mine."

"How about a cup of tea and a chat?" Cassie asked.

"Always ready. Get the tea, I'll start the water.

* * * * *

"Can you believe it? They're getting married." Ray ran his hand across his bald head and then sat on the park bench. "They just met this spring, and in a few months' time decided to marry. She barely knows him. What kind of control does he have over her?"

Terry shook his head and replied, "I've seen them together, it's not control; they're truly in love. I saw them the day they met. Believe me, he was just as awed by her as she was by him. I witnessed love at first sight that day."

Ray suggested. "This means we group her with the rest."

"Yeah, I think so too. Another thing, they spend most evenings together but he never stays the night. It's my bet they aren't sleeping together."

"That's odd in this day. He sleeps in the mansion, I suppose."

"Yeah. I'll get a chance to check out the guests and maybe link some others from the community to the group."

"That's a good idea."

"They're holding the wedding at the mansion. Tell the boss I'll get her the guest list as soon as possible."

"Will do. It'd be nice if we could crack this nut wide open."

"Yeah, I'd like something to come from all these years watching them."

Ray ground his cigarette butt out on the path, then turned and left.

* * * * *

Chapter Twenty-Nine

The morning passed quickly for Alexandra and Cassie. After breakfast they found themselves happily driving toward the goldsmith's shop.

She had taken great pains the night before to notice Jediah's hands. They were large, and compared to hers, well, they didn't compare at all. As much as she hated doing it, she guesstimated the size for his ring. His pinky compared somewhat to the size of her pointer finger. Maybe he could get it over his knuckle. Dang, she hated not knowing his size.

Mr. Snyder was as sweet as he had been the previous day and was prepared with three samples of color combinations.

"Ms. Higgins, I was anticipating your visit. I hope you find something here to your liking," he said while bringing a velvet display card into view from beneath the case.

He presented three rings. All were equally beautiful in their own right. The first ring blended the crimson gold into the rose gold with a fading effect. The insignia would have a distinct color difference when viewed from the top, and a blended appearance from the side. The second ring had distinct separation between the two gold colors; the ring would have the same appearance when viewed from the top as the first, but have a line separating the two colors on the sides. The third ring from the side was complete rose gold. The insignia viewed from the top had a rose gold border around it and the detail set inside was crimson gold.

"They are all so beautiful, Mr. Snyder. I love the way the colors blend in this one, instead of the complete separation of colors on the second one. The rose gold is just so wonderfully soft in appearance."

Cassie said, "I agree, Allie. When you were describing it yesterday, I wasn't fully grasping the look you were after, but apparently Mr. Snyder had no such problem sensing your exact thought. They are all exquisitely done."

"Mr. Snyder, each one is a work of art. I could easily choose any one and be completely satisfied, but the one that caught my eye initially is the first one. The color blends so beautifully, I find I can't take my eyes off it."

"Ms. Higgins, it was my choice as well," he said, smiling.

"I'll need to see the ring wheel to give you a size. He has large hands; his little finger should be about the size of my pointer finger."

"That looks to be eight and a half," he said as he slid the test ring on Alexandra's finger. It fit perfectly.

"I could have used that keen eye of yours last night when I was trying to measure his finger without him knowing."

"An adjustment would only take a few minutes if we've made a mistake. I'll get busy on the design immediately and fabricate it from the deeper reddish color on the top, and when I carve out the layer to make the design, the two colors will be visible. Check back with me late tomorrow for approval of the finished project."

"I can't thank you enough, Mr. Snyder. I'm sure it will be perfect."

After a short discussion on the time and cost of materials involved, the two friends departed the shop.

"What design is that anyway?" asked Cassie.

"It's similar to something I saw and really liked. I don't know if it has any particular translation or not."

"Well, either way, I'm sure he will love it."

"Let's go back to the bungalow and get ready for the rehearsal dinner. Let's do each other's nails one more time."

"Allie, that sounds super. They're delivering your gown and my dress today and it'll be a nice way to pass the time until John gets here."

"Jediah has planned the evening. I don't even know where we're going. Let's hope he doesn't show up in a leisure suit or a shirt with ruffles."

"Believe me, if he does, I'll be the last to make fun of him."

"Cassie, I'm so happy you like Jediah. Can you imagine how horrible it would be if you two didn't get along?"

"Ugh, that thought makes me shiver. Don't even say such things. It could jinx everything!"

As they pulled into the bungalow, the van from the shop in Pittsburgh pulled in alongside them. The girls quickly checked over the items to assure they were correct and sent the deliveryman on his way. They grabbed nail polish, files, polish remover and cotton pads, then grabbed sliced veggies and dip, and headed for the table under the tree.

Once ensconced, the chatter resumed throughout the manicure and pedicure, continued as they moved inside, and their antics were still going strong when John arrived.

"I could hear you two singing as soon as I got out of the car."

"John, it's so good to see you again," Alexandra said, noting the shoe was now located on the other foot and she was the third wheel as they kissed 'hello'.

"Unfair, Jediah's not here," she said.

John reached into his pocket to retrieve his cell phone, and asked, "Should I give a certain fellow a call to arms?"

"If you do that we'll never be ready in time," Cassie said. "I had to beat him with a stick to get him to leave last night. He was heading to the bedroom carrying Alexandra when I caught them. If I hadn't been there, I don't know what would have happened."

"It sounds like I should take some pointers from Jediah and carry you off," he said pointedly to Cassie.

Everyone fell silent. Had it been later in the evening, only the sound of crickets would have prevailed. The girls looked at each other, then at John.

"Hurry," Alexandra yelled. "Don't let him

catch you!"

Cassie bolted for the door, but John was quicker. He asked, "You thought you could out run me?" He led Cassie back into the living room, sat in the overstuffed chair, and pulled a laughing girl into his lap.

"I'm afraid you're in trouble now," Alexandra yelled to Cassie from the kitchen. When no response came from the living room, she decided her friend had no desire to run from the trouble she was currently experiencing.

She went to her bedroom to lay out the dress she planned to wear to dinner. It was a teal crossover-front dress with ruching at the waist, kimono sleeves, and full skirt. She bought it a year ago and it still had the tags attached. It hung in the window at Nordstrom's and when she saw it she knew it had to come home with her. It had been an extravagant purchase at the time, but there were times after the purchase that she had come across it in her closet and it had given her comfort. It gave her great pleasure to be wearing it tonight. The color would accent her eyes and hair.

She hunted through the boxes of shoes, yet unpacked, to find the box that contained Hawaiian wooden mules hand-carved in a hibiscus pattern, with a white leather strap that formed a peek-a-boo toe. Her white leather clutch with a gold shoulder chain would match perfectly.

Laid out on the bed the outfit looked like it belonged to someone else, for other than her wedding dress, Alexandra had never purchased an item of clothing that cost more than a hundred dollars.

She quickly stepped into the shower and just to be extra sure, she shaved her legs and underarms twice, used the expensive conditioner on her hair, and when done, covered her body with softly scented lotion. By the time she dressed, the scent from the lotion would have time to dissipate and not interfere with the *Emeraude* she planned to use right before stepping out the door.

Donning her robe, she stepped from the bedroom to check on the two love birds inhabiting her living room. "Cassie, your turn," she said while toweling her hair and making the turn into the room, and ran smack dab into Mr. Big, Dark, and Handsome.

He caught her around the waist and pulled her close, leaning down to breathe in her hair and skin.

"You smell wonderful," he said while rocking back and forth with her.

"And you smell...." She wrinkled her nose. "Geesh, Jediah, what have you been doing?"

"Some of us have things to attend to, unlike you who lounge around all day and paint your nails."

"Were you spying on us?"

"Not like you think, I was with Mom earlier and saw you and Cassie out of the window." He nodded toward Cassie. "Are you going to be able to do without her after the wedding?"

"Hmm, not quite sure, I might have my hands full with this elusive fellow."

"I'm elusive?" he asked.

"Well, you tend to come and go and I never

know what you're doing. What are you going to do when you have to spend the whole day with me?"

At that, he leaned in very close, brushed his lips across hers, and pressed his body close; too close when she only wore a thin robe.

"Do you really want me to answer that?" he murmured in her ear, his hot breath sending chills down her arms and legs.

"Jediah," she whispered huskily.

"I've waited so long," he said.

"And you're going to wait two more days," warned Cassie from the kitchen.

"Cassandra Hudson, you have the worst timing," moaned Alexandra.

"Depends on which side of the fence you're sitting on. I think my timing is impeccable," snorted Cassie.

"That remains to be seen, Ms. Hudson," scolded Jediah.

"Aw, cut her some slack, Jediah. Cassie is having a tough time losing her best friend," reprimanded John.

When they glanced at Cassie, they could see she had been crying. Alexandra caught her friend's eyes and her eyes filled with tears as well.

She left Jediah's arms and went into those who had held her during her most trying times.

"Aw, Cassie, I'm not leaving you. I'm expanding our circle to include Jediah. There's more than enough love to go around."

"It was just so awful when you went missing. I'm sorry for the tears. John says I've done nothing but cry since he met me. Now you're getting married and I'm crying again."

She brushed the hair from Cassie's face. "I'll always be an instant away. You're not losing me; we're gaining Jediah."

Breaking in on the tender moment Jediah announced, "You guys have an hour to get ready; I'll be back to pick you up."

"An hour!" exclaimed Cassie. "My face won't recover from crying by then." She flew into the bedroom.

John went back to the couch stating, "I only need twenty minutes."

Alexandra kissed Jediah and said, "I might be able to wait an hour for you." She turned and ran to her bedroom with Cassie.

Jediah stated to John, "Talk about scattering, did you see those two fly? Make sure they're on time, John."

"I'm no magician, but I'll try."

Precisely an hour later, Jediah was at the door of the bungalow collecting his party of three. As his eyes fell on Alexandra, she knew she'd scored a hit.

Jediah caught his breath as she looked up at him from lowered lashes and then spun slowly before him. She'd practiced the maneuver in the bedroom to show off the fabric of her dress and her hair. It worked! And he thought she couldn't acquire feminine wiles. Hah! The green dress, which clung to her body at the waist, accented her figure and brought out the color of her eyes.

Jediah had never seen Alexandra in a dress. "You are beyond beautiful."

"Thank you, Jediah." She blushed under his scrutiny and was pleased she had succeeded in pulling the outfit together.

"I love those shoes," he said.

Suddenly a picture of her purchasing them filled her mind. She looked intently at him as the pictures played out. She saw how she had debated, walked away from the store, went back a second, then a third time, and finally, purchased them. When she got back to her apartment, she took them out and put them on. She walked around in them, and then twirled as if she was dancing for several minutes. She sensed he had fallen madly in love with her that day. He was very pleased to know she wore them tonight.

She held his eyes thanking him for the memory. "I love them too. I've never been happy enough to wear them until today."

He kissed her sweetly.

She took her time in surveying her future partner. He was dashing, exciting, handsome, rakish, powerful, and gentle, all wrapped up in the only word that really came to mind, 'home'. Dressed in midnight black slacks, a soft gray crew neck top and a black dinner jacket, he was one in a million that could carry off the look and appear as if he dressed like that every day. He was relaxed in his skin, yet looked like he could strike a lethal blow at any minute. Power exuded from him, and caught Alexandra by surprise. He was splendid, and he was hers.

"Jediah," she whispered, "you are Heaven in a basket."

"I'm not too old for you then?" He remarked taking her hands in his.

Goose flesh prickled her skin as she replied, "Never."

"Then, it's good to be me." He kissed her lightly, not wanting to spoil her make-up.

Jediah had rented a limousine. The gentlemen escorted the ladies to the limo and helped them inside. As the driver took them to their destination, Jediah opened a bottle of champagne and filled four glasses.

"I'd like to make a toast," he began, "to friends and lovers."

"Quite appropriate," nodded John and raised his glass to Jediah.

The ladies smiled and joined, clinking glasses, then sipped the champagne.

"Where are we going?" inquired John.

"It was to be a surprise, but I suppose I can tell you now. It's the Saffle Family Retreat. We have a little place outside town that we use for family functions. The dinner is to be catered there."

As it turned out, the 'little place' was atop a smaller version of Alexandra's mountain nestled beautifully amid rolling hills of green pastures and bordered with immaculate white fences.

"Jediah, this is breath-taking," whispered Alexandra.

"It has been in my family for many years; each generation maintained and added a bit."

As they passed the entrance gate, John said, "The wrought iron gate is truly intricate; it has to be 'old world' craftsmanship. How old do you think it is, Jediah?"

"If my memory serves me correctly, I believe it
was forged mid-seventeenth century. The same
craftsman who forged the main gate also made the
garden gates on either side of the main house and
the design work on the balconies and railings."

"It's remarkable to have the kind of connection
throughout generations as you do," Cassie
commented. "I have no idea what my ancestors did
or who they were. I think society, as a whole, lives
in the present and stretches out to what is tangible
and goes no further."

"You may be right, Cassie," said John.
"Alexandra is the only one I know in my complete
circle of friends who has taken up genealogy."

As they drove by the stone stables with three
copper cupolas and red metal roof, Alexandra
laughed, "So that's were you were this morning."

"I have my little pleasures in life…," Jediah
said softly.

"What's his name?" she asked.

"Ob."

Alexandra and Cassie laughed. Alexandra said,
"That's a strange name."

"It's short for Obsidian."

"Ah, I see. I guess I'll have to give up my
notion of a knight on a white horse," noted
Alexandra. "I can't wait to meet him."

Lining the paved road were wispy red Japanese
and green and white variegated maples. They
passed a riding ring and jumping fences.

"The grounds are beautiful," said Cassie
appreciatively.

"Thanks, Cassie. My mother laid out the plantings and general landscaping. She's always had an eye for the pleasantries of nature."

They reached the crest of the hill. A long straight drive brought them up to a circle in front of the house constructed of stone, which had nearly disappeared under the ivy reaching to the second story. Paned windows with old-fashioned shutters peeked through the ivy.

"We're here," said Jediah.

"It's just breathtaking," said Cassie wistfully. "It makes me feel like I stepped into a time portal and just got whisked back a couple of hundred years."

Four steps led up to the covered porch, which stretched across the front and around either side. It further welcomed visitors with swings, gliders, and lounge chairs placed to gather small groups together.

Jediah escorted everyone through the house and out to the back where they discovered a conservatory where ferns, ivy, grasses, tropical hibiscus, bougainvillea, and orchids flourished yearlong. Lazy ceiling fans circulated the air, cooling in summer and warming in winter. Tiny lights intertwined with the ivy as it meandered through the overhead structure supporting the clear glass hip roof.

In the center of the room was a large circular table; a large, though short centerpiece of blossoms and candles was tastefully arranged so no one's vision was blocked from the person sitting across the table.

Ever the matriarch, Nancy Jane stepped forward to greet Alexandra with a hug. She stepped back a pace and looked lovingly in the young girl's eyes. "Alexandra, you look beautiful. You have made this old woman wonderfully happy. I am so very glad to welcome you to our family."

Nancy Jane was dressed in a pale yellow silk suit with matching shoes and hat that sported the tiniest veil. She looked regal and elegant.

"Thank you, Mom. I am so happy to be part of your family. I love both you and Jediah with all my heart."

Nancy Jane smiled warmly and then turned to the others. "And this must be your close friend, Cassandra. My dear, I am so very pleased to meet you."

"Thank you, Mrs. Saffle. I'd like you to meet my friend, John Ryan."

"John, Jediah has spoken highly of you. Thank you for joining us on our happy occasion."

"The pleasure is completely mine, Mrs. Saffle. Your country home is quite spectacular," John said.

"Thank you, John."

Jediah leaned in and kissed his mother on the cheek. "Would you care to be seated, Mom?"

"Yes, dear, that's a good idea. The others will be joining us shortly. I'll count on you and Alexandra to greet them in my stead."

John and Cassie took their seats as positioned by the name cards.

The first to arrive was James Dawson and his wife, Sarah. She was the perfect complement to James, and possessed a charming and friendly manor.

Mr. and Mrs. Hudson arrived next, bubbling over with excitement regarding their surroundings and the upcoming marriage. Jediah took them around and introduced them as Alexandra manned the door.

Next to arrive, was the good-natured Dr. Jellan, who Alexandra thought looked terribly cute and animated; he took his seat next to Nancy Jane.

The last to arrive was someone Alexandra did not recognize. She was tall, with long shapely legs, raven shoulder-length hair, and deep-set eyes; she was extremely striking in a strapless ivory dress with matching shoes.

"I see I am somewhat a surprise to you. I am Alice Jane, Jediah's sister."

The proverbial ton of bricks landed on Alexandra. Had it not been for the supporting arm that magically appeared to hold her up she would have buckled at the knees and dropped like a stone.

A chuckling sounded in her ear and Jediah said, "Say hello to my baby sister, Alexandra, she's been waiting to meet you."

"Jediah," Alexandra said sweetly, "the first chance we get, we need to have a talk." Then, immediately recovering from her shock, she reached for the dark-haired beauty with violet eyes, (why hadn't she seen those earlier?) and embraced her warmly.

Alice said, "Welcome to our family. I see Jediah's kept me a secret, has he?"

"Yes, and he will pay for it dearly. I've never had a sister before."

"Jediah, it was perfectly evil of you not to tell her about me."

"She never asked," he said with a shrug.

"He's completely irredeemable," Alice said to her. "Finally, we have someone to take him off our hands. You do realize he's an item on sale; there are no returns."

"Alice, I'm so glad you came. It might have been years before I learned of your existence had it not been for this get-together. I plan to count on you for support in the years to come when I'm ready to pull my hair out."

Alice smiled beautifully and said, "You are a delight. I would be honored to side with you against this brute."

Jediah broke in. "If you two are finished stomping on my honor, we can take our seats since we're all here."

Never before had Alexandra been to such a dinner. Jediah had flown in the chef from *Nikolai's* in Atlanta. Each course took nearly an hour. Throughout the dinner, waiters served tiny glasses of infused vodka in flavors of peach, lime and lemon as well as specially selected wines to complement each course.

Conversation among the guests was light-hearted and joyful, and continued the remainder of the evening. Shared stories and laughter filled the night. Everyone in attendance marveled at the ease of camaraderie enjoyed by all.

* * * * *

"Ray, we need to change our meeting place. We're becoming too well known."

"Yes, I know. But we've never run into any of the group we're watching here, which is good."

"Here's the list for the rehearsal dinner and the wedding." He handed it to Ray. "It's a small affair, so there's not many names to check. There's a woman from Seattle, Alice Saffle. I think she's Saffle's sister, but I've never heard her mentioned before," Terry said.

"Okay, I'll check her travel arrangements and anyone else from out of town."

"I think everyone else for the dinner is local."

"Wheeling to Waynesburg is driving distance too, but somehow Alexandra got home from the abduction. We need to know how these people get from point A to point B. We might get luckier with the guests for the wedding."

"I'll keep on it."

* * * * *

Chapter Thirty

Alexandra didn't want the night to end. The evening had been perfect. She was only saddened that her parents weren't there to enjoy it as well, but knew that somewhere, they had joined in her happiness. She was completely and utterly happy.

Alice Jane took Nancy Jane back to Larkspur soon after the dinner was over, but returned shortly. The remaining guests continued in the frivolities for an additional hour and a half. Jediah surprised the guests with a bit of after dinner music which transcended the generational divide with American folk songs such as, *'Barbara Allen'*, *'Greensleeves'*, *'Lavender Blue'*, and *'I'll Take You Home Again Kathleen'* on fife, recorder, flute and cello.

Back at the bungalow, the foursome grew to a five-some with the addition of Alice Jane who proved to be worth her weight in laughter.

"Alice," stated John, "you didn't bring a date. Has no Seattle fellow caught your eye?"

"I'm too young to be tied down," she responded. "Engineering types aren't really my cup of tea. We're too caught up in nit-picking to have two in one household. All I've been running into have been geeky space-head guys, so I'm happy right now just furthering my career."

Since Jediah, John, and Alice had engineering backgrounds, the conversation turned to one in which Alexandra found her mind wandering.

She looked around the room at the people in her life and knew she was fortunate beyond compare. Never would she have believed she could be this blessed. She knew John and Cassie would follow in their footsteps soon and join in matrimony. John looked at Cassie the way Jediah looked at her, with love and adoration. Alice Jane was a new person in her life, but Alexandra sensed she would play and integral part in their future.

* * * * *

When Jediah and Alice took their leave, it was three in the morning.

Walking back to Larkspur Alice spoke her heart. "Well, brother, she's everything you told me she would be, and she adores you."

"It was a long wait, and for a while I thought it might never happen."

"I don't know how you did it. All those years alone... You two were meant to be together. She has fire, which will keep you on your toes. I also sense a very strong will."

"Yes. She plays it down well, but if anyone is lucky enough to peek beneath the surface as I have been, they will find a formidable strength of character."

"Mom certainly thinks highly of her," Alice said.

"You should see them together. Alexandra has so much power and so many varieties to her senses it's almost scary. If I didn't know her like I do, I'd

430

be worried about so much in one package. Mom
and Alexandra communicate as if they're of one
mind. I truly had no idea Mom had so much
power."

"Yours had to come from somewhere," Alice
said.

"I suppose so. I always thought it came from
Dad. It's funny how things turn out."

She stopped and turned to Jediah. "Mom's
time is near, isn't it?"

"Yes, Alice, very near."

"I'm not ready."

"Neither am I." Silence followed.

* * * * *

Cassie and Alexandra fell into bed knowing the
next day held yet another as good as this one had
been. John was pleased to be as close as the room
next door to Cassie, even if it was on the couch.

The plan was to meet at the country house
where Jediah had offered Mr. and Mrs. Hudson and
James and Sarah Dawson housing for the event.
Jediah orchestrated activities for all to enjoy.

John was the first to arise and shower. As he
made coffee, and the girls showered, there was a
knock at the door.

Jediah announced, peeking in the door,
"Breakfast will be served on the side lawn in forty-
five minutes. Since you are ensconced with the
girls, you have the chore of ensuring they will be
outside and ready for the affair."

"I'll do my best, Jediah, but I can promise

nothing."

As the ladies rushed through their morning rituals and finished just in time for Jediah's return, squeals of delight could be heard.

Under a canopy, a table contained place settings, and a second long table, set off to the side, which held platters of bacon, ham, sausages, eggs, waffles, yogurt, fresh fruit, cheeses, coffee, milk, chocolate milk, tea, pastries, and a plate of strawberries dipped in chocolate.

Jediah greeted all, then singled out his favorite, kissing the tip of her nose then her lips, in an I-missed-you-terribly kind of way.

"I'm so happy, Jediah," she murmured, "thank you for everything. This is truly a dream come true."

He squeezed her tight and said, "The world is ours to hold in your hand. Just the look in your eyes last night and this morning is enough to warm my heart for decades."

"I didn't know it was possible to have this much joy in one heart without bursting. To have you here beside me is more than I could fathom. You are the best of my life."

"You are my life," he said.

"Hey, you two, no matter what they say about love, it's food that will keep you alive. Get over here and fill your plates," teased Alice.

"I like her," Cassie said loudly to John. "Alice, you can help me keep an eye on them until they are married."

"Nobody needs to keep an eye on us. We are perfectly capable of maintaining decorum," Jediah said pointedly to those at the table. When his declaration caused everyone to turn to look, he bent down to kiss Alexandra. It was one of those kisses impossible to turn away from, no matter how hard you tried. The kiss was so compelling, John reached for Cassie's hand under the table and gave it a squeeze, and Alice had the consideration to blush.

Alexandra, a bit off kilter from the kiss, fumbled reaching for a plate, and Jediah had to catch it.

"See," he said, "perfect decorum."

If it hadn't been for that delectable eyebrow popping up, Alexandra would have blushed to her toes. As it was, she just shook her head, incorrigible, totally.

Umm, I love you, Alexandra, almost as much as this sausage.

You love me like a sausage? You're a sick man.

Sure am, I'm deathly ill from a disease called Alexandra.

First, you love me like a sausage, then you tell me I'm a disease. I've lived all my life to fall in love with a man who thinks I'm a disease. Where's the justice?

There is no justice. Life is not fair. You are stuck with me. Get used to it.

Now you're dictating to me?

Now, and forever more.

Keep it up and I just might marry you.

You'll marry me all right, tomorrow.

Tomorrow? She felt her heart skip a beat. *I'm not ready. Jediah, are you sure you want to marry me?*

The orb appeared; he took her in his arms and looked deeply into her eyes.

I have never been more certain of anything in my two hundred plus years. Yes, Alexandra, I am sure I want to marry you.

But Jediah, I'm just a farm girl.

I wouldn't fall in love with just anybody. Step outside and take a good look at yourself. Darling, you are adorable. You have no idea how beautiful you are, inside and out. When I'm not with you, I am thinking of the next time I will be.

Jediah, it's too much happiness.

Open your soul; let it in. Bathe in it and let it seep into your pores. You deserve to be happy, to be cherished, and to be loved.

The orb disappeared. Tomorrow, she would become Alexandra Saffle, Mrs. Jediah Saffle, Jediah's wife.

"So, you two, where have you decided to go for your Honeymoon?" inquired Alice.

"Alice, Jediah has picked a very easy wife," offered Cassie. "She doesn't know where they are going, and she doesn't care. She told me so herself just yesterday."

"Alexandra is that true?" asked Alice.

"I'm afraid so," she said.

"Then we get to go where I wish?" asked Jediah.

"I'll follow you anywhere," she said, looking directly at him and catching the glint in his eyes.

"Oh." Warned Alice. "You've just sealed your fate. I have a very resourceful brother and would not want to be in your shoes after tomorrow."

"If you want to know the truth, last night was enough to keep me sated for years to come. I don't need or require a honeymoon," she said.

"Allie, you only get one chance at a honeymoon, maybe you shouldn't shrug it off so easily." said Cassie.

"I don't mean to shrug it off; I'm merely stating that I would be completely fulfilled without one. My hopes and dreams are sitting right here next to me, everything else is just gravy."

"Do you need a bacon cheese burger and fries with that?" Jediah grinned.

"Not after that meal last night and this breakfast," blurted Alexandra.

After breakfast, Alexandra asked Jediah to accompany her on a short trip to town, and indicated to the group they would be back within the hour. Alexandra drove her Jeep to Mr. Snyder's goldsmith shop.

"Good day to you, Jediah," said Mr. Snyder, coming from the rear of the store, "and Ms. Higgins, it is so good to see you again."

"Hello, William," said Jediah, with a warm smile.

"Hello, Mr. Snyder. We've come to have a look at our finished project, if you please," she said.

"I have it right here, and I must say, it came out beautifully."

Mr. Snyder handed the satin box to her, who handed it to Jediah, and held her breath as he opened the box to view the contents.

"Oh, it's beautiful!" she exclaimed. The ring was just as she had envisioned, and the work of a true artisan.

Jediah removed the ring and looked at it long and hard. He hadn't said a word. He put the ring on his right hand little finger and it slid on perfectly. He turned to Alexandra and caught her eyes in his.

"It's ideal. I'll wear it always." He leaned down to kiss her smiling lips.

"Jediah, I seem to have a package here for you too," said Mr. Snyder, handing a six-inch square velvet box to Jediah, who handed it to her.

Laughing, she said, "I should have known the Dawsons and the Saffles would use the same goldsmith."

When she opened the box, nestled in satin was a strand of the prettiest pearls she had ever seen. The luster was exquisite. A pair of matching earrings sat in the center.

"They are truly lovely. What a wonderful, wonderful gift. I've always wanted pearls. Thank you, my future husband, for making all my dreams come true." She hugged him close.

Jediah looked at the goldsmith. "William, you came through again with unparalleled quality. I've never see the technique before on the ring. However did you do it?" inquired Jediah.

"It was Ms. Higgins' idea. She requested the ring to be of two differently colored golds sandwiched together. It took me several attempts before I mastered the join."

"The pearls came out beautiful as well. Thank you for the great job," Jediah commended.

"Yes, thank you very much for your time and the quality of your work," added Alexandra.

As they turned to leave, Jediah said, "See you tomorrow, William."

"It's about time you got hitched, young fellow. We've been waiting a long time to see this happen."

"I know, I know. I was a late bloomer."

"Until tomorrow," finished said Mr. Snyder, smiling and shaking his head.

Riding back in the Jeep, Jediah asked, "The ring is truly beautiful. However did you come up with the design?"

"I see it every day in the mirror."

He sobered. "What do you mean?"

She looked at him questioningly, checked her rear view mirror, and pulled off to the side of the road. She put the car in park, unfastened her seatbelt, and turned to Jediah.

"This is feeling a bit weird, but here goes," and she unbuttoned her shirt enough to drop the material down over her shoulder, exposing the symbolic tattoo.

Jediah's eyes flew wide-open full of concern. "Alexandra, how long have you had that?"

"Since the first day I came to Waynesburg; the day I fell in the cistern. Why, what's wrong?"

"Tell me how it appeared."

She told the story about the cistern, the stone, the tingling feeling, and the mark appearing on her shoulder.

"Don't all Sensates have this mark?"

"No, only two," he answered.

"Isn't the tattoo on my shoulder the same as the design in the foyer of Larkspur?"

"Yes," he replied.

Half-afraid of the answer, she asked anyway. "What is it?"

"It's called a Hwihs. Before I answer any more questions, I need to do some research. Let's get back home; I need to talk to the high counsel."

"Do I need to be concerned?" she asked.

"No, it's just that you might be more special than even I thought."

"Well, that can't be a bad thing." She was unwilling to let anything put a damper on the day. "I'll wait for you to let me know, my future husband. I'll leave it in your capable hands."

Once they were back at the bungalow, Jediah excused himself from the group, and then returned shortly, smiling reassuringly at Alexandra. He handed her a slip of paper while kissing her, which she folded and put in her pocket to read later.

At Jediah's suggestion, they all piled in the Hummer to visit her construction site. The crew must have been working overtime, for when they rounded the top of the mountain, she was speechless. It had shape and form, the windows were in place, and the inside floors were roughed-in waiting for electric, HVAC, plumbing and then drywall.

"Are you two planning on living here?" asked Alice.

Cassie volunteered, "I quit asking, I always get the same answer, and it's 'I don't know, and I don't care'."

She turned toward Jediah and said, "Maybe we should talk about some of these things."

"You think?" said Cassie disbelievingly.

438

"I've just had other things on my mind." She shrugged.

"What's more important than deciding where to live?" Cassie retorted. "I don't know who you are anymore. It's like you met that guy named Jediah, and your brain turned to mush."

"It isn't like we don't have choices," she said. "We could live in the bungalow, the country house, Larkspur, my Jeep, this Hummer. It truly makes no difference to me."

"Not if you put it like that. I just thought it odd that you never even considered whether you need to pack before the wedding or not."

"Hmm, I supposed it is a bit odd, but I really never gave it a thought," Alexandra said. "Jediah, what are our plans?"

Cassie looked at her incredulously. "Now you ask him? One day before your wedding?"

At this point John jumped in. "One day before doesn't sound too bad if you put it in the proper context. She only had four days to choose from."

Jediah cleared his throat and began his oration, "Immediately following the wedding, we plan to stick around Waynesburg. We'll stay in the bungalow until Alexandra's house is completed. I don't think we should go anywhere during the final phases of construction in case we need to make any last minute decisions. We may slip away for a 'lost weekend' or two, but we'll essentially be here for at least two months. Also, my mother hasn't been feeling very well lately, and we really don't want to be too far away right now."

"Oh, Jediah, I had no idea your mother wasn't

feeling well. I'm so sorry for my insensitivity. Please forgive my ranting," Cassie said. "I was just stirring the pot like I normally do. I'm sorry."

"Don't be concerned. You couldn't possibly have known and you don't have a mean bone in your body. Mom has weathered through a good many years and doesn't really show her age."

"Jediah's right, Cassie," said Alice. "Mom fools us too. She never shows her distress to others."

"I understand," said Cassie, now subdued.

"Your house is truly beautiful," said Alice. I love this mountain and always wanted it to belong to someone special; I see I needn't have worried. It's found a home with you."

"What a nice thing to say," Alexandra said. "Thank you. I felt like I was home the minute I set foot here."

"Don't you mean the minute you set eyes on Jediah?" Cassie grinned. "Alice you should've seen her. She took one look at him then stumbled around like a zombie. She wouldn't even speak. I'd never seen her like that before."

"Is that true?" prodded Jediah. "Did I boggle your mind?"

"Oh, no you don't," said Alexandra, "we're not playing 'let's pick on Alexandra' today."

If it makes you feel any better, Terry slapped me on the back of the head. Like I was some fool kid or something!

Alexandra burst out laughing and everyone turned to look at her. She shrugged, and then continued walking to the arbor, one of her favorite places.

You, a two hundred-plus year-old man, got cuffed?

Yeah, he said I was acting like a ninny. Me, a ninny?

Okay, I feel better. I guess we were both ninnies.

Speak for yourself, I'll never admit to being a ninny.

She bumped into Jediah causing him to trip and almost fall, and then used the temporary advantage to run as fast as she could toward the arbor. She heard thundering footfalls behind her and although she ran at top speed, he passed her easily leaving her in the dust. When she reached the arbor, slightly winded, he was sitting with his feet propped up as if he had been waiting there for hours.

"You're pretty fast for an old man," said Alexandra between breaths.

"And you're quite lovely with your cheeks so rosy. Care to sit a while?" He offered her his lap, which she accepted readily.

It was thus the three found them, entwined as the vines in the tiles at their feet.

From there the passengers and driver headed to the country house where they found the Hudsons and Dawsons immersed in a challenging game of croquet. They all complained good-naturedly when a ball was whacked too far away.

The five-some obtained iced tea and dropped into comfy chairs to watch the remainder of the game, rooting for no one in particular and berating anyone who hit a ball, whether it was a good shot or bad.

Jediah made a quick call and arranged to have horses saddled for everyone. After the croquet game ended, they all headed to the stables for a leisurely trail ride through the countryside.

At the stables, the groomsman handed off saddled horses to each in the group. Jediah walked partially into the field, followed closely by Alexandra, and yelled, "Yo, Ob."

A magnificent Friesian reared in the field displaying perfect conformation and unbridled spirit. He galloped to Jediah, snorted playfully shaking his mane, and came to rest next to Jediah waiting for his master's command.

"Alexandra, I would like you to meet Obsidian. Ob ho."

At the command, Ob shifted his enormous weight, drew his left front leg back, and knelt, lowering his head, before Alexandra.

"Oh, Jediah, he's beautiful. No wonder you consider him one of your pleasures."

Jediah reached over to Ob and rubbed his neck, saying, "Good Ob," which released Ob from the task. Jediah grabbed a grip on Ob's mane and swung himself up bareback. The consummate horseman, he rode Ob without bridle or reins.

A bit mesmerized by the vision before her, she saw her future husband as a commander of legions, an Iroquois brave out hunting, a fierce knight of the realm, and the stinky, dirty, Pony Express rider.

As she watched him gather the group together, pride in her chosen mate swelled in her chest. She swung onto a splendid Arabian and joined the group already anxious to test their skills in somewhat uncharted waters.

The leisurely ride through the countryside proved to be a wonderful experience for all. Paths through the woods revealed a bounty of wood ferns, rhododendrons, and ancient pines.

Alexandra watched Mrs. Hudson for signs of panic due to her 'no-animal' policy, but she appeared to be quite happy sauntering along with her husband at her side. Luckily, all horses behaved themselves throughout the jaunt, and everyone returned safe and sound, none the worse for wear.

Later, seated around the table the group enjoyed another fantastic meal prepared by the country house chef.

"What a wonderful place, Jediah," said Mrs. Hudson. "There's always a nice breeze, the surroundings are picture perfect, and the staff is marvelous. Thank you for offering this place to us. It's been like a mini vacation."

"You are most certainly welcome. Feel free to visit us anytime, you too, John and Cassie. Consider this place an extension of your own."

Mr. Hudson, still filled with enthusiasm from the ride said, "Jediah, you are everything Cassie said and more, and a most gracious host. Thank you for your extended hospitality."

"I consider you Alexandra's family, as does she," he replied.

"Why don't we play Charades?" Alice suggested.

"A great idea," chimed in Cassie, "we should pit the men against the women."

"Oh, you ladies wish a trouncing?" Jediah

goaded.

She was the first to respond to Jediah's put down, "Hah, it's not over 'til it's over, and the end remains to be seen."

Although Cassie, Sarah, Alice Jane, Mrs. Hudson and she tried their very best using all their feminine wiles to gain advantage, the men won time and time again; the women gained satisfaction by swearing the men were cheating, but couldn't figure out how.

The group disbanded close to midnight, somewhat unwilling to yield the day. She left John and Cassie in the living room while she stole a few minutes in her bedroom alone. She pulled the slip of paper from her jeans pocket and read the contents:

One from pain and one from strife,
Join together guarding life.
Crossing boundaries, breaking rules,
Both are marked as ancient tools.

One alone and schooled in lies,
Anger, scorn, and hate the guise.
Taught by others to be cruel,
Hence brought forth the timeless duel.

In the heart where all hope died,
Grows the truth from deep inside.
All required is hope and trust,
Break the tide; turn hate to dust.

None will know and none can see,
Plans of secret hold the key.
If one fails, the last will fall,
One that's close could doom us all.

Jediah?

Yes, love.

What is this poem?

It's a loosely translated version of a Prophecy from over a thousand years ago. It is said two Sensates will be marked with a Hwihs and they will join forces to save our world.

Oh, Jediah, is the mark on my shoulder a Hwihs?

Yes.

Who has the other mark?

I know of no other.

Do you know what any of this means?

No one really knows, but there are many theories.

Do you know of any pressing things threatening our world?

No more than you do.

Can you tell me everything you know about the Prophecy?

Yes, Love, but not tonight.

What does the high counsel want me to do?

Marry me.

She smiled. *You goof, that's what you want. Me too for that matter, but what does the high counsel want?*

They want you to marry me too.

Alexandra smiled at Jediah's stab at levity. *I love you. You make my soul take flight.*

Ah, I love you dearly, tomorrow is all I've dreamed of for years. Be happy, my love, sweet dreams.

Join me?
With pleasure…

* * * * *

This dream was unlike any other she had shared with Jediah. They traveled through dimly lit tunnels, which were marked at the intersections with carvings of animals on the walls. At the first intersection, where they had a choice of an elk, snake, bear, or eagle, Jediah chose the bear. The second intersection where he had four more choices, he chose armadillo; thusly they moved forward with Jediah, time after time, indicating the proper tunnel to take.

After what seemed an endless amount of intersections, they arrived at their destination. Jediah unlocked a massive metal door with the touch of nine letters on a keypad, which she recognized immediately and smiled.

He gathered his future wife in his arms and kissed her as his shimmering orb encased them once again. This time, the orb climbed higher and higher until she could see all of Waynesburg and her mountain. She was still lost in the wonder of it all when…

"Wake up, Allie. How can you sleep at a time like this?" asked Cassie.

"Oh, I was dreaming."

"You're getting married today. We have so much to do. Get up, girl, and wed that man of yours. There're only seven hours left for you to be Alexandra Higgins."

"Oh, my, I was so lost in dreaming that I almost forgot."

"I'll bring breakfast to you. Jediah is not to set eyes on you until you walk down those stairs. So, up with you so we can begin our day."

Sitting cross-legged in her bed she moaned. "I can't believe the day has arrived. On the other hand, I can't believe I began this journey less than three months ago. What was I thinking? I barely know him." Then she wistfully amended as peace filled her from the inside. "No, I've known him forever."

Chapter Thirty-One

Saturday began much as the day before, with breakfast served under the canopy. The yard was busy with servers going back and forth delivering fresh trays then clearing, then setting up for the wedding.

Jediah and Alexandra decided on a self-uniting marriage ceremony with no officiant to preside at the ceremony. Their ceremony consisted of music, entrance, vows, signing the certificate, and sealing all with a kiss.

Alice declined to be part of the wedding party, offering instead to play the harp for the ceremony as her gift to the couple.

The wedding, scheduled for two o'clock, required Cassie and Alexandra to be secluded most of the morning working on hair, makeup, and the essential somethings; old, new, borrowed, and blue, and, of course, the garter.

During one of the rare quiet moments, a voice interrupted her thoughts.

Can you hear me? She hurriedly glanced around. It was the same voice from the unexplained shower episode. The voice only she had heard earlier.

Who are you?

Help me! Alexandra sensed the relieved excitement and tried to reach the imprint of the mind, but it wavered, and she was unable to lock on the source.

I can't lock on to help you. She sensed the desperation and hoped the voice knew she wanted to help, but couldn't. No response came and agony replaced the excitement in the voice. She lost the connection. Concentrating to focus her energies, Alexandra scanned for any trace of the voice; there was none. There was nothing left to do.

Jediah didn't contact her, so she must have been the only one to hear the cry for help. At a loss and feeling completely inadequate, she turned to see Cassie presenting herself to John.

"Cassie, you are simply gorgeous," John said. "I just might carry you away."

"I just might let you," she replied appreciatively. "I'm going to need your help. We need to get our bride from the bungalow to the upstairs library without Jediah or anyone else seeing her."

"I'm your man. I'll set things up then get back to you. Be back in a few minutes," he kissed her cheek and disappeared around the side of the house.

The stairs were on the second story of Larkspur, specifically, in the library. John returned a few short minutes later with the plan.

"I'm going to act as decoy to get Jediah to the other side of the house. I'll keep him there for a good ten minutes so you can choose the best time to sneak her into the house."

Cassie replied, "I knew you were the man for the job. I'll be look-out and let Allie know when to go."

It had the precision of a military operation and worked like a charm.

In the library were Mr. Hudson, who had agreed to give the bride away; Cassie, Maid of Honor; James Dawson, acting as Jediah's Best Man; and the bride. The four watched as the scene unfolded below.

Decorated with pale violet blossoms of larkspur, lilac, and lavender mixed with soft green fronds of fern, the garden's floral scent wafted through the air rendering the setting reminiscent of times gone by. An intricately designed white arbor, entwined with dainty green vines, stood in front of a large ivy-covered wall that acted as a perfect green backdrop.

Pale green petals highlighted the steps from the second floor library to the lawn below. Wide white ribbons and ivy garland adorned the railings, interspersed with larkspur and lilacs. Alexandra smiled at the fairy tale scene laid out before her.

Alice, dressed in pale blue chiffon, sat with her harp to the left of the staging area where she played a heavenly selection of *Claire de Lune, Jesu (Joy of Man's Desire), Canon in D, and Pachebel's Canon.*

Cassie snapped candid photos of those in the library, then went outside on the balcony to photograph the scene.

She returned bubbling. "Allie, I caught Jediah fidgeting with one of the studs on his tux. And, I got one of John as he looked up from below and saw me on the balcony. I think they're going to be great."

"Good. You always take good pictures."

450

"Let me get some of you before you have to
change your name," said Cassie.

"Funny girl. You'd better hurry up, pretty soon
I'll be a Mrs."

"Are you ready for this?"

She smiled radiantly. "Bigtime." Snap.

"Perfect!" Cassie said.

As Cassie took pictures of Alexandra, she
caught her reflection in the mirror over the
fireplace. Adorning her head were sprigs of a
dainty vine twisted with tiny white roses to form a
crown; her hair fell in long waves with ringlet wisps
at the temple.

Her strapless gown hugged her form from
bodice to mid hip, and was the utmost in elegance,
design, and beauty. The full-length skirt billowed
to the floor with yards and yards of satin sweeping
from the left hip, around her legs and catching back
up at the same hip in an apron-like style exposing
layers of voluminous folds, which created the long
flowing train. Completely hidden underneath her
skirt was a triple layered chiffon petticoat in the
softest shade of moss green, which was bound to be
an eye-opener when exposed during the removal of
the garter.

She wore white peep toed shoes with
Casablanca heels, leaving nothing to chance while
descending the steps from balcony to garden. At
her neck and earlobes were the pearls Jediah had
given her the day before; they radiated splendidly
from her sun-kissed skin.

Cassie approached Alexandra from behind as
she checked her make-up for the umpteenth time.

"You have a tattoo?"

She turned to see Cassie's astonished face. "It just sort of happened." Alexandra looked down at her shoulder.

"Were you drunk?"

Laughing at her friend's question, she replied, "No, I just hadn't planned on it. Getting it was as much a surprise to me as it is to you."

"Isn't it the same design as Jediah's ring?"

"Yes."

"Woman, you are full of surprises, but it's quite beautiful."

"Thanks, Cassie."

"Are you nervous?"

"Only about falling down the steps; not worried about getting hurt, but how I'd look tumbling down all those steps with so much material. I imagine it would look like some kind of puff ball rolling soundlessly in slow motion, with my screams of embarrassment completely muffled."

"I can see it all now. People are running to your aid, but they can't find you; they flip through satin and petticoats for half an hour and end up finding only an ankle. It takes them ten minutes alone just to establish head from toe."

"Good thing I borrowed your pettipants, for rump over tea kettle could be a bit exposing."

"At least you'll be cute upside down."

"I'd make a wager I won't even get bruised because there's so much padding."

Hugging her friend, Cassie said solemnly, "You are entering a new phase of your life. Jediah is a wonderful man and I know you've been mesmerized from the instant you met him. Your Mom would remind you to always honor each other."

"I love you, Cassie. Thank you for being my friend and for being here with us today."

Mr. Hudson cleared his throat. "Alexandra, if you need to back out, your last minutes for doing so are vanishing quickly. Is it still your desire to wed that handsome fellow down there?"

"It is," she replied.

"Then Mr. Dawson, would you kindly assist my daughter down these steps so we can unite our breathtaking bride with her patiently-waiting groom?"

James threw open the double French doors to the balcony. "Cassie, shall we go?" he said, and held his arm out for her to grasp.

As Alice Jane's harp resonated through the foliage and into the hearts of the on-lookers, the ceremony began.

Eyes of sparkling violet watched as Cassie and James stepped forward and glided down the steps. At the foot of the steps, they continued through the aisle where Cassie took her place to the left of the mock stage and James joined Jediah on the right.

Alice began the *Wedding March,* as the attendees rose and turned to watch the scene unfold. Alexandra and her escort stepped onto the balcony and she heard an audible intake of breath. Her beauty momentarily stunned the audience, as she slowly descended the stairs. She was a radiant, confident, and exquisite bride. The white satin gown merely accented her allure. Her eyes were transfixed on Jediah.

Ah, sweet Alexandra, come to me and be my wife.

Peace and serenity washed over Alexandra as she sensed her mate waiting for her below.

Jediah.

Yes, love?

Thank you for choosing me, and for waiting for me.

'Twas but a snippet of time.

So great is your love. I sense it wrapping around me like a glove. I wish forever to be worthy of such a love and to honor you always as you honor me.

From that moment on, Jediah's eyes never left Alexandra's, nor hers his. The love they radiated touched each individual heart with fascination and wonder.

Alexandra, you are exquisite.

Jediah, I'm so happy I think my heart will burst.

No, love, hearts stretch and encompass. The love you're radiating today is extraordinary. I am sensing those about us and everyone here is affected by your love.

Alexandra opened her senses to include those around her.

Oh, Jediah, it's ethereal. I feel like air.

As Alexandra walked toward Jediah, she began to glow, barely perceptible at first, but then growing in magnitude.

Jediah was the first to notice. Without taking his eyes from hers, he quickly sent out a signal to all

Sensates attending, except Alexandra, to help contain the incident.

He needn't have bothered. The radiation of love, which now held her in a blue sparkling aura, was apparently for his eyes only, for the Sensates instantly sent back acknowledgement of witnessing nothing out of the ordinary.

Alexandra, you are beyond belief.

The power he felt emitting from Alexandra washed over him like a ripple of time, ever growing, ever changing, ever questioning.

He returned the sensation with one of his own.

She sensed it immediately. It began as an inkling, tickling the edges of her senses, which turned into a feeling, then changed into a thought. Jediah presented her with all his memories of her since he began entering her dreams, all the ones he hadn't allowed her to remember. The flood of emotion assaulted her on every level, as she was hit full force from the impact of his love.

Jediah, I never imagined...

There's so much more...

After they spoke their vows, not a dry eye was to be found.

He kissed his bride. Alice announced the newlyweds to the gatherers. Only then did their eye contact break to take in those who had witnessed their joining.

Everyone's eyes were on the new bride and groom as they stood and clapped. After signing their marriage certificate, Jediah escorted his wife through the center aisle and around to the side of the house, where they were to greet their guests.

He turned his lovely bride to face him, and took both her hands in his and said, "I didn't think it was possible for you to be lovelier than you already are, but today, you are breathtaking. I'm honored to call you my wife. Mrs. Alexandra Saffle, I adore you."

Leaning in for his kiss, she replied, "No more than I love you."

When their lips touched, Alexandra opened her heart and soul joining with Jediah's. He felt her gift and stormed the castle walls of her heart with his admiration and love. Their minds met on a grand scale of intertwined senses, each grasping, and absorbing the others' love with the force of a tsunami.

My wife.

My husband.

Nancy Jane offered her best wishes to the newly married couple, and then quickly excused herself from the festivities. Alice Jane escorted her mother upstairs where she had a bird's eye view of the ongoing festivities below.

What followed was a whirlwind of greeting guests, eating, singing, dancing, picture-taking, and good-natured camaraderie.

She met many members of the community that were friends of Jediah and Nancy Jane, who warmly welcomed her to Waynesburg. When William Snyder danced with her, his steps were so light and smooth she could have sworn they floated on air.

About halfway through the afternoon, she made her way to Nancy Jane's rooms. She knocked lightly, and heard, "Come in dear, I've been expecting you."

Nancy Jane lay on her bed, had removed her wedding suit, and now wore lounging clothes. She looked small compared to the size of the bed, and was nearly engulfed by the double down-filled duvet.

"I just wanted to check in on you and see if you needed anything," she said.

"You have given me this day more than I thought to see; my son, completely happy, joined in marriage to you. Today, you became not only my son's wife, but my daughter as well. My heart is finally at peace."

"You honor me with your words. I'm proud to be considered your daughter."

"Alexandra, the time is near, open your mind to me, I have one last lesson for you. It will only take a few minutes' time."

As apprehension gripped her chest, she said, "I am ready."

Talking tires me, this is so much easier. What I have to share with you is remarkable. I don't believe any others exist with this knowledge or power. I recently shared it with Jediah. He had the ability through his many years, but did not know how to use it until the day you came back to us from that horrible episode with Magis. I shared it with him then in a last ditch attempt to locate you and bring you home. It is because of this power that I guarded my knowledge so dearly, and why I searched for a worthy vessel to give it to upon my demise. Only one as pure of heart as you, and only one with your sense of fairness and honesty would be considered deserving of this power, for in the wrong hands, massive devastation is possible.

Are you so very sure of me?

Yes, my daughter, I am.

Nancy Jane shared with Alexandra all she had shared with her son. She warned of the misuse, and cautioned against the moral implications. Because she had prepared Alexandra for the majority of the transfer during their lessons, the actual transfer was much quicker than it had been with Jediah.

After Nancy Jane completed the task, Alexandra stood before her in total awe; that this tiny woman had such immense power would never have entered her mind. Nancy Jane had given her an astounding power coupled with massive responsibility. The gravity did not escape Alexandra, who now felt weighted down by the sheer liability of owning such crushing might.

Six months ago, she lived a much different life. The last few months' transitions had honed her into someone able to handle the depth of power now placed on her shoulders. She no longer thought of herself as unworthy or questioned her right to have such powers; she had been born to cope and manage her abilities. Nancy Jane and Jediah had faith in her. She would own up to the challenge, rise from the girl shrouded in the pain of losing her parents, and become a true Ultra Sensate.

Jediah and Alice Jane appeared at their mother's side. All three stood facing Nancy Jane as children of the matriarch.

Nancy Jane looked first to Jediah; next, her eyes rested on Alice Jane, and lastly on Alexandra. "It is done, Alexandra. Release me from this life," she requested.

She reached into her bra and brought out the key. She held it tightly in her hand.

Jediah leaned over and kissed his mother on the cheek and said, "Good journey, Mom, I love you now and forever."

Alice Jane held her mother's hand, kissed her cheek, and said, "Pleasant journey, Mother. You have my heart."

As tears welled in her eyes, Alexandra said, "I love you, Mom. Thank you for loving me." She placed the key in Nancy Jane's hand.

Nancy Jane smiled peacefully. As she slowly vanished in sparkling lights, they heard, *I will always love you, my darlings.*

Had Jediah's arm not been about Alexandra's waist, she would have fallen to her knees at the onslaught of pure energy that rushed through her body. It continued for a few seconds and then finally abated, seeking sanctuary inside her core. The transfer of power was complete.

"Oh, she's truly gone. I am so sorry," she said.

"Don't be. All is as it should be." He hugged her tight.

Alice Jane reached over to hug her and said, "Mom was so very pleased with you. Thank you for performing such a celebrated task. We're truly blessed to have you in our family. Please consider me your sister in times of happiness and sorrow. I love you as Mom loved you."

She hugged her new sister.

Jediah dabbed her eyes with his handkerchief then reminded her. "We have guests to attend to."

Shocked at the suggestion she said, "I couldn't."

"Darling, you can and you will. Reach deep. You are made of sterner stuff than you can imagine. Let us go dance and sing, and revel in Mom's honor."

Alexandra took a deep breath, let it out slowly, and as the tears dried she looked into the depths of his eyes and said, "I consider it my duty to my new family to celebrate the life of one so loved as your mother."

"Our mother." Jediah and Alice spoke simultaneously, looking directly at Alexandra and acknowledging her place in their family. The three rejoined the guests, laughed with joy at the birth of a marriage, and revered the life of a matriarch.

Many hours later, all guests having departed, Alexandra, Jediah, and Alice Jane sat in the living room at Larkspur.

"I'll take care of closing down the house, Jediah, and then I'm going to get back to Seattle," Alice said.

"It was good to see you," Jediah said. "Please keep in touch and let us know what 're doing now and then, okay?" he reprimanded as only an older brother could do.

"Will do." She turned to Alexandra and said, "Call me if this big lug gets out of line. I think between the two of us, we can whip him back into shape."

"I'll keep that in mind," Alexandra said. "It was my distinct pleasure to meet you. Thank you for all your kindnesses."

Jediah took her hand, and in a blink, they left Larkspur to begin the next chapter of their lives.

Epilogue

Alexandra had no idea Jediah's holdings were so vast. They went from one estate to another over one month's time. They spent two days in his mountain chalet in Norway, three days in a beach house in Costa Rica, rested up for a week at his estate in the mountains of Colorado, then jumped to a castle in Scotland, and lastly to New York to a luxurious penthouse on Park Avenue.

It was every woman's dream of the perfect honeymoon. Jediah was attentive, funny, charming, roguish, and a gifted tour guide.

Her wedding night in Norway was a scene from a romance novel complete with dashing groom and beautiful bride. They arrived at the entrance of the chalet, chilled from the cold breeze and wearing gown and tux as they had at the wedding. Jediah smiled, scooped her up in his arms, and carried her over the threshold.

He kissed her lovingly before setting her down on the inside. He swung around, closed the door, then said, "Welcome to one of your many homes."

After a quick tour of the chalet, he suggested they both get into something more comfortable. Since the chalet consisted of both his and her quarters, she readily agreed, but mentioned they hadn't packed.

"Everything is at your fingertips," he

responded. "If you need something, pick up the phone. Betsy Jorgensen will answer. She speaks perfect English. Tell her what you need and she will get it for you. As for clothes, you'll have to make do with the items I've selected for you. If they're completely horrible, and not to your taste, tell Betsy what you wish and she will get it for you. I'll meet you back here in front of the fire, in forty-five minutes. Deal?"

"Deal!" She kissed her amazing husband and ran for her quarters to get out of the gown, which she felt had been wearing her, for the last few hours.

She hurriedly looked through the clothes; how anyone could be displeased with his selections was beyond her wildest dreams. French lingerie, silk blouses, dresses, skirts, pants, jeans, snow suit, leggings, boots, hand muff, and a complete selection of shoes and hats. Although she took time to primp, she still made it back to Jediah's arms within the allotted timeframe.

She was glad she chose the coral silk dressing gown and matching slippers when she saw the look of appreciation in Jediah's eyes. He was wearing black silk lounging pants tied at the waist, and a matching jacket, which he left unbuttoned and was sitting leisurely in a tufted chair.

My husband, you look so delicious you make my mouth water.

His mind had been wandering, but he sat upright at the vision coming toward him.

No more jeans or scruffy clothes for you! I'll never get enough of you in dresses and gowns. I think I'm spoiled already and we've centuries yet to enjoy.

She crossed the room and sat in his lap, a place she recently found most desirable. His arms encircled her and she rested her head on his chest. She could hear his heart beating and it lulled her into a dreamy state.

He lifted her chin to kiss her lips. The kiss was sweet and tender. As she savored each moment, he introduced her to the art of making love. Her defenses toppled one by one.

The kiss turned from sweet to one of ownership. Forevermore she would imprint as Jediah's. She felt his heart opening to hers. He lifted her and carried her to his bed.

Jediah, I can feel your heart beating inside me; your heart beats in my chest. Our senses...

Her breathing became more rapid and she could feel the rush of her power ushering forward to meet his. She sensed all he felt along with what she experienced for the first time. His knowledge met her innocence.

She heard, *Our senses are co-mingling, Alexandra. We are becoming one. Don't be afraid. It is our way.*

I'm not afraid, I just want to relish each minute with you.

He led her down a course of heightened emotions only to cease them and bring her senses to an even greater high the next time. He could feel the escalation within her; it was far greater than he had anticipated.

Jediah, it's so sensory. I'm losing my grip. Don't let me go.

He recognized the sensation immediately. He had felt it himself when he came into his full powers at twenty-five.

Darling, not only are we co-mingling senses, you're also coming into your full powers, sweetheart. Your timing is impeccable. Let your senses flow, open your mind, hold nothing back. Love me.

Her love burst forth wrapping them in a blue energy aura. Sparkling lights flickered all around them like electrical charges. His powerful senses met hers head-on in a cataclysmic bombardment of pure energy.

I'm... we're...

He continued his assault until she lost touch with her body and was completely engulfed by a sensory need that could only be sated by the consummation of their love. As he held her in his arms, they joined as men and women have done since time immortal. She sensed sensed the complete barrage of his powers as they became...

One.

With highly tactile skin, nerve endings pulsing, and the pounding rush of blood coursing through their bodies, the blue sparkling lights surrounding the couple burst into millions of miniscule shimmering orbs. The union was complete.

For these two sensual beings, their love had exploded exponentially. As the power surge slowly subsided, they held each other until their breathing returned to normal. Lying in Jediah's arms, Alexandra sensed his unconditional love.

What occurred that night neither would be able

to explain; for in Sensate history, it had never taken place. Only by combining their recollections decades later would they be able to grasp the magnitude of what happened that night.

Nestled together in his quarters, the young lovers awoke to a beautiful snowy day in Norway. He kissed Alexandra's forehead, then departed for the shower. As he walked away, she was instantly aware of the vacancy.

She took the opportunity to sneak back to her quarters, shower, and dress for a new day then searched for her husband, whom she found in the kitchen lazily sipping coffee and watching the falling snow from the huge window in the breakfast nook.

"Mmm, you look delicious," noted Jediah.

"Thank you, dear husband. You look quite yummy yourself."

"Could it be we're both hungry," he said smiling.

"I don't know why, but I feel like I haven't eaten in days."

Just then, there was a knock on the door and a man wheeled a serving cart into the nook. The man bowed slightly to Jediah, then left.

"I think we can take care of your hunger now, maybe later too," he said with a wink.

"I'm so lucky to have found you."

"No, I found you, and swore I'd never let you go."

"Lucky, lucky me."

Time passed quite quickly for the newlyweds and within a few weeks, Alexandra longed for the bungalow and Waynesburg. Late one evening, they checked out her mountain to find the house nearing completion. It was just as she had envisioned in her mind. Landscaped beds, a paved driveway, and a seeded lawn stretched before her eyes.

"Jediah, look behind that blind of hemlocks. Greg put in the secondary access."

"It's barely noticeable. Once the trees grow a bit more, it'll be completely hidden."

"He's done a fantastic job on every aspect. What do you think of my pond?"

"It's a nice touch. It won't take it long to fill; we'll get more rain with the change of seasons."

A few of her favorite trees had been planted close by so she could enjoy them. Greg had also brought in a few specimen trees to catch the eye of the beholder.

They decided to call Greg the following day to get a date of completion so she could make plans to have all her things brought to Waynesburg from storage in Wheeling.

"What do you think of a housewarming party?" Alexandra asked.

"I've never held one before, but it sounds like fun. We could get the gang from the wedding together again."

"I'm sure Mr. and Mrs. Hudson would be on board. They certainly enjoyed themselves at the wedding. Oh, my, I've been so neglectful; I wonder how Cassie and John are doing?"

"I'm sure they are on the path to wedded bliss."

"I think so too. And I miss that crazy bird, Sebastian. Are you sure Terry is taking good care of him?"

"I'm positive Sebastian is in good hands."

"Jediah, each time I see Terry I get a funny feeling inside."

"You do?" he asked.

"Yes, it feels like something festering in the pit of my stomach. I can't explain it."

"I'm sure if it's important, it will work itself out."

"How long have you known him?"

"Four years or so; we hired him as gardener for Larkspur, the country retreat, and to watch over a particular piece of land north of the city."

"I'm glad he's no longer at the mountain. He has no reason to go there now, has he?"

"None, I discharged him from that task and he seemed relieved."

"He's not a Sensate, is he?"

"No."

"Hmm, was he very close to your mother?"

"I wouldn't call it close; they consulted on the landscaping, of course."

"Did you check into his background?"

"No, but I will now that you have raised the question. Do you suspect anything in particular?"

"No. I just don't like the feeling I get."

"Okay, we'll watch him." He pulled her close nuzzling her neck.

"Jediah, I didn't want to bring it up, but now that we're approaching the end of our time away, how are we to handle your mother's passing to our friends?"

"Alice took care of everything. Dr. Jellan

signed the death certificate so all appears quite legal; a crematory was used per her request, with all applicable paperwork created. Alice notified everyone to let them know Mom preferred a private ceremony with just immediate family; and any contributions to her memory were to be sent to my mother's favorite charity."

"I hadn't thought of everything that needs to happen to maintain our secrecy."

"We've been at it for centuries. Our cover-ups would tower over one of the country's best covert operations."

"It's a shame the cover-ups are necessary," she said. "From what little I knew of your mother, she had the highest ideals and moral fiber that could be imagined. Jediah, I'm so sorry she's gone."

"I am as well. We had a wonderful life together. I miss her more than I can say."

"I'm glad I had the opportunity to spend so much time with her. She was quite the lady," she said pensively.

"I wish I had gotten to know your parents," he said.

Ruffling his hair she said, "They would have loved you." She sensed his loss, as she knew he sensed hers.

"Come over her and get closer to me, I can't hear you thinking from that far away," he coaxed.

"I'm practically sitting on top of you already. You can hear me perfectly; you just have other things on your mind."

"Don't you?" he asked.

"Always," she whispered.

"Then listen to your husband and get over here."

"Come and get me," she said tossing over her shoulder as she jumped and ran for her life knowing he was at least five times faster than she would ever be.

Even if she used her best avoidance tactics, she knew he would capture her in seconds, so as she made the turn in the hallway, she used her senses to block Jediah's vision of her, then quickly stepped aside so he wouldn't run into her. She felt his hands grabbing her waist. He tossed her invisible, giggling body over his shoulder and carried her to the bedroom.

"I see it's going to be 'me-tough-man-you-weak-woman' today, is it?"

He laughed as he deposited her on the bed and lay down beside her.

"Me-not-tough-man and you-not-weak, woman," he taunted. "Is it wrong for me to want my wife next to me?"

"I have no complaints whatsoever."

"Good. If you had any it would make the next several hundred years a very long time."

"How did you find me?"

"I recognized your ploy instantly, performed the same block on you and at the same time heightened my sense of hearing. You made the mistake of breathing."

"You cheated!"

"No rules were stipulated," he stated slyly.

"You have unfair advantages."

"Yes, love, I do."

After nuzzling her neck and placing tiny kisses all around her lips, he said, "It's time to go back to Waynesburg. Are you ready?"

She looked at him. Hah, she had it! "You want a piece of that chocolate pie, don't you?"

"It has been five weeks since I had a slice. Wouldn't you like some French fries and gravy?"

"My mouth is already watering."

She closed her eyes to accept his tender kiss, which escalated just a bit to curl her toes and tingle her nerves. When she opened her eyes, she was back in the bungalow, lying next to him in her bed. As she snuggled into the curve of his sculpted body, she traced his lips with her finger and murmured, "I half expect Cassie to come running down the hall yelling for us to separate."

"She better never..."

Alexandra rested quietly in his arms. The peace that enveloped her softened the loss of her parents, erased the horror of the abduction, and held her poised for an amazing future.

Alexandra? Her eyes flew wide open. The voice was powerful, strong. She became instantly aware of her surroundings; her pulse quickened.

Who is this? She knew the answer before the voice resonated.

Ryeth.

Ryeth

The Sensate Nine Moon Saga continues with *Ryeth*. Ostracized by his kind and his survival fueled by loathing and revenge, he lives in a world where his Sensate abilities remain a secret. Travel through time as he grows into the hardened rogue who threatens the Sensates' existence.
Unsuspecting, he is caught off guard by the allure of a dark-haired beauty who plagues his tormented mind and crosses the boundaries into his solitary existence.

Uncover his twisted fate and the depth of his desires in *Ryeth*.

Acknowledgments

To those in my life that weathered the storm: you have my most sincere gratitude.

My first mention goes to Tom who warmed my soul with his kindly offer to critique my work. It was through his inspiration I gained insight and moved forward to completion.

Next, I offer my thanks to Kimberly, who I met on a trek to reclaim my former self. Your excitement spurred me to get right back into the next two books. Thank you for your great comments and support. Get ready; we're taking the next journey together.

Without the world of love bestowed on me by my wonderful husband, I would have never enjoyed the freedom to complete this part of my Bucket List. I thank you for being the kind, supportive husband every girl dreams about, my very own 'Jediah.'

Lastly, I need to thank three very special ladies, Hazel, Helen, and Laura, for being the women who inspired me throughout my life. The strength of women often goes understated; this day I give them their due.